Welcome to Tumbling Creek Ranch.

Inside this book you'll find three novellas set in a fictional town in Montana. These are the first three novellas about two families who own neighboring ranches and the people who come into their lives, showing them love and how to continue the family legacies.

Love at Tumbling Creek Ranch

Books 1-3

Eight Seconds to Love

Love Me Anyway

Wrong Cowboy to Love

Windtree Press
Hillsboro, Oregon

LOVE AT TUMBLING CREEK RANCH
Copyright © 2020 Patricia Jager

Contact Information: info@windtreepress.com

Windtree Press
Hillsboro, Oregon
http://windtreepress.com

Cover Art by Christina Keerins - Covered by CLKeerins

PUBLISHING HISTORY
Published in the United States of America
ISBN 978-1-952447-35-8

Author's Note

These three novellas first published in anthologies with other talented authors. Now they are available individually as ebooks, or as an ebook box set or in this print collection.

Eight Seconds to Love

Chapter One

Jared MacIntyre pushed back the curtain in the ER to tend the bull rider paramedics just brought in. A disheveled blonde woman in tight jeans and a bloody, ripped, long-sleeved western shirt lay unconscious on the gurney. He checked the chart. Bull rider from the Copper Springs Rodeo. The woman was dressed like someone who would be at a rodeo.

He walked closer, caught a whiff only those who associated with cattle tolerated, and peered at her face. His chest crushed in around his lungs.

Lacey Wallis.

The last time he'd seen his best friend's cousin, Lacey had been tagging along after them at the carnival their senior year in high school. She'd been a pain, trying to one-up them in everything, even though she was five years younger and a girl. But her tenacity and smile had her popping up in his mind many times over the years as he watched men complain and beg out of things Lacey would have tackled with joy. Yes, joy and tenacity were the words that best described Lacey.

He shoved the memories to the back of his mind and went to work, doing what he'd been trained to do—discover the trauma and help the doctors make the best decision for the patient. She was unconscious, but he didn't see any bruising or abrasions on her head.

Her left arm was another story. He'd seen arms like this while a medivac in Iraq. A bomb hadn't mangled this arm; it was a two-thousand-pound bull.

"What do we have here?" Dr. Parley asked as she entered the room.

"The patient needs x-rays to see how much damage was done to the left arm. The paramedics stopped the bleeding. And a cat-scan might be in order if she doesn't wake up during the x-rays." He glanced down at Lacey, resisting the urge to sweep the blonde hair, dulled by dirt, off her forehead. He'd never seen her so still.

Dr. Parley did a quick evaluation and nodded. "I agree. Get on this stat. The longer her lower arm goes without blood, the less chance her hand will function properly."

Jared nodded and grabbed the end of the gurney, wheeling Lacey down the hall to the x-ray department as a noisy group of people entered the ER.

***

Lacey woke to hellfire in her arm and pounding in her head. Slowly, she opened her eyes. The room was white, smelled of antiseptic. Damn! She was in a hospital. It was the third time since she'd started riding bulls. Her mind shot back to what she could remember. She'd managed to stay on Red River for eight seconds. The buzzer sounded. When she'd released and landed, her feet had caught in the soft rutted dirt and she'd tumbled onto her back. The few short seconds she'd stumbled and fallen to the ground were a blur, but the image of the bull's massive hoof coming down on her left arm was as bright and clear as a high-def photograph.

That was why her left arm hurt like hell. She tried to raise it, but pain seared up her arm and caused her stomach to churn. She twisted to prop her body up on her right arm and get a look.

"Hey, you need to remain flat for a while yet, or you'll have a headache worse than when you came in."

She aimed her gaze at the sound of the voice. It had a familiar tone. When her gaze landed on the man's face, there was no mistaking those dimples or those dark blue eyes. Jared McIntyre. She continued staring, taking in the more chiseled features that proved the boy had grown into a man. His dark hair was just long enough to curl in her fingers, if she got the chance to run her fingers through it as she'd fantasized about many times as a teenager and even as an adult.

Jared was the one boy she'd wanted to notice her when she was thirteen. He'd been the handsome high school quarterback and one of the highest scoring players on the basketball team. His features had matured into an even handsomer man. And he still worked out. Muscles stretched his short-sleeved, blue, scrubs. Her cousin hadn't said anything about Jared becoming a doctor or that he lived in Bozeman. She'd only heard he'd joined the military.

"Cat got your tongue?" Jared asked.

"N-no. I'm just surprised to see you. Here. In Bozeman." Since she'd started riding bulls, she never thought much about how she looked. She needed to fit in, be tough, and not care if her hair was mussed. But at this moment, she wished she was a model or anything but a dirt sucking bull rider.

"How does your head feel?" he asked, picking up her wrist and taking her pulse.

His gentle touch sent her heart racing.

One dark eyebrow lifted, and he set her right hand back down on the covers. He held out a thermometer. "Open up. I need to monitor you for infection. That arm of yours looked like you'd been in a Jeep hit by an IED."

She shuddered, thinking her arm had to have looked pretty bad for an ex-military person to say such a thing.

He checked the IV sticking out of her right arm. "Were you really on a bull when this happened?"

The skepticism in his voice was the same she'd received every time she said she was a bull rider. She'd been riding bulls since high school. Once the boys, and now men, learned she had as much passion and heart to ride a bull as they did, they didn't give her any guff. In fact, they helped her with her technique and watched out for her when a newbie came along and talked smack about her. She'd been working her way up the circuit and trying for a shot at the National Finals Rodeo. She'd finally made it. Riding Red River and staying on until the buzzer, had clenched her spot in the NFR, but now… She turned her head to her left. "My arm. How soon can I get back on a bull?"

"Lacey, you can't be serious." His tone sounded like her parents'.

She peered into Jared's eyes. "Dead serious. This ride clenched my spot in the Finals. Do you know how long it took me to make this goal?"

He shook his head. "I don't. Brett said you were riding in rodeos, he didn't say you were sitting on top of two-thousand pound animals. Is this what you've been doing since high school?"

"Yes. I've been working my way through the ranks to be the first woman to ride a bull at the National Finals. This ride did it. I stayed on eight seconds. Red River is one of the highest scoring bulls in the circuit. My score had to have put me in the top three and that's all I needed to secure my spot." She glanced toward her strapped down arm. "I would have had a clean ride if my feet hadn't gone out from under me when I dismounted." The stumble could have cost her her dream.

"Why?" He stood beside her bed, gazing down at her with the same bewilderment she received from family.

"The victory is in knowing the beast under you is fifteen times your weight and stronger than anything you'll ever come up against. He wants you off his back, and you try your best to outwit him and stay on." She smiled. "It's the challenge. And for me, it will be riding at the Finals and showing the world a woman has the same grit and determination as a man."

"But you aren't a girl any more. You can't keep trying to outshine the boys." Jared's words sounded so much like her father, she readied her usual response.

He opened and shut the door quickly, leaving her alone with her thoughts.

She lay in bed, her arm throbbing, and contemplated how she could spin what happened into good publicity instead of bad. All these years she'd avoided interviews with announcers, papers, and the association. Most of the rodeo associations didn't like that she rode bulls, but she had her card and paid the fees. There weren't any rules that said she couldn't ride bulls. But at the same time, they were always looking for a way to keep her from riding. This accident, if it garnered too much publicity, could do that.

She drew in a deep breath. Her arm had to heal quickly, and she had to keep all publicity about this accident upbeat. Where was her phone? She needed to find out if she had qualified for NFR and then tweet how she was looking forward to the experience.

Chapter Two

Jared wasn't surprised to see Lacey's folks or Brett when they strode down the hall toward him. He'd called his friend when Lacey went into surgery the day before. All three still lived in Duncan, Montana— five hours from Bozeman. It was the reporters following behind them that bothered him.

"Where's security?" he asked the nurse sitting behind the reception desk in the ER.

She picked up the phone and spoke into it.

Jared pulled the Wallis family into the ER break room. And stood with his back to the door to keep the reporters out.

"How bad is it?" Mrs. Wallis asked. She was a daintier version of Lacey but just as tough. The Wallis family had gone through hard times while trying to make the family ranch, the Tumbling Creek, support two families.

"I told her to stop this foolishness the last time she was in the hospital," Mr. Wallis said, putting an arm around his wife's shoulders and glaring at Jared as if he were the one who put their daughter up to riding bulls. The man was nearly his height of six feet, but leaner. His graying hair made a Velcro band around his head, keeping his ball cap from sliding off his bald top.

"Mr. and Mrs. Wallis, Brett." Jared shook hands with the two men. "She's doing well considering the damage to her left arm."

"She's always been a tough one, but riding bulls…" Mr. Wallis shook his head.

Jared knew how the man felt. If he had known the feisty girl would grow into a woman hell-bent on riding bulls, he would have tried to help change her crusade. "You can't go charging in there and tell her what you think. She needs to see you love and support her. That arm is going to take a long time to heal. Maybe by the time it heals, she'll find something else she's just as passionate about."

"How long did they say it will take her to heal?" Brett asked. He had Lacey's hazel eyes, but his hair was reddish brown and his six-two frame was wiry like Lacey's dad.

"Eight to ten months with the possibility of a surgery during that time." Jared ran a hand through his hair. "I won't lie to you, I've seen arms not as damaged as hers that had to come off."

Mrs. Wallis gasped.

"Luckily, we have a top-notch surgeon in the area who worked on her. Lacey will keep her arm, but right now no one knows how much use she'll get out of it." Jared studied Lacey's parents. They nodded their heads.

"Can we see her?" Mrs. Wallis asked.

"Yes. As soon as security gets rid of the reporters. It appears her qualifying for the Finals is a big news story." He shook his head. How could anyone want to see a woman ride a bull?

He glanced out the small window in the door. Carl, the security guard, was moving the press back out to the reception area. Jared opened the door and pointed toward the ward with the recovering patients. "She's in room two-fifty-four. Down this hall and make a right at the end." Jared put a hand on Brett's arm, keeping him from following the couple.

"Is there something you're not telling my aunt and uncle?" Brett asked. His worry for Lacey was palpable. The two families had been close, every holiday they were together. Brett had told Jared that Lacey was like a sister to him.

"Why didn't you keep her from getting up on bulls?" Jared had been wondering this ever since he'd realized who she was and what had put her in his ER.

Brett stared at him, narrowing his eyes. "Don't you think I've talked to her until I was blue in the face? She won't listen. She thinks riding the bulls and besting males is her calling. She's twenty-eight years old. She should have found a man, settled down, and become a teacher by now. But she keeps following the rodeo circuits and riding bulls. From what you told us, she won't be able to ride another bull. I don't know what that will mean, now that she finally has her ticket to her dream." Brett rubbed a hand across the back of his neck. "She's wanted a chance at the Finals since she put a helmet on and shoved a mouthpiece between her teeth. The last time she ended up in the hospital she broke her leg. She'd insisted she could still ride with a cast." He shook his head. "And damn if she didn't. She even placed in the money at two of the rodeos she attended with that damn pink cast."

Jared had latched onto his friend's comment about becoming a teacher. "Does she want to be a teacher?"

"Hell, I don't know. I just threw that out there because she gets along well with kids. She helped me out at the ranch the last time she was laid up. The kids all loved her." Brett lifted the cowboy hat from his head and scratched his forehead. "I guess I'll invite her to come stay at the ranch with me and help out while she heals and figures out what she wants to do next. If she goes to her parents, they'll just keep badgering her."

"And you should, too." Jared didn't like imagining what could have happened to Lacey if the bull had stepped on her chest instead of her arm.

"Badger her?" He snorted. "It doesn't do any good. All the family did that when she was riding bulls in high school. Seemed like the more we told her not to, the more determined she became to do it." Brett tipped his head toward the reception area. "How about you take a couple weeks off, stay at the ranch, and see if you can help her with whatever her next step in life will be? I could also use help keeping her from doing things she shouldn't." He slugged Jared's shoulder. "She's always had a thing for you."

Jared stared at his friend. "What are you talking about?"

"Why do you think she followed us around during our senior year of high school? She was in puppy love with you." Brett sauntered down the hall, leaving Jared to wonder why his friend hadn't mentioned this before.

***

Lacey opened her eyes at the sound of cautious footsteps. The nurses and doctors strode into the room with purpose. If it was someone with the press, she wanted to pretend she was asleep. But her curiosity got the better of her and she opened one eye. Her mother stepped up to the bed, her eyes brimming with tears. Why did Brett have to call her parents. It always upset them to see her in the hospital. She loved her parents, but hated seeing the fear in their eyes and hearing their pleas for her to stop riding bulls. However, the adrenaline rush of riding had become an addiction she wasn't ready to kick.

"Mom, what are you doing here?" She glanced beyond her petite mother and spotted Dad. The concern and scowl on his aging brow, tugged at her conscience. Guilt became a greater pain than her physical pain. "And Dad. How did you know I was here?" The only person she put on her forms as next of kin was Brett. Had the rodeo manager called him?

"How are you, darling?" Mom asked, her hands clutching Lacey's right hand.

"Brett called us." Dad stood beside the bed, his ball cap in his hands. The bald top of his head reflecting the sunlight coming through the window.

"I'm fine. Just banged up my arm." She still couldn't raise her arm. Any effort to move any part of it brought on pain.

"What are you going to do now?" Mom asked, as Dad slid a chair behind her. She sat and stared into Lacey's eyes. "You could stay with us. We'll take good care of you."

And tell me every day you knew this would happen. Even though she felt guilty for causing them pain and fear, it was her life. She'd made that clear many times. Just as she'd told them she had no intention of working for the Wallis Excavation Company. Her younger brother, Nate, and Brett's younger brothers, Garth and Dillon, leapt at the chance to drive equipment all day rather than ride horses and chase cattle. Her parents and Brett's parents even seemed to thrive off the ranch. She and Brett were the only two who had their grandpa Wallis's love of horses, cattle, and the great outdoors. "I'll be fine once I get out of the hospital. I'm sure I can work for the feed store—"

"Not with a bum arm you can't," Dad jumped in. "You could answer the phone at the shop."

At that moment Brett stepped through the door. "Hey, Hot Rod, looks like the bull won."

She'd never been so happy to see anyone at that moment than her cousin. "I won. I stayed on for eight seconds. I just couldn't get my feet under me and ended up on the ground with the bull dancing around me."

He winced and her mother gasped.

"That ride got me into the Finals." She couldn't say or think that enough. After twelve years, she had finally made it in the rankings to ride in the Thomas and Mack Center in Las Vegas. But would her arm heal enough she could compete?

Brett glanced at her parents. They all knew something she didn't.

"What aren't you telling me?" She glared at each of them. "Who told you what?"

Brett stepped closer to the bed. "We were talking with Jared—"

"What did he say?" Lacey clenched her mother's hand so tight she squeaked.

"He said you won't be able to use that arm for eight to ten months."

She mentally did the math. That wouldn't be until May of next year. Way after the NFR. "I don't need this arm to ride. I grip the bull rope with my right hand. I want my day at the Finals." Which wasn't likely to come if word got out her arm wouldn't be healed in time. Tears burned the backs of her eyes. She'd come so close to fulfilling her dream.

"But darling, the damage you could do to it if you…you ride." Mom released her hand and glanced over her shoulder as if asking Dad to say something.

Jared stepped into the room. "Dr. Parley is here to check on the patient."

Lacey could have kissed Jared for getting her family out of the room so easily. Mom stood, thanked the doctor for taking care of her daughter, while Dad and Brett stood at the door, waiting for her.

When they disappeared, she turned her attention to the woman doctor. "Someone told my family I wouldn't be using this arm for eight to ten months. Is that true?"

Dr. Parley studied a chart then raised chocolate brown eyes to study her. "I understand you are a bull rider and think you're tough, but you will have to refrain from riding any bulls for at least eight months. Longer would be better if you want to have full recovery."

"I don't use my left arm for riding. It's in the air." *Eight months!* She'd be so out of shape it would take her a year or longer to get back into the physical condition she was in now. Not to mention mentally.

"Flinging your arm about and perhaps reinjuring it is up to you, but if you want to have as pain free a life as possible, I would recommend finding another means to support yourself." The doctor unstrapped her arm from the board underneath and raised the dressings. "We need to keep this cleaned and antibiotics on it until the wounds heal enough we can cast."

Jared nodded his head and wrote in the chart the doctor had handed him.

Lacey tried to see the damage, but the way Dr. Parley held up the bandages, she couldn't see her injury.

The doctor left. Jared pulled the soiled bandage off, giving her a glimpse of her arm. The sight churned her stomach. She stared out the window as he worked.

"You're quiet," he said.

"I'm thinking."

"Good, I wouldn't want you feeling sorry for yourself."

She whipped her head around and glared at him. "I'm not feeling sorry for myself. I'm trying to figure out what to do with myself while I heal." And how to avoid the press. She didn't want anyone speculating she wouldn't be fit for the Finals. Not until she could determine how well she could sit a bull by December.

"You could help me at Tumbling Creek," Brett said, walking back into the room.

"You have a use for a one-armed ranch hand?" she asked.

Jared strapped her arm back to the board to keep it immobile. "She can't be doing anything that will put stress on this arm."

She started to glare at Jared but caught the concern in his eyes. Her heart stuttered. Did he, after all these years, care about her?

Chapter Three

Jared found himself taking his breaks at the same time of day Lacey was in rehab. He sat in on the "torture" as she called it. Dr. Parley had given Lacey the go ahead to get her cast and leave the hospital tomorrow. Jared had also scheduled a two-week vacation and promised Brett he would bring Lacey with him to Tumbling Creek. The press had stopped trying to get in to see her once they'd realized it wasn't going to happen.

"I was beginning to think Dr. Parley was never going to release me," Lacey said as he wheeled her back to her room after a rehab session.

"If you don't follow her instructions when you get out, I'll make sure you are right back in here," he said, pushing Lacey through the door to her room. He hadn't visited her in the room for a week. It now resembled a flower shop. "You must have a lot of admirers."

And one stood in the room holding a bouquet.

The cowboy looked to be younger than Lacey. He held his hat in one hand and daisies in the other. "Hi Lace. I didn't think you were the fancy flower type."

Even his voice sounded young to Jared. He didn't like to think the other bull riders had sent her the flowers and possibly been visiting her like this young cowboy.

"Hi Skip." Lacey smiled at the cowboy. "Shouldn't you be on the road?"

"I was in Idaho last weekend, headed to South Dakota. Thought I'd check in on ya." His cheeks darkened in color as his gaze landed on her left arm. "Good thing it was your left arm ole Red River stepped on."

"Yeah." Lacey said a bit too cheerful for Jared.

He should have left, but he wanted to see if she had a thing for this youngster.

"I was surprised to hear they were keeping you this long. Usually, after an arm or leg break most of us are up and out of the hospital in a day."

Her eyes narrowed. "If you think I won't be at the Finals, you're all thinking wrong. I'll be there. The break to my left arm requires rehab, but my right hand is still strong enough to hold on to the bull rope and keep me in the money."

"Yes, ma'am. I wasn't tryin' to say…"

"You be sure and let everyone know, I'll be walking out in the arena with all the other finalists come December and showing those cowboys how to ride a bull."

He shoved the flowers at her. "I'll sure tell them. Get well." His youthfulness showed at how Lacey's bossiness sent the cowboy scurrying for the door.

"You made him tuck tail," Jared said, plucking the flowers from her hand.

"Skip is a good kid. His older brother was hurt pretty bad a couple years back. He always checks on a bull rider who goes down." She stood and walked to a pile of letters. "These are what I cherish. Letters from young girls who want to be like me and ride bulls."

Jared shook his head. "His brother was hurt by a bull and he still rides? Why would any female, or male for that matter, want to crawl up on an animal that could crush you with one step?"

She turned her hazel gaze on him. "It's like a fever that gets into your blood. When you have a good ride and the crowd cheers, it's like you conquered something few can conquer. When I'm on the back of a bull, riding out the twists and jumps, I'm not a helpless female, I'm in charge of my destiny. I've dreamed of the day when I would jump off a bull at the Thomas and Mack Center after the eight seconds and everyone would know a woman can ride a bull and make it to the biggest rodeo event."

He stared at her. Her eyes glittered as if stars had fallen in them and her smile was a mile wide. Would she ever find anything that gave her the same rush? And how did a young girl come up with the desire to ride bulls?

He walked around the wheelchair and stood behind her. "It's not going to happen now. That arm isn't going to be in any shape by December for you to ride a bull." He started to put his hands on her shoulders but heard a noise at the door and dropped them.

"Lunch," said the duty nurse, carrying in a tray. She glanced at him and then Lacey.

"I'll be by at eleven tomorrow to pick you up," he said to Lacey.

"I'll be ready sooner if you can get here before eleven," she said, sitting on the bed.

He nodded and hurried back to the ER. How had his desire to befriend her and help her family get her moving in a different path with her life, changed to a desire to be near her? He'd witnessed heat and desire in her eyes a time or two when he'd caught her watching him. And damn if it didn't arouse something in him he hadn't felt in years. Which worried him. He'd not be able to keep his hands off her for two weeks at Tumbling Creek if she kept looking at him that way. If not for Brett depending on him to help keep Lacey from overdoing it, he'd back out of this trip. He couldn't have a woman in his life who thrived on danger. The memories would return.

***

Lacey was dressed, her cards were all packed in her duffel bag, and her injured arm wore a bright green cast. Her torn skin and injured muscles had healed enough to apply a cast. She glanced at the clock. It was five minutes later than the last time she'd checked. What was keeping Jared? Dr. Parley had been in early to give her the pep talk about not using her left arm and hand for anything other than rehabilitation and to stay off bulls for eight months.

The doctor obviously hadn't heard the news. Lacey had caught a brief clip the night before by the PRCA, saying Lacey Wallis had qualified for the NFR with her ride at Copper Mountain. And while she had qualified, it was up in the air if the first woman to qualify in bull riding would be physically and mentally ready after being trampled by Red River.

After hearing that bit of news, she'd shut off the television and cried tears of frustration.

All those lonely nights, sitting in a motel room waiting for the competition the next day while everyone else went out and celebrated because she didn't want anyone to say she made her way up the ranks by sleeping with anyone. The hours with her mentor and millions of push-ups, pull ups, and abdominal work she'd done to keep in shape to ride. All for nothing.

A wheelchair entered the room pushed by Jared.

She turned her head, swiped at the tears pooling in her eyes, and pushed away any thoughts of not going to the National Finals.

Lacey picked up her duffel bag. "I don't need one of those. I hurt my arm, not my leg."

Jared strode over, took the bag, and grasped her elbow. "Hospital policy. You'll leave the premises in a wheelchair. Sit."

She would have dropped into the chair, but she'd learned early on that jarring her body, jarred her arm. Once she was seated, Jared plopped her bag on her lap and settled her feet on little platforms by the front wheels.

"Are you taking any flowers?" he asked.

"Nope. I told the nurses to distribute them to patients on the floor." She waved her good hand toward the door. "Move 'em out."

"Yes, ma'am." Jared rolled her out of the room, down the elevator, and out the back of the facility into the wonderful sunshine. They had a five-hour drive to reach her cousin's dude ranch outside of Duncan.

"I never get tired of breathing Montana air," she said, more to herself than to Jared.

"It does smell different." He opened the passenger door of a half-ton Dodge pickup. "It smells like home," he added as he helped her out of the wheelchair and into the truck.

She had to agree but wasn't going to tell him that. She'd traveled all over the states and even up to Canada a few times looking for rodeos that would boost her rankings. Every time she came back to Montana, she did get a feeling of home, no matter whether she was in the mountains, on the plains, or barely over the state line.

Jared put her duffel in the tool box in the back, ran the wheelchair back into the hospital, and slid behind the steering wheel. "Hungry?"

"I wouldn't mind grabbing a burger somewhere and eating it as we drive. I want to get away from this hospital." She noted his raised eyebrow. "No offense to you or the other nurses and doctors, but I'm tired of smelling antiseptic air and hearing squeaky shoes."

He laughed and said, "There are days after a long busy shift, I feel the same way." He put the truck in gear, and they pulled out from behind the back of the hospital.

"Did you take me out the back because there are still reporters wanting my story?" After the clip she'd watched the night before, she was beginning to think she might want to tell them she would be at Finals. Her arm wouldn't keep her from competing. But unless she sent them a notification that she wouldn't be competing, they would leave her on the roster. Would just having her name as a finalist make her happy? She'd have to think on that a bit. But her gut said she needed to get up on a bull in the Thomas and Mack Center to have accomplished her dream.

"Yeah, there are still a couple diehards who haven't left the hospital in hopes of getting your side of things." He glanced at her. "Do you want to tell your side?"

"Yes and no. I would tell them I will be competing at Finals, but I'm afraid they'll ask about my injury and figure out it's more than a break." She wanted to keep her options open and not give the association any chance to fill her spot with someone else.

"Competing? Haven't you heard a word Dr. Parley told you?" Jared's tone held a note of protectiveness.

"Haven't you ever had a dream? I finally have a chance at my dream. I can't just say, I can't compete, give my spot to someone else. December is two months away. If I stay in shape, I can still sit on a bull and fulfil my dream." She studied Jared's profile. He had such a strong face. It would be easy to sit back and let him take care of her, but she'd been on her own too long to let a man, or anyone else, take on her problems. "You didn't have to drive me to Brett's ranch." She'd been trying to decide if she was excited about spending more time with Jared or annoyed.

"I've been meaning to get out and see his place since he turned it into a dude ranch. I had some time coming." He glanced over at her. "Do you mind my being at the ranch while you're there?"

She stared into his blue eyes until he had to pay attention to the road. She'd had few boys or men look at her with such… she wasn't sure what she saw, but it stirred her insides. "I don't mind. It could be fun watching you ride a horse."

"I know how to ride a horse. What makes you think I don't?" He swung the truck into line at a fast food restaurant.

"I said I wanted a burger, but I meant from a place that actually uses beef and the juices drip down your chin."

Jared watched her. "I figured you ate at places like this all the time."

"Are you kidding! I need real food in this body, not preservatives. Keep driving. I'll shout when I see a good place to eat." She leaned back in the seat, wishing she had something to prop her arm on.

At a stoplight, Jared studied her. "Is your arm hurting?"

"A little."

"Watch out." He pulled the center of the seat down, making a rest for her arm.

"Thank you. That helps." Before she had her arm completely comfortable, he pulled into a parking lot.

"How's this?"

She glanced up at the building. "This will work. Are you going to order or are we going in?"

"We'll go in. I don't want my hands busy while I'm driving." He slid out of the truck and was opening her door before she had her seatbelt off.

"Thank you."

He nodded and put a hand on her lower back, escorting her into the restaurant. The touch was possessive and protective. His fingers heated her skin, taking her thoughts to a place other than the restaurant they'd entered.

She hadn't notice he'd brought in a coat until he bunched it up and placed it beside her on the booth.

"Rest your arm there while you eat." He brushed a wayward strand of hair off her face and sat in the booth opposite her.

Lacey's heart skittered in her chest from his thoughtfulness.

They ordered their food and talked about Tumbling Creek Ranch and Brett while they ate.

As they climbed into the truck, her cell phone jingled. Jared stood next to her, ready to give her a boost into the truck since she couldn't pull with her left hand. Lacey slipped the phone out of her back pocket and stared at the screen. She didn't know the number but it could be someone from the next rodeo wanting to drop her from the roster.

Using her thumb, she swiped across the screen. "Hello?"

"Hi Lacey, this is Dave Lathom from the PRCA. We heard about your accident and wanted to check in and congratulate you on making it to the NFR in December." His voice was cordial, but she heard a bit of reserve also.

"Thank you. I'm looking forward to participating at the Finals."

"We haven't been able to learn about your injury from the last rodeo you participated in. Will it cause you any problems for participating in the Finals?"

They were fishing to see if she would be competing. "I'll be ready to ride."

"Then you won't mind if we send someone to do a piece on you for a couple of magazines, as promotion for the Finals?" His tone was more an order than a question.

"That would be fine. I'm leaving the hospital today and will be staying at my cousin's ranch, the Tumbling Creek, outside of Duncan, Montana. You can send someone there."

"You'll remain there until NFR?"

She glanced over at Jared. "Most likely."

"I'll be in touch when someone is assigned to the story."

"Thank you." She swiped her phone off and stared ahead. An interview for publicity. She hadn't thought about that while she was working to be the first woman in bull riding finals. The thought she'd have to stay upbeat and not let on how badly her arm was damaged, took some of the starch out of her legs.

"What was that all about?" Jared asked, grabbing her arms and helping her stay on her feet.

"The PRCA is sending someone to do a story about me. You know, to help publicize the rodeo finals." She peered into his eyes. Anger and worry swirled in their depths.

"Why aren't you telling them the truth. Your left arm may not be ready for you to compete. And if you do..." He held her tight. As if he could hold her in this one place and she wouldn't be able to compete.

The pressure of his muscled body against her caused her mind to drain of all rational thought. She wasn't a virgin, but her dances in the sheets had been few and a long time ago. Her heart raced, pounding in her ears.

"Whoa, don't faint on me. If you're tough enough to ride a bull, a telephone call shouldn't rattle you this much." Jared stared into her green eyes rimmed with brown. He'd moved close when he'd noticed her legs giving out. But holding her tight, his body was coming to life in a way it hadn't in six years. As much as he'd like to explore these sensations, he knew better than to get mixed up with another adrenaline junkie woman.

His words had the effect he'd hoped for. Lacey's body became rigid in his arms. Her eyes sparked, and she shoved him away with her good arm.

"I don't like speaking to reporters. The one time I did back in the beginning of my career, the man had made comments about how in this sport, I'd have to sleep my way to the top." She put her good hand on his shoulder, using him for leverage as she pushed up into the truck seat. "I vowed then to not talk to any more reporters. I did all of this on my own."

He didn't like the idea of anyone badmouthing Lacey. Especially, saying she slept her way to the finals. That would be ridiculous. But just the accusation had triggered his anger and protectiveness. After she settled in the seat, he closed the door and got behind the wheel. "Give me the guy's name and I'll go punch him in the nose."

She laughed and said, "I don't think he'd even remember. It was a long time ago."

He put the truck in gear and headed out of town. "Do you get many of those comments?"

"Not usually. Once in a while someone who scored lower will make a comment similar to that." She frowned. "I think they want a reporter to ask questions more about if I'm fit to ride in December than anything else. That's the feeling I got from the man who called."

He shook his head. "They have every right to be concerned about you being fit enough to ride. You could have been killed. The association would get bad press if you, or any woman, died from a bull. Why do you keep doing it?"

"Why do immigrants keep coming to the United States? For freedom. The right to do what they dream of." She tipped her head back against the seat. "I'm tired."

He let the conversation drop. But his one priority the next two weeks would be to talk her out of riding a bull again.

Chapter Four

Lacey couldn't stop squirming in the seat. It had been over a year
since she'd visited Brett's dude ranch. This time of year, with school
back in full swing, it would be older couples and middle-aged single
people looking for adventure.

"I'm impressed," Jared said as they drove under the large metal
archway with curvy lines and the words Tumbling Creek. This had
once been the Wallis family ranch. Brett bought everyone out and was
keeping the ranch alive as a dude and resort ranch.

"Brett has made our granddaddy's ranch into something special.
My dad and brother and his dad and brothers didn't want anything to
do with it." She was proud of her cousin and his efforts to keep the
ranch in the family and make money.

"He's told me about all his work here over the years, but the only
time I visited was right after I came back from Iraq." Jared's eyes
dulled. "I needed some calm to think things out."

"He's made major improvements since then," Lacey said,
skipping over Jared's melancholy but locking the information away for
later when she could ask Brett.

Jared pointed to the people walking out of the main house. "It
looks like he's added some help as well."

Lacey smiled. Perhaps her cousin was finally following his heart. She'd met Melanie Trask the last time she'd visited. But for some reason both Brett and Melanie denied they had anything more than a boss and employee relationship.

The truck stopped at the end of the walkway to the large, log, main house. To the left were eight smaller cabins for the guests. Beyond that a barn, stable, and corral.

Brett pulled her door open. "Good to see you up and walking around."

She punched him in the shoulder with her good hand. "I'm never down for very long." Lacey stepped out of the truck and found Brett on one side of her and Jared on the other, carrying her duffle bag and his.

"It's good to see you again," Melanie said, walking forward and smiling.

"You, too. Are there any guests right now?" Lacey asked.

"Until this weekend, just you two and the Oatmans." Melanie stepped aside so they could enter the house.

Lacey never tired of seeing the large log home. As a child, they'd spend a week at the ranch during Christmas. All the family gathered here to be close to her grandparents. Since Brett took over, the families met at one brother or the others for Christmas dinner only.

This time she noticed doilies, fancy throw pillows and afghans that had to be Melanie's doing. "The place looks wonderful!" Lacey said, spinning and taking in all the subtle changes that made it look like a home rather than a lodge.

"Melanie has an eye for decorating," Brett said, with a hint of pride in his voice.

"This is a big change from the last time I saw the place," Jared said.

"Brett, take Lacey's things up to the guest room. Jared, we've given you one of the cabins." Melanie looped her arm through Jared's, moving him back to the door.

A sting of jealousy had Lacey spinning from the sight.

"Here, you need her things," Jared said. Within seconds he was beside her, handing her duffle to Brett. "Make sure she doesn't use that hand or arm at all." He peered into her eyes. "Don't start practicing for some other male dominated occupation."

"Mr. McIntyre, you act as if you don't trust me to take care of myself," she teased.

He narrowed his eyes. "You're too bull-headed to think past your next thrill."

She glared at him, and he spun on his heel, exiting the house with Melanie.

Brett laughed. "Have you two been going at it like this the last two weeks?" He started up the stairs.

"In a way. He doesn't understand my desire to ride bulls, and I don't understand his need to see me give up my dream." She followed him up the stairs and down the hall to the same room she'd stayed in her last visit.

Brett dumped her duffle on the trunk at the end of the bed. "You know where everything is. Dinner will be at seven. Be on your best behavior, we will have an older couple eating with us."

"I'm always on my best behavior." She unzipped her duffle as he walked out of the room. "Except when Jared is around." There was something too precise and held in about him that made her want to see him explode. She had a feeling when he let loose, he'd be as hard to ride as a bull.

***

Jared stood at the corral, mulling over why he gave a damn that Lacey might have lost her chance at her dream. He hated that she rode bulls and could have been killed, but at the same time he admired her drive.

"Nickel for your thoughts."

He turned to the voice that had sent his body tingling two weeks ago. "Not sure you'd like them."

Lacey stepped up beside him. He liked that she'd changed into a body hugging T-shirt. She looked feminine, even though he knew under those clothes was the hard muscle of an athlete.

"Hmm. Then you're either thinking about how to get me to quit chasing my dream, or what happened in Iraq that sent you here for peace and quiet." Her hazel eyes studied his face.

He was surprised she cared about why he needed solace after his last tour in Iraq. But he wasn't ready to reveal that part of his life. To tell her about Anita would open wounds and make him worry even more about Lacey. He also understood a person needed a reason to go on. His medical career had helped him ease the pain of losing Anita by showing him he could save others. He just wished Lacey's dream wasn't so destructive.

"I was wondering if that phone call is only the beginning of more. Maybe you should call a press conference and tell them about your injury and your dream."

She stared at him. "You care whether or not I get a chance to ride in the finals?"

"I don't like you riding bulls, and I don't like to see dreams crushed." He put a hand on her shoulder. "Everyone needs a dream or goal. It's what gets them out of bed every day."

"What is your dream?" She stepped closer, nearly touching their bodies.

His body sprang to life at her nearness. He cupped the back of her head with his hand and brought her lips an inch from his. "To forget the past and take charge of the future."

Her wide eyes stared into his. "How about take charge of the present?" The breath from her words whispered across his lips moments before she closed the inch between them.

She'd made her move, now it was time for him to make his. Jared opened his mouth and she followed. His tongue sought her moist heat and sweetness. He could tell by her clumsy attempts to mate her tongue to his, she had less experience. The knowledge only made him want to show her more.

The hand not holding her head, slid up her side and cupped her breast. She moaned and pressed closer. He squeezed her breast and slid his leg between hers, lifting her slightly. Her body wiggled, and he felt her desire heating his thigh.

A horse snorted and stamped a hoof.

He broke free of the kiss and lowered his leg. This wasn't the place to bring her to an orgasm.

Lacey's hand fisted in his shirt. She peered up at him. "Did I do something wrong?"

"No." He nodded toward the barn and the buildings beyond. "I'm not a fool. Someone could come along…" He ran a hand through his hair. "I don't want anyone to get the wrong impression about you or me."

"What does that mean?" She released his shirt and took a step back.

"I won't take advantage of you when you're vulnerable." The sparks in her eyes revealed he'd said the wrong thing. But he needed to keep her away. While he cared for her, and God knew his body reacted to her without provocation, he didn't want her in his life. She was too much like Anita. He couldn't lose another woman he loved.

"I'm not vulnerable. I might have a bum arm, but I am sure as hell not vulnerable. I knew what I was doing when I pressed my lips to yours." She spun away from him and marched into the barn.

The door slammed shut.

"No, you aren't vulnerable. I am." He shoved his hands in his pockets and headed out across the meadow. A walk would do him good.

Chapter Five

Lacey walked into the dining room that evening expecting to find Jared missing. But he sat at the set table, conversing with an elderly gentleman.

"Take the seat next to Jared," Brett said from the head of the table.

She walked around the end where Melanie sat and took her seat between Melanie and Jared. The older couple across the table from her smiled and nodded.

"Mr. and Mrs. Oatman, this is my cousin, Lacey Wallis. She's staying with us while her arm mends," Brett said.

"Pleased to meet you," she said to the couple.

"Were you in a car wreck, dear?" Mrs. Oatman asked.

"A bull wreck. I was riding in a rodeo and the bull came down on my arm." She smiled and tapped the green cast.

"Oh my! Were you one of the people who rides a horse and saves the cowboys?" the woman asked.

Lacey shook her head. "No ma'am, I was riding the bull."

Mr. Oatman pointed a finger at her. "I hope you showed that bull what-for."

She laughed. "I rode him the full eight seconds. It was after the buzzer I got this."

"Good for you. You don't hear much about women riding bulls." Mr. Oatman said to his wife.

"You haven't been watching the news," Jared said.

Mrs. Oatman's eyes widened. "You're the woman the news has been talking about? The first woman to be a finalist for the rodeo they hold in Las Vegas every year?"

"That's me. It's been my dream since I first sat on a bull in high school." She glanced at Brett. He had a concerned expression, but he didn't say anything.

"On my way here today, I received a call from the PRCA asking if I would give an interview for publicity. I'm not very good at talking to reporters, but I want everyone to know a woman made it to the bull riding finals."

Mr. Oatman cleared his throat. "I owned a newspaper for thirty-five years. If you want, I could help you practice what to say."

Lacey couldn't believe her good fortune. "You don't mind? The last time a reporter interviewed me, it didn't go well."

"I'll say. He put words in her mouth," Jared chimed in.

Lacey felt her cheeks burning. She didn't want anyone else to know how the man had twisted her words to make her sound like a slut, but she also couldn't help but notice how it had offended Jared as much or more than her.

"What happened?" Mr. Oatman asked.

"The man twisted my words and made accusations that were false, only I was young and didn't know how to answer them. When the story came out…" She shook her head. "I found out who my friends were."

Mrs. Oatman glanced at her cast. "Will the cast be off by December?"

"No." Jared answered.

Lacey glared at him. "You don't know. You aren't psychic."

"I know from a medical standpoint, if you don't have another surgery on your arm in November, you won't be able to use it fully. That means there will be another cast on your arm in December." Jared flashed a gaze from the older couple to Brett and back to her. "If you don't have that surgery, you won't be able to do much of anything with your left arm. Is your dream worth crippling yourself for life?"

She heard the anger in his words. "It's my dream. I'll be there arm healed, or not. I've made it this far and I won't allow anything to keep me from something I've earned."

Jared shoved his chair back and stood. "I said I believed in dreams, but I can't stand by and let you purposefully toss your life away. This time it was only your arm, what if the next time a hoof comes down on something vital?" He strode out of the room.

All eyes were on her. She didn't understand his outburst.

"Let's eat," Melanie said, passing the dishes to the Oatmans.

Lacey put little on her plate. She barely kept up with the conversation as her mind replayed Jared's reaction.

After the meal, Lacey made a stab at helping Melanie clear the table.

"Go on, you don't need to help. You're still recuperating," Melanie said, shooing her out of the kitchen.

Brett was saying good night to the Oatmans. When the couple left, he stopped beside her. "Come for a walk with me."

She nodded not really in the mood, but not wanting to go to her room just yet.

They wandered down to the stream that the ranch was named for. Tumbling Creek was named after the dozen or more small waterfalls that the water tumbled over as it meandered down the side of the mountain before flowing through the meadow.

"Has Jared told you anything about his tours in Iraq?" Brett asked, stopping by a downed log and sitting.

She sat beside him. "No. We've barely talked about anything other than my arm and my riding bulls.

"Try not talking about the bull riding around him. Ask him about why he's a nurse instead of a doctor and why he hasn't been interested in a woman since he left the military."

She studied her cousin. "What aren't you telling me?"

"I'm telling you to get to know the man. You two are giving off pheromones when you're in the same room. But he isn't going to jump into something that will tear his heart out again."

"Again? What are you talking about?"

"It's not my place. Just tone down the bull riding talk and get him to open up about his past."

She shook her head. "I already know he doesn't want to talk about it." He didn't want to talk about the past, but it had been evident in their tangled bodies by the corral that afternoon, he was interested in the present.

"I can guarantee, he will, if you can show him you aren't trying to kill yourself."

"What are you talking about? I'm not suicidal." She glared at her cousin.

"Your desire to ride a bull is to Jared." Brett stood. "Think about what I said. Act like a normal woman, not some crazy lunatic who has to prove you can ride a bull as well as a man."

She watched him walk away as the moon lit up the meadow, dancing sparkles across the creek. Lacey continued to sit on the log, watching the deer slowly step out into the meadow and listening to an owl greet the night.

Brett was trying to tell her something. She glanced back at the cabins. Two had lights on. One had to be Jared. Time slipped away, and she was that thirteen-year-old with sweaty palms, hoping Jared would look at her and see more than the tomboy.

He knew she was a woman by the way he'd kissed her that afternoon. She'd never thought riding a bull made her less feminine. When not at a rodeo, she wore dresses now and then. She'd had a few men ask her out, but they never sparked anything in her. Not the way Jared always made her body heat and her insides go all squiggly.

Her gaze landed on the opening cabin door. Golden light poured out into the night. A tall, broad-shoulder form walked out, stood on the porch a moment, and then started out toward the meadow. Her heart raced. Jared was coming toward her. Had he seen Brett talking to her, or had Brett told him she was sitting out here?

She riveted her attention on the water gurgling over the rocks in the creek. The closer he came, the more alive her body became.

Jared still wasn't sure why he was headed out to see Lacey. Brett had stopped by and said she was sitting on the log by the creek. His friend hadn't said more than that. He evidently knew the two had grown closer these past weeks and wanted them to get along while at his ranch. It was pushing their friendship, the way he'd stormed out of the dining room in front of Brett's paying guests.

The meadow grass swished as he walked through it toward the dark lump on the log. The moon was a sliver of yellow in the dark, star-filled sky.

He walked up behind Lacey. "Mind if I have a seat?"

She didn't startle. Didn't even glance up at him. "There's plenty of log."

He sat, leaving a good foot or better of log between them. "I'm sorry I blew up."

"Me, too." She continued to stare at the stream.

"You didn't blow up." He studied her profile in the faint moonlight.

"I'm sorry you blew up. Sorry my life makes you uncomfortable." She faced him. "What I don't understand is why?"

It would be easier to start with the obvious. "My living is patching people up, seeing them after they've had trauma. I understand car wrecks, accidents, but intentionally putting your body in harm…It doesn't make sense."

"You were in the military. Didn't you put your body in harm while in Iraq?"

"That was different. I put myself in danger to help others. I was a medic. It was my job to help the wounded and bring them back alive." He shut his eyes and tried shutting his mind to the horrors he'd seen and the people he couldn't save.

"I understand. But didn't you also get a thrill out of slighting death not just for you but for your patients? Helping a soldier get back home alive?" She bumped his knee with hers. "I don't ride for the sake of riding. I'm good at it. My instructor and mentor told me, 'a guy with an ear tore off looks tough, a girl with an ear tore off looks ugly,' meaning if I didn't want to cause a stink and get a bad name for women in the profession, I had to be as good or better than the men to not muck things up for any other woman who wanted to ride bulls. I wanted to help open the opportunity to more women and show the world, we are strong enough, agile enough, and have enough brains to ride bulls."

He snorted. "I would have never pegged you as a feminist."

"I'm not. I'm for equality for everyone, no matter their gender, race, or philosophy. No one should be told how they can or can't make a living. It has nothing to do with feminism and all to do with being able to do what I like and I'm good at." She put a hand on his leg. "What about you? You're an ER nurse. Typically, a female job but not so much anymore. Why not a doctor?"

Jared tried to ignore the soft, playful way she asked and the hand slowly moving back and forth on his leg. He'd not seen this side of Lacey before. His resistance to her compassion wasn't working.

"I had to make too many life and death decisions while in the military. A nurse gives their opinion and lets the doctor make the final judgement of the situation." He put a hand over hers. "It's nice to have the weight lifted off my shoulders."

She nodded. "I can understand that. A person can only take so much pressure and they need to back off."

He'd never thought of the decision making as pressure, but it had come to a boiling point. With his job now, he went home every night feeling he'd given his best and could sleep. There were times in Iraq when he hadn't slept for days second guessing a decision he'd made in the field.

Tired of thinking about the past, he asked, "When do you think that reporter will come do the interview?"

"I don't know." She exhaled. "I hope Mr. Oatman can prepare me with good answers. I really don't want it to be a 'toss Lacey Wallis under the bus' piece."

"Do you want me to be there? I can stand up beside you, maybe make whoever the reporter is think we're an item and that may keep any questions like that from arising." He didn't want her riding bulls, but he also didn't want some reporter trying to make a name for themselves to use lies about Lacey to make their mark.

"If you're here when they arrive, I don't mind, but if they ask intimate questions what are you…we going to say?" Her gaze flitted from him to the creek and back.

What was she hoping he'd say? What could he say?

"We've known each other most of our lives. Not as close as say, your cousin and you, but I would think we could come up with something that would make it sound plausible." Knowing he could help her this way made him happy.

"If you told me a little more about you, that would help."

He heard the innuendo of her trying to get more about his past and didn't like where the conversation was going. Time to change it up. "Feel up to a ride tomorrow? I'd like to see all those colorful trees up close."

"I know the perfect place to go. There's a meadow up there." She pointed up the mountain side with her good arm. "The larch, alder, fir, and spruce will be turning colors. And the pine scent…" She sniffed. "You can almost smell them down here."

Jared laughed and tugged her closer. "You can smell the pine and you can smell Montana. Makes me wonder if you aren't part dog."

"I can be very loyal."

The whispered words before her mouth covered his, stole his thoughts and sent blood rushing to his cock and whooshing in his ears. He pulled her closer. She draped her legs over his and her good arm around his neck. Jared fell into the kiss, exploring her heat and sweetness with his tongue and her toned body with his hands.

His hands skimmed over the taunt muscles on her side, back, and belly. When he slipped his hand inside her bra and grasped her firm breast, she pressed closer, tipping her head back. The invitation wasn't lost. He skimmed his teeth down her neck and pushed her shirt up, revealing the pebbled nipple he held in his hand. A flick of his tongue across her nipple caused Lacey to moan and squirm in his lap.

This added friction to his growing cock had him close to exploding, but he didn't want to stop. It had been a long time since he'd had a woman with so much fire and passion that he didn't want to think about where they were or what the consequences could be.

"Jared," Lacey said in a raspy voice.

"Yeah," he croaked.

"Can we take this to your cabin?" She stopped squirming and placed her hand on his erection.

He sucked in air, hoping he didn't lose it. "That might be a bad idea."

She continued to rub her hand up and down his length under his jeans. "Why? I can tell you are in to me as much as I'm into you."

Jared grabbed her hand, so he could think. Her ministrations had him seeing stars. He drew in several deep breaths and said, "I have a feeling it has been a while since we've both had sex." He felt her slowly pulling back. "I don't want anything with you to be a one-night stand. I have your cousin's friendship, your parents' respect, and my conscience to think about."

"So, you're saying, you'd ignore this," she dropped a kiss on his lips and pressed her bare breast against him, "Because of my family

and your conscience?”
    “Yes.”

Chapter Six

Lacey didn't know whether to be angry or happy. Her body was a burning inferno, and she had enough wisdom to know the only thing that would douse the fire was a romp in bed with Jared. And here he was being noble, stating he didn't want a one-night stand.

"Cowboy, I don't do one-night romps. If we went to your cabin, it would mean I planned to be loyal to you until you told me to take a hike."

Jared grasped her head, holding it in front of his face. "How many men have you slept with and told them you'd be loyal?"

She swallowed. She hadn't thought her lack of experience would come out. After all she was twenty-eight and a decent looking woman. She should have slept with lots of men by now. "One."

"Damnation!" Jared exclaimed and released her. "How long were you loyal?"

"A lot longer than he was. We were twenty. I thought he cared about me and my dream to ride bulls. Turned out, he thought I was just another buckle bunny. I came home from a rodeo and found him in bed with a real buckle bunny." Tears streamed down her cheeks. She'd never been so mad or ashamed as she had been that night. She'd hung her hopes and dreams on Keith and he'd tore her heart in two and her faith in men who weren't family.

"Lacey." Jared pulled her into his arms, holding her tight. She liked the way his body engulfed her, making her feel safe and loved. He kissed her cheek.

She turned her face, meeting his lips with hers. She'd never craved the touch and taste of anyone like she did Jared.

He took over the kiss. Once again, her body started humming, her senses roared to life, experiencing every touch of his hands, his lips, his body. It had been a long time since Keith, but she knew her body never came to life under his hands like it did with Jared.

He had her t-shirt up again. He'd pulled her bra up, to reveal both breasts. His wide hands spread across her back, holding her up so her breasts were near his mouth. One by one, he sucked, nibbled, and flicked the nipples, making her body shiver and wetness soak her panties.

"Jared, please, either take me here or take me in your cabin, I can't…" The words were swallowed as he captured her mouth in a kiss and swung her up into his arms.

She barely registered the movement of him carrying her as he continued to kiss her.

This was like a story she'd once read in a book. The hulking knight carrying the damsel to his lair. Only she would experience the knight's ministrations first hand, not as words on a page.

His steps crunched in the gravel walkway to the cabin. His lips left hers as he fumbled with the door knob and finally pushed the door open with her hip.

He set her on her feet and kicked the door closed. The heat and desire in his eyes made her heart leap into her throat. She'd never dreamed anyone would look at her that way.

She took a step toward him, her hand catching the bottom of his shirt.

He shook his head, moved her hand to her side, and tipped her chin up, kissing her chastely on the lips. "We're going to take this like it's your first time. Slow, easy, and memorable," he whispered across her lips.

Her body quivered in anticipation. "I don't want slow and easy. I want hard, fast, and hot."

"No. We'll do that another time. This time we do it my way or…" He glanced at the door. "You can leave here wondering what you missed."

She swallowed, even as her feet were thinking about walking just to see if he'd call her back. His big, throbbing package she'd touched earlier wouldn't like her to walk out the door. Her body pulsed with need. She'd never be able to sleep if it wasn't sated.

"I'm yours," she said, staring into his eyes.

He smiled, showing off the dimples she loved. Jared reached out, slipping his hands under her shirt. His palms skimmed up her sides. She raised her arms, and he slid the t-shirt off over her head being careful of her arm in the cast.

When she thought he would unhook her bra, he walked her backward until the bed bumped the back of her legs and she sat. He pulled off her boots and socks, unfastened her pants, and stood her up.

Shivers skittered across her skin as he slid his palms down her legs, taking the pants down to her ankles. She kicked them off and stood in front of him in her bra and panties.

She became nervous when he just stood there looking at her, not moving. "Don't like what you see?" she asked.

"The complete opposite. I've never seen a more perfect body." He stepped close, placed his hands on her back, lifting her up his body and her mouth up to his. His size reminded her of a bull. Big, strong, and uncontrollable.

She fell into the kiss, opening her mind and body to him. She'd never had a headier ride than the one Jared was taking her on. Her body throbbed and smoldered when he laid her on the bed. His hands came away with her bra. He was still completely dressed as he drew her panties down her legs, leaving her naked on his bed.

"When do I get to see you?" she asked, running her gaze up and down his body, wondering if the physique she'd imagined was hidden under those clothes.

"I told you, this was going to be slow." He grabbed her feet, pulled her to the edge of the bed, and spread her legs.

Her heart raced as she realized what he was about to do. She remained prone on the bed, griping the covers with her good hand, pressing her curls into his face, and panting like she'd run three miles. Her body arched, lightening ripped through her limps, and her mind went blank.

When she came to her senses, Jared stood at the edge of the bed in his birthday suit and a condom. His broad shoulders, wide chest, hair arrowing down to his narrow waist, and impressive package, started her body heating up all over again.

He kissed and nipped his way up her legs, thighs, belly, breasts, neck and ended up drugging her with another heart pounding kiss before he slowly eased into her.

Her body cried out for release until he was finally seated as deep as he could go.

"Are you doing okay?" he asked.

She pressed her good hand against the small of his back and thrust her hips up against him. "I want every inch of you."

He set a leisurely rhythm, pressing deep, swirling, and drawing out, sending sensations rippling through her body but not taking her over the edge.

"Faster," she begged, trying to make him go faster with her hand clenching one butt cheek.

"There is no hurry. We have all night," he said in her ear and nipped her lobe.

She liked the idea of all night, but her body was taut, tense, and ready to explode with just the right enticement.

When she began to think she would never orgasm, he increased the thrusting. Taking her harder and deeper until her body exploded, sparking her nerve endings and flashing colored lights in her head. Her hand slid to the bed, and her body slumped after the initial spasms. She'd never felt so relaxed and happy.

Jared started to rise off her.

She wrapped her arm around his neck, holding his wide body on top of her. "Next time, I'll show you how I ride a bull," she said, kissing his cheek, her heart feeling free.

***

Jared sat on the couch staring at Lacey asleep in his bed. What have I done? She told him she was loyal, and he had no doubt she would be faithful to him. He would be faithful to her as well, but what if he lost her like he lost Anita? She had the same daredevil tendencies. Hell, she was talking about riding a bull while her body was healing from a second surgery.

She murmured and flung the sheet off her body. His cock came to attention at the sight of her toned, athletic body. It was this part of his

42

anatomy that had put him in this predicament. No, he couldn't blame it all on that head. He'd talked himself into taking her to bed, making love to her, hoping he could overlook the one thing that made her exactly like Anita. Then she said she'd ride him like a bull. Damn if that hadn't turned him on and at the same time frightened him.

The pink sky heralded another day. He should get dressed, go for a long walk, and clear his head of Lacey. Her good hand skimmed down her body, drawing his gaze to her blonde curls and open thighs, showing the delights awaiting him.

He pushed up off the couch, stepped out of his briefs, and slipped into bed. He would have to overcome his fear of losing her, because after one night in her arms, his heart had toppled all the way for her.

Chapter Seven

Lacey wasn't sure whether to creep into the house unnoticed or just walk in, go to her room, and change her clothes. She'd never had to deal with family after leaving a man's bed. The rush was almost as heady as waiting to get on a bull.

She had a tiny pang of guilt over slipping out of the cabin while Jared took a shower. It wasn't like he'd asked her to stay and walk to breakfast with him. She wanted a shower and clean clothes before entering the dining room.

The main door opened without a sound. She turned, closed it quietly, and pivoted to head up the stairs.

"Shit!" she hissed, nearly bumping into Brett.

"What are you doing sneaking in here in the same clothes you had on yesterday?" His face was in a scowl, but his eyes danced with merriment.

"You scared a year off my life sneaking up like that," she said, making to walk around him.

Brett stuck his arm out. "When I told Jared you were down by the stream, I didn't mean for the two of you to jump into bed together. I wanted you to talk." The humor in his eyes was replaced with concern.

"We did talk." Lacey squared her shoulders. "We have more talking to do, because we were distracted." She raised one eyebrow.

"Distracted. Is that what it's called now." Brett gazed steadily into her eyes. "He may be my best friend but if he hurts you, I'm on your side. You're family."

She hugged him. "I'm more worried I'll hurt him."

"What do you mean by that?" Brett held her away from him. "If you get back on a bull, it could ruin any relationship you and Jared may be working on."

"I can't stop being who I am." She shoved her hair out of her face. "Jared needs someone who is safe and comfortable."

"He needs someone who loves him." Brett released her. "You've had the hots for him since you were thirteen."

She shook her head. How had Brett known about her crush on Jared? "You don't know what you're talking about."

"You can deny it all you want, but I saw the signs. I'm surprised the two of you hadn't hooked up before now."

"He went off to war, I hang out at rodeos." She shrugged. "We are opposites, and I'm not surprised we haven't run into each other." It hurt to find out now, that Jared had been back living in Montana for as long as he had and they hadn't crossed paths.

"But you're both family." He glanced out the window on the door. "Here he comes. You want to talk to him now or after a shower?"

"After a shower." She ran up the stairs to avoid Jared until she could digest Brett's words and her own emotions.

***

Jared shoved the door to the main lodge open and was surprised to see Brett standing in the entry, his arms crossed, and looking as if he were waiting for him. He closed the door with more care than he'd opened it.

"If you're here to see Lacey, she's up taking a shower." Brett nodded toward the dining room.

Jared followed. If Brett knew his cousin was showering, he'd also caught her coming into the lodge from spending the night with him. "Look, Brett…"

"Coffee?" His friend walked over to the large self-serve coffee pot in the dining room. It sat at the end of the long sideboard. There were three large tables in the room with benches and comfortable padded chairs. He wondered if the ranch ever had the room packed during a meal.

45

"Please." Brett offering him coffee was better than a fist to the jaw. Jared sat at the table closest to the coffee pot.

"I'm not mad at you or Lacey," Brett said, placing a steaming cup in front of Jared and taking a seat across the table from him. "You're both adults. But I am worried about both of you."

"Why would you be worried? We know how to take precautions." Jared sipped his coffee.

"That's not what I meant. You are two strong-willed individuals who believe it's your way or no way."

Jared took offense to that. Lacey might be strong-willed, but he wasn't. "I am not as stubborn as she is. I'm the one who will be doing all the compromising, if we make this a relationship."

Brett laughed. "If you make it a relationship? I'd say from Lacey's point of view it is a relationship. Did she tell you how many men she's been on more than one date with?"

"From what she told me, I'm guessing one."

"And that guy stole her faith in men and faithfulness. If she spent the night with you, that means she trusts you to be loyal." Brett took a sip of coffee.

This conversation was only making him angrier than he'd been when he walked out of the bathroom at the cabin and found Lacey gone. "You know me. I'm faithful."

"But will you be able to hang around if she does something you feel is dangerous?"

Leave it to his friend to hone in on the exact thing that had him worried about a relationship between he and Lacey.

"You tried to change Anita and it didn't work. Can you stay with someone you know you can't change?" Brett's question dangled in the air between them.

He didn't have an answer. Not yet. There hadn't been as much talking last night as there should have been. "I don't know."

Melanie entered the dining room, pushing a rolling cart loaded with platters of ham, eggs, toast, buns, and fruit. "You two must be hungry to be here this early." She placed the platters of food on a sideboard.

"Need help with anything in the kitchen?" Brett asked.

"No. I'm good. You two visit." Melanie rolled the cart out of the room.

Jared decided to find out about his friend and the cook. "When are you going to stop staring at her and make a move?"

Brett glared at him. "You're starting to sound like Lacey."

"Well?"

"It's complicated. I don't want to mess up our working relationship." Brett stared at the kitchen door.

"What's complicated. You're both adults, unattached—"

"That's where you're wrong. She's still married to some jerk who beat her. She ran away and is hiding here. If she files for divorce, he'll find out where she is and could come after her." He ran a hand over his face. "She's better off if we keep it platonic."

Lacey walked into the dining room. Her wet hair was pulled up into a ponytail. She wore a body skimming tank top and jeans. "You still plan on taking that ride today?" she asked, her gaze remaining on him.

"If you're up for it. We can saddle up horses after breakfast." Jared pulled out the chair next to him.

"I'll go see if Melanie needs help," Brett said, leaving the table and the room.

"I think I scared him off," Lacey said, picking up Jared's cup of coffee and taking a sip.

He grinned. He should have known she'd think nothing of leaving him to find her own shower and clean clothes.

"Why did you leave? You could have showered with me." He smiled, hoping she saw the mischief he was feeling.

"I could have, but then what would I have dressed in afterwards? I like to put a clean body in clean clothes." She stood, walked over to the sideboard, and started loading up a plate.

He followed her lead, filling a plate for himself and getting her a cup of coffee.

They both sat at the same time.

Before he put a bite in his mouth, he shifted toward her. "Brett told me he thinks we're going to hurt each other. What do you think about that? Because I don't want to hurt you."

She shifted, facing him. "There's always the chance someone will get hurt. I don't plan to intentionally hurt you, but after last night, I am scared."

He put a hand on her cheek. "What are you scared of?"

"How much I want you." The desire heating her gaze took him by surprise.

He'd never seen this depth of desire in Anita's eyes. And if he was truthful with himself, he had never felt complete with her either. Last night he was happy just lying in bed, with his arms wrapped around Lacey.

"There is more to a relationship than desire." He couldn't believe, he, the male in this relationship was talking down sex.

"There's trust." She leaned close. "I trust you to make each encounter magical."

He tapped her nose with his finger. "Eat your breakfast so we can go on that ride." If he didn't put his mind on eating, he would pack her upstairs and show her some magic he'd learned.

Mr. and Mrs. Oatman entered the dining room. "Good morning," they both sang together.

"Good morning," He responded as Lacey finished chewing the food in her mouth.

"You two look happy this morning." Lacey picked up her coffee cup.

"We had good news from our granddaughter this morning. She got engaged last night to a nice boy we both like." Mrs. Oatman's face glowed with happiness.

"Congratulations." Jared wondered if Lacey's parents would be that happy when their daughter finally wed. He glanced sideways at her. She didn't appear to be excited about the announcement.

He bumped her good arm.

"I'm sure your granddaughter picked a nice man." She put a forkful of eggs into her mouth.

Mr. Oatman said, "He is a wonderful young man. He's in the newspaper business."

"Any chance he'll be the one doing my interview?" Lacey asked, knowing it would be too much of a coincidence.

"I don't think so. The PRCA uses local reporters. It will most likely be someone from this area."

The couple focused on the buffet, insisting they should try this or that and worry about their diets when they were home.

Lacey's stomach churned. She wished someone would contact her. Then she could get the interview over with and concentrate on keeping her body fit.

***

Jared had the picnic lunch stowed in the saddlebags and two horses saddled and waiting for Lacey. She'd offered to help Melanie with the breakfast clean-up. She couldn't seem to sit around and do nothing.

He hadn't been this nervous dragging injured soldiers out of harm's way. While he'd realized Lacey wasn't Anita, there were enough similarities that he didn't think reasoning with Lacey would keep her from her dream. That was what scared him the most.

Footsteps sounded outside the barn. He faced the open doorway and waited.

Lacey stepped through the door. The smile on her face spread nearly from ear to ear.

His stomach squeezed with apprehension. He could only think of one thing that would have her that happy. His worst fear.

"Wow, I take back every thought I had about you being a greenhorn," she said, taking the reins he held out to her.

"For having a crush on me when you were thirteen, you'd think you would have known my family owned a cattle ranch. I know how to sit a horse and chase cattle." He chucked her chin and led his horse out of the barn.

She followed. He turned to help her mount since she wouldn't be able to use her left hand or arm. Before he could get to her, she'd swung up into the saddle.

"As smooth as that went, anyone else wouldn't know about your injury if not for the cast."

"And that's the way it's going to be," she said, not waiting for him to mount before heading her horse toward the meadow.

He mounted up and trotted to catch her as she started into the cottonwood trees on the other side. He pulled his horse up alongside.

"You're glowing. Is that the company you're in or something else?"

She smiled and studied him. "What do you think of Melanie?"

He hadn't expected the question and took a minute. "From what I can tell she's a hard worker, tries to please, likes your cousin."

"Yes! And he likes her. All she talked about the whole time we were cleaning was Brett this and Brett that." She frowned. "Why do

49

you think they aren't, dating or…" She glanced his way and her cheeks reddened. "Fooling around like us?"

"Perhaps you should just let them be." He hadn't meant for the words to come out like a reprimand. But he heard it the minute a scowl swept away her happiness. Melanie's past and Brett protecting her was their business, not his or Lacey's.

She pulled her horse up and glared at him. "What? On top of you telling me not to ride bulls, now, you think I should stay out of my cousin's life?" She looked him up and down. "If I'd known climbing in bed with you would make you think you can order me around, I'd have diddled myself and stayed away."

Lacey kicked her horse in the ribs, and they both took off at a lope.

"Damn!" He hadn't meant for the words to come out like they did. And there she was running her horse hell-bent, ducking limbs. "Lacey, stop!"

Chapter Eight

Jared didn't like the idea of chasing after her in the same wild ride she was taking, but he didn't want to lose sight of her either in case something did happen. He realized she needed to cool down before he could talk to her and tell her she'd heard it differently than he'd meant the words to come out. But watching her avoiding branches and trees as the horse galloped through the woods, sent his heart into his throat and his gut clenching.

She finally slowed her horse and walked.

He trotted his horse until he was abreast of the winded animal and grimacing rider. It appeared her attempt to release her anger had caused her arm to hurt.

"Let's get off and rest," he offered.

"No. I'm not getting off until I get to the spot I told you about." Her face was pinched, her eyes staring forward. She wouldn't look at him.

Fine. He'd talk and she could choose to listen or not.

"I'm sorry you took the words I said wrong. I wasn't accusing you of anything, other than being nosy. It would be best to let Brett and Melanie work things out on their own." He glanced over. She rode with her back straight and her nose pointed between the horse's ears. "Like I told Brett his morning, we needed to work things out without him interfering."

Her gaze latched onto him. "You and Brett talked about us this morning?" Her eyes narrowed.

"See how you don't like the thought of him and I talking? I bet Melanie would feel the same way if she knew you and I were talking about her and Brett." He nodded. "Let's let them figure things out for themselves." He glanced at the sweating horse Lacey sat on. "How about we talk about your need to push yourself and those around you."

She wiped at the horse's sweaty neck and for a brief moment regret flickered in her eyes. They continued walking the horses. "There's nothing wrong with striving to be the best at what you do."

"There is if you're putting your life at risk." While in Iraq, he did his job even if it meant he could be shot, but it was to help others, not because he had a need to be the best, his drive was protecting people.

"I don't risk my life. I've worked hard to be good at what I do. I'll have you know that in the last eight years, I've ridden fifty to sixty bulls a year and averaged a thirty-five-point-two-six percentage for staying on a bull. That's up there with the top-ranking bull riders. I've been injured less than most of the top riders. If I want to get back on a bull when my arm is healed, I'll damn-sure do it. Not you or anyone else will stop me." She nudged her horse into a trot.

Even though her words were what he'd expected, he still couldn't shake the fear he felt about letting himself fall in love with her. He kicked his horse into a trot and followed behind, letting her cool down.

He stared at Lacey's straight back and the way she sat the horse. Would this proud woman put her life at risk to prove to herself and the world she was one of the best?

Forty minutes later, Lacey stopped her horse in a grove of white-barked alder. The leaves on the trees were gold and orange from the cooler fall nights. On the outer edges of the grove, larch needles were turning orange, contrasting with the darker green pine and spruce mixed among them.

Jared dismounted and walked over to where Lacey had tied her horse.

"You're right. This spot is beautiful." He tied his horse and untied the blanket and saddlebag behind his saddle.

Lacey stared at the trees while he spread the blanket and placed the saddlebags on the edge.

"Come on, have a seat." He sank down, sitting cross-legged near the saddlebags.

She glanced over her shoulder and shrugged. "I was thinking about going for a hike."

He raised an eyebrow. "Do you think that's safe? This area is known for cougars."

"They could come after me here as easy as if I'm hiking."

"You know they wouldn't. You're just trying to start an argument." He patted the blanket. "Come sit down. As your cousin told me this morning, we have some talking to do if we plan to have a relationship."

Her eyes widened. "You want a relationship with me?" She walked over and sank to her knees, facing him, on the blanket.

"I can't deny the chemistry between us. It's stronger than anything I've experienced before." He picked up a blade of grass and started tying it in knots. "Brett had some valid questions I couldn't answer."

"Like what?" She leaned forward. The low neckline on her shirt revealed the lacy trim on her bra. Not the type of undergarment he would have associated with the tomboy he'd known as a teen.

It was evident she'd dressed to entice him. Even though her actions and words made him wonder if she really cared about him, there were things, like the lacy bra and the way her eyes sparked with desire that proved to him, she cared. Hopefully, he could make her care enough to be less reckless.

"Your eyes have drifted to my breasts." she said, putting a hand under his chin and tipping his face up so their gazes met.

"I was thinking about what you would look like lying on this blanket in just your bra and panties."

She laughed. "I want to know what Brett had to say about us." Her good hand grabbed the bottom of her tank, pulling it off over her head.

The sight of the hot pink, lacy bra against her creamy skin sent his mind racing to places it didn't need to go when they had so much to talk about.

"Maybe you should put that shirt back on," he said, reaching into the saddlebag to find a soda to wet his dry mouth.

"You brought it up, and I like the idea." She kicked off her boots, tugged off her socks, and soon her jeans lay on top of her shirt. "I need to work on my tan anyway."

He guzzled the soda, staring at her matching set of undergarments and her resting on her side, her good arm propping up her head and her top leg, set back behind her bottom leg, like a model in a magazine. Her bright green cast propped on her hip.

"You sure you haven't done any modeling? You strike a fetching pose."

She laughed and rolled to her back. "I don't think I'd like modeling. I can eat what I want when I want." Her good hand rubbed back and forth across her flat belly.

Jared took one last look at her and busied himself pulling things out of the saddlebags. "Care for a soda?"

"Thanks." She reached up. He placed the can in her hand and she slid it around on her body, leaving moist trails.

She damn well knew her motions were heating him up, but he wasn't going to make love to her until they'd had a conversation.

"Brett told me we needed to talk." He stared at her feet, hoping that would keep him from wandering from what they needed to do.

"So talk." She rolled to her front, reached behind her with the one hand and unfastened her bra. "I don't want tan lines."

He couldn't resist her bare back and round, plump ass barely covered in hot pink silk. Jared reached out, running his fingers up and down her spine before cupping her firm buttocks.

"What are we supposed to talk about," she asked in a husky, sexy voice.

"Our pasts." He slid closer, straddled her legs and began massaging her back.

"Oh, man. That feels so good. I could have used you traveling with me."

He liked the idea of traveling with her, giving her massages and special attention.

"Your past is longer than mine, what are you supposed to tell me?"

His hands continued moving across her back as his mind flashed to the parts of his past she needed to know to understand his fears. "I joined the military to get an education. You know I was the youngest of my family and by the time it was my turn to leave home, there wasn't any money for a college education."

"I figured you'd get sports scholarships."

"I did too, but they weren't enough for the education I wanted." He remembered how hard it had been to turn down the scholarship to Gonzaga but there wasn't going to be enough from the scholarship to make his dream come true.

"So, you went into the Army?" She turned her head to the side and glanced back over her shoulder at him.

"Yes. They trained me to be a medic which is the equivalent of an EMT."

"Why don't you work as an EMT instead of an emergency room nurse?" Her eyes closed, her head propped on her good arm.

His hands no longer massaged. He traced the lines of her muscles, ribs, and shoulder blades. "I like being able to keep in touch with the patients and see that they are recovering."

"Like you visited me." Her lips tipped into a smile. "I hope you don't give all your patients a picnic in the woods and a personal massage."

"You're the first." He leaned down, kissing the nape of her neck.

"Carry on with your story."

He skimmed his fingers down her sides, making her squirm.

"Stop, that tickles." She swatted at his hand on her right side.

"While I was in Iraq the second time, I met a photographer. Her name was Anita Sullivan."

Her breath hitched. "Was? As in she…"

"Yes, she was killed while traveling with a caravan." He raised up and rolled Lacey to her back, while his legs still straddled her. Her bra was up above her pert breasts. The sunlight kissed the pink nipples. "She was a thrill seeker like you. Always chasing the best photo even if it took her to places much too dangerous for her to be." He shoved away the memory of Anita running toward enemy fire to get an action shot. Her actions were something he could see Lacey doing. He leaned forward, placing his hands on either side of Lacey's head. "When I see how you light up at the mention of riding a bull, it squeezes my chest and brings back memories of her telling of close escapes." He pressed a soft kiss to her neck. "I don't want to lose you."

Chapter Nine

Lacey better understood Jared's fear. But she wasn't this Anita. She wrapped her good arm around his neck and kissed him. She drew back. "I want to tell you I will never put my life in danger on purpose, but you also have to agree that all our lives are in danger every single day. When we drive a car, when we walk down a street, even going into a building with many other people, we could catch a disease. I can't live as if everything I do could take my life."

"I'm not asking you to do that. I'm asking you not to take unnecessary risks." He raised up.

She went with him, drawing her legs up from between his and wrapping them around his waist. "You told me your fear. I understand."

He lowered his body, pressing her into the blanket and the ground. "Do you really understand? I know we've only reconnected the last few weeks, but Lacey, I feel like there were never any years we were apart. You're the same smart-mouthed, aggravating—"

"Hey!"

He caught her mouth in a mind-numbing kiss of tangled tongues. As quickly as he started the kiss he ended it.

"—stunning girl that I can't get out of my head."

Her heart raced in her chest. "Really? You've thought of me over the years?”

“You were jail-bait back when I was a senior, but I never forgot your face or your determination to best your cousin and I.” He slid a hand under her panties, touching her throbbing clit. “If you take these off, I’ll show you I can be just as determined to best you.”

Just his words started her body vibrating. The last time she’d visited the ranch, she’d lain in this spot and fantasized about Jared making love to her. That her dream was coming true, filled her with happiness.

She unwrapped her legs from his waist, and he slid the garment down her legs, tossing it onto her pile of clothes. Next, he tossed her bra on the pile. She reclined on the blanket, completely naked, enjoying the kiss of the sun on her skin and watched Jared shuck out of his clothes and slip on a condom.

She started giggling at a thought.

He glanced at her, his eyes dark with desire. “What’s so funny?”

“I hope there aren’t any biting flies out right now. We could be in a world of hurt.” She laughed even harder as he scanned the perimeter of the blanket.

“Roll over,” he ordered, helping her move to her front.

“Are you going to massage me some more?” she asked, having enjoyed not only the kneading of her muscles but the heat of his hands on her earlier.

“Something like that,” he said before trailing kisses from behind her ear all the way down her spine. He spread her legs. This time as he retraced the kisses, his fingers found her moist center.

“Oh!” Her one and only other intimate partner had preferred no foreplay, and he usually received the satisfaction of their coming together. Jared’s touch and giving nature turned her on as much as his talent.

His other hand slid under her, cupping a breast and then squeezing her nipple. Her lower body rose up, and he slid his hand out of her and under her hips, holding her up. That’s when she felt him entering.

The sensation of being filled from a different angle, shattered her body. He continued to hold her up and stroked in and out with such a frenzy that her body heated, sparked, and exploded at the same time Jared did.

He held her tight to him as his shaft flexed. He ran a hand down her back, and slowly drew out, placing her on the blanket.

"That was better than my fantasy," she said, before realizing the words had slipped out.

Jared lay on his side next to her. He raised up on one arm. "What fantasy?"

Staring into his face, she couldn't tell him anything other than the truth. She ran a hand through his hair, feeling the length and softness. "The last time I was at the ranch, I came up here, and fantasized you made love to me, here, in this spot."

He leaned down, kissed her thoroughly, and raised back up. "Any other fantasies we can work on?"

"Well, there is the barn, my room in the lodge, and behind the chutes at a rodeo." She raised an eyebrow, daring him.

"We can take care of the first two while I'm here, as for the rodeo," he grimaced. "Not sure I could do that."

A bit of happiness leaked out of her heart. "Why not the rodeo?"

"I don't like an audience."

She burst out laughing.

Jared started tickling her sides. "What's so funny?"

"Stop, stop, I can't breathe!" she cackled, and he finally stopped the assault on her sides.

"We wouldn't do it while a rodeo was going on." She rolled her eyes. "There are too many people and things happening during a rodeo to be able to do anything other than climb on a horse or a bull."

"That's good to know. I really do have performance anxiety in front of a crowd." He reached over and rubbed a nipple between his fingers. "I, however, like this. Fresh air and sunshine."

She glanced down as his enlarging shaft. "I do, too."

They had another romp in the sunshine, this time with Lacey taking control. While Jared's version had been much better than her fantasy, she decided to see how far she could go toward fulfilling his desires.

***

Jared tied the saddlebags and blanket onto his horse. Lacey was tightening the cinch on her saddle. They'd shared two electrifying romps and had talked about everything that they'd seen and done since his senior year in high school. He'd known bits and pieces of her life by asking Brett about her. He'd told her the truth, when he said she had always been on his mind all these years. He didn't know if it was because he'd hoped that someday they would be as close as they were now or just because she had been a constant while he and Brett were friends.

Lacey swung up into her saddle. She grimaced and he put a hand on her leg.

"Do I need to be gentler?" He dropped his gaze to her crotch.

"No. I'm just not used to having sex this much in a short period of time." She leaned down, turned her head so their hats didn't bump, and kissed him. "The more we do it, the more I'll be in shape." Mischief danced in her eyes.

"The more we do it, the more likely you'll end up out of commission." He didn't like the idea of their love making hurting her.

"That won't happen. Anything that makes me feel tingly all over can't be bad for me." She headed back down the mountain. "Come on, Lover."

He knew she was kidding, but he wanted to be more to her than a lover. "What are you going to tell your family?"

"About?" She didn't look over her shoulder, only said it loud enough he could hear.

When the trail widened, he rode up alongside of her. "About us. Friends? More than friends?" He knew unless he placed an engagement ring on her finger, they were friends, but he wanted to hear what she was thinking.

"Good friends." She waggled her eyebrows.

He laughed. "Honestly? That's what you're going to tell your parents?"

She stopped her horse and studied him before she said, "I don't plan on telling my parents anything about you until I know in my heart, you aren't just trying to distract me from my dream—"

He ran a hand across the back of his neck and stared at her. "After last night and what just happened back there in broad daylight, you think I'm just trying to distract you from killing yourself?"

"For the last time, I am not suicidal. I know what I'm doing when I crawl on a bull. I had a mentor who taught me well." She swallowed. "And for what happened last night and just now. It was the best sex I've ever had and if it's all I get, I will die a happy woman."

Jared wrapped his arms around Lacey, dragging her over onto his lap. "That wasn't just sex, Lacey. That was me showing you I care about you." He held her chin and kissed her soft and long. "Don't ever think I only want you for the sex."

She nodded. "Good, because while sex with you is fantastic, I need a friend." Her eyes glistened with an emotion he'd witnessed in the mirror. Loneliness.

Chapter Ten

Lacey hummed as she went about one-handedly saddling horses for the Lister family to go on a ride this morning. Three families had arrived Friday morning. It was a long October holiday weekend. The families were getting their last vacation before the snow came and the ranch wouldn't have as many activities.

She no longer stayed in the main house, she and Jared were sharing the cabin. Monday he was driving her to Bozeman for her doctor's appointment to see if her arm was healing as it should. She didn't want to think about the few days they had left together before he went back to work.

Brett and the Lister family walked into the barn together.

"Did you all put on your long johns and heavy coats," she asked. The last couple of mornings, frost had coated the ground and new snow appeared on the mountains. The cold air was slowly creeping down into the valley.

The three kids, two girls and a boy, all laughed and said yes.

Brett walked up to her. "I'll take them. A newspaper just called and there is a reporter on her way up here. Should be here in an hour."

Lacey stared at her cousin. She'd forgotten about the interview. Since she hadn't heard from anyone at the PRCA, she'd figured they'd changed their minds. "Okay. I'll—do you know where Jared is'?"

"He's waiting for you in the main room." Brett put a hand on her shoulder. "Don't worry. Just be yourself, answer like Mr. Oatman taught you, and everything will be fine."

She nodded and walked away. Brett didn't know how badly the last interview had gone. Her feet dragged as she slowly made her way to the house. There had to be a way to take her mind off the interview.

In the house, she hung up her coat and stocking hat and placed her boots below her coat. She padded on stocking feet into the main room. Jared sat at the game table with a chess board set up.

He glanced up when she entered the room. "I thought we could play chess while waiting."

"Chess? You think that will keep my mind off all the possible questions I could be asked?"

Jared raised an eyebrow. "We could make the game more interesting and you more invested in winning."

The gleam in his eyes caught her attention. "How, exactly?"

"We could take this to the cabin and play strip chess." His voice was low and husky.

She liked the idea but knew they would lose track of the time and the reporter would arrive and they would be all tousled and glowing from their antics. "I like that thought. Maybe save it for another time." She walked out of the room and into the dining room. After being out in the cold, she wanted a cup of hot cocoa. The tall pot of hot water was full and packets of the mix sat in a basket next to the pot.

Jared came into the room. She glanced up from stirring her drink. The worry wrinkles across his forehead stilled her own nerves. There didn't need to be two of them nervous during her interview.

"Let's go back in the other room and see if I can beat you." She knew he had a more intellectual mind than she did, but there were times when cunning and reading the opponent's moves did you more good. Just like riding a bull.

"Is that really what you want to do?" he asked, filling a cup with coffee.

"You know what I'd really like to do?" She peered into his eyes over her cup of cocoa.

"What?"

"I'd like to start working out again. Do you think they'll clear me to do that on Monday?" She sipped the hot liquid and studied his face.

She could tell he was trying to come up with an answer that would appease her.

"It will depend on how you are healing. Why do you want to start working out?" He'd followed her back into the room with a cup of coffee. It was his turn to study her over his steaming cup.

"I think that's why I feel restless. I'm used to being active. Push-ups, sit-ups, pull-ups. Stretching and running. I think that helped settled my nerves." She sipped her cocoa. A run right now would calm her and show the reporter she was keeping in shape. "How about it? Can I go for a run?"

"I can make a sling that will keep your arm from dangling or swinging around." He narrowed his eyes. "And I'm going with you."

"Great! Can we go now? To help use up this nervous energy that is making me crazy about the interview?" She stood.

"I guess so. Let's change into running clothes." Jared walked out of the house, carrying his coffee, and she followed.

Yes! It was about time she resumed her active lifestyle. This sitting around visiting with people and taking them on horse rides was too calm and sedentary. She needed action. The only action she'd been getting was at night in Jared's bed. She smiled. And that was pretty darn amazing.

They dressed in running pants, put on running shoes, and Jared made a sling that hugged her arm to her body.

"Let's go," she said after stretching. She wanted to make an entrance after the reporter arrived.

Jared let her take the lead. She stayed on the most used riding trails, circling the ranch and giving them one small incline. She was sweating halfway through the three-mile loop. Once Jared went back to work, as much as she was going to miss him, she would need to start in getting back in shape. There was no way she was going to fly off a bull the minute the gate opened at NFR.

They jogged out of the trees and toward the main house as a car pulled up to the front of the building. A petite woman of an island descent stepped out.

She turned to them, her gaze flashing over Lacey and ogling Jared. The woman held out her hand. "Lacey Wallis, I'm Jessica Rahn. I was sent here to do an interview with you."

Lacey shook hands with the woman. "Pleased to meet you."

The woman's dark eyes wandered to Jared as she held her hand out to him.

"Jessica Rahn. Are you Lacey's trainer?"

Jared scowled, shook hands, and said, "No, I'm not her trainer. I'm a friend."

The woman's eyes lit up. "I see." She returned her attention to Lacey. "Would you like to clean up before we do the interview. I do want to take photos."

"You could take one now if you like, and then I'll get cleaned up. You know, to show how I am staying in shape." She smiled at the woman.

"May I include you in the photo?" Jessica asked, pulling a camera from her car and pointing it at Jared.

"No. This is Lacey's interview." He touched Lacey on the shoulder. "I'm going to go change."

She nodded. It was best they didn't both walk to the cabin together. She didn't want this reporter doing any more speculating.

"Okay, how about you walk back there a bit, and I'll get some shots of you jogging toward me." Jessica took at least thirty shots. Some with her slinged arm as the focus and others with it slightly hidden. She wasn't sure what angle this woman was going to take.

Jared returned, cleaned up and looking not as angry. "Ms. Rahn, how about a cup of coffee or tea while Lacey gets changed?"

"That would be great." The woman beamed at Jared and headed into the house with a backward glance at Lacey.

Which was fine by her. That way the woman wouldn't see her go into the same cabin as Jared. She jogged to the cabin, took a quick shower, dressed in her rodeo clothes, and pulled her hair into a ponytail, before heading back to the house.

Jared poured the reporter a cup of coffee while dodging all of her questions about whether or not he and Lacey were a couple. He didn't want the world to know about them when he still wasn't sure what they had. The nights were the best he'd ever had with a woman and the days, as long as they didn't talk about bull riding, were pleasant and fun. But while bull riding was in her blood, he didn't see a future with her. And that put an ache in his chest he couldn't cure.

Melanie entered the dining room. "Oh! I didn't know we had another guest." She walked forward, her hand extended. "Welcome to the Tumbling Creek Ranch."

"This is Jessica Rahn. She's the reporter interviewing Lacey," Jared said, at the same moment Lacey walked into the dining room.

"Well, I'm pleased to meet you. Do pick up a brochure on your way out." Melanie shook the woman's hand, mouthed good luck to Lacey, and vanished through the kitchen door.

"Who was that?" Ms. Rahn asked.

"That is my cousin's cook. He owns this ranch. It's a dude ranch for people to vacation and enjoy the outdoors on horseback." Lacey walked over to the hot water pot and stirred up another cup of hot cocoa.

"I see. I thought you had hidden away here to avoid the publicity your last ride drew." The woman sat down at a table and pulled out a notepad and pen.

"No, I came to my cousin's ranch to recuperate." Lacey knocked on her cast. "This arm needs to heal and this is a nice place to relax and do that."

Jared didn't know whether to stay or go. Lacey seemed to be doing well so far. He glanced her direction. She appeared relaxed, but he knew her. The fingers on her good hand were tapping her cocoa mug on the side the reporter couldn't see.

He picked up a magazine, someone must have been reading during breakfast, and sat down a couple tables over from the two ladies. He was out of the reporter's vision but where Lacey could see him. All she'd have to do if she wanted him by her side would be to motion.

"How long before your arm will be healed? Will you be able to ride at the National Finals?" The reporter honed right into the tough questions.

Lacey glanced his direction, then stared at the woman. "I'm not sure about my arm. I have an appointment on Monday to see how it has been healing. I'll have a better idea then. But whether this arm is healed or not, I plan to be at the Finals. It has been my dream since I sat on my first bull in high school."

He knew she'd planned to fulfill her dream, but damn did it have to be this year? She needed to heal before she got on another bull. It took all his will power to not jump into the conversation.

"I read your bio. You've been at this ten long years. How did it feel when you realized you'd made the Finals?"

"I knew the minute the buzzer went off and I was still on top of Red River." Her face lost its glow. "When I dismounted, I stumbled backward and ended up on the ground. I couldn't believe that such a great ride would end with me on my butt and a bull breathing in my face." She avoided eye contact with him. "Before the bullfighters got to me, that dang Red River came stomping my way. He landed on my arm and kicked my head. The safety helmet saved me from who knows what, but he mangled my arm pretty bad." She licked her lips, staring at her cast. "I didn't fully realize I'd made the finals until I was lying in the hospital bed and heard it on the news." She glanced at him and then back at the reporter. "Nothing is going to keep me from getting to the Finals."

And that was why it was a good idea for him to get back to work and try to forget Lacey. He didn't need to be worrying about her. Wondering if she'd come home from a rodeo in one piece or not at all. His gut clenched. He didn't hear the rest of the conversation. His mind was trying to figure out how to avoid Lacey and still be friends with Brett.

"Let's get a few photos in here and then maybe out by the corrals and horses." Ms. Rahn said, pulling out her camera.

Lacey stood and did as the woman directed her. He stood, planning to go for a walk.

"Jared, why don't you let me get a photo of you and Lacey." Ms. Rahn waved for him to join them at the door.

"I'm not a part of her rodeo life." He peered straight into Lacey's eyes. Sorrow filled her hazel orbs. His heart squeezed knowing he'd hurt her, but it was better now than a week before the damn rodeo.

"Let's get those photos by the corrals," Lacey said, leading the reporter out of the main house.

"Damn!" The next few days before he went back to work were going to be hell.

Chapter Eleven

Lacey had trouble getting through the rest of the photos with a smile on her face. Jared had pretty much, in front of the reporter, told her he was dumping her because she wouldn't quit the thing she loved. Anger and sorrow were warring inside of her as she smiled and answered the reporter's questions.

"I thought it looked like you two were a couple," Jessica said, tucking her camera away. "But his comment about rodeo…" The reporter stared into Lacey's eyes. "You sure you want to lose him by trying to be the first woman to ride a bull at the NFR?"

She wasn't sure what she wanted. But she'd set her sights on the National Finals Rodeo and she was so close, she couldn't see giving that up. Not now. No one in her life had ever believed in her dreams. She'd hoped Jared would want her dream for her as much as she wanted it. But it wasn't going to happen.

"If it's meant to be, we'll get together when I'm done chasing the gold buckle." She smiled and made light of their relationship when in her heart, she'd be crushed if when she did give up rodeo life, he had moved on.

Jessica studied her then shook her head. "Some people don't see what they have until it's too late. I wish you luck at the Finals and in keeping that man."

She watched the woman walk to her car and drive away. Her heart told her to find Jared and talk things out. Her gut said he wouldn't be willing to listen. Frustration sent her to the barn.

The first place she'd started working out was in a barn. Helping Dad feed and take care of the animals, she'd packed buckets of feed and water, did pull-ups from anything she could grab and dangle from.

She walked over to the bow gate leading into a stall. With her feet planted under the metal piping, she jumped and caught hold with her good hand. It was the hand that needed the most strength to hold onto the bull rope. After ten pull-ups, she dropped to the ground. Sweat beaded her brow and her arm felt like a cooked noodle. How could she have gotten so out of shape in such a short time? At the wall, she put the palm of her good hand flat on the boards and leaned in. Feeling her pectoral muscles strain, she pushed her body back. It wasn't as good as push-ups on the floor but would have to do until she had two arms.

A decision needed to be made about the next month and a half. Stay here at the ranch or go home. She knew the answer. Stay here. She loved her parents, but they would badger her every day about quitting the rodeo life. Here, Brett let her be, with only an occasional lecture on what she planned to do the rest of her life.

A bucket sat under the spigot. She filled it with water and lifted, doing reps, using different muscles.

"What are you doing?" Jared's tone caused her to drop the bucket and slop water over her legs and boots.

"Not trying to get wet," she replied, and stared down at her wet jeans. It was that or glare at him. She didn't need to add more fuel to his anger. Walking in on her exercising would have only made him even more upset.

"You know what I mean. You don't even know if your arm is healing. Your whole body needs to rest so it can heal." He stomped up to her. "Don't you give a damn about your body?" His gaze drifted the full length of her.

"I do care. That's why I'm exercising. I need to be fit to do what I do. I can't let one muscle go flabby." She raised her injured arm. "This is useless, but I'll make sure the rest of me is ready by Finals."

He shook his head the same way her father did when he didn't understand her drive. "You can't be serious. Even if your left arm isn't healed, you'll climb on the back of a bull?"

"I worked damn hard to get where I'm at right now—"

"Injured?" he cut in sarcastically.

"No! The first woman to ride a bull in the finals." She stepped closer to him, peered into his eyes. "Haven't you ever worked for something that you wanted as much as you wanted to breathe?"

His gaze softened, then heated. His arms wrapped around her, drawing her tight to him. "Yeah, I want you. But without the worry of you riding a bull. That is my dream." His mouth crushed down on hers.

Her first instinct was to fight him off, not allow him to make her lose focus of the argument. But once his tongue breached her lips and started seducing hers, she barely remembered her name.

Her good arm looped around his neck, and her body pressed against him as if his warmth was needed to keep her alive.

A throat cleared loudly, and giggles slipped into her conscience.

Jared heard the approach of several people. He wasn't going to let anyone think what they were doing was wrong. He slowly eased out of the kiss and held Lacey against his side with an arm around her waist.

"Brett, everyone, did you have a good ride?" he asked, ignoring the grin on his friend's face and the wide-eyed stares from the children. Mr. Lister was frowning, but Mrs. Lister had her hands clasped against her chest.

"It was a good ride." Brett's gaze drifted to his cousin. "How'd the interview go?"

Lacey straightened, trying to put some space between them, but he held tight. "She was nice. Asked good questions, took a lot of photos." Her gaze flashed to him, then back to her cousin.

"Tie your horses to the rail and head on in for lunch," Brett told the family. Commotion ensued as kids argued over where they had found their horse and the adults sorted things out.

Lacey tried to pull away from Jared, but he kept a firm hold on her. The only way she could leave was to cause a scene. She wouldn't do that and cause trouble for her cousin. Jared kept her tucked against him, enjoying her warmth and curved hip under his hand. He had a feeling Brett wanted to talk to them, and he was going to stick around. His friend seemed to be the only person who could get Lacey to listen.

When the kids and adults were gone, Brett stopped uncinching the saddle on his horse and faced them.

"You two might want to cool it outside the cabin while we have so many families here." Brett tipped his hat back. "We walked into a scene out of an R-rated movie. Another minute and it looked like you two would have moved to the hay stack and started throwing clothes."

Jared grinned. That idea had been in his mind. "We'll keep that in mind the next time."

Brett and Lacey shook their heads at the same time.

"There won't be a next time," she said, rolling from his arm. Fire sparked in her eyes and it wasn't from passion.

"What's going on?" Brett stepped forward. "You two were just kissing like you were going to devour one another. What are you ticked off about?" He directed this question to his cousin.

"We were discussing an issue we can't agree on and then he…he…" Lacey glared at Jared. "He grabbed me and started kissing me and I forgot."

He couldn't stop the grin forming on his lips. "You forgot what?"

She shoved him with her good hand. "You know what you did. You did it on purpose to get me to stop talking."

"I kissed you because it was that or shake the livin' daylights out of you." He crossed his arms and stared at her. She was the only person he knew who could get him to have every emotion, and then some, in the matter of several minutes.

"It's clear you two have some talking to do. Take it to the cabin or saddle up horses and take it to the mountain, but don't keep at it here, where my young guests may see more than their parents want them to." Brett turned back to the horses and continued unsaddling.

Lacey walked to the horse farthest from Brett and him and started unsaddling.

"Do you want to take a ride?" Jared asked her.

She nodded. "It's better than being in the cabin with you. At least I'll have a horse to run away from you."

Fear punched his lungs. He didn't want her galloping through the trees like their last disagreement when they were riding.

***

Lacey's face heated thinking of the Lister family walking in while Jared was kissing her senseless. That was why she was now riding a horse, to avoid him getting a chance to put his arms around her and make her forget they had a major problem with their relationship.

"You haven't said one word since we left the barn." Jared's voice carried on the cold air.

She rubbed a hand over her running nose and didn't reply.

"Brett told us to talk out our problems. Can't do that if you don't talk." Jared moved his horse up beside hers.

"There is nothing to talk about. You don't believe in my dream. I have made it this far on my own and I'll fulfill my dream without you or anyone else by my side." She glanced over at him. Why did he have to be so damn handsome? And the emotions in his eyes…No. She couldn't let her body have her falling in his arms again.

"Think about it from my perspective. I patch people together. It goes against everything I'm made of to stand beside you when you are putting yourself in danger every time you crawl on a bull and challenge your dream." He put a hand on her arm. "It would make me ill to watch you ride a bull."

"I'm not asking you to watch me. I'm asking you to support my dream." Knowing what he'd witnessed in his career as a medic and now as an ER nurse, to say watching her ride a bull would make him ill, told her how much he cared about her.

He shook his head. "I can't support something that puts you in danger." The sorrow in his eyes shattered her heart. "When I leave here, we'll have to say good-bye. I can't pretend you aren't going to ride bulls and love you when you're around." He released her arm and turned his horse back to the ranch.

Lacey sat atop her horse, staring into the woods, tears rolling down her face, until the sun disappeared.

Chapter Twelve

Lacey rode in Brett's truck as they followed Jared to the doctor's office in Bozeman. Because of the discomfort their tangled relationship was causing at the ranch, Jared had decided to call his vacation short and remain in the city after her appointment. But he'd insisted on going to the appointment with her. He said to help her and Brett understand what the doctor had to say. She knew it was because he cared.

Sitting in the waiting room, she glanced at Jared more than she should. But it would be her last chance to drink in his features. Once she returned to the ranch, she had a feeling she would never see him again. It would be too painful for both of them.

"Dr. Parley will see you now," the nurse said, motioning for them to follow her.

"You have quite the support system," the nurse said.

Lacey smiled but didn't comment. Brett looked nervous. Jared had changed the minute they entered the hospital and walked to the doctor's waiting room. Many of the women and men in uniforms greeted him. He was in his element here.

"Lacey, good to see you," Dr. Parley said, as they all walked into what appeared to be the doctor's office. "Jared, I see you are still with the patient." The doctor's eyes twinkled.

"I'm surprised you're seeing us in your office," he said, sitting

Lacey in a chair in front of the desk.

"I had an emergency surgery this morning, making me backed up. I wanted to visit with Lacey first then we'll take the cast off, take x-rays, and decide what will happen from here." she motioned to the two chairs to the side of the room. "Gentlemen, have a seat."

"Lacey, how is the arm feeling?"

She wiggled her fingers with a lot of concentration. "It doesn't hurt, but it tingles at times."

Dr. Parley nodded. "That's because we had to reconstruct some nerves, tendons, and muscle. I'm surprised at the movement you have in your fingers. That's a good sign."

Lacey grinned and looked over her shoulder at the two men. Brett grinned back. Jared's brow furrowed as he met her glance.

A nurse walked in.

"Rachel, take Lacey to a room where you can get her vitals. Jared, you can go with her and help take the cast off. I'll want to see the arm before you send her to x-ray." Dr. Parley stood. "Mr. Wallis, I'll escort you back to the waiting room until after we get the x-rays back."

Lacey stood and walked over to the nurse. Jared followed them down hall.

"You're the lady bull rider, aren't you?" the nurse asked.

"Yes." Lacey smiled at the woman.

"Why do you want to ride a bull?" she asked, holding open a door to a room.

"Because I'm good at it and the thrill I get when riding a bull is unlike any other." Her gaze darted to Jared and flicked back to the nurse. Except for when Jared made love to her. It was thrilling, heart melting, and just as intoxicating as staying on a bull for eight seconds.

"I still don't understand." The nurse became busy taking her vitals and discussing with Jared the business of taking the cast off.

When the cast rested in a bucket and the nurse had gone off to tell the doctor she was ready, Jared caught her by the chin and stared into her eyes. "Don't get your hopes up that you'll be able to ride a bull right away just because Dr. Parley was pleased you could move your fingers."

"I hadn't thought that." His thinking she'd hop on a bull because she was healing well had her jerking her chin out of his grasp. "I'm in no shape right now to ride a bull and I know it." She glared at him.

"I'm not stupid."

He nodded his head and stood, moving away from her. She hated the way he was treating her today. Where was the gentle loving man she'd spent so many wonderful hours and days with?

The door opened. Dr. Parley and the nurse walked in, crowding the room.

"I'll be out with Brett," Jared said, leaving the room.

She stared at the door as the doctor examined her arm. How had they become so close only to feel like they were a universe apart?

"Everything looks like it is healing well. Once I see how the bone fragments are doing, I'll know what the next course of action will be." Dr. Parley motioned to the nurse. "Take Lacey down for x-rays."

***

Jared sat in the waiting room feeling out of place. He was used to being the person moving around in the background, helping the patients and being busy. Not sitting.

"What is up with you and Lacey?" Brett asked, putting down the year-old *Field and Stream* magazine he'd been reading.

"Nothing. Absolutely nothing." Knowing it and then voicing it out loud, tore his heart. She was the first woman to come along that made him forget his past and look toward a future. But there was no future with a woman who was hell-bent on putting herself in danger.

"Nothing? I don't believe that. I've seen you two twined together and lost to the rest of the world. And I've seen you laughing and having a good time. That's not nothing." Brett leaned forward his forearms resting on his thighs. "This have to do with her career choice?"

Jared stared at his best friend. "What do you think? I patch people up for a living, how do you think I could overlook that she puts herself in danger every time she rides a bull?"

"She's good at what she does."

"Good? Then why is she in there having her shattered arm examined?" Jared didn't need to hash this out with Brett. He and Lacey had talked the whole thing to death. Neither one was willing to compromise.

"You are both too strong-willed." Brett leaned back, picked up another magazine, and ignored him.

He didn't know which was worse, talking about Lacey or being

74

ignored by Brett. It felt like half the day had gone by when the nurse called them back to Dr. Parley's office.

Lacey sat in the chair in front of the desk. Another chair had been placed beside it. He motioned for Brett to take the chair. He stood on the other side of Lacey.

"The mangled nerves, tendons, and muscle are healing. They will require some physical therapy as soon as all the bones are set."

Lacey gasped. "You mean healed?"

"No, set. We were only able to piece part of your bone together. We need to do another surgery to graft on the bone that was too shattered to put back together." Dr. Parley glanced at Jared. "I had assumed Jared told you about all of your injuries."

Lacey shook her head and peered up at him. The questioning in her eyes caught him off guard.

"I didn't see any sense in telling you everything. I told you, you would need another surgery."

"But you failed to explain why. Instead of telling me to stay off a bull, you should have been explaining my medical injuries to me." She flashed him a glare and shifted her attention to Dr. Parley.

He mentally knocked himself upside of the head. He should have told her the truth rather than harping on the one thing that was making her stay focused on healing.

"The x-rays show the large breaks we put back together are knitting nicely." She held up an x-ray. "See the white spaces here and here. Those are the spots we need to graft the bone. I think you are a candidate for the allograft, which means we won't have to take any bone from you. I have a packet of brochures made up for you to take home and read." Dr. Parley looked at each of them and returned her gaze to Lacey. "I would like to do the surgery within the next three weeks."

Lacey nodded her head.

Jared put a hand on her shoulder. She shrugged it off. He didn't blame her but it hurt.

"What is the recovery time after the surgery?" Lacey asked, pulling out her cell phone and opening the calendar app.

"You'll find most of your answers in the material in the brochure. If you have any questions just call." Dr. Parley opened her laptop and started typing. "I can schedule you now."

He didn't listen as they set up the dates. Instead, he was kicking himself for not pulling his head out of his ass and telling Lacey exactly what her injuries were and what would be happening in the next few months.

"Sounds good. I'll have her back here November first," Brett said, shaking hands with Dr. Parley.

"My nurse will send you the information for pre-op and what to expect after the operation." Dr. Parley put an arm around Lacey. "Don't worry. We'll have you as good as new in eight months. You're healing nicely."

"Thank you."

He saw the wheels spinning behind Lacey's eyes. What was she thinking? It couldn't possibly be riding at the National Finals in December. She would have only a little over a month since the surgery.

Brett and Lacey headed down the hall.

Jared caught up to them. "Hey, if you need a place to stay before, during, or after the surgery, you can stay at my place. In fact, it's been a long day. You could crash there tonight and get off first thing in the morning."

Brett stopped and faced him. "I like the idea but it's up to Lacey."

The stubborn woman had kept on walking.

"It looks like a 'no' from her." Brett slapped him on the back. "I'll see what I can do to talk you up, but you may have to dig yourself out of this hole." He pivoted and jogged down the hall to catch up with his cousin.

He watched them turn the corner. The best thing he could think of was throwing himself back into his work. He'd stop by the ER and let them know he was back in town and ready to work whenever they needed him. Work had eased the pain when Anita died. Work had kept him sane when he returned to civilian life. And work would help him get over Lacey.

Chapter Thirteen

Lacey sat in the upstairs room at the ranch. The pre-op and after surgery information sat on the bed beside her. She had a tough decision to make. One she wished she could talk to someone about.

She glanced at the phone on the bed beside her. Calling Jared was out of the question. They'd had only one brief conversation since he returned to Bozeman. She and Melanie had become close the last few weeks, but she'd also witnessed how close the woman was with her cousin.

"You're avoiding the people you know will tell you to go ahead with the surgery." Her voice echoed in the silence. She had to face it. Her desire to talk was with someone who would tell her to put the surgery off, keep getting in shape, and head to the Finals in December.

Right now, her arm didn't hurt. The cast kept it stable and the only way it would get hurt worse when she rode, was if she landed on the ground. That wasn't going to happen. She picked up her phone and punched Gabe Perkins' number.

"Hey, Princess, I was wondering when you were going to call me," the gruff ex-bull rider said.

Lacey laughed. "I'm ready to train for the Finals," she said. "Do you have a spare bungalow where I can stay until December?"

"You know I do. How's the arm?" His gruff voice softened.

"Getting better every day." So, she lied a bit. It was getting better. It wouldn't be normal until she had the graft done.

"I'll pack up tomorrow and be at your place Thursday." Anticipation at getting back into riding mode had her nerves jingling.

"I'll be waiting for you. I already have videos of all the bulls that are going to be at the Finals. Kit and Tad are here."

"Great!" She hung up and started packing. Gabe had never let her down in her dream of making the Finals. He'd get her whipped back into shape and ready for the bulls she drew.

***

"What do you mean you're leaving?" Brett stared at her from the head of the table and Melanie watched her from straight across.

"I'm going to Gabe's to get ready for Finals." She had waited until breakfast to say anything. Better to not let Brett think on things too long.

"Gabe's? Your trainer? What about your surgery?" He looked so much like her dad at that moment, Lacey had a hard time coming up with the words.

She swallowed twice, took a drink of her coffee, and said, "I'm postponing it until January."

"January?" Brett stood up and paced back and forth. "You could make that arm worse by riding and not taking care of it."

"I read the information they sent me. I could be in the hospital from one to five days. And no strenuous exercise for three months. That means I wouldn't have a chance in hell to be at Finals. I'd have to start all over again trying to get where I'm at now. If I postpone the surgery, I can ride this year, and no matter the outcome, I'll have achieved my dream." She stood up and walked over to him. "There is no guarantee that after the surgery I can still ride or that I'll be as good as I was this year."

She spun toward Melanie. "I want to achieve my dream. Then take a year off to let my arm heal and decide if I want to continue or not." She pleaded with the woman. "Is that so wrong?"

"Will you do more damage to the arm if you ride and don't have the surgery?" Melanie asked.

"I don't think so, but I plan to stop in and see Dr. Parley and tell her I'm moving the surgery to late December or January."

Melanie glanced over at Brett, then back to Lacey. "If you won't cause any more harm, then go for your dream. Get it out of your system and move on."

She hugged Melanie. "Thank you!" Lacey faced her cousin. "I can't promise this is the last rodeo for me, but I have to finish this year."

Brett nodded. "I still don't agree. And I damn sure won't tell your mom and dad, you'll have to do that. But if you have to do this, get well prepared, Hot Rod."

She grinned at the name he'd given her when she was eight and raced her bike and horse everywhere she went. "I'll call them tonight."

"Don't forget to call Jared," Melanie said.

Lacey stared at the woman. "Why would I call him?" The last person she wanted to call was the man whose voice turned her to a puddle of desire and who had contempt for her dream.

Melanie shook her head. "Because he cares about you and might like to know what you've decided to do."

"He'll only get mad and tell me how stupid I'm being." She sat down and finished her breakfast. A voice in the back of her mind asked her the same thing.

***

Jared walked out of a room and did a double take. The tall woman with a swinging blonde ponytail looked a lot like Lacey from the back.

"Get it together," he told himself and headed to the desk to get the paperwork to check out the man he'd just finished bandaging. Since leaving Tumbling Creek Ranch, he'd spotted Lacey everywhere he went, only to have it turn out to be a woman he didn't know. He couldn't get her off his mind or out of his heart, no matter how many hours he worked or how he exhausted himself at the gym.

A glance down the hall as the woman turned the corner and his heart started racing. It was Lacey. Had she come here looking for him? He handed the clipboard to the other nurse. "Take this to the patient in three."

Long strides carried him down the hall and around the corner. Lacey stood at the reception desk for Dr. Parley. Was she having problems with her arm? He lengthened his stride and walked into the waiting area as a nurse took Lacey through the door to the rooms and Dr. Parley's office.

He smiled at the receptionist and took a seat. The minutes passed.

Five. Ten. Fifteen minutes later the door opened and Lacey stepped through. Her expression was one of deep concentration.

"Lacey." He stood.

Her gaze flashed to him. Happiness lit on her face a moment before annoyance replaced it.

"How did you know I was here?" She grabbed his arm, leading him out of the waiting room and into a corner of the corridor.

"I saw you walk in. Is your arm bothering you? Is that why you were talking to Dr. Parley?" He put a hand on her arm and all the empty nights without her washed away.

"My arm is fine." She gazed into his eyes. "How have you been?"

"Busy." He leaned forward. "I've missed you."

She swallowed and tears glistened in her eyes. "I've missed you, too."

"I can take an early break. Can we go somewhere and talk?" He willed her to say yes. The last few weeks had been the most miserable he'd ever spent.

Lacey worried her bottom lip between her teeth and watched him.

"Come on. We can go someplace public. I promise to behave myself." He cupped her cheek. "I just want to hear your voice and see you're well."

"You can do that standing here," she said, rubbing her cheek against his palm.

Damn! She was getting his blood racing.

"Come on." He took her hand in his and led her back toward the emergency wing. He stopped at the desk long enough to tell them he was taking his lunch break and led her out the doors not waiting for the women he worked with to contemplate the cowgirl he pulled out of the hospital and over to his truck.

"Are you hungry?" he asked, opening the passenger door for her.

"A little." She stepped up into the passenger seat and he closed the door.

Lacey! He had her in his truck and she was going to talk to him. His heart raced as he started the vehicle and headed to a nearby, quiet bar. This time of day there would be few patrons.

"Where are we going?" Lacey asked, studying him.

"A quiet bar not far from here." He glanced over. Her color was good, her eyes shining. Her soft lips were tipped in a wistful smile.

"You're looking healthy. Brett's ranch seems to be good for you."

"Yeah, the fresh air and working with animals are two of my favorite things." Her hands fidgeted.

"Did you come down here today for tests for your surgery?" He pulled into the parking lot. As he'd figured, only two cars were in the lot besides the cook and bartender's vehicles.

"No, I didn't come down for tests. I was passing through and stopped in to ask Dr. Parley some questions." She was out of the truck before he could round the front and get her door.

He escorted her into the dimly lit interior. He helped her out of her jacket, and they sat at a small table in the corner.

"What can I get you two?" the bartender asked as he approached the table.

"Lacey?" Jared asked.

"Hot tea and a BLT, please."

"I'll have coffee, a burger with all the works, and fries." Jared leaned back in his seat as the man hurried away.

"What questions did you have?" He reached toward her cast.

She pulled it back but not before he noticed all the wear. It looked like she hadn't listened to the doctor about her arm not being healed completely; the need for another surgery.

"What do you do here in the city when you're not working?" she asked, avoiding his question.

"I work twelve-hour days and go to the gym. My days off, I usually go hiking, skiing, or kayaking."

Her eyes narrowed. "You ski and kayak, two potentially dangerous sports and yet, you frown on my riding bulls? Boy, is that hypocritical."

"Wait a minute. There is a difference. They are hobbies. I do them for enjoyment and I don't take risks." He leaned back as the bartender delivered their hot drinks and a basket of condiments. When the man left, Jared reached across the table, capturing Lacey's good hand. "I don't want to talk about anything that makes us argue. I've missed you."

Her eyes softened, the stormy dark green of moments before changing to a light green with brown specks. "I've missed you, too. Brett and Melanie are so wrapped up in the ranch and each other that I didn't have anyone to hang out with."

He moved his thumb back and forth across the underside of her wrist. Her pulse raced under his thumb. He wanted to pack her out to the truck and take her home. But he'd learned from the beginning, with Lacey he had to turn down his caveman instincts. Except in bed. She liked it rough, hard, and fast. Just thinking about it, had his cock throbbing.

"I have four days off next week, I could come hang out with you."

Her eyes widened a second before her lids lowered halfway. "I'd enjoy that but I won't be there."

"That's right, you'll be here, having your surgery. It's good my days off coincide with that. I can keep you company while you recuperate." He waggled his eyebrows, thinking of the things he could do to take her mind off the pain of the surgery.

She shook her head. "I won't be here either."

"What do you mean you won't be here? Your surgery is scheduled for the first."

"I'm not having the surgery then. It's rescheduled for December twenty-first." She stared into his eyes. "I'm postponing the surgery so I can participate at the NFR."

As the words sunk in, his heart squeezed with fear. "Why? You can't be serious?"

Anger shot from her eyes and she ripped her hand from his. "I am serious. This is my chance to go to the Finals. I may never be as good. I can't fall short of my dream when I'm this close." She put her hand on his arm. "I'll get the surgery done in December. Then I'll take a year off from riding and see how I feel after that. But I can't take a year off now and then never get another chance at the National Finals Rodeo. I couldn't live with the knowledge I was right there and didn't go all the way."

He understood her conviction to her dream. But damn! Her dream could kill her. "How do you know you'll be strong enough to even stay on a bull?"

"That's why I'm going to stay with my mentor, Gabe Perkins. We'll study videos of the bulls who will be at the finals, and I'll work on form and build my muscles." She dug her fingers into his arm. "I can't not try." Her gaze beseeched him. "You have to understand. If I don't try, I'll be kicking myself for not following through."

He had to admit her tenacity had always been one of the things that had endeared her to him. "There's no way of talking you out of this?" He leaned back as their food arrived.

Lacey shook her head. "I've made up my mind. I'm riding at National Finals and I'll worry about the future after that."

Chapter Fourteen

Lacey stood beside Jared's truck in the hospital parking lot. She'd been surprised when he didn't raise a stink over her riding at the Finals. He'd asked her questions about Gabe's place and where she'd be staying while there as they ate.

He walked over to her. "I'd like to visit you at this Perkin's place. May I?"

A part of her was thrilled that he wanted to see her, another part was skeptical that he'd talk Gabe into not helping her prepare. She was leery of his tamed down attitude toward her riding.

"I'll ask Gabe when I get settled in and let you know."

A heated smile spread across his face and started her body humming. "I'll wait for your call." He stepped closer, wrapping his arms around her. "Or I could call you tonight?"

She shook her head. "I'll be going through an area with limited service tonight. I'll call you when I'm settled in at Gabe's."

"I've missed your lips. Any chance I can get a kiss to last me until I see you again?" He didn't wait for an answer before capturing her mouth.

She clenched his scrubs in her good hand and hung on as her body caught fire and she dallied her tongue around his. The kiss reverberated through her body like a herd of stampeding cattle. She wanted more.

A horn honked.

Jared drew out of the kiss, holding her up with his arms. "I didn't realize how much I'd missed you until I saw you walking down the hall today." He rested his forehead on hers. "Promise you'll call when you get settled."

She locked her knees and used her hands to shove away from him. "I promise. But you aren't going to talk me out of riding at the NFR."

He studied her. "I do understand wanting to fulfill your dream. I'm working on my fear of losing you." Jared ran a finger down the side of her face. "You don't know how hard I'm trying."

The flash of pain she witnessed in his eyes had her wondering how she could be so lucky to have him in her life.

"I'm grateful you are trying." She glanced over his shoulder to the emergency room doors and her face heated. "You might want to go back to work so the others will do their jobs." Several nurses and a couple other people in uniforms stood at the emergency room doors watching them.

Jared shook his head. "Now they are going to want to know all about my cowgirl." He grinned. "I think I'll keep them guessing." He kissed her lips. "Call me."

She nodded, her heart thumping in her chest like a jackhammer. Her legs were a bit wobbly after his thorough kiss, but she managed to get to her truck and behind the wheel without making a fool of herself. She glanced at the emergency doors and saw the employees crowding around Jared. A laugh burst out of her. It was about time he was in the spotlight instead of her.

Minto, North Dakota was a good twelve hours away. She'd stop when she became sleepy and pull into Gabe's place tomorrow afternoon. For the moment, it felt as if a burden had been lifted. Jared wanted to visit her at Gabe's, and he didn't fight her on not getting the surgery done now. Was he possibly coming around to see she was not giving up on her dream?

***

Jared stood in the airport scanning the crowd for Lacey. When he'd discovered how long it would take to drive and he'd only have four days, he'd purchased a plane ticket and asked Lacey to pick him up in Grand Forks.

His gut started to twist when he'd stood at the arrival gates for fifteen minutes and no sign of Lacey. Why wasn't she here? Did she have an accident? He pulled out his phone and sent her another text, saying he was waiting at the arrival gate.

Another ten minutes went by and he was the only one standing by the exit. A man of about sixty with bowed legs, gnarled hands, a limp, and a cowboy hat walked toward him. He stopped back about ten feet.

"You Jared from Bozeman?" he asked, his voice raspy and gritty.

His heart started to race and panic squeezed his chest. "Yes. Where's Lacey?"

"I dropped her off at the store to get the groceries. Don't like sticking around this town too long." He stuck out a hand. "Gabe Perkins.

"Jared MacIntyre." He was still concerned about Lacey not picking him up.

"Come on." Perkins spun around, heading back the way he'd come.

Jared shouldered his backpack and followed. He was surprised Lacey hadn't met him and even more surprised at the limping man ahead of him. He didn't seem to be too hospitable.

Once they were in the truck and headed out of the airport parking lot, Jared asked, "Why is Lacey getting groceries here?"

The man glanced at him, then focused back on the traffic. "Cuz there ain't much for shopping in Minto. I come here once a month to shop."

In their phone conversations, Lacey had said Minto was a quaint little town, but he'd thought there would be all the stores the people living there would need.

Perkins navigated the traffic and pulled into a large warehouse store parking lot. He circled several times until a spot near the front opened. He pulled in and parked, tugged his hat down over his face, and slid down as if to take a nap.

"Don't we need to go help her?" Jared asked.

"Can if you want."

Jared shoved his backpack to the middle of the seat and stepped out. He didn't have a clue how long she'd been in the store or where to look for her, but he'd start with the check-out stands. After entering the store, he headed straight for the lines. Her signature ponytail was the first thing he spotted. Four lanes over, she stood beside a large rolling cart.

Making his way to her, he eyed the cartons and large quantities on the cart and became angry with the man sleeping in the truck. She had an arm in a cast and he sent her in here to lug heavy boxes.

She glanced up and smiled.

When he stood beside her, she said, "Good, I'm glad Gabe found you."

Jared scanned her face. She looked good. "Why did he leave you here managing all of this by yourself?"

"I told him to go pick you up. I didn't think you'd like hanging out in the store with me while I shopped." She put a hand on his chest. "It's good to see you, too."

"I don't mind helping you shop as long as we're together." The line moved up, and he moved behind the cart, shoving it forward. "You shouldn't be lugging these boxes and this cart."

She frowned. "Don't start telling me what I can and can't do. You came here to be supportive." Her hazel eyes stared into his. "Didn't you?"

He shoved out a heavy sigh. "I came here to be with you and see for myself if you really are ready to climb on a bull."

A dazzling smile shot heat through his body. Something he'd said had made her very happy.

"I could kiss you right now, but we seem to lose track of where we are when we kiss." Her eyes sparkled with desire.

"Don't worry, I've been thinking up all sorts of wonderful ways to show you I've missed you."

He shoved the cart forward and twenty minutes later, he pushed the cart and all the boxed food out to the truck.

***

Lacey couldn't believe Jared stood in her bungalow on Gabe's ranch. She wasn't the only bull rider here at the moment. Two other cowboys who had trained with Gabe were going to the Finals as well. Kit Marlow and Tad Neevers. They were both younger than her by at least five years. When she'd arrived, they had both jeered and made comments to one another. But after a week, they regarded her as an

87

equal and listened when they all sat around watching bull videos and talking strategies.

"I was happy to know you had a bungalow. I wasn't sure Perkins would like us fooling around in his house if that was where you stayed," Jared said, dropping his backpack on the bed and wrapping her in an embrace.

"He wouldn't have heard anything. He sleeps like the dead because he takes pain pills."

Jared's eyebrows rose. "He need the painkillers because of too many spills from a bull?"

She shook her head. "Ironically, it was a car accident that crippled him, not riding bulls. It also ended his career when he was at his peak."

"Now he trains up-and-coming bull riders?"

"Yes. Three of his students are in the Finals this year. Me and the two you'll meet at dinner."

"What are the other two like?" He sat on the bed, pulling her down onto his lap.

"I don't want to talk. We have a couple hours until dinner." She started unbuttoning his shirt. When he'd walked up to her in the store as if they'd just parted while she'd shopped, her body had started tingling. His scent swirled around her and she couldn't wait until they were alone. "Gabe said I could have the rest of today off, but tomorrow, I have to keep with the routine."

"Routine? Are you riding bulls here?"

"No. No one wants to get injured before finals. But we're working out and watching videos."

Jared's eyes gleamed. "I can give you a much better workout."

"That's what I'm counting on." She pulled his shirt tails out of his jeans and flung the shirt toward the chair.

His fingers went to work on her shirt, but the snaps popped free much easier than the buttons she'd worked loose. It took extra time to work her shirt over her cast. As soon as he had her bra flinging through the air, his tongue and teeth teased her nipples.

Her arms dropped to her sides as she reveled in his touch. "I've missed you." Her voice was breathy and low.

"I don't like thinking about you constantly. It makes doing my job hard." He grasped her head, peering into her eyes. "When these finals are over, move in with me."

Her heart stuttered and beat harder. He'd asked her to move in with him. "I don't know what will happen after—"

"Let me take care of you after your surgery. I have good qualifications." He lowered his head, capturing her lips and drugging her with a long, slow, sensuous kiss.

He held her head back, running soft, wet kisses down her neck, across her collar bone and down to her breasts.

She wanted to say yes, to have him with her every night and to help her through her mending. But would he agree if she decided to return to bull riding?

His fingers worked her zipper loose. She stood and he shoved her jeans down her legs. Her boots stopped the downward motion at her calves. He pulled her back down on his lap and worked the boots off her feet, along with her socks and the jeans.

"You are overdressed now," she said, working the button of his jeans through the hole and grasping the zipper.

He stood, placed her on the bed, and shucked out of the rest of his clothes.

Lacey stared at his body. She had never seen a more muscled, magnificent man. And he was hers.

She reached down to shove her panties off.

He stopped her actions. "Not yet." A smile played on his lips as his gaze moved up and down her body. "You wore those just for me, didn't you?"

All she could do was nod. The heat in his eyes had brought a lump to her throat. She had purchased this bra and panty set with him in mind. The way he'd enjoyed seeing her in the hot pink set, she thought he'd like this black lacey set with pink ribbons.

He settled on the bed next to her and ran his hands over every inch of her that wasn't covered by the panties. Her body hummed, heated, and throbbed. Need clenched her insides.

"Jared, please," she pleaded, wanting him to enter her.

His hands slid to her hips and his thumbs hooked the sides of her panties. Slowly, he slid the garment down her legs, when she would have rather he ripped them and slammed into her.

When the panties hung from the chair arm, he flopped onto his back and slid on a condom. "How about you ride me like I'm a bull?"

He couldn't have said anything that would have made her hotter. Before he had his hands back to his sides, she scrambled to her knees and straddled his belly. She could make the tempo as fast and hard as she wanted.

She raised up, settled over his shaft, and lowered with one fast motion.

His eyes widened, and he shoved upward, making sure she was taking in every inch. She rotated her hips, swirling around him, her arm in the cast held in the air and her other hand, locking in his. His other hand settled on her hip, driving her down onto his shaft. She rode him like he was a bucking bull. Rocking, swirling, rising up and slamming down.

A sheen appeared on his brow as his eyes closed, his hand on her hip tightened and he shoved up hard and held it. He pulsed, and she rocked, sending her body into a spasm of delight.

Spent, she lay on top of him, their bodies still connected.

"Riding you is as exhilarating as riding a bull," she said, kissing his chin.

"Remember that," he said, pulling her up and kissing her until her body was on fire and needy once again.

Chapter Fifteen

Jared watched the two young men and Lacey hang upside down from a bar and do inverted sit-ups. Three sets of twelve reps. He didn't think he could do that many. Then they twisted their bodies and did two sets more. He'd spent the morning watching them work out harder than he'd worked out for high school football and damn near what he'd done in boot camp.

He had to admire how Lacey did everything the cowboys did except the push-ups on the floor. She did other things to work the muscles on her right side. He was glad to see she was taking care of the injured arm.

"Time for lunch," Perkins said, walking into the barn where the three had been working out.

So far, he'd seen very little that Perkins did for the three other than tell them when it was time to work out and when it was time to eat. Lacey said all he asked of them was that they paid for room and board while they prepared for the finals.

He didn't understand why she couldn't have accomplished all of this at Brett's ranch. He would have felt more comfortable there. Perkins made him feel unwanted, the two young cowboys gave him knowing looks, raised eyebrows, and nods.

"Come on, let's eat," Lacey said, looping her arm through his and walking out into the cold November air. He worried snow might fall in the next couple of days. He didn't want to get snowed in here. The extra time with Lacey would be great but not the inactivity during the day.

Mrs. Perkins stood at the back door, waving them all in. He liked the woman. She was not plump but not slender either. A smile was always on her face and she spoke softly. How she put up with the crusty old cowboy, he didn't know.

When they were all at the table and Mrs. Perkins had said the blessing, Perkins glanced around the table at the cowboys and Lacey. "We'll look at videos this afternoon. That will free up the evenings while Lacey has a guest."

The cowboys gave him that knowing look and Lacey smiled and said, "Thank you, Gabe."

The old cowboy nodded, and his wife smiled at Jared.

Jared had a feeling Perkin's wife told him to give Lacey and her friend more time together.

"You can sit in on the videos," Lacey said. "They are of the bulls that will be at the finals."

He glanced around the table. "You sit and watch bulls?"

"It shows us how they act when they come out of the chute," said the cowboy called Neevers.

"Then you're watching other people ride the bulls?" He would never understand this sport.

"Yes, in some cases we've each ridden the bull and can also give pointers that we remember," said Marlow, the other cowboy.

He studied Lacey. "Are you riding any of the ones on the videos?"

"A couple." She sat a little straighter and stared him in the eyes.

That was a challenge if ever he saw one. She wanted him to watch the videos of her riding. His gut clenched, and his chest squeezed. He didn't think he could watch.

"She does real good on the Double T Ranch stock," Perkins said.

His whole body was screaming "no!" but his head told him if he wanted her to believe he was here to stay, he'd have to face watching her ride sometime. And the videos were of past rides. She'd be sitting beside him reminding him she'd made it through without harm.

"I'll watch. I want to see all that you do to prepare for riding." He said the words and his body slowly relaxed.

Lacey's face lit up. "Good!"

The cowboys were smiling like they had some sideline joke. Perkins was frowning, and Mrs. Perkins was shaking her head.

Now his gut was twisting again.

***

Lacey sat down on the couch with Jared on one side of her and Gabe on the other. Tad and Kit sat in the two arm chairs.

"This is a rodeo down in Arizona where the Double T bulls were rode earlier this year." Gabe had the remote in his hand. He clicked buttons and the television started up.

Jared's body tensed.

She put a hand on his thigh. "I wasn't at this rodeo." The muscle under her hand relaxed.

Gabe stopped the video when he wanted to point out something or ask a question, seeing if they were paying attention to the bull's movements.

The next rodeo he had on tape was where she'd placed third. She'd made two of the three rides that weekend and her top score placed her in the money. Her first ride had been bad. She was surprised the crowd hadn't booed her out of the arena.

The third bull on the video was her first ride. "This is me. I didn't make the ride so don't get worried." She squeezed Jared's leg where her hand still rested.

Gabe stopped the video just as she started to come unseated. "See what he did?"

She shook her head and glanced at Tad and Kit. They also shook their heads.

Gabe rewound and started it again. "Watch close."

They all leaned closer to the television, even Jared.

"There, he shoved his weight as if he was going right and he swung left. That would have unseated anyone," Gabe said.

As he said it, she did see how the bull had shifted under her, making her think he was going the opposite of what he was. Snowball. A fun name for a crafty bull.

"If any of you draw him, you'll have to stay on your toes and not try to outthink him." Gabe hit the play button.

When she hit the ground, Jared flinched. The bull fighters had been right there, keeping the bull away while she picked herself up and hobbled back to the chutes.

"I don't land on the ground as much as these two," she told Jared.

And sure enough, they had been at the same rodeo and both were only able to stay on one bull out of three. She stayed on two of the three.

Gabe stopped the video after that rodeo. "What can you each tell the other about the bulls you rode? How were they in the chute? Did they have any tells?"

The next forty-five minutes they discussed the bulls until they each had a pretty good idea of those seven bulls. She and Kit had ridden two of the same bulls.

"Do what you want until supper," Gabe said, shoving to his feet. Kit and Tad shot out of the room like they had a girl waiting for them somewhere.

Lacey shifted on the couch, curling into Jared. "What do you want to do?"

He kissed her softly. "Are you up for a walk?"

"It's cold out there. We could snuggle in the bungalow until dinner." She wanted to be someplace warm where they could get naked if they had a mind.

"We can put on coats. Come on. I haven't had a chance to see this place." He stood and pulled her to her feet.

If he hadn't kissed her, she'd be thinking he had second thoughts about the two of them after watching her ride.

Jared held onto her hand as he led her to the front door and their coats, hanging on the hall tree. They bundled up and stepped into the cold air.

"You sure you want to walk in this?" she asked, moving closer to him.

"Just a bit." He put an arm around her, drawing her tight to his side.

They sauntered close together down to the corrals where half a dozen horses stood around, their tails to the wind.

Jared stopped at a spot behind the barn, out of the wind. He pulled her into his arms and kissed her. It was a sweet kiss. A caress of lips.

"I wanted to talk to you out here, where layers of clothes will keep us from losing track of the conversation."

She leaned back and stared up into his eyes. "Was that a good-bye kiss?" Her heart thudded in her chest as fear tickled the edges of her mind.

"No. It was an I'm so glad you're still alive kiss." His eyes shut for several seconds and he drew in a long breath before studying her face. "Seeing you on those bulls, then on the ground and seeing their size…" He held her tighter. "It was all I could do to watch. Watching those videos was scarier than seeing a Jeep ahead of me blowing up."

She wanted to ease his fears but couldn't find the words. She cradled his face in her hands and stood on her toes to kiss his lips. The kiss started soft and caring like his, but within seconds it turned into a hungry, all-consuming need to taste him. To show him how much she wanted and needed him.

He grasped her arms and set her away from him. His breathing was as erratic as hers. "This is what I'm talking about. We can't have a conversation without one of us heating the other up and nothing gets settled."

"Settled?" She shook her heated thoughts from her mind. "What are you talking about?"

"Those weeks we were apart, I thought of you day and night. I wanted to forget you, but I couldn't. You'd wiggled your way into my life, my senses, my heart."

Some of her irritation vanished when he said 'my heart'. "Your heart?" Hers fluttered and started the tap dance only Jared brought on.

"Yes. My heart. I wanted to ignore it and told myself over and over I wasn't in love, I was just feeling protective." He pulled the hood of her coat up onto her head. "Then I saw you in the hospital hall, and I knew what I felt for you was more than protectiveness. Happiness filled my heart at the sight of you."

"You do that to me." She tried to step into his embrace, but he held her back.

"We aren't hugging or kissing until I finish what I have to say."

She did something she hadn't done since she was eight. Her bottom lip came out and she pouted.

Jared laughed. "That won't work on me. I have something to say to you and I won't be distracted."

"Fine. Spit it out so we can go get naked and celebrate our feelings." She smiled as sultry as she knew how.

He laughed again. "Is that the only way you know to celebrate?"

"It is with you." Happiness filled her to overflowing. He loved her and would stick by her until she accomplished her dream.

His gaze became heated and hungry. Her body responded with a shiver of anticipation.

"I like a woman who has strong convictions." The fire left his eyes. "Except for the conviction you have to ride in the National Finals. Sweetheart, isn't knowing you made it as a finalist enough? You've already made the rodeo hall of fame by being the first woman to make it that far. Why risk your life and possibly the chance of having children by riding another bull?"

Her jaw dropped, and she stared at him. How could he stand there and say he loved her and her convictions then turn around and ask her to not ride another bull?

"You are more wishy-washy than a woman!" She stomped several feet away then back. "How can you tell me one minute you love me and the next ask me to not do something that I love."

"Do you love riding a bull more than you love me?" He watched her.

She swallowed and battled to find the right words.

"It's taking you a long time to answer. I'm beginning to think you have love and lust mixed up." His face grew red and angry.

"No, I don't." She swung her arms and smacked her casted arm into the corner of the barn. "Damn!" Tears came to her eyes as pain shot up her arm.

"This is why I don't want you on a bull. If you fall off, or your arm slams into the chute or the bull's head, who knows what kind of damage you can do." He grasped her left arm, holding it against her body, stabilizing the weight and pull.

He plucked the tears from her cheek with his finger. "Lacey, I love you and I want you to be safe."

She raised her tear blobbed lashes and peered at him through the blur. "I know what I feel for you is love. But I can't stop now. I'm so close to a goal I've worked ten years to attain. I'm not a quitter. A quitter wouldn't climb onto a bull's back." She touched the hand still holding her arm. "If you want to walk away now, I'll understand." Her heart ached more than her arm. The tears were from a deeper pain.

"We'll sleep on it and see how we feel in the morning," he said, leading her back to the bungalow.

Chapter Sixteen

Jared walked to the house to see if Mrs. Perkins would put together a tray of food for them to eat at the bungalow. After their talk outdoors, Lacey was cold and wanted to take a hot bath. He'd decided if this was their last night together, he wanted to make it special. Just the two of them.

"Jared, are you here for a snack?" Mrs. Perkins asked, stirring something on the stove.

"No. I was wondering if you could fix a tray for Lacey and me. We have a soul-searching conversation to have, and we'd like to remain in the bungalow." He sat at the kitchen table.

Mrs. Perkins turned the flame down on the pot and took a seat across from him. "I don't see that light of love sparkling in your eye. Did you two argue?"

"It's not so much an argument as a difference of opinion that we can't sway the other on." He watched the woman. "Were you married to Gabe when he was riding bulls?"

She nodded. "I know what your problem is. You don't like the idea of Lacey doing something so dangerous."

"Yes. But she is so darn stubborn about attaining her goal of riding at the Finals that she can't see the possibility that something worse than her arm getting crushed could happen." Even as he said it a prick of fear tightened his muscles.

"I had the same fears all those years ago when I first started dating Gabe. He was the most handsome cowboy I'd ever seen. Stole my heart the first time he smiled at me." Her expression softened, and her eyes lit with the memory. The wistful smile vanished, and she stared at him. "The first thing we fought about was him riding bulls. I wanted a husband and a father for my children, he wanted to win a Finals buckle." She shook her head. "You can't change their mind about that buckle. It's something they have to try for, just like you and I try to keep them safe." Mrs. Perkins stood. "But I can guarantee, that as soon as Lacey has her chance and makes her mark in history, she'll be ready to settle down. Your fears just have to stay hidden through the Finals. I had five years of worry before the car accident took away Gabe's chance to make it to the Finals. He'll be the first to tell you he's found as much satisfaction out of teaching the sport to others as he did beating up his body. Give her time, Lacey will find something else that rewards her, but let her have her moment to shine."

She pulled a tray out of a cupboard. "I'll get that tray ready."

Jared sat at the table, staring into space, swirling the woman's words around in his mind. Could he condone her riding, knowing she could give up the whole thing after the Finals?

"Here's the tray. I made chocolate cream pie today. You might want to put those slices in the fridge when you get to the bungalow."

"Thank you for this," he held up the tray, "and our talk."

She smiled and patted his arm. "You two love one another too much to let this come between you."

"I hope so." He trudged out of the kitchen and back to the bungalow.

Holding the tray in one hand, Jared grasped the door knob and shoved the door open.

Lacey sat on the bed in one of his t-shirts, tears trickling down her face.

His chest constricted at the sight. "What's wrong?" He set the tray on a table and plopped on the bed beside her, wrapping his arms around her shoulders.

Her good arm circled his neck and her body pasted to his. "I thought you'd decided to find someplace else to spend the night."

"Shhh, I'm not leaving you. Everyone has bumps in their

relationships." He smoothed her hair and kissed the top of her head.

"We don't have bumps, we have boulders." She sniffed, rubbed her nose, and sniffed again. "Did you bring back dinner?"

"Yeah. I wanted us to spend tonight here, alone, and see if we can't figure out how to make us work."

Lacey's heart expanded with love for the man and his willingness to try a relationship with her. "Thank you." She kissed his willing mouth. He deepened the kiss, pushing her back onto the bed and covering her with his body.

"You looked damn sexy sitting here in my shirt." His hand skimmed up her thigh, over where her panties should have been and on up to her bare breast. "I thought you were naked under this. I won't be able to wear it without thinking of your skin touching it."

Her body heated at his words and hand cupping her breast.

"Knowing it was your shirt made me even sadder, thinking I'd lost you." She wrapped her legs around his waist. "You have way too many clothes on for this dinner party."

"I don't know. I thought you were the appetizer." He drugged her with another kiss then sent her shooting to the stars with his tongue and fingers.

She lay on the bed, spent and happy as he took a shower, put on pajama bottoms, and brought the tray over to the bed.

They ate the cold ham, scalloped potatoes, and carrots. Jared put the pie slices in the refrigerator for later consumption and cleared away the tray holding the empty plates and silverware.

"Let's sit on the couch and see if we can carry on a conversation without making out," he said, leading her over to the apartment size piece of furniture.

Lacey started to sit, but the fabric poked her naked legs. "I need a blanket." She turned to get one off the bed and Jared caught her wrist, spinning her around and down onto his lap. "I thought you wanted to put distance between us and lustful thoughts." She didn't mind sitting on him, feeling his muscled body under her.

"We are to keep our hands to ourselves." He placed his hands on the couch beside his thighs.

She folded her hands in her lap. "Why do we need this talk? Give me your blessing to ride in the Finals in Las Vegas and after that I'm all yours."

He peered into her eyes. "Do you mean that? Once you've ridden at the Finals, you'll hang up your bull rope?"

Her innards twisted a bit at the thought of not riding, not following the rodeo circuit and settling in one place. Could she do it? "I'm going to give it my best shot. Maybe go back to school."

His eyes lit up and his smile started the flames of desire coursing through her. "What do you want to go back to school to learn?"

"I don't know, but I can't sit around and do nothing. That would drive me crazy."

He nodded. "We can figure it out the next few weeks and get you signed up for online classes while you are recuperating from your surgery."

How was she to figure out what she wanted to do in the next few weeks when she'd only just now decided to stop doing the only thing she knew? Lacey nodded, unsure how to answer.

"I'm going to stay here until the Finals and keep getting in shape." That, she was positive would happen no matter what Jared thought.

"I agree. If you're going to ride, I want you in the best condition you can be in. I don't want any chance you get hurt because you are unprepared."

Her heart danced, thumping into her ribs. "That sounded sincere. Like you are okay with me riding." Happiness gave her a giddy high.

"I'm not okay with you riding, but I had a talk with Mrs. Perkins while I was picking up the tray. She made me see how that the part of you that wants to ride the bulls is part of why I love you. I don't want you blaming me on our fortieth anniversary that you didn't get the chance to try for that gold buckle."

Forgetting the no hands rule he'd made, she grasped his head and brought it down to her lips, kissing him with all the happiness and love she had for the man.

His hands grasped her head and the kiss turned into the molten tongue tangling that always burst their bodies into flames of need.

He pulled her shirt up over her head. His hands and lips covered her in lightning speed, kissing, caressing, squeezing. Need swirled in her belly. She slipped her hand into his pajama pants and took hold of his growing desire.

Jared raised up, sliding his bottoms down his legs. She took this moment to slide onto his hard, throbbing shaft.

When he was seated all the way, she moaned and started riding him. They both came, exclaiming the others name and collapsing together on the couch.

Jared recovered faster, lifting her and carrying her to the bed. They spent their last night together until after the Finals, loving until the golden rays of dawn filtered into the cabin.

Chapter Seventeen

Lacey finished watching the videos with the boys and Gabe, then hurried to her bungalow. Jared had promised to call tonight and let her know if he could get the time off to come to the Finals.

She placed her phone on the vanity and striped off her clothes, sliding into the wonderful bubble bath she'd drawn. Every bungalow had a good soaking tub. It was one of the best parts about working with Gabe.

Her eyes closed, and she pretended Jared was in the room watching her. She'd learned since meeting Jared, he was happy to recreate her fantasies.

The jingle of her favorite country song, drew her attention to her phone.

Flinging her hand to rid it of bubbles, she slid her finger across the cell screen and hit speaker. "Hello, good looking," she said, in a singsong voice.

Jared's deep chuckle brought her body to life. "Hello Gorgeous. You're in a good mood."

"I'm chin deep in a bubble bath and fantasizing about what you would do if you were with me." Just telling him her thoughts caused her nipples to peak.

A groan sounded through the phone. "You're killing me, Lacey.

Now all I'll be able to do while I talk with you is envision you naked with bubbles touching all the places I'd like to touch."

A sly smile tipped her lips. "Want me to tell you what I'm doing?"

"I don't know if I can handle phone sex with you."

"You know you want to know where my hands are since they aren't holding the phone."

He groaned.

"One is sliding down my body and settling over my throbbing mound." She said in a husky tone, "Your voice sets me to throbbing."

"Lacey, I can't take this. I want you here, with me."

"Do you have yourself in hand?" she asked, wondering if he would admit he jerked off.

"As hot as you are making me, it's that or die."

She laughed at the strangled way he said it and the image. Oh. The image started her other hand playing with a nipple. "Jared, I'm tweaking my nipple and pretending it's in your mouth. It feels so good."

"You have the sweetest taste. I've never had anything that satisfies me like tasting your skin and sweetness." His deep throaty words shook her world. "Slide a finger into your hot sweet center and pretend it's me filling you."

Without hesitating, she did as asked, and her body clamped around her finger. "Oh!"

"That's it baby, come for me."

"I can't…"

"Come on baby. I'm rocking in and out, harder, faster."

Sensations grew as she moved her hand and pinched her nipple. The explosion hit and she called out his name.

"Oh, yeah. Sweet Lacey!" he exclaimed, and she knew he'd come as well. "Damn, you're good even when you aren't here."

"Don't get any ideas. I plan to be in that big bed of yours soon." She splashed the cooling water. "Did you find out if you can get the week of NFR off?"

"I'll have to fly into Vegas the first day. I can't get off any sooner than that, we're going to be short-handed."

"But you'll be there. That's all that matters." Her heart swelled. Jared would be with her when she accomplished her dream. "When will you fly in? I can't guarantee I can meet the flight. There are lots of sponsors that request we do talk shows and signings during the day."

"I haven't made my flight yet. I wanted to make sure it wouldn't be a problem with you before I did." Jared's tone was all business.

"You come whenever you can. I'll either meet you or have Gabe meet you. He and Kate will be there." She had invited her parents and Brett, but no one had said if they were coming or not.

"I'll let you know tomorrow night what the flight will be. Are you flying or driving down with Gabe and Kate?"

"I'm flying down. They are leaving a few days before I need to be there, and I don't want to be a third wheel as they relive their lives as newlyweds." She'd noticed how the older couple had been acting like youngsters when they spoke of driving down early for Finals.

Jared laughed and said, "I didn't think you were such a romantic."

"Just wait cowboy, I'll show you romance when I have the time." She had to admit, until she'd met Jared, she hadn't had any kind of romantic notions. "You bring the romance out in me."

"I think that's a pretty good recommendation for me." His voice dropped low and sultry.

The water was getting cold. She stood, splashing.

"What are you doing now?"

"Getting out of the tub. The water is cold. That's not good for strained muscles." She didn't want to tell him she'd tried a few one-armed push-ups from the floor. Gabe had rigged up a weighted pulley system to hold up her left shoulder while she did the push-ups. Her right side was pretty sore from holding up all of her upper weight.

"Don't over-do-it. If your muscles are overworked they won't respond when you need them."

She rolled her eyes. "I know. I'm going to get my pajamas on and go to sleep. I'm tired tonight."

"I hate to let you go, but understand. I'll call you tomorrow night."

"Looking forward to it," she said and made a kissing sound.

"Sleep tight, Cowgirl."

"You, too." She hit the off button and stared at her phone before finally drying off, dressing, and climbing in bed. Jared would be at the National Finals Rodeo with her. She'd never had anyone in the crowd beside Gabe or the other riders rooting for her. It put a new pressure on her to make sure she was in shape and didn't have any accidents.

***

Jared heard the excitement in Lacey's voice when he'd told her he would be at the rodeo in Vegas with her. Her enthusiasm was hard to ignore, but he didn't really want to watch her ride. He didn't think his heart could watch a bull toss her around for eight seconds, every night for ten nights. He'd read up on the rodeo and knew every contestant performed for ten days straight. Getting ten days off in December had taken a lot of smooth talking on his part. Especially since he'd already asked for a week off after Lacey's surgery to take care of her. What he had in his favor was the fact hospitals had a hard time getting ER nurses that had the experience he'd had.

There were two more days before he'd catch the plane for Vegas. Lacey hadn't mentioned her parents or Brett when she said Gabe would pick him up.

He picked up his phone and called Brett.

"Yo. I was wondering when you'd call me." Brett answered.

"We go back far enough I don't have to call you every week and tell you what I'm doing, Mom," Jared said.

"Melanie has been harassing me to call you or Lacey and find out if you're still seeing each other." Brett cleared his voice. "She sent us tickets to the rodeo in Vegas, but we can't get away."

"I wasn't sure if she sent you tickets or not. That's why I was calling. When I told her I'd be flying in on the first day, she said Gabe would pick me up. I figured family would."

"I told her we couldn't make it. I know she sent tickets to Uncle Melvin and Aunt Sally, but her dad refused to support her 'need to kill herself.'"

Jared shook his head. "If they would support her, she would be less likely to get hurt."

"I'm glad to hear you are going. Does this mean you are good with her riding bulls?"

"No. It means I support her dream. She said once she does this, she'll quit. That is why I'm supporting her. To make sure she doesn't end up in the hospital again." His chest constricted at the thought of anything happening to her now, when they had a future.

"I'm glad you two finally realized the torch you were carrying." Brett laughed. "I can't believe you didn't realize it in high school."

"She was too young for me then, but I was always impressed with her." She'd been a gangly teenager the last time he'd seen her before he headed off to play soldier. Something Brett said registered. "How did you know I had a thing for her back then?"

"Not as a teenager, but every time we talked as adults, you always asked about her. No one else in my family you'd met, only Lacey. I figured if you two didn't meet anyone before you met again, I'd have a best friend for a cousin."

Jared laughed. "I can't believe you knew how we both felt all these years and never nudged us together."

"I believe in fate, not pressure." Brett's voice trailed off.

"You talking about you and Melanie? As tight as you two seem I would think you and her were sleeping together."

"Not that I don't want to, but she doesn't need to get in trouble for already being married and she's afraid if her husband does find her, he'll do something to me if he discovers we sleep together."

He could hear the frustration in his friend's voice. "You really like this woman."

"Yeah, I can't see my life with anyone else. It's hell living like we are and only getting an occasional kiss on the cheek."

"You believe in fate. Maybe something will happen to her husband and you two will be able to marry." He wanted his friend to be as happy as he was.

"I'm thinking about hiring a private detective to learn a bit about the man."

"That's a good idea. Let me know if you need help with anything." Jared glanced at the clock. It was time to call Lacey. "I have to go. I'll keep you posted on how Lacey is doing at the rodeo."

"Thanks. Tell her we wish we could have come but December is a big month for us until the spring. We can't turn people away."

"I will."

He hung up from his friend and called Lacey. If he was lucky, they'd have another virtual bubble bath together.

Chapter Eighteen

Lacey stood next to the PRCA chairman. He'd set up a special press meeting just for her, the first woman to make it to the National Finals Rodeo as a bull rider. She wished Jared was here for support, but he'd be here later today. Gabe knew to pick him up at the airport at eleven. That would get him here to watch her sign autographs before she had to get ready for the rodeo. She could show him around and show him where to sit in the stands where she could see him when she finished her ride.

The press had all read the article Jessica had written. Several asked about the man mentioned in the story.

"He'll be here later today to watch me accomplish my dream." Her cheeks hurt from smiling and carrying on a positive conversation even when one male news reporter tried to insinuate her making it this far was because the judges were easier on a woman.

"I don't know where you get that kind of information. If anything, and you can ask several of the other contestants, there were some rodeos where I thought the judges were tougher on me. If you hadn't noticed bull riding is a boy's club of sorts. I didn't get any recognition for how well I rode until I'd been at this for five years." She raised her cast. "I'm riding with a fractured arm that needs surgery when this is over. Don't talk to me about being handed my scores. I have worked hard for every single point and dollar."

The women in the group applauded.

"Thank you, Lacey Wallis for taking the time to visit with the press." The chairman escorted her out of the room. "We would appreciate you keeping any mention of this being a boy's club to yourself. We don't need a bunch of women's libbers picketing. We have enough trouble with the animal rights activists."

"I didn't mean to put the organization down, I just wanted that man to see, I did not sleep my way to the Finals. I put in years of patience, learning, and getting in shape." She didn't want to tick off anyone in the PRCA. She needed them on her side.

"Just smile from now on and say how happy you are to have made it here." He studied her.

"Yes, sir."

He walked away.

She wiped at the sweat beading her forehead. Don't let your big mouth get you kicked out of here before you even get a chance to ride.

***

Thomas and Mack Center was rocking with cheers, music, and the sounds of metal chutes, panels, and bellowing cattle.

Lacey stood behind the chutes waiting for her ride. Her mood was fluctuating between mad and frustrated. She needed to focus on her ride. The bull she'd drawn for the first round was one of the toughest in the Double T rough stock. But Gabe returned from the airport without Jared. He'd promised he'd be here. While her riding a bull wasn't something he wanted to watch, he said he'd be in the stands cheering for her.

Did he have a change of heart before getting on the plane?

"Hey, Lacey. You have a great draw. Go get 'em cowgirl," Kit said, stepping up to the platform behind the chute housing Thunder, the bull she'd ride. He and Tad were her helpers. She'd be there for them when it was their turns to ride.

She nodded and climbed up to stand on the walkway behind the chute. Ignoring her nagging heart, Lacey focused her mind on the videos she'd watched of this bull. He had a tendency to twirl right then shift to the left. She'd have to feel him with her legs.

"Here is the first ever woman to ride enough bulls and earn the money and points to make it to the Nationals Finals. Give a big

Thomas and Mack welcome to Lacey Wallis!"

As the announcer said her name, she settled down onto Thunder. She'd rosined up her glove as the man talked, and now she wrapped the rope around her right hand, pounding her stiff glove and fingers, curling them for a tighter grip.

The two thousand pounds of beef under her quivered. She drew in a deep breath, focused on his head, and nodded.

The gate flew open.

She used all her muscle and wits to stay on the bull through the buzzer.

Eight seconds sounded, the crowd roared, and she bailed off the beast. The bull fighters moved between her and Thunder, diverting him as she scrambled for the chutes. Kit pulled her over the panel.

"Damn that was good! You're the first one to make eight tonight."

Tad came running up with her bull rope. "Man, I hope I can ride that good."

"And that, ladies and gentlemen, is how this little lady from Duncan, Montana made it to the Finals. The judges gave her an eighty-two. Nice ride, young lady!" the announcer said.

While she was pleased with her first outing at the Finals, her heart was breaking that Jared wasn't here to share it. Would he be here for the next nine rides?

***

Back in her room after the rodeo, Lacey picked up her phone and dialed Jared's number for the fifth time. Still ringing and going to voicemail. "What is going on?" She took a shower, put on her pajamas, and crawled into bed. Something had to be wrong. Even if he'd changed his mind, he would have called and told her. He had too much honor to hide from her.

The phone sat on the bedside table. She picked it up and dialed Brett.

"Hey, Lacey," he said.

She heard what sounded like a truck engine. "Where are you driving this time of night?"

He let out a whoosh of air. "To the MacIntyre place."

Her senses went on alert. "MacIntyres? Why? Is that why Jared didn't show up in Vegas and isn't answering his phone?"

"He made me promise not to call you, but you called me so that

109

makes my promise invalid. Some guy high on meth walked into the emergency room with a gun. Jared stopped him from shooting anyone else, but he took two bullets."

Her heart stopped beating and her breath caught. "How-how is he?" She forced through her constricted throat.

"They were taking him into surgery after he called. One of the bullets hit organs that needed repaired. I'm driving to his family's ranch to tell them. The weather here has knocked out phone lines and I don't know Lee or Kendal's cell numbers."

"I'll be in Bozeman as soon as I can catch a plane." She hit the speaker button and started stripping out of her pajamas and putting on clothes.

"He told me not to call you. He wanted you to stay and finish riding."

"How can I ride knowing he's been shot?" She pulled on her boots. "I'll call you when I know what flight I'm catching." She punched the off button, threw a set of underwear and her toothbrush into her purse, and grabbed her room key. On the street, she hailed a cab and headed to the airport. She willed Jared to gain strength and prayed harder than she'd ever prayed for anything in her life.

***

Jared's gut and thigh hurt like a son-of-a-gun. He knew from the doctor's comments the bullets were extracted and he'd been patched up inside. As consciousness grew, he realized someone held his hand and there was weight on his chest.

He opened his eyes and looked down his body. His heart expanded at the sight of Lacey's ponytail. But he also knew he hadn't been out long enough for the rodeo finals to be over. He placed a hand on her head. "Lacey, sweetheart, wake up."

She stirred, her fingers squeezing his hand, and then slowly sat up. "I'm sorry, did I hurt you?" Her eyes widened and glistened with tears.

"No. What are you doing here?"

"I came to make sure you're going to live." She brushed at the tears in the corners of her eyes. "And you thought what I did was dangerous," she quipped.

He wanted to laugh but that would hurt too much. "I guess the joke is on me."

Lacey stood and leaned over him, kissing his lips briefly. "When

Gabe came from the airport and said you weren't on the plane, I'd thought you'd changed your mind about being able to watch me ride. It was my anger with you that got me a good ride."

"Glad I could be of help."

She grinned. "Then afterwards, I kept trying to call you. I wanted to give you a piece of my mind." Her eyes saddened. "But when you weren't answering, I got worried. I knew even if you decided you couldn't come to Vegas you would still talk to me. When I called Brett, I could tell he was in his pickup and asked him what was happening. That's when he told me about the guy shooting you." She swallowed. "I thought my heart was going to break thinking about the possibility of losing you."

He grasped her head, pulled her down into a kiss that told her he had felt the same way.

A throat cleared.

Lacey straightened and backed away as Dr. Layman walked up to the bed.

"I see you're feeling well enough to make your guest feel better." The doctor glanced Lacey's direction then zeroed in on Jared. "From the way you were kissing this woman you don't mind if she hears what I have to say, do you?"

Jared held his hand out to Lacey. She placed hers in it and scooted closer to the head of the bed.

"We're in this together whatever you say." Jared squeezed Lacey's hand and she nodded.

"The first bullet was a clean hole through your right quadricep. That was taken care of first to staunch the bleeding. It hit a main artery. Being in an ER, once the man was apprehended, everyone jumped into making sure you didn't lose too much blood."

Lacey squeezed his hand. He witnessed the fear flicker in her eyes and lighten her complexion.

"Once that was stable, we went to work finding the other bullet that was still inside. It had lodged in your rib but hit a few organs before stopping. We stopped the bleeding and extracted the bullet. You should be able to get out of here in a couple of days. We need to monitor you for internal bleeding in case we missed something."

"Thank you," Lacey said to the doctor.

"Don't thank me. Thank the ER staff and this man being in such good shape. I'm sure if one of the female nurses had tackled the man, they wouldn't have lived through it. I heard even with the bullet wounds you managed to subdue the man until security arrived. Your actions saved nearly twenty lives." The doctor held out his hand. "Thank you for taking charge of the situation."

Jared was embarrassed that this man thought he was a hero. He'd done what needed to be done. The threat taken out. He shook hands with the doctor. "I only did what needed to be done."

The doctor shook his head. "There's not many these days that would react like you did." He pivoted and walked out the door.

"That was brave of you to put your life last," Lacey said, her eyes glowing, her lips curved into a soft smile.

"The waiting room and exam rooms were full. There were too many people at risk to not do something." He'd been taken back to Iraq and the times he'd had to protect the injured soldiers. Seeing the man wielding the gun had brought back memories. He'd moved on instinct.

"Did you ride last night?" he asked to take the subject off his actions. "And what about tonight and the rest of the week?" He was also worried she'd get kicked out of the rodeo.

"I did ride and had a good score. The Finals doesn't matter. Making sure you get well matters." She settled on the chair next to the bed.

"It does matter. It has mattered to you for ten years. You can't quit now."

"I'm not a quitter," she said emphatically.

Just the reaction he'd hoped for. She had to go back and finish her rides. "I'm fine. I'm in good hands. You need to get back there and make a run at the buckle." He tried to raise up on his elbows. Pain shot through his body. He'd have to take it slow. The pain meds were going to make him think he was better than he was.

"Stay put. I'm not going anywhere." She handed him the lever to make the head of the bed go up.

"I want you to go back to Vegas, get on those bulls, and show the world what Lacey Wallis is made of." He'd never meant anything as much as he meant what he was saying right now. He didn't want his actions to take away from her dream.

"I can't leave you."

"Why not? You know where I'll be. Safe and sound here in this bed healing and resting up to give you a welcome home you'll never forget." Visions of what he could do to welcome her home came to mind, making his heart beat faster.

"You sure you'll be well enough to do any of what you're thinking?" she asked, leaning her face towards his. "I can tell you're thinking something mind blowing because your gaze has become heated like when we make love." She whispered the last few words and captured his lips with hers.

As much as he wanted to have her slide into bed beside him, he had to stay focused on getting her back to Vegas to fulfill her dream. He couldn't pull out of the kiss, plastered to the bed, so he grasped her ponytail and pulled her face away.

"I'd love to carry on like this until they send me home, but you need to get back on a plane and finish what you set out to accomplish."

She shook her head. "I'm staying here with you."

"Lacey, I'm not worried about you riding. I want you to go show those bulls what-for and to show the world a woman can conquer a bull." He grasped her head in his hands. "I want you to stride into my apartment when the rodeo is over and in that cocky way you have, tell me all about every ride and how you wowed the crowd."

She studied him for several minutes. "You really want me to do that?"

"Yes. It might seem strange, but while the people in the ER were patching me up, all I could think of was I would miss seeing you ride. I wanted to see your caginess and your athleticism. I may not be able to to see it in person, but if you go back and ride, I can watch it on the T.V." He kissed her lips and stared into her eyes. "I want to witness history in the making."

Her eyes glowed and her smile grew. "That's what I'm doing, isn't it?"

"It sure is and I want to tell our children that their momma was the first woman to ride a bull at the National Finals Rodeo." He meant every word. He wanted her to be proud of her courage and athleticism.

"And I'll be here to make sure the big pain in the ass does as he's supposed to do," said a voice.

Jared glanced toward the door and grinned. "What the hell are you doing here?" He couldn't believe his eyes. His oldest brother, Lee, strode into the room.

"Brett came over and told us you were hanging around bothering the nurses after hours." Lee walked up to the bed, his gaze locked on Lacey.

"Lacey Wallis, my oldest brother, Lee." Jared couldn't believe someone from his ranching family took the time to come see if he'd made it through surgery. They had never been a close family. When their dad died, the two oldest had fought over the ranch. He'd never wanted anything to do with ranching and joined the military.

"Pleased to meet you," Lacey said, holding out her hand.

Lee shook hands and glanced between them. "How come we haven't heard about you two?"

"It's still new to us," Jared said, watching his brother study Lacey.

"Lacey Wallis. Aren't you the woman trying to ride bulls at the NFR? What the hell are you doing here?" Lee hooked the cowboy hat he'd been holding in his hands on Jared's foot at the end of the bed.

"She's headed back now." Jared said, nodding to Lacey.

"You'll make sure he follows the doctor's orders?" she asked his brother.

"Yeah, I know he can be hard-headed at times, but I'll make sure he does what he's told. You're going to miss tonight's ride."

"I know. But I never had a chance at the buckle. There are too many good riders. It will be a no ride tonight, but I'll do my best the rest of the week." She kissed Jared. "I'll call when I land."

"Go get 'em, Hot Rod." He knew it was Brett's pet name for her. As well as it fit when she was a child, it fit her as a woman. Just thinking about her made his rod hot.

She laughed, picked up a purse, and flew out of the room.

Jared shifted his attention to his brother. "Mom send you down here?"

"No. She doesn't know you were shot. Her heart isn't doing well." Lee took the chair Lacey had sat in.

"Why didn't anyone tell me?" He started to lean forward and stopped at the stab of pain.

"She doesn't want anyone fussing over her and didn't want you running home when she felt your work is important." Lee glanced around the room and shivered. "How can you spend every day in this place."

"I know most of the people who come through the doors are healed." Trying to change his brother's perspective of a hospital would never happen. He'd lost his wife and unborn child five years ago in a hospital and hated the things. That was why it had surprised him to see this brother at the door. "What aren't you telling me? Something's up that you came to my rescue and not Kendal."

"Kendal and Jane are having another baby. He didn't want to leave the ranch with her due in a month. And I wouldn't let him." Lee hid the pain that briefly reflected in his eyes.

"That makes sense. But you didn't need to come at all. I'll be fine." All he wanted was to get out of here in two days and recuperate in his apartment watching Lacey ride and getting ready for her return.

"I talked to the doctor. He doesn't want you using that leg too much and your insides have to heal. I'll stick around until your cowgirl comes home." Lee leaned back in the chair and crossed his arms.

Jared closed his eyes and pretended to sleep. It looked like he and his big brother were going to do some much needed bonding.

Chapter Nineteen

Lacey was as jazzed for this tenth ride as she'd been for the first. They'd given her a no score on her second night because she'd been a no show, but every night after that she'd ridden her best. She was tossed off four bulls before the buzzer sounded and had decent rides on the rest. Her right knee ached, her left arm ached, and she wasn't excited for Jared to see the bruises on her backside and her shoulder from one of the falls. But she had shoved the pain aside with a little help from some pain relievers and was ready for this last ride.

Tonight, she'd drawn Showboat. He fit his name. The bull liked to pirouette more than buck and then high-step out of the arena. He would be an easy ride for the last night and she knew, even if she stayed on, the score wouldn't be high because the bull never scored well. He was more for entertainment and the fans, than for a rider to score well.

"Boy, did you get a raw draw this round," Tad said, as they stood behind the chutes, waiting for her turn to climb on the back of a bull. She'd not only drawn a poor bucking bull, she was the very last rider of the event.

"I'm okay with it. I'll be able to stay on till the buzzer. To me that is more than any score." She glanced over at him. "Your jaw's hanging open."

"I can't believe you don't care about the score." He puffed out his chest. "I got on Ace in the Hole planning to come up with a big score."

"And you did. Eighty-four was a great score. I didn't come here to win the buckle though I told people that was my goal. I came to fulfill my dream. I'm here, I've been riding and competing, and I can go home, hang up my rope, and be content."

He stared at her with suspicion in his eyes. "You're really going to hang up your bull rope and not crawl on another bull?"

She nodded. Every night after her ride, she'd found a quiet spot and called Jared. They'd talk for an hour, or more, if he shut himself in the bedroom where they could talk more intimately. Those talks, and knowing he was waiting for her, she was ready to walk away from this body torturing career and start something new.

Showboat entered a chute and she hustled over. She had nerves, but knowing this was her last hurrah and he was a bull known to look for the gate as he twirled, she was ready to enjoy the ride.

"I honestly didn't think you'd make it to this round," said one of the rodeo officials as she shoved on her helmet.

A grin tipped her lips. "I knew I couldn't make all ten rides, only one man in history has done that, but I'm pleased with how many I've stayed on."

The official slapped her on the back. "Good luck."

"Thanks." She shoved the mouthpiece in and climbed up the panel as the bull and rider in front of this chute bounded out.

"Hey there, Showboat," she said, standing over the bull, her feet on a panel and the chute gate.

"You ready to rock this arena?" Kip asked, helping with her rope.

She nodded and took her position on top of the big white bull.

The music roared to life, she nodded, the gate shot open, and everything but the movement of the animal under her became background to her motion and the feel of the bull. He was predictable. The ride played out as if she'd ridden him a hundred times. The buzzer sounded, she released the bull rope and sailed off with one of his spins, landing on her hands and knees, jarring her injured knee, shoulder, and arm, and rattling her brains. She scurried to the side of the arena even though she was pretty confident Showboat was headed for the gate.

One of the bull fighters grabbed her arm and pulled her back toward the middle of the arena.

She spit out her mouth guard. "Hey, what are you doing?"

He pointed to a gate at the side of the chutes.

A man on crutches hobbled through the gate. His bent head and cowboy hat prevented her from seeing who he was. There was something familiar about his build. When he was ten feet in front of her, he raised his head.

"Jared? What are you doing here?" She pulled off her helmet and walked through the soft dirt to him, knowing how it can cause pain to an injured leg. Her heart stuttered. He'd come to watch her ride, something she'd never thought he'd be able to do in person. But why had they allowed him in the arena?

"I can't get down on my knee, but…" He reached in a pocket and pulled out a ring. "I was wondering if you'd do me the honor of marrying me?" His voice boomed over the speakers in the building.

Tears burned her eyes as she stared into the face of the man she would give her life for. She loved him with every atom of her body.

"Yes!" She held out her shaking hand. He placed the ring on her finger and hauled her up against him with one arm, kissing her until her knees grew weak.

"And that, ladies and gents, is how a hero proposes to his gal," the announcer boomed. As the man related why Jared was on crutches, she helped him out of the arena.

"I can't believe you're here. Why didn't you tell me you were coming?" She kept an arm around his waist and he had an arm around her shoulder, with both crutches under his other arm.

"I wanted it to be a surprise once it was arranged." Jared kissed her temple, and they stopped in the area behind the chutes.

"Congratulations!" Kip and Tad said, smacking Jared on the back and hugging Lacey.

Jared wrapped his arms around her when they were off to the side out of the way of the buckle ceremony. "That was some ride you made tonight."

"Thank you. That was some entrance you made. How did you pull it off?" She remained snuggled against him, ignoring the new aches from the last ride.

He nodded to his left. She glanced over and spotted Lee, Brett, Melanie, Mom, and Dad. "You got all of them here?" She kissed him. "You are a hero."

"Lee knows quite a few of the NFR people and arranged for you to be the last ride tonight so I could propose."

"What if I'd have said 'no'?"

"I don't think anything could have been as bad as standing there watching you ride for eight seconds and hoping you weren't trampled into the ground. That would have made asking you hard to do." He kissed her and swung her toward their family. "Let's go celebrate and get back home."

"I like the sound of that." Her heart was overflowing with love for Jared. "I'll take love over eight seconds of an adrenaline rush any day."

Chapter Twenty

Jared stared down at Lacey. Dr. Parley said the surgery went better than she'd expected, and Lacey should have full recovery in eight months as long as her body didn't reject the synthetic bone grafts.

He was glad they were able to get her surgery a week after nationals. He was still on medical leave from his gunshots and wouldn't lose any time tending to her. Giving him time to take off for a honeymoon.

Her lashes fluttered and she moaned.

"Hey, I'm right here. You're going to be as good as new," he said, grasping her right hand.

Her gaze was foggy, but a smile curved her lips. "I knew you'd be here. My own personal nurse."

He kissed her and sat in the chair by the bed, holding her hand, waiting for her to come out of the anesthesia completely.

"How's our girl doing?" Mr. Wallis asked, entering the room with his wife.

"She'll be fine. A few weeks of rest and then some rehab and in eight months she'll be as good as new." Jared smiled at his soon to be in-laws.

"Have you set a date for the wedding?" Mrs. Wallis asked.

"We're thinking September twelfth. The day we reconnected." He glanced down at Lacey. The day he fell in love with a bull rider.

"That's a wonderful date. Just enough time to make all the preparations." Mrs. Wallis glanced up from her daughter. "Have you picked a location? Those can be hard to get if you don't have enough notice."

"I'm pretty sure the place we picked will be no problem." He squeezed Lacey's hand. "We want the wedding and reception at Brett's ranch."

"Oh, that's wonderful! The family will be delighted!" Mrs. Wallis beamed with happiness.

"Have you told Brett? He may already be booking people," Mr. Wallis said.

"He knows. We told him before Lacey came in for the surgery." Jared had told Brett his plans for the proposal, and he'd made sure to get Lacey's parents to the last night of the finals. It was also his friend's idea to have the wedding at the ranch. "Keep it in the family," he'd said.

Lacey heard familiar voices. Her right hand was warm, secure in the grasp of Jared's. *Jared.* He'd been showing her what she meant to him ever since they returned from Vegas. And now, here he was holding her hand and keeping her company as she came back to consciousness.

Opening her eyes, she smiled. Mom and Dad. They said they would be here the day of the surgery and they were.

"Hi," she said in a hoarse voice.

Jared released her hand and held a straw to her mouth. "Small sips to ease your throat but not upset your stomach."

She did as told and smiled at her parents. "Thank you for coming."

"We've come every time you ended up in a hospital, this is no different," her father said gruffly. She knew it was his way of not sounding like he cared when he did.

"You two must be happy I'm not going to ride any more bulls."

"Yes!" her mother exclaimed, then pressed her fingers to her mouth.

Jared laughed. "It's okay. Lacey understands the fear you and I felt when she rode bulls."

She peered into his eyes. She did. They'd had long discussions since the Finals about how she'd nearly lost him and how it corresponded to how he and anyone who loved her felt when she was sitting atop the bulls.

"I never understood the power of love until now." Her heart raced at the love she saw staring back at her in Jared's eyes.

"I always knew you two would make a good couple," Mom said.

Everyone nodded, and the room filled with laughter.

Lacey scanned the faces of her family. "Everyone knew my deepest secret?"

Jared shrugged and added, "Apparently mine, too."

***

Love Me Anyway

Chapter One

Melanie Trask stood beside Brett Wallis as the last of the wedding guests drove away with Brett's seven-month-old herding dog, Kool, running alongside the vehicle. Kool stopped at the archway inscribed with the words TUMBLING CREEK RANCH. The wedding and reception had been bittersweet. Her heart ached knowing she could never marry the handsome man standing beside her. Over the last eighteen months, she'd fallen in love with her boss. If she didn't need this job to support herself and remain hidden from her abusive husband, she would have moved on and tried to forget the caring cowboy.

"What are you thinking?" Brett asked, putting his arm around her shoulders. He'd started touching her more the last six months as they'd worked with his cousin Lacey, planning her wedding to Brett's best friend, Jared. He'd even kissed her twice. Not the soft kiss of affection, but toe curling, set her body on fire kisses. Both times, it had taken her days to quiet the need in her body.

"I'm happy for Lacey and Jared. Happy the wedding and reception went so well." She ducked out of his arm and headed toward the kitchen. "I'll start cleaning up the food while you direct the football team in cleaning up the barn."

After watching the wedding and seeing the longing in Brett's eyes when he glanced her direction, she wished there was a way to get a divorce from Steve without him finding out where she lived. Once he had an address, her husband would arrive and break as many of her bones as he could and probably kill Brett for harboring her. She'd been so starry eyed and ready to leave the small town she'd grown up in, that the telltale signs of Steve's possessiveness and anger hadn't registered until they were married, and he'd thrown her against a wall for laughing with a man at a bar. She'd tried to tell him the man had told a joke that was funny and wasn't hitting on her, but Steve wouldn't listen. The memory of that first glimpse of the man she'd married sent a flash of fear up her spine.

She shivered and hurried to the array of dishes on the work counter. Melanie had covered one bowl of salad when Brett's determined strides echoed under his boot heels down the hall along with the click of Kool's nails behind him as they entered the room.

"You can't get away from me that easy. Why didn't you answer my question?" He kept his distance, but his intense hazel gaze made her feel as if he were standing toe to toe with her.

"The football team…" She tried once again to keep distance between them. To grow any closer would only end up with them both being physically and emotionally injured.

"Knows what to do. This is the third wedding they've cleaned up after." Brett was always respectful of her space, moving slow and pensive around her.

He was also as tenacious as his bull-riding cousin, Lacey. She wouldn't get him to leave her alone until she'd answered his question. "I was thinking what a lovely wedding it was and hoping the chemistry those two have can outlast both their stubborn ways and Lacey's quick temper."

Brett laughed, caught his breath, and said, "Yeah. I've never seen a couple who are ripping each other's clothes off one minute and fighting the next." He sobered. His eyes softened. "You know I would never hurt you. I would always put you before myself."

She nodded, unsure what to say. They'd had long talks during the winter evenings when there were few guests at the ranch. The conversations were about their childhoods and the ranch. He'd never pushed to know more about her adult life other than she'd run from an abusive husband. Despite knowing her past and that she was married, he'd shown her every day how he cared about her. And that was what had been her undoing. She'd never had a man care for her with such kindness.

"I know you're married and you fear your husband finding you." Brett took a step closer and grasped her chin, tipping her face up, peering into her eyes. "But I'm jealous of what my best friend and cousin have." He chuckled. "Not the fighting but being there for each other and having that someone in their bed every night. Seeing the person you love in bed beside you every morning."

She gulped as her heart rampaged in her chest. Even though she and Brett spent many hours a day together, she was lonely. It was the type of lonely he was talking about. Wanting to be with the person who brought you the most happiness. Melanie opened her mouth to say the opposite of what she was feeling.

Brett's face swept down to hers and their lips met.

After all the wedding vows, family, and love radiating from the ranch today, she allowed herself to believe that she could marry Brett and be his wife. With that thought chasing away her fears, she fell into the kiss, allowing him access to her body, her soul, and her heart.

She stood on her tiptoes and slipped her arms around his neck, pressing her body to his and feeling his long, lean torso.

He groaned and pulled out of the kiss but held her tight. "I knew you were feeling the same thing I was. I could see it in your eyes." He dropped a kiss on her forehead, eyelids, cheeks, and recaptured her lips.

Denying his accusation was senseless. She had been dreaming of walking into the barn and seeing Brett at the makeshift altar when Lacey walked up the aisle to Jared. Even during the first dance, she'd wished she were in Brett's arms.

This time, she eased out of the kiss. "This type of behavior doesn't get the work done, nor does it make it any easier to work for you."

He raised an eyebrow. "You mean I have to fire you to be able to marry you?"

She took a step back. "We can't marry, you know that."

"We can if you'd allow me to have a solicitor in Billings handle the paperwork. He can be discrete. Your husband will never know where to find you." Brett put his hand out toward her.

Melanie retreated two more steps, bumping into the counter. "You don't know Steve. He'll find me. He'll ruin you, the ranch, and never let me go." She wrapped her arms around herself to stop the tremors she hadn't had since landing the job of cook and housekeeper at Tumbling Creek Dude Ranch. The thought of Steve showing up here and ruining everything Brett had worked so hard to establish made her physically ill.

She ran past Brett, down the hall, and into the guest bathroom. The hard tile floor hit her knees, chattering her teeth when she dropped down in front of the toilet and lost the wedding cake and punch she'd eaten during the reception.

"Hey. I didn't mean to upset you," Brett's deep soft voice said, moments before water ran in the sink.

The clack of nails and a wet tongue on her arm didn't stop the helplessness she felt. A cold cloth wrapped her forehead and Brett knelt beside her. Kool pushed his head under Brett's arm, his brown eyes with small blue specks peered at her with more empathy than she'd ever seen in a person.

The two males giving her support made her want to cry. And wish she hadn't forgotten to close and lock the door in her hurry to reach the toilet. Brett's charm and quiet demeanor could make her believe that Steve would never find out where she lived and she'd be safe.

But she knew better.

Steve wanted more than having her back as a wife. He wanted the money she'd stolen to leave him. All ten thousand of it.

Chapter Two

Brett didn't want to think about the violence Melanie's husband must have treated her to, that would make her stomach toss up its contents at the mention of contacting him. But after watching the wedding between his best friend and cousin today, he wanted that union of a man and a woman. And he wanted it with the woman hanging her head over the toilet.

"Hey, if it upsets you that bad, we don't have to talk about it. Not now. But, Melanie, I will have you for my wife one day. I hope it's before we both have gray hair." He kissed the top of her head, drinking in the scent of her floral shampoo.

She grabbed the washcloth from her forehead and wiped it across her mouth. It was a good thing she'd wrapped her long brown hair up into a comely bun thing on her head today, otherwise she would have needed a shower.

Before she'd darted from the kitchen, her brown eyes had reminded him of a frightened calf.

"Come on." He grasped her by her elbows and raised her to her feet. She stood a good six inches shorter than his six feet. "Forget I said anything. I don't like seeing you scared."

He released her elbows and waited for her to look at him or say something.

She only ducked her head and walked out of the bathroom, Kool at her heels. He hated how bringing up her husband turned the fun, warm woman into a scared rabbit.

If he ever met her husband, he'd knock him around and let him see how it felt. Brett slowly released his fisted hands and walked down the hall. He peeked in the kitchen, where Melanie moved about putting food away, and continued to the back porch. He pulled on a jacket and grabbed his work Stetson. Kool stared at the door, knowing when his master put on the work hat, they were going to do something fun. Brett smiled at the dog and opened the door. Kool shot toward the barn, where the Duncan High School football players were cleaning up.

Brett didn't like seeing Melanie so frightened, but from previous conversations with her, he knew that it was best to leave her alone after bringing up her husband. She listened better after working things out in her head first.

At the barn, he shook hands with the Duncan football coach, Mark Shaffer. "Looks like you brought the whole team this time."

"I did. We didn't have a game this week, so I told them this was mandatory." Mark nodded toward the teenaged boys folding chairs and tables and stacking them in the small room used for such event items. "And we appreciate the money you donate to athletics at Duncan High."

"My pleasure. My brothers and cousins all benefited from participating in sports in school." Brett frowned. "Though whoever talked my cousin Lacey into getting on bulls will never have my gratitude."

Mark laughed. "That wasn't a teacher. It was the boys, teasing her about being a tomboy. I guess she had to prove to them and everyone else that while she was a girl, she was more than a tomboy."

"That sounds like Lacey." He glanced around the barn. "It looks like you have this under control. I'm going to see what damage all those cars did to my pasture."

Brett left the cleaning of the barn in the football team's capable hands and wandered to the front pasture that allowed guests arriving at the ranch to see cattle on one side as they drove in and horses on the other. The publicity firm he'd used to get the ranch publicized in all the right places had suggested the visual as people drove up to the ranch. He had to admit, most people commented on the cattle and horses as soon as they stepped out of their vehicles.

He'd moved the heifers out of the field closest to the barn to allow parking for the wedding. His brother Garth's truck still sat at the far end. He'd been one of the first to arrive and had helped direct parking.

A quick glance around the horse pasture and he knew where his brother had gone. Garth's favorite horse, Vortex, was missing from the pasture.

Brett walked over to the small shed off the side of the barn and fired up the four-wheeler. It would be quicker to catch up to his brother with this than to catch and saddle a horse. He twisted the throttle and headed through the meadow with Kool running between the ATV and Tumbling Creek, the meandering creek that the ranch was named after. As he'd presumed, Vortex, the blue roan Garth favored, was tied to a tree by the first small waterfall.

Garth stood up from the rock he sat on. Kool ran up to his brother, barking and acting tough.

"Kool, you tough dog, it's me."

Hearing his name, the dog stopped barking and trotted over for an ear scratching.

Brett cut the engine and sat astride the four-wheeler as Garth walked over to him.

"Something wrong?" he asked, stopping ten feet back.

"You tell me? Everyone has left and you're up here brooding at your favorite teenage hangout." Brett had found his brother here nearly every day as the teenager had tried to find his way in a world he didn't feel he fit in.

"Just clearing my head. All that mushy wedding stuff had me thinking about the women I've dated and wondering if there's something wrong that I'm twenty-seven and haven't felt a need to drag a woman into matrimony."

Brett swung his leg over and sat sideways on the cushioned seat. "Nothing wrong with you. We can't all crave women like our cousin Nate."

Garth laughed. "I can't keep up with the tales he tells about the women he takes home." He sobered. "Do you think it's because he grew up with a sister? Maybe us not having a woman around other than Mom made us...I don't know."

"Speak for yourself. I have my eyes on a woman. I just have to get her to realize I'm not like the men of her past." He chuckled. "And I don't think having an older tomboy sister would have made a difference in Nate's desire to date every woman he meets."

"Yeah. I think that's all he thinks about as he drives the excavation equipment." Garth crossed his arms. "The woman you're talking about is Melanie, isn't it?"

"Yeah. She's got some garbage from her past that's keeping her from seeing what we could have." Brett wished he could tell his family about her past, but she'd sworn him to not tell a soul. She'd be disappointed to know, he'd told his best friend Jared. It was his confiding in Jared, that helped them find the lawyer Brett had told Melanie about earlier.

Garth nodded. "Mom thought as much."

"That Melanie and I like each other?" He didn't hide the fact, but he hadn't thought they'd given off the signals that Lacey and Jared had.

"That. And that she has a rough past."

"Really? Mom said that?"

Garth grinned. "She's pretty intuitive."

"True. So, you want to stay and help us eat some of the left-over reception food?" Brett swung his leg over the handlebars and started the engine.

"I'll be there shortly." Garth sauntered back to the rock he'd been sitting on.

Brett watched his youngest brother a few minutes, whistled for Kool who had disappeared in the trees, and headed back to the barn when the dog came charging out of the trees. Something was eating at Garth. He was pretty sure it was more than his brother's lack of interest in women right now. Maybe Dillon knew. The two worked together at the Wallis Excavation Company in Duncan. His family and Lacey's family owned the company. Well, everyone but him and Lacey. He preferred the family ranch.

At the barn, he put the four-wheeler away, checked on the animals, and waved to the football team as the van that brought them pulled out of the driveway with Kool racing the vehicle to the archway.

Maybe now, Melanie would be ready to listen to his idea for setting her free from her abusive husband.

Chapter Three

The food had been put away in the large commercial refrigerator and the dishes had been run through the commercial dishwasher. Melanie sat at the kitchen island, sipping tea and thinking about leaving a note for Brett to find his own dinner. She was tired and with no guests, now that the wedding was over, she could spend the evening in her room reading or latch hooking a special wall hanging for Brett's mom.

She rose to walk over and get a paper to write on when Brett walked into the room followed by Kool. Before she could think quick enough to make evasive maneuvers, he had her caught up in his arms.

"You look tired." He kissed her temples.

"I am. I was just leaving you a note to fend for yourself this evening."

He held her at arm's length. "You aren't trying to avoid me, are you?"

A guilty look must have crept across her face because his dark blond eyebrows nearly touched as he frowned.

"You were. Melanie, you can't stay married to a man you fear. You can't be a martyr and avoid happiness because of that fear."

She put a hand on his chest. He sucked in air as her fingers felt his firm pectorals under his white shirt. "We can talk about this tomorrow when I'm not tired or emotionally drained."

An eyebrow raised, and he placed a hand over hers. "Emotionally drained? Why?"

Melanie narrowed her eyes and tried to pull her hand out from under his.

He pressed her fingers tighter against his chest.

"You know why." She stared at him, not wanting to voice her feelings out loud.

"I want to hear you say it again. I want you to realize what you want. I want you to fight for it. For us." His gaze softened, and he drew her hand to his lips. He kissed her knuckles and peered at her. "I know we can have a wonderful life together, here, at the Tumbling Creek. You would never have a day that you woke fearful." He turned her hand, kissing the palm.

Her heart stuttered. Her knees weakened at his soft kisses and gentle touch. His emotions reflected in his hazel eyes, and she wished with all her heart, she could tell him what he wanted to hear.

She eased her fingers from his and took a step back. "We'll discuss this tomorrow." Without looking back, she headed down the hall to her room next to the office.

When she'd interviewed for the job, she'd been hesitant about working here after meeting the handsome ranch owner, not much older than herself. But she'd witnessed the gentleness in him then, and when he'd shown her the room she'd live in downstairs, far from his room, she had decided this was the place she could heal and hide.

Now, she wondered at her sanity for staying. The gentleness she'd felt from Brett that day had turned into love. A profound desire to always be with him, permeated every waking moment and filled her dreams with thoughts of being loved by him. But she couldn't give in to her desires. She couldn't hurt such a wonderful, kind man because of her stupid mistake five years ago.

She slipped out of her clothes. A pretty dress she'd purchased in Duncan because it was Brett's favorite color. Everything she did was with Brett in mind. And that was why she had to keep him from pursuing a divorce for her. Steve would never agree. Even if she wanted nothing from him, just his signature on a paper, he would make sure Brett regretted it the rest of his life. And he would come to hate her. She couldn't bear to witness hate in his eyes towards her.

***

Brett sat on the couch in the great room, sipping a beer and flicking through the channels on the television. Kool lay on the floor beside the chair. If Garth didn't come in and join him, he was going to go crazy and storm into Melanie's room, ruining his chances of getting her to agree to the lawyer and divorce.

The main door opened.

"Anyone here?" Garth called out.

"In here. Want to watch football or rodeo?" he asked, sitting up straighter in the chair.

"Of the two, I prefer football. Rodeo sours my gut these days."

He glanced over at Garth. "Because of Lacey?"

His brother, six years younger than him, shook his head. "My girl problems."

This was more interesting than brooding over his and Melanie's predicament. "I thought you were worried you don't like girls?"

Garth pointed to the beer bottle. "Got more of that?"

"Yeah." Brett rose out of the chair and motioned for his brother to follow him to the kitchen. "We might as well eat as long as we're drinking."

Garth walked over to the refrigerator and pulled out a platter of small sandwiches. He placed them on the counter as Brett snagged a couple more beers.

They sat at the kitchen counter, helping themselves to the food and beer.

Brett waited until Garth had drank half the bottle of beer before asking, "Your girl problems a cowgirl?"

"Yeah. She barrel races. Thinks because I don't drive her to all of the weekend events, I don't care enough." Garth stared at the bottle in his hand. "She's got me thinking, maybe she isn't the one because I don't want to follow her and hang out at rodeos."

"But you see each other during the week?" Brett wondered at his brother talking to him and not Dillon, their middle brother, about this girl.

"When she's not working or practicing and I'm not working." He shrugged. "Usually one or two nights a week."

"Do you want to see her more?" He had a feeling the woman was into Garth more than the other way around. He tossed a chunk of a sandwich in the air. Kool jumped up and caught it.

"I enjoy being with her, but after watching Lacey and Jared, and you and Melanie today, I feel like I'm giving her false hopes."

Brett was stuck on the 'him and Melanie.' "What do you mean, watching me and Melanie?"

"A blind man could see the secret looks you two gave each other and how you couldn't be near her without touching her." His gaze turned earnest. "That's what I want to feel. I don't with Darla."

Brett grinned, realizing it was noticeable to everyone but Melanie that they were meant for one another. He'd have to keep at her until she agreed to the divorce. Because they both deserved happiness.

He tapped his bottle against Garth's. "Then she isn't the one for you. But there's nothing that says you can't be friends with a woman while waiting for the right one to come along."

Chapter Four

Melanie woke the next morning feeling as if she hadn't slept more than an hour all night. Her thoughts had bombarded her mind, keeping her tossing and turning until the early morning hours when she'd finally dropped off to sleep only to have her alarm startle her awake at five-thirty.

She shuffled about the kitchen, starting the coffee, making breakfast for Brett, and checking the schedule for guests. They had two retired couples arriving today. She'd need to make sure cabins one and three were in order and a welcome basket of fresh cookies, fruit, and beverages was placed in each.

The main door opened and closed. Brett's footsteps echoed down the hall. Her heart sped up. She'd become accustomed to the sound, looking forward to his entrance every morning.

"Good morning," he said, striding across the room and placing a kiss on her head. He'd made this a morning ritual as the guests grew fewer this month and she wasn't frantically making breakfast for a larger crowd.

"Morning. We have guests arriving this afternoon. Could you make sure there is firewood in cabins one and three? I'll check them and place the welcome baskets in the rooms by eleven." She placed a plate of bacon, eggs, hash browns, and toast on the counter in front of the stool Brett used when they didn't have guests. Tomorrow, he'd eat in the dining room with the guests and discuss the adventures he'd take them on.

Brett grasped her hand. Not tight, but firmly. "When would be a good time to talk about our future?"

Peering into his caring, more green than brown eyes, she wanted a future with him. But her past wouldn't allow her a future with anyone. She didn't want to see his life ruined because of her. "We don't have a future." The thing that had kept her up all night popped out of her mouth. "If you don't stop talking that way, I'll have to leave."

The good humor in his eyes and the smile on his lips disappeared. "I don't understand. Why would wanting to make you my wife cause you to leave?"

Her fists pressed down on her hipbones as she said, "Because Steve will never just let me go. It doesn't matter how careful your lawyer says he'll be, there's bound to be some way my whereabouts will come up. He'll come here, see you, and go all possessive. He'll hurt you, then he'll drag me away, and I have no doubt he'd rather kill me than have me leave him again." She spun around, avoiding the empathy in Brett's eyes. "You don't know how long it took me to plan my escape from him. I won't do anything that could put me back with him." She glanced over her shoulder. "And that includes sending someone to get his signature for a divorce."

Hands rested on her shoulders, massaging her tight neck muscles. "I don't want you to be fearful he'll find you or that you'd have to go back to him. All you have to do is tell the courts what he did to you and file a restraining order. Then if he does show up, we can call the cops."

Melanie spun around, her gaze locking with Brett's. "How do you know all of this?"

"I told you. I've been talking to a lawyer in Billings. He was telling me all the precautions we can take to keep Steve away from you and keep you safe until the divorce is final."

She shook her head as her stomach twisted. "You don't understand. Steve doesn't care about the law. He won't care if there is a divorce or even that I married you. All he'll care about is making sure I suffer for leaving him and that you suffer for taking me in."

"This isn't the wild west anymore. He can't harm us." The

determined expression on Brett's face wasn't enough to convince her.

"He doesn't like to lose…at anything." Melanie wanted the subject changed. "I heard another voice out here last night."

Brett released the stubborn woman. He realized what she was doing, and he'd let it go for now. He'd talk some more with the lawyer. Yesterday was the first time she'd slipped up and told him her husband's first name. Now they could hire a private investigator to find the man discretely and see if he was even attempting to find his wife.

"That was Garth. He's having some girlfriend issues."

"And he came to you for help? I would have thought he'd have asked Nate." She placed a cup of juice by his plate.

"That's what I said. But Garth isn't the love 'em and leave 'em type like Nate." Brett sat at the counter and waited until Melanie slid onto the seat beside him before digging into the now cold food.

"I agree. Garth is too gentle hearted. He wouldn't go out with a woman just to get her in bed. When he falls in love, he won't let her go." She put a bite of egg into her mouth.

Brett waited for her to chew the food and grasped her hand. "Just like me." He peered into her eyes. He wanted her to know, he would do whatever it took to make her his wife. If that meant putting her husband or soon-to-be ex-husband in jail, then he would.

"D-don't—"

"What? Love you? I can't stop my heart from feeling what it feels for you." From the first sentence out of her mouth when she'd called about an interview, he'd known she was special. Her voice had tugged at him. When he walked out of the barn the day she'd arrived and she stepped out of the car, he'd known the second he peered into her brown eyes that she wasn't leaving the ranch.

"Please, don't say that."

"Why? So it's easier for you to not think about what you are throwing away by not allowing me to help you get away from your husband?" The words came out harsher than he'd planned.

Her eyes widened, and she slid off the opposite side of the stool.

He grasped her hand gently, keeping her feet from taking her out of the room.

"I'm sorry. I didn't mean for my frustration to come out so harsh in my words." He rubbed his thumb gently across the back of her hand. "I would never hurt you. And I would never speak cross words to you. They were of frustration not anger."

She didn't accept his apology, but she also didn't tug her hand from his grasp.

"Come on. Sit down and eat. We have a lot of work to do before the guests arrive." He released her hand and turned his attention to his breakfast.

By the time he'd finished his meal, Melanie had sat back down and picked at her food. He would have given the ranch to know what was going on inside that pretty head of hers. From what she'd told him of her childhood, he understood her taking the first offer of marriage that came along. She was looking for a chance to make her own family. One much different than she had. But he didn't understand why she was so sure the man would find her and harm them. Maybe once the investigator found him, there would be a clue to this man's hold over Melanie and his disregard for the law.

Chapter Five

Melanie liked the fact Brett insisted she sit with him and the guests during dinner. It was a welcome respite after cooking and serving, to sit a bit, and enjoy the conversation before having to clean the dining room and kitchen.

She glanced at her employer. He was telling a story she'd heard many times since being the hostess at the dinner table. Every time he embellished the story just a tad more. Soon he'd be facing off a pack of wolves, rather than one pup as the true story went.

"That is some story," Mr. Barnes said, elbowing his wife. "It reminds me of a trip we took to Yellowstone some five-six years ago."

"I'll say. We went on a hike and came back to our camp and found two marauding bears." The woman nodded. Her gray bobbed hair swinging on both sides of her narrow face.

Melanie glanced at Brett and shared a smile. Mr. Barnes finished the story with his wife interrupting every other sentence.

The other couple, Mr. and Mrs. Gallerie, were enthralled with the tale. While checking the two couples in that afternoon, she'd learned that the Barneses had traveled a lot and liked rustic adventures and the Galleries were just beginning to enjoy their retirement by traveling.

"Excuse me, I'll go get the dessert," Melanie said, standing. All three men at the table stood. Her cheeks heated from embarrassment.

When the dining room was full of people, no one seemed to notice her slipping from her spot to refill bowls and deliver desserts. This show of courtesy surprised her. She hurried through the door joining the kitchen and dining room.

Before pulling out the apple pie she'd baked earlier in the day, Melanie drew in a deep breath and centered herself. The morning had started with Brett's determination to terminate her marriage to Steve, then she'd worked continually to ready things for their guests and keep her mind on anything but her past. The men's one simple act of standing as she left the room, had cold cocked her. No one, before working at this ranch, had ever shown her a miniscule of that respect.

"Do you need help?" Brett asked, walking through the swinging door that joined the dining room and kitchen.

She drew in one more breath and spun to the refrigerator. "No. I was just taking a moment to breathe."

"Let me help." Brett opened the freezer door as she placed the pie on the counter. He set the carton of vanilla ice cream beside the pie.

Melanie ignored his nearness, cutting the dessert and putting it on small plates. She popped five desserts in the microwave for a minute, to take the chill off the pie and fill the room with the scent of apples and cinnamon.

Brett scooped the ice cream and she placed the desserts on a tray.

"I'll bring along coffee," he said as she headed for the dining room.

A smile tipped her lips. They worked well together. Had from the first day they'd met.

"My, that smile on your face tells me that you and Brett are more than employee and employer," Mrs. Gallerie said when she stepped into the dining room.

That snatched her moment of happiness away. "We aren't. We just work well together." She walked around the table, setting the dessert plates to the left side of the guests' plates.

The door swished open and Brett arrived carrying a tray with a coffee carafe and teapot with hot water, along with cream, sugar, and tea bags.

"You do work well together," Mrs. Barnes said, winking.

Melanie filled the tray with empty plates and hurried back into the kitchen. These weren't the first guests to insinuate there was more than a working relationship between she and Brett. She would give anything to be able to slip on his ring and slide into his bed every night, but that couldn't happen.

She scraped the plates and started stacking dishes in the dishwasher. If only she truly believed that she and Brett would be safe from Steve's wrath. But she'd witnessed his anger too many times before leaving and knew he would not give up until he felt vindicated.

***

Brett found it hard to follow Mr. Barnes' conversation when his mind was dissecting what could have sent Melanie charging to the kitchen after delivering the pie. They'd fallen into that easy work comradery they'd had in the kitchen putting the desserts together, from the moment she'd started working at the ranch. But something had happened before he'd returned with the coffee.

"I'm looking forward to the horseback trip tomorrow," Mrs. Gallerie said. "I've never been on a horse, but it has always been one of my dreams. And taking my first ride like this…through a forest with the leaves turning colors… I'll be the envy of all my friends."

"You do have horses that a beginner can ride?" Mr. Gallerie asked.

"Yes, our horses are gentle and know the trails. Even if you get lost from the group, the horse will bring you back to the barn." While the horses weren't barn sour, they did know that at the end of the day there was a treat waiting for them.

"Have you lost many riders?" Mr. Barnes asked.

Brett leaned back and picked up his coffee cup. "There have been a few riders that wandered off when I was trailing a large group. Once the rider realized the horse knew where it was going, they would show up in time for the horse to get his evening grain."

The couples laughed and pushed back from the table.

"Please tell Melanie, it was a wonderful dinner," Mrs. Barnes said, her eyes twinkling.

"I'll do that. You all have a good night. If you plan to go out to the meadow star gazing, be sure to take a flashlight with you. Wouldn't want anyone falling in the creek or tripping over a rock." He started clearing the table.

"It's wonderful to see how you two work so well together," Mrs. Gallerie said. "You might want to put a ring on that woman's finger."

He grinned and bit back the retort, "I'm trying." Carrying the dishes into the kitchen, Brett wondered if the woman had said something similar to Melanie.

She was hunched over the sink, scrubbing on a pot. That was why her shoulder and neck muscles were so tight. All the scrubbing and cleaning she did around here. If she'd agree to be his wife, he'd hire another person to take over the cleaning. He'd have Melanie help him with the books and keep cooking. He didn't think they could find anyone to cook as well for a crowd without spending twice as much for a professional chef.

"Hey, want me to take over the pots?" he asked, placing the tray of dirty dishes on the drain board by the dishwasher.

Melanie started and pushed stray strands of her long brown hair off her face. "I'm fine. You should make sure everything is ready for your ride tomorrow."

He grasped her shoulders. "About that ride. I'd like you to go with us. I think getting out, enjoying the fall air will do you some good."

She shook her head.

"Why not?" He stopped her side-to-side movement by placing a palm on her cheek.

Her eyes darkened a moment before she moved her face away from his hand. "I wouldn't be able to relax. Those two women would be looking at everything I do and thinking I'm doing it because I care about you."

"I see. They must have said the same thing to you that they did to me." He put his arms around her loosely. "Melanie, we can't hide our feelings. That's becoming clear as more and more people keep telling me we are meant for each other, or I should put a ring on your finger."

She sucked in air and started to pull back.

"Don't. Don't run from me or my love for you."

Her eyes widened.

"Yes, I said it, and I'll keep saying it until the day I die." He lowered his head and captured her mouth, kissing her with all the pent-up desire he'd built since meeting her.

She sagged against him. Her arms wrapped around his neck and she clung to him, taking and giving with the same intensity.

Brett released her mouth and leaned his forehead against hers. "This is why you need to agree to a divorce. I can't go on just kissing you." Her body didn't stiffen at the word divorce. He was making progress.

She pressed against him. "Why can't we be like other people and not care about whether I'm divorced?"

"Because I want more than living together. I want to be your husband." He grasped her head in his hands. "I want the world to know we're together. I want to not have to worry about someone making a comment that could make you tuck tail and run."

Her gaze flashed from staring at his lips to his eyes. "Is that how you see me? A woman who tucks her tail and runs at the first sign of trouble?"

"No, but you do get uncomfortable when people talk about how well we work together." He peered into her brown orbs, seeing her uncertainty. "We should be able to kid one another, bump shoulders, and enjoy working together, without worrying someone will make a comment that upsets you."

"It doesn't upset you to have strangers commenting on our closeness?" Her brow wrinkled, but she didn't pull from his grasp.

"No. I like that what we have is seen by others. It means our feelings for one another are real."

"I do enjoy working here, with you. And I care for you enough I don't want anything to happen to you or the ranch."

There was the fear creeping back into her eyes and voice.

"Nothing will happen to me, the ranch, or you. I promise." He kissed her again. This time a soft, lingering kiss that heated his body nearly as much as the first one. "Will you give me permission to have my attorney write up the divorce papers?"

She gave a half nod. "Steve will never know where I am?"

"The attorney assured me that he won't know where you are or even know my name." Brett had made that clear with the attorney when he'd met him in Billings on one of his tuxedo fittings for Jared's wedding.

"I do want to be your wife. Curl up in bed with you every night." Her eyes took on a heated gleam.

"You don't know how many nights I've had to force myself to not come down here and beg you to let me in your bed." Brett meant every word. He'd spent many nights lying awake, thinking about Melanie sleeping in the room by his office. He'd thought of making excuses to wander to the office and make enough noise to wake her and perhaps… those were thoughts better left for another time.

"Really? I've had similar thoughts. Wishing you'd come down to work in the office, and I'd slip through the door and ease your tired muscles with a massage." Her breathing picked up.

He rubbed his hands up and down her sides, grazing the sides of her breasts. His cock grew with each innocent brush of his thumbs.

The dishwasher beeped.

Melanie stepped away from him. "I have dishes to finish and things to get ready for breakfast."

"I'll go check on the gear for tomorrow." He stopped at the kitchen door and faced her. "I'm saddling up a horse for you tomorrow. Plan on bringing a picnic for everyone."

Seeing her desire and knowing she'd had the same dreams as him, only strengthened his resolve to get her divorced as quickly as possible. This was a family friendly ranch and he couldn't with good conscience sleep with Melanie without a marriage license.

Chapter Six

Melanie dressed in jeans and a flannel shirt and pulled on a pair of cowgirl boots Lacey had given her on the woman's first visit to the ranch. The sassy bull rider had told Melanie if she planned to live and work on a ranch, she had to wear boots when working outside or riding a horse. She grinned. Lacey had become her best friend. Really, her only friend besides Brett.

Breakfast was over. Brett had led the guests to the barn to practice riding before they all headed out on the trail ride. She stood at the counter with her back to the kitchen door, making sandwiches for the picnic.

The fax machine in the office clacked and whirred. She finished wrapping the sandwiches and headed to the sink to wash her hands when Brett appeared in the doorway.

"You ready?"

"Just about. I need to add drinks to the cooler." She wiped her hands on a towel. "The fax machine just made noise. Might be more guests."

He nodded and disappeared.

She finished putting everything in the cooler, carried the cooler to the back porch and pulled on a thick, hooded sweatshirt with the Tumbling Creek Brand logo on it. Brett had given her the sweatshirt the first winter she'd worked at the ranch.

"What is this?" he asked, walking into the room, waving a paper.

"I don't know. I told you it just came over the fax."

He held it out to her and she saw the logo and name of an attorney. She glanced at the address, Billings.

"It appears to be something from the attorney."

"Yes. It says there are no such persons as Steve or Melanie Trask who ever married or lived in Oregon City. Have you been lying to me?" His stony gaze started her gut clenching and her heart racing with fear.

She took a step backwards and raised her arm to ward off a blow.

He dropped the hand threatening her with the paper and his gaze softened. "I won't hurt you," he said, softly.

Her mind flashed to the time Steve had caught her in a lie. He'd nearly sent her to the hospital with the beating he'd given her.

"Why can't the attorney find you or your husband in the town you say you lived?" His voice was low, unthreatening.

"Because there is no Steve or Melanie Trask. Trask was my father's mother's maiden name."

He studied her. "But your driver's license and social security card had that name."

Her cheeks heated as well as the tips of her ears. "I told you, I'd worked up to leaving. I found a person who makes fake identification."

Brett couldn't believe the lengths to which Melanie had gone to leave her husband. Most women went to a shelter or asked family for help. He knew she had no family left. But surely, she could have found a shelter and been safe.

"You have illegal identification? You could go to jail for that." The thought of the quiet, gentle women he'd come to know ending up in jail for trying to get away from an abusive husband brought her plight sharper into perspective. "I can't help you if I don't know who we are dealing with."

Melanie's gaze had drifted to the pointy-toed boots Lacey had given her. It was clear she didn't want to look at him. He'd found her truthful, or had thought her truthful till now. He wasn't sure if she was embarrassed by being caught or thinking about how to cover that she'd been caught. Either way, he had to get to the bottom of why she'd lied to him after how close they'd become.

The main door opened and the sound of several feet, reminded him he'd left guests out by the corrals. "We'll talk about this later." He picked up the cooler and headed toward the main room. Over his shoulder, he said, "Come on."

He heard her boot heels following timidly behind him. His heart skipped, hoping that meant she'd be ready to tell him the truth when they had the time.

"We wondered what happened and came to see if you needed help with the lunches," Mrs. Barnes said, glancing beyond him to Melanie.

"I was taking care of some business that came in on the fax machine." He stepped aside and nodded for Melanie to head out ahead of him.

Mrs. Gallerie linked her arm with Melanie's and led his cook and housekeeper toward the corrals. Kool trotted behind them a short distance, then pivoted and ran back to sniff at the cooler.

Mrs. Barnes pulled the door closed behind Brett and fell into step with him. "Not to butt in, but as a psychologist, I've dealt with women like Melanie. If you'd like me to visit with her…"

His heart lodged in his throat. It was one thing to tell the attorney he'd hired about what Melanie had done to get away from her husband, but would the woman be bound by some legality to tell the law Melanie had purchased fake identification?

She stopped. "I know you aren't her abuser. She trusts you."

He shook his head. "I value that trust. I don't want her thinking I sicced you on her."

"Oh, I would never tell her that or insinuate you said a thing to me. I figured it out from watching her." Mrs. Barnes hurried off ahead of him.

Brett wasn't sure whether he was relieved or upset the woman had realized Melanie's history. He arrived at the group and noted everyone was on a horse but Melanie. She stood beside the older gelding, River, he had saddled for her. This was her horse whenever she rode. He'd given her lessons on the horse and the two were comfortable with one another.

"Mount up," he said, nodding to her horse.

She swung up into the saddle as if she'd been riding her whole life.

He strapped the cooler on behind her saddle and walked up to Woolly Bugger, his horse, and stepped into the stirrup, throwing his leg over the big quarter horse gelding.

"Let's go." He led the way with Kool running up the trail ahead of him, knowing Melanie would fall into the end of the line. They'd set up a system where if she saw someone having trouble with a horse, she'd whistle and he'd stop and check on the riders.

Once they were moving across the meadow, he glanced back and noticed Mrs. Barnes had positioned herself alongside Melanie instead of in the line. Before the younger woman saw him watching, he set his sights forward and led the group up the side of the mountain, stopping every half hour to point out the trees and underbrush as well as dismounting to relieve the beginners' backsides and to point out wildlife prints and scat.

"You mean that's a wolf pile?" Mr. Gallerie asked, peering into the forest around them. "It's bigger than our dog's piles I pick up in the yard."

"Yes. We see the wolves in the winter more frequently than I like." Brett glanced at Melanie. "Tell them about last winter."

She studied him a moment, not smiling and her eyes had a distant glint to him. Damn! She thought he'd put Mrs. Barnes up to speaking to her.

Kool sat down by Melanie's horse and peered up at the woman still astride River.

Melanie smiled at the dog. "Last winter, I went out to lock up the chickens after dark. The hens were making more noise than usual. I shined the flashlight into the trees beyond the chicken coop. Two red glowing eyes reflected in the light and I made out the shape of a grayish white wolf."

"No! What did you do?" Mrs. Gallerie's face lost its color.

"I yelled and swung my arms like Brett and Lacey taught me and the wolf ran away." Melanie glanced his direction a moment. "Shortly after that Brett brought Kool home." She swung her gaze to the trail and reined her horse back onto the path.

Mrs. Barnes started his direction.

"Mount up," he said, mounting Bugger and waiting for the others to pull themselves up into the saddles. He wanted to make sure Melanie didn't see him and Mrs. Barnes speaking alone again. But he was damn sure going to make time alone with Melanie to discuss her false name and her husband's real name. They couldn't proceed to get her legally away from him until he could give the attorney all the specifics.

Chapter Seven

After Mrs. Barnes asked her questions about her past and made comments that sounded a lot like Brett had put the woman up to trying to get her to talk about her husband, Melanie kept herself quiet and away from the guests and Brett.

They'd been on the ride for nearly two hours. That meant they were getting close to the third waterfall up from the ranch. It was the usual place they stopped for a picnic. She glanced around. While they might have been on the trail for that long, it appeared with Brett stopping every half hour to teach the riders about the wildlife and plants on the mountain, they were still a bit below their stop.

She peered at Brett's back. He was a natural at explaining and patiently listening to questions. Seeing him like this and with the kids that came with families, she could see him as a wonderful father. She snorted. "How would you know what one was?" she chided herself. River twitched one ear back as if he were interested in her conversation with herself. She patted his dark brown neck. "I could have used someone like you when I was growing up. Someone I could talk things over with and not feel like an idiot."

The sight of Riffle's dapple gray rump, the gelding Mrs. Barnes rode, came into her view. Not again. Why was the woman so set on digging into her past? Melanie stared at Brett's back. He would never have told anyone her past. She'd told him about it in confidence and over the year and half she'd lived at the ranch, she'd seen how loyal he was to his family and friends.

"Did I hear you back here talking to yourself?" the older woman asked.

"No. I was talking to River. He's a very good listener." Melanie patted his neck again and marveled for the millionth time at how satisfying it was to work with the horse and other animals on the ranch.

The woman smiled. "Animals are the best therapists. If more people knew that I'd have been out of business long ago."

Melanie stared at her. It all became clear. "Did Brett invite you to the ranch to talk with me?" She couldn't stop the accusing tone. It hurt to think Brett would try to push something on her she didn't need or want. His need to help her was almost as smothering as Steve's possessiveness.

"No. Brett had no idea what I did before I retired. I, on the other hand, have been watching you and feel you need to get over something before you can move on and have a good life with that man who cares for you very much." The woman nodded toward the front of the line of horses.

Brett's wide shoulders had always been a source of amazement to her. He carried so much on them. His family, this ranch, and now her.

"We're working on it." Melanie stared the woman in the eyes.

Mrs. Barnes returned the stare for several minutes. Their horses stopped.

Melanie glanced forward and noticed they'd arrived at the waterfall.

"We'll have our picnic here. You're welcome to wander around, take photos and enjoy the scenery while I make the horses comfortable and Melanie gets the picnic laid out." Brett had twisted in his saddle to peer down the string of horses and riders. His gaze met hers briefly.

Everyone started dismounting. She couldn't get down until Brett removed the cooler tied on behind her horse. Which was why at all the stops she had stayed on her horse while the others walked around.

He grabbed the reins of each person's horse as he made his way back to her and River. Brett dropped the reins of the horses and reached up, unbuckling the cooler and lifting down.

She swung her leg over the horse's rump and stepped to the ground. Her knees buckled a little from the strangeness of locking them straight as opposed to being bent slightly for the last few hours.

Brett's arm wrapped around her waist. He pulled her back against him, holding her up until her legs didn't feel like soggy cotton.

"You ready to stand?" he asked in a low husky voice.

"Yes." She stepped out of his hold.

"Hang on to the horses and I'll pack the cooler over closer to the waterfall." Without waiting for her to grab the reins, he picked up the cooler and strode away from her.

She used the time to loosen River's cinch and scratch Kool's ears.

Brett returned, taking the reins. "Are you doing okay other than not getting a chance to stretch your legs?"

"I'm fine. I didn't need you holding me up. All I had to do was move my legs a bit."

He grinned. "But I like finding reasons to hold you."

Her cheeks heated as she walked over to the cooler. She unbuckled the blanket strapped to the lid and spread it on the ground.

Mrs. Gallerie hurried over and took a seat on one of the corners. "That was my first time on a horse and I have a new respect for the men who practically lived in their saddles back in the days of cattle drives. My backside is numb."

Melanie chuckled. "You might want to do some more walking around before we get back on the horses to return to the ranch."

The woman waved her hand. "I'm more thirsty than numb."

Melanie raised the cooler lid and handed the woman a bottle of water. She'd brought one bottle of water and a soda for each person along with sandwiches, chips, grapes, and brownies. She handed the woman her lunch and as each person wandered to the blanket, doled out the rest of the lunches. She waited until Brett arrived and handed over his before pulling out her sandwich and eating.

Between bites, Brett told the story of how his great-grandfather had homesteaded the land on this mountain and the meadows and valley where the buildings sat.

"And you're the only family member who wanted to continue at the ranch?" Mr. Barnes asked.

"My cousin Lacey loves it here and is welcome to come help out and live here when she wants. But she just got married and is beginning a new life after being a bull rider."

The love and admiration in his voice when he talked about Lacey always amazed Melanie. There had never been a member of her family who talked about her or cared for her the way she'd witnessed the love and respect in both the Wallis families. Her mother had continued the best she could when her husband went to jail for trafficking drugs and they'd been shunned because several teenagers in the town had died from overdoses caused by the drugs her father had brought to town. She'd hated the town and couldn't wait to get out. When her mother was diagnosed with cancer and was gone six months later, a month after Melanie graduated from high school, she'd sold everything that had a value, gave the rest to the church thrift store, and loaded her belongings into her mother's old car and drove until it quit. That's when she'd ended up in Oregon City.

And fell for the first man who said she was pretty and acted as if she mattered.

"A bull rider? Really?" Mrs. Barnes said, with the same amazement as everyone who met Lacey.

"She competed at the National Finals Rodeo last year." The pride in Brett's voice drew Melanie's gaze to his. "She didn't place, but it will go down in the Rodeo history books."

"And she did it with a broken arm," Melanie volunteered.

"She must be one tough woman," Mr. Gallerie said.

"We all are." Mrs. Barnes winked at Melanie.

She wasn't sure what the woman meant, but it was good to be seen as a woman of strength. She'd been working on it here at the ranch.

Brett liked the small interchange he witnessed between Melanie and Mrs. Barnes. Perhaps the woman had broken through whatever barriers his housekeeper had built up over the years. Even a crack for him to keep wedging himself into would be a bonus.

"Now that I have the ranch and have built it into a guest ranch, I think it will be easier to keep it successful and in the family." He couldn't stop his gaze traveling to Melanie. He wanted her to be a part of this ranch, raising their children here and having one of them take over as he and Melanie aged.

"It's always a grand idea to have children take over, but from experience, they don't always want the same things you do." Mr. Barnes nodded at his wife.

"I agree. That's why I bought out my uncle and father. They no longer wanted to deal with the ranching life. They and my brothers and cousin love the excavation business they started. Myself, I can't see the fulfillment of driving around big equipment." He shuddered at the thought of not being able to ride the hills and enjoy the mountain as part of his job.

"That's what I mean. Everyone has their own dreams." Mr. Barnes studied Melanie. "And you? Do you plan to stay on here or is this a resting place before moving on?"

Brett's heart stopped as he waited for her answer.

Melanie's gaze darted to him, then to Mrs. Barnes and finally landed on Mr. Barnes. "I enjoy working here and living at the ranch. I don't know what the future holds for me."

Kool walked up behind her, placing his head on her shoulder. Everyone laughed.

"I think Kool is trying to tell you something," Mrs. Barnes said.

Melanie's cheeks darkened in color. The woman had embarrassed her.

Brett turned to Mrs. Gallerie. "What did you think of your first horse ride?" He caught a mouthed 'thank you' from Melanie.

Mrs. Gallerie went into an excited monologue about her experience. By the time she'd finished everyone had eaten their lunch and were beginning to stiffly stand.

"Before we get back on the horses for the ride back, I'd like to take you on a short hike I think you'll find interesting."

Melanie, placed all the containers and wrappings into the cooler and stood. "Where are we going?"

Brett grinned and held out his hand. "Somewhere I haven't shown you before."

He was surprised when she grasped his hand and fell into step beside him. The two older couples followed, and Kool darted past all of them and took the lead up the faint deer trail.

It had been years since he'd been to the place he was taking everyone. He would have preferred it were just he and Melanie, but knowing his guests' occupations, he had a feeling they would enjoy this excursion if for no other reason than prolonging getting back on the horses.

The trail opened up to a small clearing. Across the clearing were three large rocks. His grandfather had shown him these when he was about eleven.

"This land was one of the summer homes of the Blackfoot. On the back of these rocks are carved pictographs, telling what they hunted here and a bit of the ceremonies they held and even slaves they captured."

"Really?" Melanie tugged on his hand, leading him behind the rocks.

The others followed and soon there was a deep discussion on what certain carvings meant and how this was a historical treasure.

"It's wonderful that this is your land and not public. No one can come up here and wipe out this story of history," Mrs. Barnes said.

"I agree. And that's why I only show it to a few people who I know will respect the history and not tell others who may come up here and deface it." His brother, Dillon, had told a friend. One night when half a dozen of them had been drunk, they'd made an attempt to find this place and had ended up lost on the mountain overnight and half the next day.

"I imagine you would rather I didn't take photos then?" Mr. Barnes asked.

"I don't mind as long as you don't say it was on this ranch that you saw them."

"That could be a selling point to get more guests," Mr. Gallerie said.

"We're fine. We have just enough guests to keep the ranch going. I don't want to be so overrun we have to hire a bunch of people." He didn't want to lose his private time with Melanie.

Mrs. Barnes nodded. "I agree. You have just the right touch of family atmosphere to make this a splendid place for families to vacation. Without being tied down."

"That's the way we like it." He glanced at Melanie, still standing by his side.

She nodded but her cheeks had darkened again. She blushed more than any woman he'd ever been around.

Chapter Eight

Melanie followed the horses back down the trail. She'd enjoyed seeing how Brett coveted the carvings on his ranch and having the privilege to see them. She would have preferred he'd showed her when it was just the two of them, but he'd held her hand the whole time and made her feel as if he had wanted her close to show her it had been for her.

This day had been filled with so many wonderful memories. She knew, tonight when the guests had gone to their cabins and the two were left to clean up from dinner, he'd be after her for more information about Steve and her illegal actions.

She sighed. If only she could wipe out that one bad mistake and pretend it had never happened. And she could have, if she hadn't told Brett about her husband, used her fake name and married him. But she would have been looking over her shoulder the rest of her life, knowing that any day Steve could find her and ruin everything.

And he still could. Brett hadn't asked her where she came up with the money for the fake identification. He knew she didn't have a job, she was surprised as smart as he was, he hadn't started asking more hard questions.

They were back down at the ranch by three in the afternoon,

giving her plenty of time to get vegetables ready to go with the roast she'd put in a roaster that morning.

Brett took the cooler off the back of River and handed the empty container to her when she'd steadied her legs.

She grabbed the cooler and started for the ranch house. There were kitchen chores and tidying to be done before dinner could be served.

***

Everything was cooking and the table was set when Melanie sat down at the kitchen island to breathe and sip on a cup of tea. She heard the click of Kool's nails on the tile hallway and knew her peaceful break wouldn't be so peaceful.

Brett entered the kitchen, picked up his usual mug with a four-point elk on it, and filled the mug with coffee before sitting down beside her. "It was a good trip today."

She nodded, sipping her tea.

"Did you enjoy seeing the pictographs?"

"Yes. It is amazing how creative the Indians were to carve their activities into the rocks for future generations to see." She put the cup down. "It was like looking at a living room wall with family photos."

He grinned. "That's what I thought the first time I saw them."

She smiled, peering into his eyes. They had so much in common it made her realize how naïve she'd been to marry Steve. They had never agreed or liked the same things.

Brett spun his stool and faced her. He put his hands on her leg, spinning her stool. When they were face to face his expression became serious. "We have to talk. You need to give me your husband's name and where to contact him. I'm not going another eighteen months pretending there is a future for us. I want to *know* there is a future."

She gulped, shoving the lump of emotion back down her throat. "I-I want a future too, but you don't know my husband. He doesn't take no for an answer and he doesn't like to lose."

"He's going to lose you. I won't let you go on living half a life because you can't commit to anyone. Even if you don't marry me—" his eyes dulled, "—I want you to be happy with someone."

She reached out, capturing his hand. "Steve is not a nice man."

"I have friends at the sheriff's department. He's not going to hurt you or me." Brett squeezed her hand. "Wouldn't it be easier to get through this with someone you know cares about you?"

Tears burned behind her eyes. She'd dreamed since the age of fifteen about finding a man who would love her. That she had one sitting in front of her made her chest ache with happiness and sadness. "I-I'm touched you care about me."

"Don't pull away."

She stared at him. "I'm not—"

"Maybe not physically, but your eyes say otherwise. Give me his name and we'll see what the investigator for the attorney can find out."

"No one will contact him? Make him suspicious?" She knew Steve. He was so crooked, he'd know there was a reason an investigator was asking about him.

"I promise. All we want to do is discover if he is looking for you and the best place to serve him with divorce papers."

A chill slithered up her spine. Divorce. Steve's words still rang in her ears and chilled her bones. *I'll kill you before I'll let you divorce me.*

"Hey, it's okay." Brett reached over, pulling her into his arms.

She couldn't stop the tremors. She'd lived with them a year before she'd made up her mind to get out of the hole she'd dug.

Brett rubbed his hand up and down Melanie's back, trying to warm her up. This was the second time she'd started trembling at the mention of getting the divorce. He had a feeling her husband had threatened her if she ever did.

"Just tell me his name and I'll do all the rest. You won't have to do anything but sign papers."

She rubbed her nose and face on his flannel shirt and tipped her face up. The uncertainty and fear in her eyes was like being run over by a stampeding steer.

"I'm scared for me and for you," she whispered.

"Let me deal with it. There is no need for you to be scared." He leaned down and kissed her softly. "Let me do this for you."

"Steven Perret."

"Thank you. Giving me his name means you are stronger than you think." He kissed her again, eased her back onto her stool and stood. "I'll call the attorney and come back in to help you serve dinner."

She nodded and wiped at the tears trickling down her face.

Brett wanted to shout hallelujah. He'd broken through her fear and had her working with him, instead of against him, to get her free of the man who had a strong hold on her but not her heart.

In the office, he pulled out his phone and dialed the attorney. It was a few minutes before six. He hoped the man was still working.

"Hemstead."

"Mr. Hemstead, this is Brett Wallis. Melanie told me the reason we couldn't find her or her husband under Trask is because she had false identification records made so her husband couldn't find her. His name is Steven Perret."

"It's a misdemeanor to have false identification," the attorney said. "But if no one is pressing charges, she should be okay. But I would suggest she start using her real ID now that we have a name and can move forward with the divorce proceedings."

"I'll tell her. Any idea when you'll know anything more?" He was anxious to get this behind them both, so they could move on.

"It will depend on how much time the investigator has to spend on looking into the man's background. I can get a check from police through my connections."

"Melanie was adamant that if her husband even smells something wrong, he'll discover where she is. Please tell the investigator to not stir anything up when he is digging."

"I understand given the woman's fear of her husband. Now that I have her real name, we can also look for hospital records if she was ever tended in an emergency room." The attorney's enthusiasm gave Brett hope they could get this whole thing taken care of easily.

"If you can ask Melanie about any medical care she underwent for her injuries that will make it faster."

"I'll do that and leave a message on your phone."

"Sounds good. Hopefully, we'll have something for you tomorrow night." The line went dead.

Brett sat a minute staring at the name Steven Perret on the notepad in front of him. It was safe to say in his thirty-three years on this earth, he had never felt hatred for anyone. But staring at the name and knowing what the man had put Melanie through and the lengths she'd gone to get away from him…he had violent thoughts about the man.

He shoved his phone into his pocket and wandered back to the kitchen. He'd offered to help haul the platters and bowls of food into the dining room.

"Brett," Mrs. Barnes said, stalling him from entering the kitchen. He shifted and walked to the dining room door where the woman stood.

She pivoted and walked toward the great room. It appeared she didn't want the others to overhear the conversation.

Once they were both over by the fireplace in the great room, she faced him. "My husband and I have been discussing Melanie and we'd like to stay on another week. That would give me more time to get her to warm up to me and perhaps talk more candidly with me."

He studied the woman. "Why would you care about helping Melanie?"

She stared back at him not blinking an eyelash. "I'm not just helping her, I'll be helping you as well."

He rubbed a hand over his head and stared at the painting of the old homestead that hung over the mantle. "But why?"

"I'm retired. I miss helping others and I can see you and Melanie belong together but there is something in her that is keeping you apart."

He nodded. But it wasn't his place to tell this woman anything about Melanie. "I don't mind if you stay on another week. But it's not because I believe you need to help Melanie or me. We're doing just fine."

She raised her gray eyebrows. "You are?"

He grinned at her sarcasm. "Ma'am, we are."

Mrs. Barnes shook her head. "We'll stay a bit longer anyway."

"Suit yourself. I promised to help carry in the meal. Excuse me." He strode down the hall and into the kitchen.

Melanie was just stepping from the dining room into the kitchen. She was hesitant, almost shy when she glanced at him. Almost as if she feared he'd already learned something about her husband.

"I made the call. Now we just wait and see what the lawyer digs up."

She cringed, did one quick nod, and picked up a bowl of mashed potatoes and a pitcher of gravy.

Brett picked up the platter with a juicy roast and followed her into the other room.

Mrs. Barnes sat next to her husband, their heads bent together.

He placed the platter on the table in front of his place setting and waited for Melanie to sit.

***

The meal was nearing time for Melanie to clear plates and get the dessert when Mr. Barnes took over the conversation.

"After the ride today, Miriam and I decided we'd like to book another week. That is if you have room."

Melanie's gaze shot to Brett. He pulled out his phone and checked the calendar for scheduled guests. "It appears your cabin isn't booked until the following weekend, but then you'd have to leave because it is a family reunion and all the rooms in the house are full and all of the cabins have been booked."

"We'd like to do that." Mrs. Barnes smiled at Melanie.

He noted she did not smile back. Brett had a feeling Mrs. Barnes was not becoming as chummy with Melanie as she thought.

Chapter Nine

Melanie was up at four in the morning making cinnamon rolls to go with breakfast. She'd barely slept as everything that happened the day before kept spinning in her mind. Giving up trying to hide anything from Brett had become exhausting. He had worn her down to telling him Steve's real name and about her illegal activity. She was still annoyed that Mrs. Barnes had butted into her life and now planned to stay longer. But she was a guest and could stay however long she wished. Melanie would just have to do her best to stay away from the woman's prying. She still wasn't sure Brett didn't have something to do with it.

She punched the dough and heard the click of nails coming down the hall. It was a little after five. Kool entered the kitchen, his tail wagging.

"Morning to you," she said, kneading the dough.

Brett appeared at the door. He looked as tired as she felt.

"Didn't you sleep well?" she asked, shoving her hands into the dough.

He stopped beside her, brushed his thumb lightly under her eye, and said, "I think I could ask you the same thing."

"It's noticeable?" She hadn't really studied herself in the mirror this morning. She'd crawled out of bed, into her clothes, and stopped long enough in the bathroom to pull her hair up into a ponytail. She hadn't had the energy to braid it.

"Yes. Tell me what kept you awake, and I'll tell you what kept me up." He kissed the top of her head and filled a cup with coffee.

She shrugged. "This and that."

He narrowed his eyes over the rim of the mug of steaming coffee. "You'll have to be more specific or I won't tell you what kept me up."

Kool whimpered out on the back porch.

"Hold that thought." Brett strode to the porch, let the dog out, and returned to the kitchen, picking his coffee up off the counter where he'd set it.

"You really want to know?" Melanie asked, not glancing at Brett. Even though he looked rough from missed sleep, he'd still sent her heart racing when he'd walked through the door.

"I wouldn't ask if I didn't want to know." He leaned his backside against the counter next to where she worked the dough.

"I was tired enough I dropped off quickly, but then I had a dream Steven found me." She darted a glance at Brett. He was watching her intently. "He was stalking me through the trees. He had a gun and was taunting me that he'd killed you and wanted me to suffer knowing I'd caused your death."

Brett pulled her into his arms. "Hey, I never want you to feel guilt over anything that has to do with me. I'm the one who has pushed you to get clear of this man. If I get hurt it's on me, not you."

If only she could believe that. Her dream had felt too real. "But I don't want you hurt. If Steve ever finds out, he'll want you and me dead."

She couldn't stop the trembling.

"Shhh. You can't allow him to ruin your happiness." He tipped her face up. "When you came here, you reminded me of a scared doe. Now, you're stronger, braver. I'll stand with you against him. Together we are strong."

Her heart thudded against her ribs. If only she could believe that they were strong enough and smart enough to out think Steve.

His face lowered and their lips locked. She'd never needed the solace and promise his kiss signified more than she did now. Without reservation, she delved into the kiss, allowing him access to her soul and her heart.

He groaned, pulling her tight against him. His desire was hard against her belly. It was at that moment she realized, that they were both wasting time ignoring their desire. They could both be sleeping better, holding one another and enjoying the company. If her husband did find her and took all of this away, if she slept with Brett, she would have those wonderful memories to hold with her.

She pulled out of his kiss and rubbed her body against his length. "Tonight, I want to come to your bed," she said in a whisper.

His desire-heated gaze peered into her eyes. "Are you sure?"

"I've never been more sure of anything."

He captured her in another kiss, drugging her, until she dropped onto a stool when he backed away. "I have to check on the yearlings. I'm thinking about taking the men with me. Can you find something to entertain the women?" he asked.

She nodded.

He kissed her cheek. "I'll go feed the horses."

The back door opened and closed. Cool air swirled around her ankles. She sat on the stool a few more minutes before rolling out the dough and finishing the rolls. Her heart soared. Tonight, she would finally know what it was like to be connected mind and soul with the man she loved.

***

Brett whistled as he fed the horses and set out the tack necessary for the ride today. He didn't know what had brought this change to Melanie, but he wasn't going to try and dissuade her. His goal was to love her so well, she'd realize he would always be here for her and would always put her first.

He entered the dining room as the Galleries were filling coffee cups. "Good morning," he said, picking up a cup to fill.

"Good morning. I believe there is more of a nip in the air this morning." Mr. Gallerie had on a sweatshirt with a college logo.

"Yes, it won't be long and we'll start seeing heavy frost in the mornings." Brett took his place at the head of the table.

Mrs. Gallerie sniffed. "Is that cinnamon rolls I smell?"

"Melanie was working on them early this morning." Brett couldn't stop the grin that tickled his lips.

"Fresh cinnamon rolls! I've died and gone to heaven. I've ridden a horse and now I'm getting fresh out of the oven cinnamon rolls." She turned to her husband. "This is the best trip you've ever taken me on."

Brett laughed as Mr. Gallerie blushed.

The Barneses walked into the room.

Melanie came through the door from the kitchen pushing the rolling cart. She placed a platter of fresh cinnamon rolls, a platter of ham, a bowl of scrambled eggs, and a bowl of hash browns on the table. "How is everyone this morning?" she asked.

Mrs. Gallerie snatched a roll with her fork. "Dying to taste this."

Everyone laughed.

Melanie rolled the cart back into the kitchen.

Throat clearing, brought Brett's eyes from the swishing swinging door and his mind back to his guests.

"What do you have planned for us today?" Mrs. Barnes asked.

"I need to go check on some yearlings. Anyone who wants can ride along."

Mrs. Barnes' brows wrinkled in thought.

Mrs. Gallerie had finished off the first roll. "I could just sit here and eat these all morning."

"Wouldn't you like to go for another horseback ride? You said how beautiful you thought it was yesterday and today I'll bring along my lighter camera," her husband said.

Brett held back a chuckle. It was obvious the man was trying to save his wife from the agony of realizing how many rolls she'd eaten.

Licking her fingers, Mrs. Galleria studied her husband.

"Fern, I bet if you asked, my Larry would take photos of you and your husband on the horses and think of the wonderful Christmas cards that would make?" Mrs. Barnes had a huge smile on her face.

It didn't take but a second for Brett to realize the woman was maneuvering people to be alone with Melanie. He damn sure hoped the woman's interfering didn't change Melanie's mind about tonight. He'd been dreaming of this night for over a year and believed in his heart that once she saw how gentle he was and how good they were together this way, as well as working together, she'd have even more incentive to get the divorce.

Mrs. Galleria smiled at her husband. "That would be a wonderful photo for our Christmas card." She added eggs to her plate. "Yes, the more I think about it, I like it. I'm going on the ride."

Mrs. Barnes leaned back in her chair with a satisfied smile.

Chapter Ten

Melanie pushed the cart into the dining room and found Mrs. Barnes stacking the dirty dishes. "Where is Mrs. Galleria?"

"She went riding." Mrs. Barnes set the stacked dishes on the cart. "I can help you with the dishes. I have nothing else to do."

The woman was a manipulator. Melanie had lived with one long enough to see it. She'd made up her mind about spending the night with Brett. Nothing this woman said was going to change that.

"I can always use help. You can follow me as I do my duties, I guess, or you could go for a walk or read a magazine." She put all the empty platters and bowls on the tray and pushed it into the kitchen.

The soft pad of the woman's sneakers followed her into the room.

Melanie prepared the dishes to wash and cleaned up the kitchen as Mrs. Barnes kept up a running dialog of some of the trips she and Mr. Barnes had taken over the years. Every once in a while, Melanie gave a non-committal "uh-huh, or really" and kept on working. When the kitchen was clean and she'd taken care of any prep for lunch and the dinner meal, she picked up the tote of cleaning items, towels, and other items to replenish the cabins and placed it in the garden wagon outside the back door.

"You have quite the system set up for doing your duties," Mrs. Barnes said, following her down the trail to the cabins.

"It only took a couple of days to figure out the most effective way to deal with the chores that need to be done every day." The first couple of days at the ranch she'd been a bit overwhelmed by what was being asked of her. She'd made lists to categorize what had to be done first and what had to be done every day as opposed to once a week. Using the lists, she'd discovered she could have free time every day.

She pulled the wagon up to the first cabin. The one the Barneses were staying in. "Do you need fresh towels?"

"If it's not a burden on you." Mrs. Barnes opened the cabin door.

Melanie picked up a stack of two bath towels, two hand towels, and two washcloths. She carried them and the cleaning caddy into the cabin.

She snickered at how the older woman hustled about putting things away and tidying the room. Melanie tossed the dirty towels in a pile on the bathroom floor, cleaned the room, and hung the clean towels.

"Would you like me to vacuum?"

"Oh, no, there's no need for that. I've been sweeping each night."

Melanie nodded. There was a broom and dust pan in each cabin allowing the occupants to clean up after themselves if they carried in pine needles and dirt. She picked up the pile of towels and carried them out to the wagon and pulled it down to cabin three.

Mrs. Barnes remained in her cabin.

It was a relief to not have someone watching her every move. Melanie repeated everything in this cabin and hauled out the dirty towels to find Mrs. Barnes standing by the wagon waiting for her. So much for hoping the woman had found something to keep her entertained.

"What do you do after the cabins are cleaned?" The woman fell into step beside her as they walked back to the main house.

"I start laundry and make sure everything is ready for preparing the rest of the meals, go over the menu for the upcoming reunion and clean the main house." Her days were full of enough things to keep her mind off the anticipation of spending the night with Brett. But she kept circling back to that every other thought.

"I hope Brett pays you well."

The insinuation in the woman's voice had Melanie wondering if sleeping with her boss was a good idea.

"You two are sleeping together, aren't you?" The woman asked.

Melanie stopped at the back door. "If we were, I wouldn't tell you and that's hardly something you should ask someone you've only known a few days." She opened the back door, picked up the towels, and headed to the laundry room off the south end of the porch.

Thankfully, the woman didn't follow. Maybe she finally figured out she'd gone too far with her questions.

Melanie hauled in the cleaning tote and put the wagon back in its place beside the porch before entering the kitchen and making her grocery list for the coming week. The best part of this job was being able to make a list, send an email to the grocery store in Duncan, and all Brett had to do was drive to town, load up everything, and pay. She didn't have to leave the ranch. In the winter when there was little to do and no guests, she'd ridden with Brett to town. They'd had lunch and she'd done some personal shopping, but the rest of the year she was content to stay right here. There was enough interaction with the guests that she didn't need to go to town to socialize.

Not sure if Mrs. Barnes would come wandering in to ask more questions, Melanie went in the office and closed the door to type up her list and email it to the store. As she was sitting at the desk typing, the fax machine whirred to life. She jumped and spun toward the machine.

Several pages spit out into the tray. Thinking they were guest registrations, she went over and picked them up to see if there were openings on the dates they wished to visit.

Her husband's face stared back at her on the top page. She dropped it and wiped her hands on her pant legs to rid them of having touched his face. This had to be the information the attorney was gathering for her divorce. An odd sensation rippled through her. She picked up the papers and read. It was as if she were reading about the life of a man she didn't know.

He had been in jail for assault before she'd married him. Why hadn't anyone told her? There was a string of abuse charges filed against him, and he had been picked up for distributing drugs.

Her stomach twisted. He was like her father. A man she'd loathed for years, how had she been so stupid to fall for the lies of a man just like him?

She dropped the pages and headed to the office door. Air. She needed air.

Melanie didn't even stop for a jacket. She shoved open the back door, drew in two deep cleansing breaths, and strode toward the walking trail behind the main house.

She'd made a huge mistake with Steve. Could getting intimate with Brett be just as big a mistake?

***

Brett returned with his guests at noon. He walked into the dining room expecting to find lunch waiting for them. Instead it appeared Melanie hadn't refreshed the coffee or drinks and there wasn't even anything set out in the kitchen.

He left the Galleries and Mr. Barnes getting drinks while he tried to find Melanie. The computer in the office was on, a half-written email on the screen. Papers had fluttered to the floor around the fax machine. He picked them up, scanning the information. Damn! She must have read this and…what?

Fear pierced his chest. Had she left? He strode to her room next to the office. Everything appeared to be in place and her suitcase was in the top of the closet. The room had her flowery scent.

Where had she gone? He had guests to tend to, then he'd go looking for her.

***

Melanie caught sight of Mrs. Barnes ahead of her on the trail and started to turn but didn't get out of sight soon enough.

"Melanie!" the woman called.

She stopped and waited while Mrs. Barnes hurried to catch up to her on short stick-like legs.

"I saw you take off. You looked upset." Mrs. Barnes stopped in front of Melanie. The older woman's faded blue eyes studied her.

Talking to this woman was the last thing she wanted to do, but at the same time, she had a loving husband who seemed to treat her well. That meant you could trust some men, didn't it?

"I spent forty years as a therapist," Mrs. Barnes said, pointing to a downed log about twenty feet off the path.

Melanie walked over and sat.

The woman followed and sat with about a foot between them. "I know you have been keeping something in, perhaps speaking with someone who has heard everything would help."

"You're a therapist?" She thought of all the times she'd found their guest studying her. *Does she think I'm crazy?*

Mrs. Barnes nodded. "And I don't think you're crazy."

Melanie started and peered at the woman. "How did you know I was thinking that?"

"That's what everyone who has never been to see a therapist or counselor thinks." She shrugged. "I do believe in talking about what is bothering you. I don't always know how to answer, but eighty percent of the time just talking helps you discover something you couldn't see while mulling it around in your head."

She studied the woman. "Did Brett ask you to do this?"

The woman's gray bob swung as she shook her head. "No. I told him I was a therapist and wanted to talk to you. He said it wasn't his place to say anything."

Her heart swelled knowing she'd been correct about his loyalty. Perhaps, she was correct about him being a good person. "That sounds like Brett."

Mrs. Barnes smiled. "I hear how much you like him in your voice. What is holding you back from moving on your feelings?"

Melanie stared at her hands, rubbing up and down her thighs. "I'm married." She glanced up. How much should or could she tell this woman.

"I see. Why did you leave your husband?"

"Because I wasn't going to let him control my life or hit me again." Anger, an emotion that had been beaten out of her and replaced with fear, reared up.

"You had the strength to leave an abusive husband, but you haven't severed the marriage?"

Melanie told the woman the whole story. About getting the fake identification, the car, ending up in Duncan, and finding this job. "Brett has been pressuring me to get a divorce. He's found an attorney who is working on that now and will make sure my husband doesn't know where I am, but I'm not completely convinced my husband won't find us. He's vindictive and mean. My fear is he'll find me, hurt or kill Brett or ruin his ranch and then beat me and kill me." Her heart raced as fear started to bubble through her veins causing her limbs to grow cold.

"Have you taken out a restraining order on this man? If you do, it gives the law more leverage to take care of him if he does show up." Mrs. Barnes said.

"That's what Brett's attorney said, too."

The woman nodded. "Come on. I'll help you with this. There is no reason your abusive, soon-to-be ex-husband should ruin your future with Brett." Mrs. Barnes headed down the trail to the house.

Melanie stood and spotted Brett walking up the trail toward them with Kool trotting ahead of him. When he came abreast of the older woman, she waved up the trail and continued.

Brett strode up to her, putting his hand on her cheek. "I was worried when lunch wasn't made and you'd left the email to Mossby's unfinished."

She'd forgotten her hasty departure and lunch. "I'm sorry! I saw the fax with Steve's face and I panicked."

"He'll never hurt you again." Brett pulled her into his arms.

She snuggled against his denim jacket. This was a solid healthy relationship. "I know."

Chapter Eleven

Brett released Melanie and grasped her hand, leading her down the trail to the house. "I managed to set out cold cuts, bread, cheese, and the stuff you spread on the bread and left them making their own sandwiches."

"I'm sorry you had to do my job." She no longer sounded frightened when apologizing. The first few months, she'd sounded like a child fearing punishment.

"What were you and Mrs. Barnes talking about?"

"Things." She leaned into his arm. "How wonderful you are."

He grinned and raised their joined hands to kiss the back of hers. "You can tell me I'm wonderful all day long and I won't stop you."

She laughed.

He loved her laugh. It was something he was hearing more frequent lately.

"You still planning to spend the night with me?" He asked the question that shouldn't have had any significance over his search for her, but had been hounding him.

"Yes."

His heart raced. They were within sight of the ranch house. He wanted to kiss her, giving her a show of what to expect but knew how she felt about others seeing such displays. "Good. How about some lunch? The men want to learn how to rope after we eat."

"I'm sure their wives will want photos of that." She squeezed his hand, and they walked in the back door of the main house.

He released her hand and wandered into the dining room. Mrs. Barnes smiled and went back to talking to Mrs. Gallerie. Brett walked over to the sideboard and put a sandwich together.

"George says you're going to teach him how to rope," Mrs. Gallerie said, as Brett sat down at the table.

"I'll show him and Mr. Barnes how to throw a loop. Whether they learn or not is up to their hand-eye coordination." He bit into his sandwich.

Melanie entered the room, carrying a tray with a variety of bar cookies. "Sorry I didn't have a regular lunch waiting for you. I thought this might work as my apology."

The guests all grabbed at the desserts.

Brett winked at Melanie. She blushed, and it made his chest ache with happiness. Tonight, he would show her how gentle and loving he would treat her the rest of her life. And he'd make her understand that he wouldn't allow anyone to hurt her.

***

Melanie finished the dinner dishes by herself. Brett had offered to help, but his phone had rung, and he'd wandered into the office to take the call. She wasn't sure if her heart raced at the thought of spending the night with Brett or that the call could be information about Steve and rather than anticipation her heart beat with fear.

She placed the rags over the racks, did one last spin to make sure everything was in its place and the prep work for breakfast had been done. The dry ingredients for muffins had been measured and sat in a bowl waiting for the wet ingredients to be added first thing in the morning. She loved the convection oven that cooked quickly. There would be fresh blueberry muffins with the omelets in the morning.

A flick of the light switch threw the room into darkness. She sauntered down the hall, peeking into the office. Brett was still on the phone. It was one long conversation and from the scowl on his forehead, she had a feeling it was about her husband.

They may not have a night together after learning more about her husband. She wouldn't blame him. Who would want to become the enemy of a drug dealer? She sat on her bed, her arms wrapped around her middle. How had she not seen it? The attorney's information explained why he had so much cash in the safe in the garage. She knew he kept money there, but he'd said it was wheeling and dealing in cars. There had been a lot of cars in and out of their garage and she'd believed it. He didn't allow her to come into the garage while he was talking "cars" with a buyer. He'd told her she wouldn't understand.

All that time he'd been hiding the real way he made money. She shuddered. It could have been worse. He could have got her hooked on drugs. Then she would have never had the strength and desire to leave him. Why hadn't he? He had to have known she would get smart some day and leave.

A soft knock pulled her out of her thoughts. "Yes?"

Brett opened the door and stuck his head in. "Can I come in?"

She smiled shyly. "Yes. But I thought we were going to be in your room."

"We need to talk first."

His blank expression and clenching hands sent her flight instincts into action. She popped off the bed, ready to run.

"Sorry." He rubbed his hands together. "I would never hit or hurt you. The clenching fists are for your husband, not you." Brett motioned to the bed. "Go ahead, sit."

She cautiously sat on the edge of the bed. In her heart she knew he wouldn't hurt her, but her mind had been tricked so many times into thinking the anger had passed only to have Steve attack again.

"That was the attorney. Besides the information he faxed over earlier today, he's learned your husband is looking for you. He's hired several private investigators. Your fake I.D. was a good idea. They are having a heck of a time trying to find you."

She sucked in air. She'd known Steve wouldn't let her be.

Brett sat on the bed and faced her. "What our P.I. did find out is that your ex thinks you may have evidence against him for something." He stared into her eyes. "Do you? Did you take something that you hoped to use as leverage if he did find you?"

She shook her head. "I didn't even know he was a drug dealer until I read that report today. He kept me locked up in the house unless he wanted to take me to a dinner or a party. He told me the cash he had was from selling cars. I saw different ones go in and out of our garage all day long. I thought he sold cars.”

"You didn’t take anything?” He peered into her eyes as his hand rubbed up and down her arm.

"Money. I needed money for the I.D., to pay cash for the car, and to travel.” She dropped her gaze. “If I had known he was a drug dealer, I would have never married him. My father ruined my childhood with drug trafficking.”

Brett nodded and pulled her into his arms. “How much money did you take?”

"Ten thousand dollars. The I.D. cost three thousand, and I wanted a car that wouldn’t break down.” She pulled away. “Can you love me, knowing everything I’ve done?”

His eyes grew darker and a hand came up to cup the back of her head. “I couldn’t stop if I wanted to.” He captured her mouth in a blood-scorching kiss.

Her toes tingled and her heart melded with his. He loved her unconditionally. Now if she could do the same.

With her fingers splayed across his chest, she felt the pounding of his heart. He didn’t give her false words. This man would never do anything to harm her.

He drew out of the kiss, breathing heavily. “How about we take this up to my room?”

She peered into his eyes. “You’re sure you want me?” A small part of her feared he’d find fault with her in bed, just as Steve had. She didn’t want him to find her lacking.

"Why is there fear creeping into your eyes? Did he hurt you in bed as well?” Anger started narrowing his eyes.

"He said I was too placid. That it was like making love to a doll.” She dropped her gaze to his chest.

Brett placed a hand under her chin, making her gaze connect with his. “I would bet this ranch against the wildcat you’re going to be in bed.”

She stared into his eyes. The love and encouragement that sparkled in their depths shoved away her doubts and added to the fire he’d built in her center with the kiss. “That’s some bet. Why do you think I’ll be a wildcat?”

"Because you’ve never been loved like I’m going to love you.”

Chapter Twelve

Melanie straddled Brett's naked body, running her hands up and down his chest, feeling the silky curls of his chest hair slip between her fingers as she massaged his pecs. He was right. There had been no craving to know every inch of her husband's body. She'd feared going to bed with him after the first month of marriage.

Brett lay under her, his hands kneading her hips and her breasts, igniting a fire as she rubbed her hot center against his hard shaft sheathed in a condom. They had been touching and tormenting one another longer than she'd thought possible, intensifying her need to have him take possession of her body.

"Now," she said, lying on top of him and pressing her moist center to the tip of his shaft.

"I don't think I'm ready," Brett said, raking his teeth along her neck and capturing her mouth in a hot molten kiss that intensified the throbbing between her legs.

She felt her body shatter into a thousand sparkling lights and a split second later, he filled her. The sensation sucked the air from her lungs.

"Did I hurt you?" He stopped, his hands cradling her head as he stared up into her face.

"No. Don't stop. I've never…"

He rolled, pressing her under him, but taking his weight onto his arms and began a steady slow rhythm. She grasped his backside, forcing him deeper as she raised up to meet him. She'd never had love made to her in such a measured way. The anticipation of the next sensations drove her crazy as did the gradual build of tension in her body, released in a scream as her body exploded with electrical currents running out to her toes and flashing in her head.

Brett held onto Melanie. She had been the wildcat he'd predicted. Right down to the visceral scream as she released. Allowing her to take control of the experience and witnessing her wonder at the sensations she'd encountered, had swelled his heart. That he had given her a new experience, one that he knew she'd not had before, gave him hope she wouldn't look at him with fear again.

"We work so well together on the ranch, I knew when we came together like this it wouldn't be any different." He rolled, drawing her up on top of him.

Her long hair veiled her face and shoulders. She propped her body up with one arm and ran a hand over her face, pushing the hair back, revealing her palm-sized breasts and glowing face. "You took me to a place I've never been." She grinned. "And I'm ready to go there again any time with you."

He grasped her head, pulling her down into a slow soul-searching kiss. This was what he wanted every night for the rest of his life. Now, if they could only get Melanie's divorce without her husband finding her.

***

Melanie woke, feeling safe and loved in Brett's arms. She snuggled against his body, reveling in having his love and his security. Her thoughts descended to memories of her marriage. The first month, she and Steve had snuggled in the morning. By six months into the marriage, he rarely was home all night and the nights he did stay, he took what he wanted, told her she was worthless in bed, and would leave after having sex. She knew he went looking for someone else and she hadn't cared. When he was gone, she didn't fear a fist coming at her or a foot tripping her.

"I love the smell of your hair," Brett's deep sleepy voice said, before soft kisses fell upon her shoulder and neck.

He would never go looking for another woman. He had enjoyed

their love making as much as she had.

She rolled in his arms, capturing his mouth in a kiss she hoped told him how much he meant to her. Kissing wasn't enough. She squirmed against him, trying to get closer. His hands cupped her cheeks, rubbing her curls against his growing shaft.

The radio blasted country music.

"Oh! Breakfast will be late." She tried to roll away, but he kept her pressed firmly against him.

"I'm the boss and after the night we had, I think we need a shower."

"Oh!" She clung to Brett as he picked her up and carried her into the bathroom. He didn't let go as he turned on the water and stepped in.

She'd never had anyone give her a shower. His hands lathered up the soap and her body. When she thought she'd melt in a puddle of molten desire, he wrapped her arms around his neck, her legs around his waist, and backed her up against the shower wall as the water sprayed around them. He took her on a heady ride. One she would never forget and wished to take again.

Coming down out of the clouds and wiping away the steam on the shower door, she peered at the clock. "I have to get the muffins mixed and in the oven," she said, squirming out of his hands and out of the shower.

"You won't get fired for being late," Brett said, from inside the shower.

"No, but the guests will wonder, and I don't want them speculating." She'd brought her clothes for today with her last night. She quickly dressed and braided her hair before hurrying down to the kitchen and getting the morning meal started.

***

Brett whistled as he went about his chores. Loving Melanie was easy. She had a good heart, fun personality, and made his body come to life in a way no other woman ever had. His phone buzzed. He stabbed the pitchfork into the bale he'd been forking and stared at the number. The attorney.

"Brett," he answered, his happiness being tamped down by concern.

"Brett, sorry to bother you in the middle of the day, but I heard

178

from the P.I. I put on Perret. The man is as dirty a dealer as he's ever seen and nasty. I can see why Melanie left him."

"I had a hunch when I read the reports you sent. What could be worse than what you've already sent me?"

There was a pause and a deep sigh. "He's not only looking for her, he has a reward for anyone who brings him information about her whereabouts." Hemstead continued. "And that's not all of it. He claims she ran off with drugs and money."

Brett shook his head. No. He believed Melanie only took money. But she had been slow in telling him about the sum. Could she also have taken drugs and sold them on her way across the states? "But he hasn't a clue where she is?"

"No, but you know once we serve him with the divorce papers, he'll try even harder to find her." Hemstead didn't pull any punches.

That was what Brett had liked about the man when he met him. "Do you have an acquaintance who you could run the papers through in another state? You know, to help keep her whereabouts secret?" His mind was racing. They had a huge family reunion next week but after that there weren't any people scheduled until the first two weeks of December.

"I can see if a friend of mine will do it. But you have to be prepared if this Perret figures it out. Melanie needs to get that restraining order and turn in any drugs if she does have them. If she testified to where she found them, she could put her husband away in jail."

That was a slice of encouragement. If he could talk her into giving a statement about how she came to have the drugs, if her husband came looking for her, all they had to do was call the police. "I'll see what I can do to talk her into going to the police. She was afraid having the false I.D. would get her in trouble with the law."

"As far as I've been told, she only used it to get out of a bad situation. No fraud was committed. Especially since she used her deceased grandmother's information. Talk with her and let me know if I need to represent her at the local police station if she goes in to talk to them."

"I will. And thank you for helping us."

"Jared said you needed help and now I see why. I'll be in touch."

The line went silent. Brett stared at the wheel-barrow and the hay he'd pitched in it to take out to the horses in the corral.

Would Melanie go to the police? Did she steal drugs from her husband? He'd find out tonight, when they were in his bed. He stopped short. But could he build a life with a woman who could be such a good liar that he believed her story when, in fact, she'd stolen from her husband and possibly sold drugs?

Chapter Thirteen

Melanie cleared the dinner dishes feeling as if there was something off with Brett. He'd carried on conversations with their guests, but his gaze kept wandering to her. If he'd sent her a smile or his eyes had held a hint of heat, she'd have thought he was thinking about tonight. But his gaze was speculative. Perhaps, he'd reconsidered sleeping with her and couldn't figure out how to tell her.

He carried in a stack of dishes. "Want some help?"

She started the rinse water and faced him. "Why have you been giving me strange glances all night? Are you sorry you slept with me?"

Brett reached around her and turned off the water. "No, I'm not sorry I slept with you." As if to prove it, he pulled her into his arms and kissed her with the same passion he had the night before.

His actions relieved her plagued mind. She didn't know which would have been worse, to have to leave because Steve found her or to leave because Brett didn't care for her as she'd believed.

He eased out of the kiss, but kept his arms wrapped around her. "We have some things to discuss when the dishes are done."

His tone spun all happy thoughts from her head. "What do we need to discuss?"

"It's something we need to talk about in private."

As if to emphasize his remark, Mr. Barnes pushed through the kitchen doors. "Brett, I—"

She backed out of Brett's arms and went to work scraping plates.

"What can I do for you?" Brett asked, walking toward the man.

"I wanted to talk to you about booking a fishing week with my brother next summer." Mr. Barnes' voice sounded apologetic.

Melanie remained with her back to the room, putting dishes in the dishwasher.

"Let's go to my office and see what is available."

The two men left the room. Even though they were gone, she didn't stop working. The sooner the dishes were put away and breakfast prep was finished, the sooner she could go to Brett and discover what he wanted to talk about.

***

Brett hadn't returned to the kitchen by the time Melanie had the dishes done and the dry waffle ingredients measured, sausage in the fridge, and had checked over what she needed to do tomorrow for the evening meal.

She flicked off the lights and headed to her bedroom. Wandering up to Brett's alone didn't feel right and she'd need her clothes for tomorrow and her toiletries.

At the office, she stopped and peered in the door. The light was off, but the fax machine light was blinking. Had he received more information on Steve? She had one foot in the room when Brett's boot heels and the click of Kool's nails grew louder.

A quick about-face put her two strides from her room.

"Hey, where are you going?" Brett caught up to her, putting a hand on her arm. "I still want you upstairs with me."

"I was just getting my clothes for tomorrow." She studied his face. There was still something bothering him. "And it felt awkward to walk up to your bedroom alone."

"We could move your stuff in my room and there wouldn't be any reason to feel awkward." He put an arm around her waist.

"I'm not ready to make that move. And next week, there will be the family reunion. I don't want to be seen sneaking in and out of your room. I'll stay down here." She didn't want to give people the wrong impression of her.

"While the family reunion is here, I'll stay down here with you." He grinned.

182

"But that's no better than me sneaking upstairs." She spun out of his arm and walked into her room, switching on the light and heading for her closet.

"There will be a big difference. I'll bring down my clothes for a week and my other stuff I'll need. We both are up before any of the guests. They won't know where I slept." He followed her into the room.

When she faced him with clothes in her hands, she caught him scanning her room. "You've been in here before. What are you looking for?"

He had the decency to blush, but took a step closer to the closet. "According to your husband, you took money and drugs with you when you left."

Her heart hammered in her chest and her mind and stomach spun as if she'd just stepped off a carnival ride. "Drugs? And you believe him?" She sat on the bed, crushed. Not only had her husband made her a target, saying she had drugs, but he'd set Brett against her. The ranch no longer felt like a haven. She sucked in air but felt like she was suffocating.

The sight of Melanie's blue lips and her gasping for air, shot Brett into motion. He grasped her arms and gave her one quick shake. "Breathe," he said, harsher than he'd intended.

Melanie let out a cough and drew in one huge breath of air as if surfacing from water, knocked his hands off her arms, and stood, all in one motion.

He was pleased to see her square off at him with anger in her eyes rather than fear.

"I don't believe your husband. I believe you. But we have to discuss this new development." He reached out, moving a hand up and down her arm in a soothing motion. "What Hemstead told me is we have to contact the police. If your husband discovers where you are, which it sounds like he isn't going to give up, then we have to take steps toward keeping you safe."

There was the fear. It was a small consolation to know it was her husband she feared and not him.

"W-what steps?"

He lowered Melanie to the bed and sat beside her. "If he believes you have drugs, then he believes you have the power to put him in jail.

That is the one card we hold."

She shook her head. "I didn't know anything about the drugs until I saw that report from the attorney."

"But your husband doesn't know that. We'll go to the Duncan police tomorrow and tell them who your husband is, why you ran, and how he's looking for you. Hemstead will put a restraining order in the system, and if you want, he said he'd meet us at the police station."

Her brown eyes grew round and child-like. "But he's in Billings. He wouldn't get here until late tomorrow. And I'm not sure I want to go to the police." She wrung her hands together on her lap.

"You have nothing to fear from the police. I've known the sheriff of this county for years and the police chief in Duncan was my little league coach." He grasped her cold hands and rubbed them between his. "Can I call Hemstead and see when he can come? Would that make you feel better about going to the police?"

She nodded.

He pulled out his cell phone and dialed the attorney.

"Hemstead," the man answered.

"This is Brett Wallis. Is there a chance you could come to Duncan and meet with Melanie and I before we go to the police?"

"With the information I've been acquiring on this Perret, I've wanted to meet with her. I was looking at my schedule and I can fly my prop plane up there tomorrow afternoon. Any chance you could put me up at your ranch for the night and we can go to the police the next day?"

Brett smiled and squeezed Melanie's hand he still held. "That sounds perfect. What time will you be landing at the airport?"

"From what I can figure about four-thirty."

"I'll be there to pick you up. See you tomorrow." Brett stood, drawing Melanie up beside him. "Hemstead will fly in tomorrow afternoon, spend the night here, and then go with us to the police the next day." He motioned to the things she'd been gathering before he'd mentioned the stolen drugs. "Gather your things, I'm ready for bed."

As he escorted Melanie up to his room, his mind raced over what more the attorney could have found out about the man Melanie ran away from. Would her husband prove to be more trouble than they could fend off?

Chapter Fourteen

Melanie stayed hidden away in the kitchen all day. She didn't want to run into Mrs. Barnes. She'd made sure a room at the farthest end of the hall from Brett's room was ready for the attorney. They would be arriving soon. Now as she finished up the last preparations for dinner, she jumped every time Kool raised his head and listened.

"You're as anxious for your master to return as I am," she said to the dog, patting his head as she walked by. She picked up the pitchers of water and juice, carrying them to the dining room. The table was set. They were down to just the Barneses and the attorney until Wednesday when the Slater family arrived for their reunion. The family had been coming to the Tumbling Creek for their reunions since Brett opened it as a dude ranch. She'd met the family last year. They were a clan of jokesters, which meant she'd have to be on her toes and not be surprised by springing and flying objects.

"Woof! Woof!" Kool ran by the dining room door and down the hall to the main room.

Brett was back with the attorney.

She glanced about the dining room. Everything was on the table but the food. She returned to the kitchen to set out the serving dishes. Her hands shook. She clutched them to her belly and forced her nerves to calm.

"Melanie." Brett walked through the kitchen door, followed by a man not much older than himself with blond, crew-cut hair, and the build of a football player. If she'd seen this man on the street she would have never guessed him to be an attorney. "This is Daryl Hemstead."

The man held out his wide hand. She put her trembling one against his palm and shook hands.

"Pleased to meet you, Mrs. Perret."

She winced. "Please, call me Melanie. I don't like my married name. Especially, after learning more about my husband."

The man nodded. "Brett was filling me in on what he knows about you and what you did and didn't know about your husband." He sniffed. "But given you have what smells like a delicious meal ready, we'll go into all of that after dinner."

She nodded. Grateful she didn't have to talk about her husband, yet.

"I'll show you to your room." Brett headed for the door and said over his shoulder, "The Barneses were headed this way when we came in."

"I'll get the food on the table."

Once the two men left her kitchen, she let out a huge sigh and started dishing up dinner.

***

Brett couldn't help but notice Melanie's nerves through dinner. She was preoccupied and ate little. Mrs. Barnes had sent him several pointed glares. No doubt she felt Melanie's distraction was due to him. And it was in part. He'd brought the attorney to the house and was pushing her to move forward in her divorce.

When Melanie stood to get dessert, he excused himself and followed her into the kitchen.

"Hey, everything will be all right," he said, walking up behind her and putting his arms around her waist.

She spun in his arms, snuggling against him. Her body trembled.

"Your husband isn't going to hurt you, not if I have anything to say about it." He kissed the top of her head.

"You don't know him. He isn't going to let me go without a fight. He told me he'd see me dead before he'd let me go." Her tremors grew more noticeable.

"I won't let him lay a hand on you." He held her tight, trying to still her shaking body.

"But he won't stop with me. You helped me. He'll want to kill you as well." She pushed against his chest, putting space between them. "I don't want him hurting you because of me."

"We have the law on our side." He said it with more conviction than he felt. They were forty miles from the nearest town, which had a small police force. They were off a dead-end county road that was rarely traveled by the county sheriffs. The only protection they had was family. And he couldn't ask them to come stay at the ranch in case her husband came after them. He'd have to come up with something. He didn't want Melanie to be frightened all the time and he couldn't have guests getting caught in the middle.

"The law. You read the reports on him. He's not going to care about the law." Her fear had turned to anger.

"That's it. We're going to need anger and not fear to get through this." Brett released her and picked up the tray with plates of cake. "Bring in the coffee," he said, packing the tray to the door adjoining the kitchen and dining room. "And stop worrying. We'll get through this."

He stepped into the dining room and found Mr. Barnes and Hemstead discussing the accuracy of a rifle. Brett placed the tray on the table and passed the dessert around.

Melanie stepped into the room carrying a tray with a coffee carafe and five cups. The conversation stopped as soon as she entered.

Brett studied the two men. Why, exactly, were they discussing a rifle?

***

Melanie finished the dishes and took her time cleaning the counters and getting things ready for the morning meal. She was stalling. Her mind was telling her to back up and move on before any of this got to Steve. If she continued using the fake I.D., he'd never find her. But her heart tugged at her to stay and fight for Brett. He was the best thing that had ever happened in her life and she should do what she could to keep him.

Her desire to remain in Brett's life won out. She clicked the kitchen light off and wandered down the hallway to the main room. The first day she set foot in this room, she'd fallen in love with the large log beams, huge river rock fireplace, and the over-stuffed western print chairs. She'd added the fringed pillows, log-look lamps, and crocheted throws.

Brett and Mr. Hemstead sat in the chairs closest to the fireplace. Brett rose and motioned for her to take his chair. Once she was settled, he sat on the arm of the chair, grasping her hand in his.

"Brett and I have been discussing the fact you say your husband threatened to kill you if you left him. That and the records I've acquired from your visits to the hospital after he beat you will be more than enough to get the restraining order in place immediately. I've already told my associate to get it signed tomorrow morning." He smiled. "I took the liberty of having it written up and waiting to go to the judge."

She blinked, hardly believing this man who had never met her was already working so hard to help her. "I only have the money I've been saving from working here to pay you," she said, realizing yesterday when Brett said the attorney would be flying his plane up here, that he wouldn't be cheap.

"Money's not an issue," Brett said.

Melanie glared at him. "I won't have you paying for my attorney."

"Our attorney. I pushed you to do this, so we can be married. I feel I should be the one to pay." Brett squeezed her hand and gave her a look that said don't fight me on this.

"We'll worry about the money after we have you divorced," Mr. Hemstead said. "Right now, it's about keeping you safe." He pulled some papers out of the briefcase sitting on the floor beside his chair. "These are copies of the papers I've sent you about Perret's activities. I've reached out to the Oregon City law enforcement. They'd like to take him down as badly as you want out of this marriage. From their accounts, they agree you have never been involved with his illegal dealings."

Melanie stared at the man, then up at Brett. "Did you think I had, even though I told you I hadn't?"

He shook his head. "I believed you, but Daryl wanted to have proof when we go to the local police."

She nodded and felt the tremors coming on. Could she be strong enough to hold up to the questions the police would have for her tomorrow?

Mr. Hemstead studied her. "Don't worry about tomorrow. As your attorney, I'll do all the talking. All you have to do is sign the papers I ask you to sign."

She nodded, thankful she had these two men on her side. But also, still worried that her husband would come after them.

"Is there any way to make sure Steve can't find me?"

"We're doing our best to make sure he doesn't learn where you are.

But there are no guarantees. We can only ask those involved to not leak the information." He must have seen her fear. "I have an attorney friend in South Carolina who will be the liaison for the divorce papers. By routing them through there, we should be able to keep him from finding you." Mr. Hemstead glanced from her to Brett. "From what Brett's been telling me, you should have a new name soon after the divorce is finalized."

Her cheeks heated. How much had Brett told this man?

"That's my plan. I figure the sooner we can get her name changed, the less likely her ex-husband will be able to find her." Brett squeezed the hand he still held.

Her confidence was slowly building, knowing Brett believed in her and would stand by her no matter what.

"Do we need to talk about anything else? I'm tired and would like to go to bed. Five A.M. comes quickly." She stood.

"No, I think we'll be ready for whatever the police might ask tomorrow. Get a good night's sleep and don't worry. I'll handle everything." Mr. Hemstead stood, holding his brief case in one hand. "If you're up that early when is breakfast?"

"Melanie is up early preparing the meal. We start serving at seven, but given the Barneses don't wander in until eight, you can sleep in if you like." Brett put a hand on her back, easing her toward the hallway to her room.

"I'll be down by seven. That will give me time to work on some briefs. What about coffee?"

"It's ready when I'm in the kitchen," Melanie said. "Or I can bring a carafe up and leave it outside your door if you'd like."

"That would be great." Mr. Hemstead glanced from her to Brett and back. "I'll have to tell my clients about this place." He headed to the sweeping pine stairway.

Brett followed her down the hallway to her room. "Are you still worried about tomorrow?"

"A little. But he does seem competent and set on helping me get my divorce without Steve finding me." She faced him. "I think it would be best if we spent the night in our own rooms."

"Why?" Brett moved closer, gathering her in his arms.

"Because, I would feel better not having the man upstairs speculating on our sleeping arrangements, and I just feel the need to spend some time alone."

His brow furrowed. "You aren't planning on taking off in the middle of the night, are you?"

She glared at him. "I thought you knew me better than that. No. While I had contemplated it, to keep Steve from finding me, I don't want to run away from you."

His eyes heated and a grin brightened his face. "It's good to hear you can't resist me." He lowered his face to kiss her.

She put a hand up, stopping the contact between their lips. "I didn't say I couldn't resist you, I said I didn't want to resist you. There is a difference."

"There is. And it makes me want you even more." He nudged her hand away and kissed her until her body hummed with desire.

Without thinking, her fingers began unbuttoning his shirt and soon she felt his hard muscles under her kneading hands. His warm calloused hands scraped across her bare back and sides, moments before she realized they were both topless and he was lying her down on the bed.

"I didn't…" her voice trailed off has he slipped his hands inside her pants, sliding them down her legs. She kicked off her shoes and arched her back, pressing her curls against his hard belly. There was no way she could resist his gentle loving. Every time they made love, he showed her how much she mattered to him.

As had become their ritual, he allowed her to explore and take control of the love making. She'd become bolder each time. Tonight, she wanted to show him just how much she trusted and loved him. Prove to him, she would never leave him.

Chapter Fifteen

Brett ran his hands up and down Melanie's body, savoring her soft skin. Tonight, she was revering his body and taking her sweet time before taking him home. Because that is what her body had become to him. His home. The place where he found contentment, joy, and love. Her small hands had heated every inch of his body. Her lips had followed, kissing and nipping his skin until his cock was rock hard and standing at attention. And then….

He groaned as she licked him as if his hard-on was a giant peppermint stick. And the whole time, her eyes remained locked with his. He'd never had a more intoxicating aphrodisiac.

"Don't think I can take this much longer," he said, through gritted teeth.

She smiled and shimmied her body up his, dragging her curls across his sensitive skin.

He growled, rolled her to her back, and spread her legs. But before he plunged in and brought them both to ecstasy, he cradled her head and tangled his tongue with hers in a kiss that took him to a higher plane of desire.

Her body wiggled under his, pressing her hot wet center to his tip.

When he knew to hold out any longer would only torture them both, he slid home. Her body surrounded his in a welcoming hug. She had been put on this earth to bring him happiness. He knew that as well as he knew this ranch had been preordained to be his from the first day his parents brought him here.

The rhythm started slow and built until they both released in a chorus of exaltations. He kissed her face and watched as he pleasured her more and she had another orgasm. There would never come a time he'd tire of watching the surprise and pleasure that crossed her face at each orgasm.

"You are beautiful, hot, and I can't get enough of you," he said, kissing her lips softly in between each word.

Her eyelids covered half of her glistening eyes. She wrapped her arms around his neck and clung to him. "I wonder every day how I was so lucky to have landed here, on Tumbling Creek with you."

"Fate brought you here." He believed that. He'd been thinking about finding a wife, someone who cared as much about the ranch as he did. And he'd found one in the timid woman who'd shown up on his doorstep inquiring about his cook and housekeeper job.

"I like that." She kissed him and closed her eyes.

"Can I stay here tonight?" he asked, not planning on getting up any time soon.

"Mmmhmm." Melanie snuggled closer to him as if she were cold.

He raised up and she protested.

"I'm getting the light and covering us up." He picked her up, opened the covers, and placed her in the middle of the bed. Two strides and he flicked the light off before sliding into bed and gathering her in his arms.

***

Melanie walked up the stairs with Mr. Hemstead's coffee. Brett had slipped out of her bed when she'd showered. Last night had proven to her she could not leave Brett. He had become her anchor in a life that, until now, had never felt grounded.

At the top of the stairs, she turned to the right. The sound of a door closing behind her had Melanie casting a glance over her shoulder. Her heart pattered in her chest. The man who had shown her in so many ways he would always be there for her, strode down the hall.

"Morning, Sunshine." He kissed her on the lips and slid the tray out of her hands. "I'll deliver this."

She nodded, smiled, and headed back down to the kitchen. How had she gone so long without knowing how wonderful being loved could make her feel?

192

The popovers were in the oven. She peeled the eggs she'd cooked the day before, cut them up along with ham, and began making a white sauce. Breakfast this morning was creamed eggs and ham served in buttery popovers. The night before, she'd cut a pineapple and mango into slices to be served as well.

Humming she went about her tasks. Once the sauce was cooked, she added the eggs and ham, let it warm through and poured the mixture into a warming dish. Glancing at the clock, she wheeled the cart with the coffee pot, hot water pot, and the tub of ice with the pitchers of milk and juice, out to the dining room.

Seven o'clock and both Mr. and Mrs. Barnes and the attorney were already in the dining room. "Good morning," she said, stopping the cart by the sideboard where the beverages, minus the milk, would sit all day.

"Good morning. What are you making for breakfast this morning?" Mrs. Barnes asked.

"Popovers with creamed eggs and ham." Melanie set the tub of ice, juice, and milk on the sideboard and grabbed the cart to wheel it into the kitchen.

"I'm definitely recommending this place to clients. I had the best night's sleep I've had in months," Mr. Hempstead said.

"Oh, we love this place," Mrs. Barnes started in telling the attorney about all the wonderful things about the ranch.

Melanie smiled and returned to the kitchen. The popovers were ready to come out of the oven. She plucked them off the pans, placing them gingerly in the basket she'd made ready with a cheery tea towel draped over the edges. When those were transferred she placed the basket on the cart, along with the chafing dish keeping the creamed mixture warm, and the platter of fruit. She wheeled that out, placing the food on the sideboard next to the drinks.

"You can dig in whenever you're ready," she said, grasping the empty cart.

"Are you joining us for breakfast?" Mr. Hemstead asked.

"No. I have too many things to do in the kitchen if we're going to town today." She pushed the cart to the kitchen and through the swinging door. If the man knew how tied in knots her stomach was, he wouldn't have mentioned her eating.

Melanie pulled out the recipes for the evening meal. There was some prep that needed done so when she returned from town she wouldn't be feeling behind. And she needed to make sandwiches for Mr. and Mrs. Barnes since she wouldn't be here to serve them lunch.

***

Brett glanced in the rearview mirror for the hundredth time since leaving the ranch. Melanie sat in the back seat, worrying her bottom lip and looking like a deer ready to bolt at the first sign of danger. Daryl had asked questions about the ranch and the area non-stop from the ranch to Duncan.

He parked in front of the city police station and noticed that Sheriff Landry's vehicle was also parked there. He'd called his little league coach this morning and asked if he could meet them here. It would save having to put Melanie through telling her story twice.

Hemstead was the first to exit the suburban. Brett took this moment to try and bolster Melanie.

"Once we get this day over with, the rest will be easy." He caught her gaze in the mirror.

"You're sure they won't throw me in jail?"

"You have done nothing wrong. Daryl will make sure they understand the gravity of your situation and help." He smiled. "Come on. I'll be right there with you."

She half smiled and opened the door.

He stepped out, captured her hand and they followed Daryl into the police station.

Melanie's hand trembled. He gave it a squeeze when he wanted to stop and pull her into his arms. She wouldn't have to deal with the police alone.

Sheriff Landry stood to the side of the lobby, drinking from a cup and talking with one of the guys Brett had played ball with in high school. He nodded to them and followed Daryl to the desk.

"We're here for a meeting with your police chief and—" Daryl nodded toward the sheriff "—Sheriff Landry."

Landry walked over to them. "Come on back." He nodded to Brett. "Good to see you Brett."

"You, too, sir." Brett shook hands with the man.

The sheriff led the way to the back of the building. A small conference room had the door standing open. "Go on in and make yourselves comfortable, I'll get Chief Taft."

"Why is the sheriff here?" Melanie asked as Brett led her to a chair.

"I thought if all the law enforcement in the area knew what was going on you'd be safer." Brett moved a chair closer to Melanie and sat.

Hemstead took the chair on the opposite side of Melanie.

Her eyes were wide, her hands clenched between her knees. Brett wanted to touch Melanie to comfort her, but refrained from giving away how close they were.

"Don't worry. This is just to let the authorities know what is going on and to be on the lookout." Daryl patted her shoulder.

"You both don't think I can remain hidden from Steve, do you?" Her gaze bounced from one man to the other as she pivoted her head.

"We're just taking precautions in case he does learn your whereabouts and to let the locals know about the restraining order, which has already been signed and is being faxed to me here." Daryl flashed a confident smile at Melanie.

Brett had no doubts with this man in their corner they wouldn't have any trouble.

The sheriff and chief stepped into the room and closed the door.

After introductions, Chief Taft said, "Why did you request this meeting?"

As he'd indicated, Daryl laid everything out to the two lawmen.

A knock brought the chief to his feet. He walked over and opened the door. There was a brief discussion and his hand disappeared, returning with papers. He crossed to the table and set the documents on the table. "It appears the restraining order is in place."

Daryl grinned.

Melanie shrank back against the chair. Brett leaned her direction.

"From what I gather, if we can catch this Perret person with drugs, we can nail him good," Sheriff Landry said.

Daryl nodded. "That would be the ideal situation. All we need to do is catch him within fifty miles of the Tumbling Creek Ranch. Given the medical records shown to the judge, she was the one who placed the larger than usual distance Perret has to stay from Mrs. Perret."

Melanie flinched at the use of the name. Knowing how she hated to be called the man's wife, made Brett want more than ever to get the man caught by the law and out of her life for good.

"If he shows up in our town we can get him. Any idea if he'll be driving one of his vehicles?" Chief Taft asked.

"I'll have my P.I. send you the license plates we know of," Daryl said.

"When will the divorce papers be served? That will set him off from the sound of things." Landry nodded to Melanie.

"As we speak, he is being served with the papers." The satisfied smile on the attorney's face, gave Brett the feeling the man was hoping Perret would make a move toward Melanie.

He didn't like the idea of her being used as a pawn in her own divorce proceedings.

"H-he could come looking for me today?"

The fear in her voice softened the expressions of all the men in the room. Brett put an arm around her shoulders.

"Remember, he's not going to know where you are. We've gone to extra lengths to make sure."

She shook her head. "He'll figure it out. He said he'd see me dead before he'd let me go."

"He's going to have to get past us before he can get to the ranch. I'll have a deputy posted twenty-four hours a day on the county road leading to the ranch." Sheriff Landry leaned over the table. "We won't let anything happen to you. You're one of us now."

"O-one of you?" Melanie asked.

"A resident of Duncan. We take care of our own." His wide white mustache rose, showing his teeth as he grinned at her.

Brett knew that the lawmen in this room were helping because he was a Wallis. A family that had homesteaded this area. "Thank you." He stood and shook hands with the sheriff and the chief.

"Say hi to your parents for me," Sheriff Landry said.

"I will." Brett grasped Melanie's hand and helped her to her feet. Daryl followed as they walked through the lobby and out onto the street. "That wasn't so bad, was it?" he asked Melanie.

She shook her head. "But I'm still not convinced he won't find me."

Chapter Sixteen

Melanie had been surprised by the show of concern for her and offers of help. Then at the end when Brett had shaken hands, she realized, they weren't doing it for her. They were helping Brett and the Wallis family.

Mr. Hemstead put a hand on her shoulder. "I'll have my contact in Oregon City keep an eye on Perret. If he leaves the city, I'll know, and I'll let Brett know."

She peered into Brett's face. "And you'll let me know?"

"Yes. If we know the man is coming, I want you to be safe." Brett led her to the bronze suburban with the Tumbling Creek Ranch logo painted on the door. "We'll drop Daryl off at the airport and get something to eat before we head back to the ranch."

Her stomach didn't feel like she would be able to eat anything for a week, but she wasn't going to tell him that in front of the one man who had done everything possible to make her feel safe and get her out of her marriage.

They climbed into the vehicle and the two men talked about the area as they drove out to the small landing strip on the edge of town. Both men exited the vehicle before she did. When she stepped out, Melanie caught a fragment of the conversation.

"I can send a man to stay at the ranch until we see what happens," Mr. Hemstead said.

"That's not necessary. I plan on telling my family and the neighboring family about what could happen. They'll keep tabs on us, and I'm sure they won't let Melanie and I be alone." Brett nodded toward her and she walked over, wondering if he wanted her to hear his concerns. "We have a family reunion coming this next week. There will be too many people roaming around the ranch for Perret to try anything. And I don't see him finding out where Melanie is until long after the divorce is final, and we are married."

He put an arm around her shoulders, drawing her close. Without apprehension, she wrapped her arms around his waist. He was her shelter. He wouldn't let anyone hurt her.

"I'll keep an eye on him and let you know his actions." Mr. Hemstead smiled at her. "After what you've been through, I'm glad you found Tumbling Creek and this man."

"I agree." She hugged Brett and smiled at her attorney.

Mr. Hemstead strode to the closest hanger and tossed his bags into a small plane.

"I like him," she said. "Knowing you two are looking out for me takes away some of my fears."

Brett tipped her chin up, meeting her gaze. "But not all of them."

She shook her head. "You haven't seen the look Steve can get in his eyes." A shudder rippled cold through her body. "I wouldn't doubt he's killed people, so I wouldn't be the first."

"I won't let that happen. Come on. I'll take you to lunch." Brett's arm remained around her shoulders as he escorted her to the passenger side of the vehicle. "We also need to make a stop at the drug store. You can think about anything you might need while we eat."

The short drive to the restaurant was quiet. They were both deep in their own thoughts. Brett parked and opened her door. Even when she'd been dating her husband he hadn't held her door, or shown her the courtesy that Brett had from their first meeting. How could she have been so blind to the nasty side of Steve?

Brett escorted her into the small diner. The red and white checkered table cloths and brands burned into the backs of the chairs and the walls of the building, let her know this would be a good place to eat a burger.

Everyone in the place said hi to Brett and studied her. One woman gave her a thorough up and down, before walking over with a pad and pencil.

"Hi Brett. Haven't seen you around much the last year." The woman's dark brown hair was pulled back in a short ponytail. She wore a t-shirt with lots of sparkles and tight jeans that showcased her wide hips. Scuffed cowboy boots gave her more height.

Melanie estimated the woman was a few inches shorter than her five-six.

"I've been busy out at the ranch. Guests just keep showing up." Brett tipped his menu towards Melanie. "What would you like to drink?"

"Hot tea, please."

"I'll have coffee and a ranch burger. Melanie, what would you like?" Brett kept his attention on her.

She liked that he was making it clear he was more interested in her than the woman taking their order. "Cheeseburger, please."

"Fries?" the woman asked in an icy tone.

"We'll share mine," Brett said.

The woman's finely plucked eyebrows raised before she spun and headed to the kitchen behind a counter lined with men, watching them.

"Why are those men watching us?" Melanie asked in a whisper.

"Could be because you are the prettiest woman in the place."

She narrowed her eyes. "The truth."

"That is the truth. But they aren't watching us. They're watching me and Belinda. We dated a bit until you started working at the ranch." He picked up a spoon and wiped it with a napkin.

"You dumped her for me?" She wasn't sure if her heart fluttered with happiness or anxiety. "If she puts two and two together she'll spit in my hamburger."

Brett laughed, causing even more people to look their way. "I would say, she'd spit in mine and probably add some hot sauce as well. But she's over me."

Melanie studied him. "How do you know?"

"Because I have it on good authority that several months after I stopped calling she was in my cousin Nate's bed."

"That doesn't bother you?" She'd only ever known Steve's possessiveness. All she had to do was look at a man or have one say hi to her and he would call her a whore and teach her a lesson not to look at anyone but him.

"Nope. That's how I knew you were the one I wanted." He stretched his hand across the table.

She placed her hand in his and asked, "How?"

"Because I knew if I had heard you were with Nate, I would have messed up his pretty face."

She sucked in air and started to pull her hand back, but he held on.

"I wouldn't have, but just thinking it made me realize how much you meant to me. We will get through all of this."

A glimmer of hope seeped into her heart. If anyone could make her feel there was a happy future ahead, it was this man.

"Cheeseburger, hamburger and fries." Belinda plopped the baskets of food on the table. "I'll get your drinks."

Melanie grinned at Brett as she plucked a fry from his basket.

***

Brett glanced over at Melanie. After leaving Duncan, she'd fallen asleep. He didn't mind having the time to watch her sleep and think about the morning's events. He grinned. If Belinda had known how quickly he'd realized Melanie was the one for him, she would have hopped in Nate's bed sooner, trying to make him jealous.

He'd dated Belinda because she had been someone who didn't seem to care if he popped in unannounced. He'd liked her, but never had he felt the way he did about the woman sleeping in the seat next to him. Whatever hurdles they had to leap to get married and start a family, he was willing to take.

What nagged at him was Melanie's insistence that her husband would come looking for her and hurt her. Rage boiled in his guts when he thought about it. A family meeting this weekend would get everyone up to speed on what obstacles were in his and Melanie's way. And a trip over to the MacIntyre Ranch. Their closest neighbors could keep an eye out for anyone lurking around. He didn't doubt the chief and sheriff would do their best to watch for Perret, but from everything he'd learned about Melanie's husband, he was slippery.

He drove under the Tumbling Creek arch and Kool came charging out from beside the barn.

"Hey sleepyhead, we're home." He smoothed the back of his fingers down Melanie's cheek.

"Huh?" Her dark lashes fluttered up and her eyes, the color a rich dark chocolate, were hazy with sleep.

He parked the vehicle and leaned over, kissing her lips. "We're home." Cupping her chin, he stared into her eyes.

"Home?" Her gaze focused on him and she smiled. "Yes. Home."

Happiness rushed through his veins and he captured her lips. Her calling him home was as intoxicating as her kisses. He cupped a hand behind her head, and tangled his tongue with hers, driving himself, and he hoped her as well to the edge of desire.

Knocking on the passenger window broke the kiss.

He peered at Mrs. Barnes standing outside the passenger door. The grin on her face revealed she knew exactly what she'd interrupted.

Melanie's face turned every shade of red he'd witnessed on fall trees.

"I'll distract her, while you get in the house." He kissed the tip of her nose and slid out the driver's side. "Mrs. Barnes, what can I help you with?"

"Your dog dragged a half dead rodent onto our porch. Mr. Barnes wanted to know how to dispose of the creature." The woman reluctantly followed him down the path to the cabins.

He glanced over his shoulder and caught a glimpse of Melanie slipping into the main lodge. "What kind of rodent did he catch?"

"I don't know. It was furry and ugly." The woman shivered.

If Kool had tangled with a rat, he was glad the dog was caught up on his shots. The dog now stood to the side of cabin number one, staring at something on the ground.

A field mouse.

Brett stared at the woman. "Your husband can't dispose of a field mouse?"

"He can, but I needed an excuse to talk to you." She handed him a shovel. "You know, in case Melanie is watching."

"You don't have to manufacture ways of talking to me." He took the shovel and scooped up the miniscule rodent. Several strides took him to the trees bordering the backside of the cabins. He flung the small body into a chokecherry bush high enough Kool couldn't reach the creature.

"Was that lawyer here to help Melanie with a divorce?" Mrs. Barnes asked, putting a hand on his arm to keep him behind the cabin.

"Yes." He didn't see any point in telling the woman anything else.

"Why did you all three have to go to town? Is her abusive husband a threat to her?" Mrs. Barnes didn't pull any punches when she asked questions.

"He could be. If he found out where she is, but we're making sure he can't find her." He folded his arms over the top of the shovel handle.

"Anything else you want to know?" While it was a question, the inflection of her being nosey rang in his voice.

"I care about her well-being. You can't fault me for that." The woman huffed and marched to the front porch of the cabin.

Brett chuckled and followed. He didn't fault her. It seemed anyone who met Melanie was compelled to make sure she remained safe. Which reminded him, he had some calls to make.

Chapter Seventeen

Melanie had expected to have Sunday off. The Barneses had left, leaving her Monday and Tuesday to prepare for the family reunion that started on Wednesday. However, Brett informed her Saturday night that they were hosting his family for Sunday dinner. Everyone, even Lacey and Jared, who would spend the night and leave the next day.

"Why did you invite everyone here? Is it your parents' anniversary or a birthday?" she asked, wondering if she needed to bake a cake.

"I asked them here to tell them about your husband and divorce." Brett put his hands on her shoulders. "I know you don't like people to know about your marriage, but we are going to need help if, as you believe, Perret comes after you or me."

The last two days she'd led herself to believe Steve didn't care anymore and would not cause problems. "Do you really think he'll come after me?"

The anguish in his eyes made her heart stop. "What haven't you told me?"

"He refused to sign the divorce papers and had the person who served them beat up, trying to find out where you are."

Her legs folded. Brett caught her, easing her onto a chair. "He refused and hurt someone?" She stared into his eyes. "I don't want to be Mrs. Perret. I want to be Mrs. Brett Wallis."

Brett cradled her face in his hands and kissed her. "I want that too. Hemstead said you can do a contested divorce. There will be a hearing and if Perret doesn't show up, you will be awarded the divorce. He's already put the paperwork in motion. In the meantime, my family needs to know what is going on and the danger you are in." He kissed her again. "What can I do to help you with dinner?"

He had to be as devastated as she was that they wouldn't be able to marry until after a hearing. And what if Steve did show up? Would she never be able to get out of that marriage? They would always have the threat of a crazy man searching for her. "How can you remain so calm?"

"Because I know we are meant to be together."

"What about your family? I'm sure your parents want you to marry. You can't marry me, not if Steve won't give me a divorce." What if his family refused to help, knowing he would never be able to marry her? Mr. and Mrs. Wallis would want grandchildren to pass down their name and legacy. Not illegitimate children.

"I know Hemstead will do everything in his power to get you away from your husband. We have the medical documents and your own words of his abuse, and he's a drug dealer. No one is going to believe a word he says. I plan on making you my wife as soon as the ink dries on the divorce papers." He dropped to one knee. "Melanie Elaina Trask, would you marry me?"

"I can't—"

He held out a ring with a setting of colorful stones. "For now, we'll call this an engagement ring."

"Don't you feel that is lying?" She loved the colorful stones and the love shining in Brett's eyes. "We can't say when we'll get married."

Brett shook his head and pulled her to her feet and into his arms. "Not when I can't see a future without you in it. I'll pretend we're married until the day we die, if it's the only way I can have you by my side."

Her heart ached with happiness and trepidation. If Steve found them pretending to be wed, that could be more dangerous for Brett than her working for him. "I want to be your wife, but I couldn't live with myself if you were hurt because of me."

"That's not going to happen. Come on. We'll have guests arriving soon. What can I do?"

She'd planned an easy meal of roast, roasted vegetables, mashed potatoes, rolls, and a salad. She'd made a large pan of apple crisp and a large pan of cherry crisp for dessert. The good thing about having family, she could put everything on the table and the dessert on the sideboard and not have to serve everyone.

Lacey and Jared were the first to arrive an hour before dinner. Lacey gave her a long hug and offered to help set the table. Jared and Brett wandered into the main room.

"I understand there are some complications with you and Brett marrying," Lacey said, always ready to hit whatever was in her way head-on.

"Brett invited the family here to tell everyone." Melanie wasn't sure she was going to be able to sit at the table and not squirm while Brett revealed her less than perfect past life.

Lacey put an arm around her shoulders. Melanie's head came to her friend's shoulder. "Hey, we all know you've had some tough times. If you're going to become a Wallis, we'll have your back, no matter what. That's what we do for family."

Tears burned the back of Melanie's eyes. She'd never had a family that pulled together like Brett's family. She'd had to face all her battles on her own. And there had been many through school and then with her poor choice in a husband.

"Hey, are you upsetting my fiancée?" Brett asked, striding into the kitchen and gathering her into his arms.

"I saw that gorgeous ring but wasn't sure if it was an engagement or promise ring." Lacey kissed Brett on the cheek and squeezed Melanie's shoulder. "Congratulations!"

"Do you need any help in here?" Brett's mom and Lacey's mom entered the kitchen.

"What's this, tears?" Lacey's mom asked, holding a handkerchief out to Melanie.

She didn't know whether to laugh or cry more at the attention she was receiving. What would happen when they all learned about her past?

"I hope those are happy tears," Brett's mom said.

"I think they are," Lacey said, winking. "Mom, Aunt Carolyn, why don't you help me carry this food into the dining room." With the same efficiency and tenacity the woman had used to ride bulls, she herded the older women, with hands full, into the dining room.

"I thought they'd never leave," Brett said, his eyes twinkling.

Before she could respond, he captured her lips in an earth-shaking kiss.

He drew back and grinned. "That put some color back in your face."

Before she'd regained her composure, he grabbed up the platter with the roast and shoved through the dining room door. Within seconds it swung inward, and Lacey picked up another bowl.

"You know we have a cart to haul all this food to the other room," Melanie said.

"Load it up with the desserts and come join us." Lacey disappeared.

She loaded the desserts on the cart, grabbed the gravy boat, and pushed her way through the door. All the smiling faces took her by surprise. She'd met each member of the Wallis families at various times, but seeing them all together at one time, overwhelmed her. She had set eleven places at the two tables they'd moved together, but seeing them, it struck her at what she would have living as Brett's wife.

He helped her place the desserts on the sideboard and took the gravy boat, motioning for her to take the seat to his left. Her usual seat at the opposite end of the table was taken up by Brett's father, John, with his wife, Carolyn, to his right. Their two boys, Garth and Dillon, and Lacey's brother, Nate, sat on the same side. The other side had Lacey's parents, Dorothy and Allan, Jared, and Lacey, sitting next to Melanie.

Brett scanned the people he loved. This would be what holidays would be like from here on out. He and Melanie hosting Thanksgiving and Christmas. His parents' anniversary. He captured Melanie's hand under the table.

Her fingers were cold as ice. Best to start with the good news.

"Thank you all for coming on such short notice." He smiled at his family. The women had knowing expressions, but the younger men appeared bored.

"First, I'd like to announce that Melanie and I are engaged." He heard her intake of air and squeezed her hand.

His mom rose out of her seat, ran around the table, and hugged both of them. "It's about time, even a blind person could see how much you two care about one another." She hugged them again and patted Brett's cheek. "You've picked a good one."

He couldn't agree more with his mom. "I did." He raised Melanie's hand and kissed the back.

She peered at him with uncertainty in her eyes.

"Have a seat, Mom." He stood and carved the roast. When all the plates were filled and the room has grown quiet with everyone eating, except Melanie who stared at the food he'd placed on her plate, he glanced over at Lacey and Jared. The two members of the family who knew about the complications.

Lacey nodded her head, as if telling him to say more.

This was the hard part, but he knew they would all help. He captured Melanie's hand and cleared his throat.

Everyone stopped with bites or drinks half way to their mouths.

"While I said we are engaged there is a hurdle we need to clear." That got everyone's attention. Utensils and glasses were placed on the table and everyone watched he and Melanie.

"What hurdle?" his dad asked.

"Melanie is still married, and her husband refuses to give her a divorce." Melanie's hand he held trembled. He went on to explain her circumstances, barely keeping his anger in check as he told of her abuse and getting away from the man.

A glance at Melanie and he noticed, Lacey held her other hand. It relieved him to know his cousin would help the woman he loved.

"If she isn't divorced, how do you propose to marry?" Aunt Dorothy asked.

"We have an attorney working on a contested divorce. If all goes well, we can marry as soon as that paperwork is done."

"I'm glad you're telling us everything," his dad said. "But what if her husband discovers where she is?"

Brett peered around the table. "That is Melanie's biggest fear. He told her he would kill her before he'd let her go."

The older women gasped and anger flashed on every man's face at the table.

"You've served divorce papers. That means he knows where she is," Jared said.

"Yes, the papers were served, and he beat up the person serving him, trying to find out where she is. But the lawyer you suggested has done a great job of covering up all the ways her husband could track her down." Brett would be forever grateful to Jared for suggesting Hemstead.

"But?" Dillon asked.

"My husband has money and resources to find me." Melanie spoke up, releasing both his hand and Lacey's. "I love Brett, but I don't want him harmed or this beautiful ranch ruined." She stood and turned to him. "You have been the best thing that has ever happened in my life, but I can't put you or your family through the terror Steve could cause finding me here. I have to go."

It felt as if he'd fallen into a rock crusher. "No. I told you, you don't need to run." He stood, grasping her arm before she could flee. "You are worth any trouble your husband could bring."

"No. Your life or the life of anyone at this table isn't worth my happiness."

"I disagree." His mom stood up. "If you don't stand up to this man, which you did already by getting away, you'll be running your whole life and never find peace." She waved her arms to encompass everyone at the table. "What do you all think? Is Brett and Melanie's happiness worth a little trouble?"

"He's not a little trouble—" Melanie started.

"It doesn't matter how much trouble he is. We're family. You are family, have been since the day you arrived and helped Brett get his dream off the ground." Dad waved his fork. "We help family. Now sit down both of you and eat. After dessert, we'll discuss what needs to be done to keep you both safe."

Brett drew Melanie down into the chair. Tears glistened in her eyes. He hoped it was from happiness that she was being welcomed into the family and not because she feared neither one of them would live to an old age together.

Chapter Eighteen

Melanie still couldn't believe how the whole Wallis family had rallied around her and Brett. They'd come up with a plan that wouldn't leave them alone at the ranch and Brett's dad would stay in contact with the sheriff to make sure they knew of any outsiders in the area. He was also calling in help from the truckers that worked for them to keep an eye out for out of state or rental cars in the area.

Everyone said they'd be looking forward to a wedding within the year.

Brett crawled into bed beside her. "I told you my family would help." He wrapped his arms around her, giving her warmth with his body.

"I would walk away to save you." That had been spinning in her head for days. She would not allow Steve to hurt Brett. She would do whatever he wanted to keep the man she loved safe.

"I don't want you to sacrifice yourself for me. I want you to be free of fear and abuse. If Steve comes, you are to hide and get out of here. Don't look back. Go to Lacey and Jared's in Billings and wait to hear from me." He released her and stared into her eyes. "I mean it. You do not sacrifice yourself for me."

She narrowed her eyes and studied him. "But isn't that what you would be doing for me?"

"No. I won't sacrifice myself. I'll beat the living daylights out of him and turn him over to the police." The ferocity of his words and the anger in his eyes told her he would do just that if given the chance.

"Let's hope he's caught by the cops before he gets near either one of us." She truly hoped the police found him before he reached the ranch, but there were no guarantees. Their best hope was that he wouldn't discover the restraining order or the divorce proceedings which had to happen in the county where she lived. If he learned about either of those, he would know where to find her.

"I don't want to think about him. I want you to make me forget." She pressed her body to his and was rewarded with a marathon of gentle, mind-blowing love making.

***

The week with the family reunion went by quickly. With so many people to feed and tend to, she fell to sleep as soon as her head hit the pillow. But it was wonderful to wake lying next to Brett every morning. He was right. No one even noticed they were sharing a bed.

Sunday afternoon, as the last member of the Slater family drove out through the archway, Brett pulled her into the great room and they both collapsed on the couch.

"What a fast and furious five days!" Brett held her in his arms as they reclined, enjoying the peace and not moving.

"I think they planned even more events than last year." The matriarch of the family made sure no one sat still long enough to play on a device or grumble they were bored.

"I felt like all I did was saddle and unsaddle horses for hours as they all went on that scavenger hunt." Brett kissed her cheek. "Now we have two weeks of just us. What do you want to do?"

"I have to strip all the beds and clean before you can make plans for us to do anything." With all the laundry and cleaning that needed done over the next few days, she wouldn't get far from the main house and the cabins.

"You know, I've been thinking that come spring when things pick up again, I think we need to hire someone to do the laundry and do the cleaning."

She spun in his arms. "Really? I mean I don't mind doing it but that would free up more of my time." Her mind went to the new recipes she'd been wanting to try and had planned to spring on Brett this winter when they didn't have guests.

"Since you'll be Mrs. Wallis by this time next year, I think you should start helping with the books and leave the cleaning to someone else."

"I'd like that." She snuggled against his chest and nuzzled his neck. "I won't be so tired every night."

He raised her chin and peered into her eyes. "That's what I'm working on." His face lowered and his lips caught hers in a heart-stopping kiss.

She came up for air and snuggled closer. "We don't need dinner tonight, do we?"

Brett grinned and his eyes sparked with heat. "At least not for a couple of hours." He rose off the couch, gathered her in his arms, and carried her down the hall to her room.

***

Monday morning, Brett wasn't surprised to see Dillon's pickup driving under the archway. Their dad had set up a schedule where either Dillon, Garth, Nate, or Lacey would be staying a few days at the ranch. He figured with an extra person around to get Melanie to safety and call the police, they would keep the harm to anyone down.

Brett had been feeding horses. He met his brother halfway to the house.

"Melanie know about the equipment I brought?" Dillon asked.

"I hadn't said anything. She'll figure it out when we put it up." Brett slapped his brother on the back. "I try not to be antsy around her, but this waiting, which could go on for who knows how long, isn't fun."

"I can imagine. Too bad the cops in Oregon City can't catch him dealing."

"Yeah, I wish there was a way to make it happen, too."

They entered the main house and hung up their coats before entering the dining room.

"I'll get you a cup of coffee. With just the two of us, Melanie doesn't put out the beverages." Brett entered the kitchen and his heart raced. Melanie had a dusting of flour on her cheek and was intently frosting a small pan of cinnamon rolls.

"You look good enough to eat." He scooped some frosting out of the bowl with his finger and spread it across her lips, then took his time tasting her sweet kisses.

"You roasting and grinding—"

Dillon's voice reminded him why he came into the kitchen.

Melanie sprang out of his embrace.

He reached over, pulling her to his side with one arm. "The coffee's over there," he pointed with his free hand. "I came in to get him some coffee and tell you Dillon is here to stay for a few days."

"I'll have an upstairs room ready by noon," Melanie said, not looking at either of them.

"Don't make up a room for me. I'll clean up cabin one and stay there. I like my privacy as much as you two do. And I'm working on a new song. I like to keep my music private until I'm happy with it." Dillon filled a cup with coffee and wandered back through the swinging door.

Brett grasped her shoulders and peered into her eyes. "I saw you standing there, looking so delicious and I forgot I came in to get him a cup of coffee. Do you forgive me?"

She licked her bottom lip. "It's hard to stay mad at a man who can kiss like that."

He grinned and slid his finger around the edge of the frosting bowl. "Want to try another kiss?"

Melanie's cheeks deepened in color. "I'll save some for tonight. Right now, I need to get some eggs scrambled and feed you two." She ducked out of his arm and straight to the refrigerator.

His mind was tripping all over itself, thinking about what use she had in mind for the remaining frosting tonight. Best not to think on that too long. He filled a cup with coffee and joined Dillon in the dining room.

"Melanie is whipping up some eggs to go with the cinnamon rolls," he said, taking a seat across from Dillon.

"I'd say you were trying to whip something up when I walked in." Dillon snickered.

"I can't help it the woman I love is so darn cute when she's cooking." Brett sipped his coffee and thought about Dillon's comment about cabin one. "You really want your privacy, or did you take the cabin for another reason?"

His brother cast a glance toward the kitchen door and said, "Dad suggested I set up some game cameras around and I brought the technology to keep tabs on them. I'll set it all up in cabin one and everyone who comes to stay will be in that cabin." He nodded toward the kitchen. "Didn't want to upset Melanie by saying anything."

He understood his brother's discretion. Melanie was already a bundle of nerves wondering if her husband would show up. He wasn't sure all the precautions they were taking would make her feel better or worse. "Probably best not letting her know."

The door swished open and Melanie pushed the cart out with plates, silverware, eggs, and the cinnamon rolls. "Breakfast is ready."

She placed everything on the table and took the seat next to him.

"This looks great! Living on my own, I tend to eat stuff that's quick and doesn't take a lot of thought." Dillon dug into the eggs and placed two rolls on his plate.

"Then I'll have to make sure you get plenty to eat while you're here." Melanie didn't make a move to put food on her plate, so Brett dug in.

"How long will you be here?" she asked.

"Three days. Then Nate will be here for three—"

"That's going to cut into his weekend fun. Did Dad plan it that way?" Brett laughed.

"No. Garth had a mechanic class he's taking Thursday nights and Lacey can't get free from her classes until next week."

"This is a huge inconvenience for all of you," Melanie said.

"But it's worth it to keep family safe." Dillon nodded at both of them. "Even if you two hadn't fallen in love, you would still be considered a part of this family. You are one of the reasons Brett's ranch, the family ranch, is a success."

Chapter Nineteen

Melanie ran Dillon's words over and over in her head as she stripped beds and cleaned rooms. She was an integral reason why this ranch was a success. She'd never felt she'd made a difference at anything before and here she was one of the factors Tumbling Creek Ranch was successful. She pulled the sheets off the bed in the room next to Brett's. She'd spent the whole morning, moving from room to room on the second floor of the main house, stripping beds and cleaning. She had a load washing and one drying as she worked.

She glanced out the window and stopped to watch Dillon and Brett secure what looked like a camera to the corner of the barn. Had all the boxes she'd watched them carry into cabin one been more than instruments for Dillon to work on his music?

When the room was cleaned and she'd put new sheets on the bed, she hauled the dirty ones down to the laundry. At the back porch, she pulled on a thick warm sweatshirt and tied the hood. The weather had turned off colder over the weekend. Brett said soon they'd see snow.

Brett was climbing down the ladder as she approached.

"Why are you putting up cameras?"

Dillon jumped and faced her.

Once Brett's feet were on the ground he took a couple steps toward her. "We're putting this one, one at the back corner of the main house, and one on the archway, to be able to monitor who is around here." His gaze traveled over her face. "It's to keep you safe."

She was getting tired of this being about her. "Don't you mean, us safe?"

"Both of you," Dillon said, taking a step closer. "This was Dad's idea. I set up monitors in cabin one. That's where everyone who comes will stay."

Melanie stared at Brett. "Were you going to tell me this if I hadn't noticed you out here?" She hated that he thought she'd fall apart knowing they were preparing for a visit from her husband.

"I was going to tell you after they were all installed." He grinned. "That way you wouldn't ask us to take them down. I know how you feel about wasting time."

She slugged him. "There are times I wish you didn't know me so well." She pivoted, called over her shoulder, "Lunch in twenty minutes," –and marched back into the house. Now, not only did she have to fear her husband showing up, but she'd have to remember there were cameras watching. She never knew when Brett would sneak up on her and give her a toe-curling kiss. She doubted his family would want to watch that.

A chicken was cooking, and she'd rolled out homemade noodles earlier in the day. The loaves of bread she'd left to rise while she worked upstairs were ready for the oven. She slid them in. There would be homemade chicken soup and fresh bread for lunch.

The cooler weather put her in a baking mood. Waiting for the bread to bake, she started mixing up batter for cupcakes. They would be a nice dessert for the three of them tonight, and if the two men didn't eat them all, lunch tomorrow.

The whirr of the fax machine caught her attention. She wandered into the office wondering if someone wanted to spend a snowy Christmas at the ranch. Seeing the pile of papers on the desk next to the printer, she shuddered. Maybe hearing the fax was going to become less and less exciting. Lately, the only papers the machine spit out had to do with her husband. This was no different.

She plucked the two papers from the tray and scanned the contents. He'd made bail from beating the poor man who had taken her divorce papers to Steve. She put that paper to the back and read the next one. THE P.I. HAS LOST TRACK OF STEVEN PERRET.

Her hands shook, making the paper rustle. He'd given the private investigator the slip to find her.

***

Brett entered the back porch and immediately heard the shrill beep of the convection oven and smelled the burning bread. He hurried into the kitchen, pulled the smoking loaves from the oven and dumped them in the stainless-steel sink. Where was Melanie?

"It smells like lunch is burnt," Dillon said, walking into the kitchen.

"Did you see Melanie?" Brett scanned the room and saw the chicken cooking, the noodles still drying, and batter in a bowl. It was as if she'd left in a hurry. Had her husband snuck in while they were out by the horses?

"Something's wrong." Brett strode down the hall to Melanie's bedroom. He spotted her through the open office door. She sat huddled on the floor, a paper in her hand.

Damn! He'd have to ask Hemstead to call or text him from now on. Having her find bad news before him wasn't helping him keep her confident her husband wouldn't find her or hurt her.

"Melanie, honey, what's wrong?" He sat on the floor beside her, waiting for her to look at him before he put his arms around her.

"He's looking for me."

"We already knew that." He pushed the stray strands of hair off her face and kissed her puffy eyes.

"No. He's really looking. Himself." She held up what he thought was one piece of paper, but there were two.

Brett took the sheets and read. He was out on bail and he'd slipped the man watching him. Double damn! He placed the papers on the desk corner and pulled her into his arms. "We aren't going to let him ruin our lives. We go on as we have been and if he shows up, we'll deal with him."

She pushed on his chest. "What if he doesn't find me for a year? Or two years? Can you go on as if nothing will happen, knowing he won't stop until he finds me?" Her voice didn't sound as stable as usual. She'd been sitting here thinking about all the bad things she could think of and made herself frightened.

"You were strong enough to give him the slip once, you're strong enough now to make sure he doesn't influence the rest of your life." He kissed her with the conviction he felt that they would beat this man. "You are a strong woman. One I'm proud to love and call my best half."

"Aren't you scared?" she asked, studying him.

"Yes. I'm scared that he'll come here and catch you when I'm unaware and hurt you. I would never be able to live with myself if something happened to you." He grasped her chin and stared intently into her eyes. "But if we live every day scared until he does show up, look at all the wonderful times we'll have missed."

She blinked, raised her hands to cup his face, and said, "I want to forget about him, but it seems every day there is a reminder he could be getting closer. It's hard to think about facing him—" she gulped "—knowing how angry he will be."

"Then don't think about it. Think only of the future you'll have here on the ranch with me. Let me worry about Perret." Brett pulled her onto his lap. "I want you to think of only one thing."

She played with the top snap of his shirt. "What's that?"

"How fully I love you and how I will show you every night and every day what you mean to me." He meant every word. There was nothing he wanted more than to show the shy, vulnerable woman on his lap how much he loved her.

Her gaze rose to his, and a smile twitched on her lips. "I did save the frosting."

"That's what I'm talking about. We are going to have one sweet lovefest tonight. That's where your mind should be. Only on the good times." He kissed her again, tangling her tongue with his, running his hands up and down her side, teasing the edge of her breasts, and making her squirm. He wanted her so full of desire for him she didn't have time to think about her abusive husband.

His hand slid under her shirt, sliding across her silky skin and capturing a breast. She moaned into his mouth and his cock started straining against the zipper of his pants.

The office door closed quietly. Dillon had just given him the go-ahead to make love right here on the office floor. Thankfully, Melanie hadn't heard the door shut or she would have been on her feet and flying out of the room in humiliation.

Brett continued massaging her breasts and worked her bra loose, to give him more access. Her hands moved across his chest now that she'd unsnapped his shirt and pulled the tails out of his jeans. Her hips moved slowly back and forth against his straining cock.

He drew out of the kiss. "I'm going to lay you down right here."

Her hazy eyes widened, and a smile tipped her swollen, wet lips.

That was the sexiest invitation he'd ever received. He lowered her back to the floor and unfastened her pants.

Her hands stalled his downward motion to relieve her of the clothing.

"Are you sure we should be doing this?"

"I've never been more sure. We don't have any guests, and I want to show you how you affect me."

She dropped her hands, and he removed her pants before he captured her mouth for another body humming kiss.

Her hands worked at the button on his jeans. His patience was just about at its limit when the button gave way and the zipper just about peeled open from the pressure of his hard-on.

"Oh, you are in dire need," Melanie whispered, as he shucked out of his pants and balanced over her.

"I'll try to keep my weight off you."

She opened her legs, and he dove into her sanctuary. He held still for several seconds not wanting her to miss out because he couldn't hold back any longer. As he held still, holding his body above her, she moved under him, undulating, teasing his ready to explode cock with the movement.

"Hold still," he hissed between gritted teeth.

She stopped and stared wide-eyed into his face. "Am I hurting you?"

"No. You have me so worked up, I want to make sure you enjoy this."

A mischievous grin spread on her face and she rose up, drawing him in all the way, then lowering and thrusting up again.

"Woman, if you want to come—"

She cut him off by seating him all the way in, wrapping her legs around his waist and her arms around his neck and kissing him as if she'd spent her whole life waiting for this chance to kiss him.

There was nothing he could do but take charge and hope she came as fast as he would. He grabbed her legs, unlatching them from his waist, and held on to them as he thrust, staring into the desire flaring in her eyes. She clamped around him and he leaned down, covering her mouth with his as she moaned her pleasure and her body contracted around him, finally allowing him to get release and follow her to the clouds of fulfillment.

He'd never made passionate love on the floor before, but he had to admit the novelty, along with her innocent desire, had made it a moment he wouldn't forget.

When his limbs worked again, he rolled, bringing her on top of him.

Melanie shoved her hair out of her face and looked down into the face of the man who had taken her to new heights and they never left the ground. "Are you sure Dillon isn't going to know what we were doing in here?" She was worried Brett's brother would know what they'd been up to and she'd blush and want to avoid him the rest of his stay.

"If he has any idea, he won't say anything. Now, when Nate gets here. We can't do any of this day time stuff. He'll rag us both the whole time he's here." Brett ran the back of his fingers down her cheek. "It will be hard to resist you if you look at me the way you did a few minutes ago."

She studied the fire building in his eyes. "How did I look at you?"

"Your lips were wet and swollen from our kisses and your eyes were hot with desire. Honey, if you looked at me like that in the middle of a church service, I'd take you right there in front of the whole congregation."

She giggled even though his words meant more to her than he'd ever know. "I hope I don't look at you that way in church. I'd never be able to set foot in a church or look at any of the people who would be present."

He laughed. His chest rumbled under her breasts. It was a comforting feeling.

"We should get dressed." She glanced up at the clock on the desk. "Oh! It's after one. The bread!" She tried to sit up, but his arms banded around her.

"I pulled them out of the oven when I came in the house. They might be salvageable."

"I'm sorry. I…" It came back to her why she'd been sitting in the office having a near nervous breakdown.

"Don't. Don't replace that pretty smile and those sweet eyes with fear." He leaned up and kissed her lips. "Remember, we're in this together. We're going to love and go on living and not worry about Perret until he shows up, if he shows up." His hands cupped her naked bottom. "If I have to make love to you twenty-four hours a day to keep your mind off him, I will."

She laughed and wiggled her mound over his hardening shaft. "I really don't think lingering in here any longer is a good idea." She tried to push on his chest, but he only slid her up and back down over his shaft.

The exquisite sense of fullness every time she took him in, filled her with awe. And desire. She couldn't have scrambled off him even if she'd wanted to. This man made everything they did together feel right. She pushed up to straddle him and rode him as expertly as she'd seen Lacey ride a bull. Sweat beaded his forehead and lip before she ground down and sent her body shattering. The same instant he exploded and grasped her head, pulling her down into a body-numbing kiss.

Moments later, when they both emerged from the cocoon of passion, stickiness flowed down her legs and she froze.

In their moment of passion, they forgot to use protection.

Chapter Twenty

Brett stared at the saddle he'd pulled out of the tack room to repair. What would they do if their passionate encounter in the office a week ago made a baby? Melanie had turned white as a ghost when she'd realized what they'd done.

"What are we going to do?" she'd whispered.

"We'll worry about it if you become pregnant." He'd kissed her softly. "It's not a bad thing. I want to have children with you."

Her gaze had softened. "I've dreamed of carrying your babies, but Brett, what if Steve finds out? He'll hurt our baby to hurt us."

That had struck him even harder than knowing the man would harm Melanie. That the man could have that much evil in him that he would harm an innocent baby to get back at the woman who left him. It also made him wonder at the sanity of loving a woman who had a man so desperate to find her. To have children with her when there was the threat of her past swooping in and taking everything he loved away. The thought of losing so much made him wonder if he was being naïve to think Melanie's past didn't matter.

Their unprotected love-making had happened a week ago. Lacey was here now, and he could tell by the looks she gave him, Melanie had told her. What would they do if Melanie was pregnant? He'd thought about selling the ranch, changing their names, and moving some place the man would never find them to keep Melanie and the baby safe. But could he give up one thing he loved for the other? The ranch or Melanie and their child? He'd spent more than one night tossing and turning, wondering which meant more to him. The ranch was a family legacy. Melanie was his heart.

Boot heels echoed on the hard-packed dirt floor. He didn't need to turn around to know his cousin had finally chosen the moment to confront him.

"What brings you out here, Hot Rod?" He used the name he'd given Lacey when she was a child always racing everywhere trying to do everything he and their male relatives did.

"From the sound of things that name fits you better." Her delivery was a pure, full on statement of fact.

"I take it Melanie told you about being forgetful?" He didn't take his gaze from the leather he laced on the saddle.

"How could you have put more guilt on that poor woman?" Lacey stopped in front of the saddle. Her arms crossed, and her face said she wasn't here for small talk.

"Guilt?" He dropped the leather and peered across at his cousin.

"Yes, guilt. Now she fears for your life and the baby's, if there is a baby. I told her I'd have Jared bring pregnancy kits and we'd see if she needs to worry." She pointed a finger at him. "Until then, you need to use protection and reaffirm to her that her husband will not get near her or the baby."

He took off his ball cap and ran a hand through his hair. "I tell her that every time I see her. But I don't feel like I'm getting through."

"She says the man dropped off the face of the earth and no one knows where he is."

"Perret gave the P.I. Hemstead had watching him the slip, and from all the feelers the attorney has out there, no one has seen him. His second in command is running the drug business, which worries me even more that Melinda's fears are real. That he would take off looking for her and not stay to take care of his business, means he is out to make a point with her." He unclenched his hands. "I don't like it."

"Neither do I. That's why I'm staying here, and Jared will come up on his days off. We both want you and Melanie safe. I can take my online classes from here and keep Melanie company." Lacey peered at him as if waiting for him to argue.

"I like that idea. It will give Melanie someone to talk to besides me, and she won't be alone during the day while I'm busy. The guys follow me around and help me when they're here." He liked the idea of Lacey hanging around. She was tough and wouldn't let anyone hurt Melanie.

"Good. Jared will be coming up in two days, bringing me more clothes and the pregnancy tests."

Brett nodded. It would be good to know if there was a child coming. If so, they would need to step up the divorce. The last he talked with Hemstead, they had a court date set for the week before Thanksgiving. Hemstead had also made sure there would be police at the hearing. If Perret did show up, they wanted to take precautions he couldn't hurt Melanie and knew he was being watched.

"I better get back in the house." Lacey walked by him.

"Lacey, thanks." He meant every syllable of the word.

She gave him a hug. "I'm only making up for the times you helped me out."

He watched as Lacey walked out of the barn. She was a tough woman and had bonded with Melanie from the first time the two met. They would be good for each other. If only there wasn't the threat of Perret.

***

Melanie couldn't control the shaking of her hands as she chopped the lettuce for the tacos she'd planned for dinner tonight. Jared was arriving in an hour, and Lacey had told her he was bringing pregnancy tests. She had a pretty good idea what the tests would say. Living in this body for twenty-eight years, she knew something was off or different. She hadn't missed her period yet, but if the test wasn't conclusive, next week she'd know for sure.

"It smells good in here." Brett walked across the kitchen and pulled her into a hug.

"Careful, I have a knife." She tried to hold the blade away from their bodies.

He grasped the utensil, pulled it out of her hand, and placed it on the counter. "There, now you don't have to worry." His lips lowered to hers. She forgot they were in the kitchen and had any worries at all for

223

the minutes that he took control of her senses.

Brett came up for air and she inhaled, filling her depleted lungs with the spicy aroma of chili powder and cumin.

"My! What was that for?" she asked, not at all sorry he'd walked in and kissed her.

"Because I can't resist you and I want you to know every minute of the day I am thinking about you." He leaned down as if to kiss her again.

Kool barked and they both peered at the door.

"That must be Jared." Brett started to release her.

"Stay. Give Lacey and her man a few moments alone. They haven't seen one another for a week." She'd want alone time with Brett if they were apart for that long, and they weren't married.

He grinned. "Then let's finish what I started." His head dipped down and he drew her mouth into another body heating kiss.

Her arms circled his neck and she pressed her body to his. She could never get as close to him as her body craved. Even when they were naked, and he was seated deep in her, she wanted more.

His hands moved up and down her back, pressing her close, molding her curves to his muscles.

She squirmed, pressing tight.

"Woof."

The bark jerked her back to where they were.

"I see more goes on in the kitchen than baking," Jared said, in an amused tone.

Her face heated from embarrassment.

Brett tucked her against this side and held out a hand. "Good to see you, Jared." They shook hands. "Wish it was under better circumstances."

That was what she could never forget. Her husband was out there somewhere looking for her and would kill the man she loved if he found them.

"They'll catch the guy and things will go back to normal." Jared sniffed. "Tacos. Haven't had homemade ones in a while."

Lacey stepped out from behind her husband. "That's because I haven't been home."

He shook his head. "No, you use a mix. There's something that Melanie puts in her meat that is better than the mix."

Melanie's cheeks had just started to cool from being caught kissing in the kitchen and now with Jared's compliment, they warmed again.

Lacey grinned. "There is something better in everything Melanie cooks. What's the secret?"

"Love." Brett said. "She loves cooking."

That she could agree with. "I do. It has always been one of my favorite things to do and when there are people who enjoy the food, it makes me pour even more into the meals."

She stepped out of Brett's arm and stirred the meat simmering on the stove. "I'll have dinner ready in about twenty minutes."

"I'll help," Lacey offered.

"Guess that means we have time to drink a beer and catch up." Brett plucked two beers from the refrigerator and the men left the kitchen.

"I thought they'd never leave," Lacey said, pulling two boxes out of her back pockets.

Melanie stared at the objects in her friend's hands. "Are those?" She was almost afraid to hope her suspicions were wrong and the tests would be negative. She wanted to carry Brett's baby, but she feared the consequences should Steve find her.

"These are the test kits. Jared says it's best to wait and use one in the morning. Then again in a few days." Lacey set the kits on the island.

Melanie chewed on a fingernail, staring at the boxes. "I have to wait until morning?" She didn't think she'd be able to get through dinner knowing she could have her results.

"If you want a true reading, it's best to do it in the morning." Lacey put a hand on her arm. "I know how anxious you are, but one more day and if you are pregnant you'll have better results."

She nodded. "I'm pretty sure I know what the results will be." Melanie picked up the knife and continued cutting the lettuce.

"You do? How?" Lacey asked, peeling the plastic off a block of cheese.

"It's hard to explain, but my body feels different, odd."

"It could just be your imagination." Lacey ran the block of cheese up and down the grater.

Melanie put the lettuce in a bowl, cleaned up the mess, and faced her friend. "No. If the test doesn't test positive in the morning, it will next week." She nodded and grabbed the boxes, holding them in front of her as she ducked down the hall to her bedroom and private bath.

Her hands shook as she placed the boxes on her bathroom counter. She ran a finger over the image of a positive result. Her heart fluttered. Having Brett's baby would be wonderful. She could already feel the weight of him in her arms, smell his soft baby scent. Tears burned in her eyes. She'd only have this if they could get Steve caught by the police before he found them.

Chapter Twenty-one

Brett sat on the end of the bed waiting for Melanie to step out of the bathroom. She'd been in the room long enough to have peed and discovered the pregnancy results. He couldn't stand the wait any longer. He stood, and the door opened.

"Well?"

Her face was flushed, and her eyes glistened with tears. "It's a yes."

"Woo hoo!" He grabbed her around the waist and lifted her in the air. "We're going to have a baby."

A smile spread across her face. She grasped his head in her hands and kissed him.

Brett plopped onto the mattress still holding her close. Melanie wrapped her legs around his waist and they continued kissing and grinning until Kool whined at the door.

"I think he wants out," Melanie said.

"In a minute, I'm not through showing you how happy I am." He captured her lips in a deeper, lingering kiss. The type he reserved for when he wanted to take her mind off everything else.

She wiggled closer and his hands cupped her bottom, clad in short silky pajamas.

Kool whined again, this time with more intensity.

Brett drew out of the kiss and moved his hands up to Melanie's waist. "I think he really needs to go out." He sat her on the bed. "I'll be back and reward you for the good news."

"I should go get breakfast—"

He placed a finger on her kiss-swollen lips. "Lacey and Jared can fend for themselves. We're going to celebrate." Straightening, he grinned down at her. "Stay just like that. I'll be right back."

At the door, he glanced over his shoulder at the enticing sight of Melanie, leaning back on her forearms on the bed, her hair falling around her shoulders, and her face glowing.

"I'll be quick." He opened the door and Kool bounded down the hall and the stairs. Brett followed right behind, not wanting Melanie to think about dressing.

He opened the back door as someone pounded on the front door. Hitching up his pajama pants, he walked into the great room and unlocked the front door.

"Jared—"

A deputy sheriff stood on the porch. "Sorry to bother you, Brett."

"It's okay, Art. What are you doing out here so early this morning?" Brett didn't like the way the hairs on the back of his neck started prickling.

"Sheriff wanted me to tell you there's been a rental car spotted around Duncan. I'll be cruising the county road during my shift and someone else will be out here after me." Art glanced past him

"Thank you for letting me know." He hoped Melanie hadn't come downstairs in her nearly nothing pajamas. He was sure her working here already had people talking even though his family had told everyone about the engagement.

"I'll let you know if I see anything of the car." The man didn't even have the decency to look at him when he was talking.

"I appreciate that." Brett closed the door and turned around.

Melanie stood in the entryway, wearing a robe. Her face had lost the glow and color.

"Hey, what's wrong?" He was beside her in three strides, wrapping his arms around her.

"What did that deputy want?" Her voice was barely above a whisper.

"There's been a rental car spotted in Duncan. No one knows if it's your husband. They just wanted to give us a head's up." He led her into the main room and sat her down on the couch. "Don't let this upset you. We have a future and a family to think about." He placed his hand on her belly.

She clasped her hands over his. "I don't want anything to happen to you or our child."

"It won't."

The front door opened. Jared and Lacey both burst through, closing the door with a resounding thud.

"Brett!" Lacey called.

"We're in here." He grasped Melanie's hand and kissed the back.

"We saw the deputy leave. What's going on?" Jared asked as Lacey sat on the couch next to Melanie.

"They said there's been a rental car hanging around Duncan. Art came to let us know. He will be cruising the county road for his shift and another will take his place when he's off duty."

"Do they know for sure it's Melanie's husband?" Lacey asked.

"No. They haven't determined who it is." Brett squeezed Melanie's hand. "They are just letting me know. It's what Hemstead asked them to do."

Jared took the seat across from the couch and studied them. "You're still in your pajamas. I suppose that means I have to rustle up my own coffee?"

Lacey tossed a pillow at him and faced Melanie. "What did the test results say?"

Melanie felt as if she'd been on a roller coaster and couldn't get off before it crashed from the rails. Her euphoria of carrying Brett's child now felt like a burden she wasn't sure she could handle.

"We're going to have a baby," Brett said, pride and happiness dripping from his declaration.

"Congratulations!" Jared said, standing and giving Brett a high-five.

"But you aren't as excited," Lacey said, tapping her on the shoulder.

Melanie shook her head. "It will just give one more reason for Steve to be mad at me when he finds me." She wrapped her arms around her middle. "He'll make sure we're all dead." She couldn't stop the shivers. They had been a daily thing, before she'd found the courage to work out a plan and leave her husband.

"We aren't going to let him get near you." Brett put an arm around her. "You have the law on your side and the whole Wallis family."

"Look at how he slipped away from that private investigator. He's too clever. Look at how long he's been on the police's radar for selling drugs and they haven't caught him?" Her heart was slowly shriveling. "We can't win against him."

"This isn't a good attitude for the baby or you," Brett said. "We will win, and we will have a family. You, me, and the baby." He pulled her to his chest and held her tight. "I promise, we will come out of this stronger. Look at how you escaped all by yourself. Now you have the whole county police force, the Duncan police force, and the people who live in Duncan to help you stay safe. I'm sure by now my parents and Lacey's parents have told everyone that there is a lunatic after you. Everyone will have their eyes and ears on any strangers in town."

She stared into Brett's eyes. "Your family told everyone my past?" She wasn't sure what horrified her the most, that everyone now knew her business or that his parents would tell everyone everything about them.

"They only said you ran from an abusive husband and he could be looking for you," Lacey said. Her tone indicated, she was irritated with Brett. "They didn't tell anyone the whole story. That's family business. They only said enough to make sure people are on the look-out."

That made her feel a little better. "Everyone is watching out for us?" She studied Lacey.

"Yes. That's what people do in small towns. We look out for our neighbors. This ranch has supported this community a long time and being a dude ranch and resort, it continues to add revenue to Duncan. No one wants to see anything happen to you, Brett, or the ranch."

Melanie thought about that. It made sense. They did spend a lot of money at the grocery store and the guests who came to the ranch usually fueled up and purchased souvenirs in town.

The ringing of the phone in the office sent Brett to his feet. "I'll be right back."

Lacey grasped her hand. "So the test was positive. Don't get too excited and tell too many people until you do it again next week. There can be false positives."

Melanie glanced over at Jared. Even though she knew he was an ER nurse, talking about this seemed too intimate for him to be listening in. He nodded in agreement with what Lacey said.

"I understand." Melanie pulled her robe tighter. "I'm going to go put some clothes on." She started for the downstairs bedroom and remembered that they had moved her things to Brett's room, what he now called, "their room."

Before she reached the office door, she heard the concern in Brett's voice.

"Yes, Dad, I know there has been a rental car spotted. No, the police don't know who he is, and they can't do anything until he heads out the county road if it is Melanie's husband." He let out a full-bodied hiss. "No. We do not need the whole family here. Melanie and Lacey just finished getting everything cleaned up from the family reunion that was here. I want her to have a break, if you bring the whole family here that will be more work." There was silence. "Yes, I know that Mom and Aunt Dorothy would help, but really, Jared and Lacey are here now, and they are just about as much company as we want."

She liked that he was keeping their life private from his family. If they were all here, she would have to work, and she'd have a hard time keeping the secret of the baby from them. They didn't need that news carried on the Duncan grape vine. If the word reached Steve's ears, he'd come raging for them.

Melanie walked softly back down the hall and up the stairs, avoiding the chatter of Lacey and Jared in the dining room.

Chapter Twenty-two

Brett and Garth were in the barn feeding animals when the crunch of tires on the drive caught their attention. It had been three weeks since the sighting of a rental car that was gone the day after its sighting. Thanksgiving was coming up and he'd invited all the family, but right now he was curious who would be coming.

The rental plates on the vehicle started his heart racing. "Go out the back of the barn and in the back porch. Keep Melanie in the kitchen until I find out who this is."

Garth nodded and hopped over the corral fence, running to the back of the house.

Brett walked out of the barn with a pitchfork in his hand. It was the closest thing to a threatening weapon he had within reach.

The vehicle stopped at the walkway to the wide front porch.

His long strides had him at the bumper of the vehicle when the driver stepped out.

The man turned and smiled.

Hemstead.

"Daryl. What are you doing here?"

He narrowed his eyes. "Tomorrow is Melanie's divorce hearing. Here in Duncan. Did you forget?"

Brett mentally slapped himself. He'd been so caught up in keeping

Melanie positive and making sure she didn't do anything to upset her or the baby, he'd completely forgotten the court date. "I did forget. There has been so much going on…" He waved to the house. "Come in. The room you used before is ready."

Once they were both inside the house, Brett called out, "We have a guest."

Hemstead studied him a moment, then greeted Melanie with enthusiasm when she walked into the great room. "Good morning, Melanie. Brett forgot about your court date tomorrow. Did you, too?"

Her face lost color. "Oh! I did. Have you heard. Will Steve be there?"

Hemstead's lips turned up in a colluding grin. "It seems no one was able to find him to serve notice of the hearing."

Brett slapped the man on the back. "That is good news!" He glanced at Melanie. She didn't seem as happy. "Your husband doesn't know about the hearing. He won't be there to contest and you'll be free."

She shook her head. "Legally, I'll be free. But he won't give up looking for me."

Brett put his arm around her shoulders. "He won't get his hands on you, I promise."

"You and your family can't continue to watch me twenty-four-seven."

"The police in Oregon City caught his second in command for selling. The man has to go back or lose his business." Hemstead headed to the stairs. "I'll get settled in and we'll talk about what will happen tomorrow."

When the attorney was out of hearing, Melanie said, "I'm sorry to not believe a divorce will keep me safe."

Brett pulled her into his arms. "But we can marry, and I can legally make sure that he never comes near you." He placed a hand on her belly. "Our family will be safe, I promise." His continually having to reassure her and promise something he planned to do even if he went to jail for killing the man didn't seem to give Melanie any hope. When they'd discovered she was pregnant, he'd hoped she would be even stronger to keep the baby and her out of her soon-to-be ex-husband's hands, but she seemed more melancholy and distracted.

He'd talked with Jared and knew stress wasn't good for the fetus.

He had to find a way to prove to Melanie she would be safe.

***

Melanie sat on the bed in the room she shared with Brett. She'd prepared breakfast, served it to the men, and now was upstairs pretending to get ready for the trip to town and the hearing. Her stomach hadn't stopped twisting and churning since the attorney arrived and reminded her of the divorce. She wanted that paper more than anyone knew, even Brett. It meant she had wiped out one of the biggest mistakes of her life. It gave her a clean slate to start over with Brett and their child. But her churning gut told her the paper wouldn't matter to the man who wanted her dead rather than let her go.

He would find her one of these days. She shivered as the vision of his twisted, enraged face came to mind. Clutching her middle, she feared for the baby conceived of love. She wanted nothing more than to give Brett a son, an heir to take over the Wallis legacy.

Tears trickled down her cheeks. "Please let me live to deliver this baby and see him grow up."

"Melanie! We need to get going." Brett's voice just down the hall had her swiping the tears from her cheeks and rushing to the sink to splash water on her face.

He would want to know why she was crying. Even though he was doing his best to keep her positive, she knew her fear and worrying was beginning to tax his patience. She wasn't a Wallis. She didn't grab her bootstraps and carry on as if nothing affected her.

The door opened, and he stepped inside, closing the door behind him.

She walked into the bedroom. Her heart thudded in her chest just as wild as it had this morning when he'd walked into the kitchen dressed in a fancy western shirt, tight jeans, and his town boots. He was a cowboy any woman would be proud to call hers.

"I thought you were going to change or something? Though I don't know why. You look wonderful." He met her, pulling her into his arms, and kissing her as if they had all night to make love.

When he eased out of the kiss, she laid her head on his chest.

"I know I've not been very cheery lately. I do love you and want to marry you and have your baby." She sighed and raised her head. "I just have lived with fear for so long and not knowing when Steve could show up has made me a bundle of nerves."

"Honey, I am trying my hardest to understand. And Mom said pregnant woman have mood swings from the hormones going wild in your body—"

"You told your mom? I thought we were going to wait until I started showing? You know so word didn't get around too soon." Having a family that never shared anything, she struggled with how much the Wallis family shared.

"I didn't tell her. Not out right. She said you were glowing, and she'd noticed you touching your belly and asked if you were pregnant." He kissed her lips and grinned. "I couldn't lie to my mom."

"No, but now everyone in town will know." Making it that much easier for Steve to hear about it.

"I told her she wasn't to tell a soul." Brett plucked her good coat off the bed and held it out for her. "Come on. Let's get this divorce over with and start planning our wedding."

She slid her arms into the coat sleeves and walked down the stairs beside him. Tonight, she would no longer be Mrs. Perret, a name she'd loathed after her first month of marriage.

***

Mr. Hemstead stayed over one more night to help them and the whole Wallis family celebrate the divorce. The courtroom had been packed with family members, but no one showed up for Steve. Hemstead's fancy talking and piles of papers had the judge signing abandonment papers on the divorce, since the person contesting the divorce could not be found to serve him papers on the hearing.

"You sit tight," Carolyn, Brett's mom, told Melanie. "You are the guest of honor tonight and we'll do all the cooking and serving." She winked and sat Melanie down in a chair in the great room with a cup of hot cider in her hands.

Brett walked over and kissed the top of her head. "I think Hemstead was worth every penny he billed me for."

She had to agree but felt bad not knowing how much the attorney had charged Brett. It had to have been a huge bill considering all the people he pulled in to help. "I don't know how I will ever be able to pay you back."

He sat on the chair arm and leaned down. "By loving me and the family we're making," he whispered.

Her lips met his in a brief kiss. "That I can do."

235

John, Brett's dad, stopped in front of the chair where they were having the intimate conversation. "Now we can start talking wedding plans."

She giggled. "You want to help plan the wedding?"

The man's face turned crimson. "No. That's for you ladies. I want to help decide when it will happen."

"Is Christmas too soon?" Lacey's mom asked.

"What about New Years? That date will make it hard for Brett to forget his anniversary," Nate chimed in.

Melanie didn't know if they were all talking such early dates because they knew she was pregnant or just to make sure the wedding happened. "I-I, well, we haven't thought that far ahead." She glanced at Brett. "Have we?"

"Melanie's right. We've just been working toward this hurdle. Now we need time to realize she is free and we can marry." He kissed her. "But I can guarantee, you'll all be the first to know when we come up with a date."

The room erupted with laughter and everyone wandered off talking.

"That was smooth," she said, finally relaxing and enjoying the day.

"I got rid of them hounding us, didn't I?" He laced his fingers with hers. "But we do need to come up with a wedding date." His gaze settled on her belly a moment then met hers. "Do you want the wedding before the baby comes or after? I don't care as long as I know there will be a wedding."

She felt the same, but wondered how the rest of the family would feel about a wedding after the baby had arrived. "Maybe you need to feel out your parents and see what they think about an illegitimate grandchild."

He shook his head. "That doesn't matter to them. They know why we've had to wait and they know how much I love you."

"Then let's not rush into a decision today. We should look at the guest registrations and work it around when no one will be here." She scanned the great room. "Because this is where I want to be married."

"I agree."

Chapter Twenty-three

Brett fought his way through the howling wind and snow to feed at the barn. The family had all left this morning after making gluttons of themselves over the Thanksgiving dinner the day before. While he took care of the livestock, Melanie cleaned up the rooms and did the laundry, getting ready for guests that would be arriving the week before Christmas.

He'd wanted to ask Melanie to drive the tractor for him as he fed the cattle, but after all the work she'd had the last few days preparing for yesterday's dinner and taking care of his large family for two days, he didn't want to bring her out into the cold weather and make her susceptible to a cold.

He'd spent all his alone time with Jared asking questions about how to take care of his pregnant fiancée. To his delight, they had decided the best time to have a wedding would be in January. There were two consecutive weeks after the New Year when they wouldn't have any guests. They could have the wedding and take a honeymoon without needing someone to cook and clean. But his brothers would have to stay here and take care of the livestock while they were gone.

He'd plugged the diesel tractor in earlier that day in preparation for feeding the hay. The engine roared to life and he pulled the trailer loaded with large four foot by eight foot bales out of the hay shed.

Feeding the animals always gave him pleasure. That he could help the animals that supported him and his family when the weather became too cold and snowy to forage, was a sense of pride.

Most of the horses were out in the pasture along the driveway. He only had half a dozen in the stalls off the barn. They were the horses that never gave him or guests any trouble and the two Percherons who would soon be pulling the sleigh if this storm were any indication of the coming weather. Guests loved being pulled around in the sleigh.

The feeding went easier than he'd expected. Driving back to the barn, he thought about how nice it would be to have Melanie all to himself after the last two months of always having someone around.

Lacey had promised to be back on Monday but wanted to go to Billings to attend an event Jared's hospital was hosting. And Dillon had gone to town to play at the local bar tonight and Saturday night. He said he'd be here Sunday morning.

He planned to spread a blanket in the main room and have a candlelight picnic in front of the fire. It was the one room he'd dreamt of making love to Melanie in but had yet to accomplish the deed. The fire…big windows where they could watch the snowflakes fall…

Kool growled, slapping Brett back to reality.

A flash of color moving from the cabins toward the house made him slam the tractor into park and open the door.

"Sic'em, Kool!" he shouted, jumping out and running through the thick veil of snow behind the racing dog.

He hoped Melanie had remembered to lock the doors as he'd told her to do when he was outside. Kool was catching up to the person running.

The same moment Kool yelped, Brett heard the sound of a four-wheeler engine start up. He ignored the ache in his lungs from sucking in the cold air and ran to where Kool lay in the snow beside wheel tracks.

"Damn!" There was only one person who would have been hiding a four-wheeler behind the house and who would viciously kick a dog.

He pulled out his cell phone and scrolled to Sheriff Landry's number. Kool lay on the ground whimpering. The sound ratcheted his anger.

"Sheriff Landry," the man answered.

"Sheriff, this is Brett Wallis. I just chased a man who kicked my dog and took off on a four-wheeler.”

"Is it the Perret guy?”

“I don’t know. I didn’t get a look at him, but I can’t think of anyone else it could have been.”

“I’ll get a deputy out there right away and seal off all the roads leading out of that area. We’ll get him.”

“I hope so.” Brett shoved the phone in his pocket and picked up Kool.

At the back door he kicked several times. “Melanie, let me in.”

Hurried footsteps thumped across the back porch and the door unlatched, swinging inward.

“Oh! Did a cow kick him?” She immediately backed up, allowing him to carry the whimpering animal into the room.

She’d just given him a way to keep her from worrying, but if the man was out there, she needed to know so she would take precautions.

He shook his head and lowered the dog to his bed in the corner of the room. “No. We were chasing someone who kicked him before taking off on a four-wheeler.”

Her face drained of color. “Steve?”

“I don’t know. I didn’t get a good look. He came from behind the cabins and ran to the back of the house, just inside the trees. That’s where he had a four-wheeler sitting.”

Kool whimpered.

“Let me see if we need to take him to the vet.” As he moved the dog’s leg checking to see if it might have been broken, he explained about calling the sheriff and how she was not to go outside for any reason and all the doors were to remain locked at all times.

“He’s found me. Locked doors aren’t going to keep him out.” Her voice was flat, devoid of any emotion or inflection.

“Kool needs us. I don’t think anything broke. Go get the heating pad Dad was using for his back. We’ll put it on his leg and see if that helps.”

She nodded and walked down the hall.

He pulled his phone out and texted all the men in the family, letting them know someone had been on the property, kicked his dog, and got away.

Melanie returned with the heating pad, they settled it on the dog’s hip and Brett took off his outdoor clothing.

"Come on, I could use a cup of coffee," he said, escorting Melanie down the hallway with a hand on her lower back. After seeing the man, he wanted to keep a hand on her until the sheriff found him.

"I'll make a fresh pot," Melanie said, moving to the coffee maker.

He started to follow when his phone rang. Lee MacIntyre, Jared's older brother.

"Hello?"

"Brett, thought you'd like to know I saw a four-wheeler tearing out of your property at our corners that adjoin the BLM. Thought it was you until I saw the color of the ATV."

"That is good to know. I chased him away from the house before I could get a good look at him."

"You think it's that no-account husband of Melanie's?"

"Ex and that's the only person I think it could be. I told the sheriff about him. If I send a deputy over there can you show him where you saw the trespasser?" This could be the break they needed. If it was Perret and he was caught on the BLM and he could prove he saw him here, the man would be in jail for breaking the restraining order.

"Yeah, send him over. I'll have a horse saddled and ready to go." Lee clicked off.

Brett chuckled. Lee wasn't fond of motorized vehicles. The poor deputy who went over there would have a cold afternoon ahead of him.

"Who was that?" Melanie asked, placing a cup of coffee in front of him on the island.

He wrapped his arms around her, drawing her close to his body. Her warmth and knowing he had her close, warmed him. "That was Lee. He saw the man on the four-wheeler cross their property."

Drawing her to his side with one arm, he scrolled down his contacts and pressed Sheriff Landry again.

"Did he come back?" the sheriff asked, by way of answering.

"No. But Lee MacIntyre called. He spotted the four-wheeler crossing their property. If you send a deputy over there, he'll show him where." Melanie started to tremble.

"We'll do that. I'm also gathering a search and rescue team. When this storm passes, we'll go looking for the guy. He has to be camping out on the BLM because there hasn't been a buzz about any strangers in the county."

"Sounds good." Brett hung up the phone and pulled Melanie into his arms again. "Shhh, he isn't going to get to you. We have the county law enforcement after him, our neighbors are looking out for us, and—" Before he could say family, pounding on the front door stopped his words.

"Brett open this door, it's your father!"

He grinned at Melanie. "Family."

"How did they know so soon?" Melanie stared at the snow coming down thick outside the window. The whole lot of them, other than Lacey and Jared, should have been tucked into their homes by now.

"I texted I'd seen an intruder." Brett released her. "You might want to make more coffee." He kissed her head. "Sorry." And left the room as his dad continued to bellow and pound on the door.

She couldn't stop the grin, even though she knew the only person out in this weather who would be lurking around the ranch had to be Steve, and she'd been worried sick he'd show up some day. Knowing he was here, and she had all these people looking out for her, she was glad the time had finally come.

Hopefully, with so many witnesses, he wouldn't attempt to hurt her or Brett.

Carolyn bustled into the kitchen. "Oh, Melanie. I'm so glad you are all right." The woman pulled her tight to her cushioned body and held on.

Melanie extracted herself from the hug, feeling a bit embarrassed. "I'm fine. I'm not the one who saw him or was kicked by him."

"I heard about Kool. Poor boy. But a good dog to chase the man." Carolyn helped herself to the coffee mugs and started filling them with the coffee Melanie had just brewed.

She counted five cups. "Who all is here?"

"John, Allan, Dorothy, and Garth." She placed the filled mugs on a tray. "We all hopped right back in the cars and headed back here as soon as we got Brett's message." Her gaze dropped to Melanie's waist. "We can't have anything happening to any member of this family." She nodded to the door leading into the dining room. "Come on. We're having a strategy meeting."

"I'll be there in a minute. I want to check on Kool and make a cup of tea."

"Don't be long. That man of yours will come looking for you." She stopped with the kitchen door half open. "He loves you and will worry if you stay away from him too long."

"I know. I'll be right in." Melanie started the kettle heating and wandered out to the back porch to check on Kool. He whimpered and sat up.

"How's your leg?" Tears trickled down her cheeks. "I'm sorry you had to take the beating I know he wanted to give me." She sat down beside the dog and ran her hand over his smooth head.

Chapter Twenty-four

Brett was glad his family had headed straight back to the ranch, but he worried about them being stuck here with the weather and the excavating business having no one to run it.

"Dad, you can't stay here indefinitely. Lacey will be here on Monday and Dillon will be here on Sunday."

"We'll stay until you hear from the police that the man is caught, or we feel you have enough people present to keep the man from getting to Melanie." His dad nodded at his mom. "Right, Carolyn?"

"Yes." His mom had pulled out her knitting and taken up the straight-backed chair by the fireplace.

He glanced at the hearth rug. So much for his plans of a romantic evening with Melanie. He glanced over at his fiancée. She'd taken a long time coming in after his mom had ushered them all into the great room to drink coffee and discuss logistics. Now she sat with her legs curled up in one of the over-stuffed chairs. She held the delicate teacup she liked to her lips, but he'd yet to see her swallow a drop.

"I can stay down in cabin one." Garth said. "In fact, I should go see if we caught the man on tape."

"Those cameras tape?" Brett asked. He thought they only showed real time.

"Yeah. Dillon set them up to record. It's not on a tape, it's on the computer, but we can copy and send it to the cops if we need to." Garth set his coffee cup on the tray. "I'll go do that now."

"Is it safe for you to be out there walking around by yourself?" Melanie asked.

"If Lee spotted the four-wheeler going through his property, the only way back is through him and the deputy that went out there. With this storm the sound of the engine would be easy to hear and track." Brett walked over to where Melanie sat. "He won't be back today."

She nodded and sipped her tea, which as he'd suspected, she hadn't touched.

Garth headed to the coats hanging near the front door. "Lock this behind me. He may not have had time to get back here, but I don't want to take chances."

Dad walked over and locked the door.

Aunt Dorothy stood. "I'll go see what I can rustle up in the kitchen for dinner."

His mom looked up from her knitting. "Did you already change all the sheets in the rooms?"

Melanie nodded. "There is still a load in the washing machine and one in the dryer."

"I'll take care of cleaning up the rooms before we leave. I don't want you going to extra trouble for us." His mom stood and waved at the suitcases sitting by the front door. "John, Allan, take our bags to the rooms."

Within minutes, he and Melanie were the only two in the great room.

"Your mom sure knows how to clear out a room," Melanie joked.

"She did it to give us time alone." He knew his mom and had seen the twinkle in her eye as she'd ordered the older men about.

"Why would we need—"

He sat on the arm of the chair and cut off her question by cupping her head with one hand and kissing her. He'd wanted to kiss her from the moment he found her safe and sound in the house, but so much had to be dealt with that he'd held off. Now, he caressed her lips, brushing his back and forth, dipping his tongue into her mouth to taste the mint from her tea and her sweetness.

Tearing his lips from hers before he forgot the house was full of people, he peered into her eyes. "Melanie, don't ever forget you are safe with me, and my family will always be there for us."

She nodded. "I'm beginning to see that." She sighed. "I know this will sound awful, but I'm glad he's finally showed up, if that was him. The waiting has been like an abscess that won't heal. It hurt to always be frightened and wondering. Now, we know he has found me and it's a matter of someone finding him."

"We have lots of people looking for him. He'd have to be stupid to come after you. But if we can catch him within fifty miles of this ranch, he'll go to jail. And if we're lucky, they will find something to keep him in there for a long time."

She raised an eyebrow. "I've heard animal abuse can get a person a harsh sentence."

He grinned. "I like the way you think." He kissed her and pulled out his phone. "I'll have Garth look at the footage on the camera at the back of the house. I don't know if the four-wheeler was in picture, but he can find out."

Melanie watched Brett stride out of the room, his phone to his ear. It would be wonderful to have Steve out of their lives before the wedding.

Carolyn entered the great room. "I have the two bedrooms ready for Allan and Dorothy and myself and John. I'm sure Garth will want to stay out in the cabin."

"I didn't get out there and clean it up from Jared and Lacey staying out there." Melanie stood, thinking about gathering the supplies and clean sheets.

"Oh no, you don't. You can gather what is needed and Garth can take care of it when he goes back out there after dinner."

"He shouldn't have to clean up someone else's mess," she argued.

"Look at the pot calling the kettle black. You clean up after strangers and family all the time. It won't hurt him to clean up where he's going to stay." Carolyn put an arm around her shoulders. "Come on, let's go see what Dorothy is putting together for dinner. Don't tell her, but she's a better cook than I am."

Melanie chuckled and allowed Brett's mom to keep track of her until after dinner. They both handed the cleaning supplies and sheets to Garth.

"I'm sorry, you have to clean the cabin," she said.

"I've been cleaning up after Lacey her whole life," Garth said, laughing. He shoved the sheets under his arm and grasped the cleaning caddy. "Tell Brett I'll have something for him to see in the morning. I'm still figuring out how to get the images out of the software and onto a flash drive."

"I'll tell him." She was surprised Garth told her this rather than his brother. But then John had monopolized the conversation during dinner with stories of family gatherings at the ranch when he was a child.

She returned to the kitchen to find the two older women had the dishes cleaned and put away and all the countertops shining. "I feel bad about making a mess, but I thought I'd whip up some cinnamon rolls for breakfast." Melanie walked to the pantry and pulled out the ingredients for the rolls.

Carolyn excused herself, while Dorothy pulled up a stool. "Do you mind if I watch? I like to bake but find my cinnamon rolls always turn out a bit dry."

"I'd love the company. You and I haven't had as many chances to visit." Melanie asked lots of questions about Lacey as she prepared the dough. Her friend always appeared tough and ready to take on anything life handed her. She would have never fallen for the charms of Steve. Melanie wanted to be more like Brett's cousin.

"That daughter of mine was a handful from day one. She never wanted to be held, and she was always trying to best her cousins, her brother, anyone who said she couldn't do something, she'd prove them wrong." Dorothy sprinkled the cinnamon on top of the brown sugar.

"Is that how she ended up riding bulls?" Melanie rolled up the dough.

"I think so. Some boys told her girls couldn't ride bulls and she proved them wrong. First in high school, and then at the National Finals Rodeo." Dorothy leaned forward. "Between you and me, I was proud she was whipping those men, but I was scared too. She could have been hurt much worse than she was. But through it all, she fought for what she loved—riding bulls."

Melanie stared at the woman. She would have never guessed how proud Dorothy was of her daughter. "Have you told her that? How proud you are of her?"

"Heavens no! I don't want her finding something else just as dangerous thinking I condone destructive behavior."

Melanie laughed.

Dorothy placed a hand over her heart. "When you become a parent, you'll understand. You hurt when your children hurt. You'll do anything for them. Why do you think Carolyn and John are here right now? They don't want to lose their son or the woman he loves. It would be like losing their heart."

Instinctively, Melanie's hand rested on her belly. She already loved the person she carried and would do whatever it took to save her child.

Chapter Twenty-five

Monday morning, Dillon set up residence in the cabin surrounded by even more monitors. He'd brought more cameras with him when he'd arrived on Sunday.

Brett scanned the monitors and noted how all angles of the house were covered, as well as the path from the cabins and all sides of the barn. There was no way anyone would get into the house without someone seeing them. But it would also mean someone had to remain in the cabin all the time watching the monitors.

"You okay with sitting out here all day?" he asked.

Dillon grinned. "Are you kidding? I can work on my music and watch the monitors. But if Search and Rescue and Lee haven't found him, he's long gone. I bet he saw how many people had rallied around Melanie and tucked tail."

"I hope you're right. I feel bad keeping all of you from your regular lives." Brett not only hated that his family had changed their schedules to help him, but he and Melanie were only alone at night in bed. While he cherished the few hours they had alone, he also missed their intimate meals, and playful conversations that were awkward with family around.

"Don't sweat it. If we didn't want to help, we'd tell you."

Brett laughed. "Yes, that's one thing a person can count on from this family. Direct truth."

He walked through the eight inches of snow to the barn to check on the horses. Dillon had helped him feed the animals earlier. Lacey and Melanie were in the house looking at wedding dresses in a magazine Lacey had brought with her.

While he was as anxious as anyone for the wedding, he wondered if his family would insist on coming on the honeymoon to keep them safe if Perret wasn't caught before then? The thought gave him a gut ache.

At least they were down to just Lacey and Dillon until Jared returned on his days off and Garth took over for Dillon on the weekends. His dad had insisted there had to be someone watching the cameras and someone staying with Melanie at all times. He didn't mind having Lacey around, it freed him up to take care of the chores. And she knew when to make herself scarce, so he and Melanie could have a bit of alone time. He guessed being a newlywed, his cousin understood.

Kool hobbled out of the barn.

"What were you doing in here, buddy?" He walked down the middle of the barn and spotted something torn up by a hay bale.

Kool walked over, sniffed, and growled. He picked the object up and shook it.

Brett recognized it as a glove. When he tried to take it from Kool, the dog growled and shook the garment more.

"Is this from the person who kicked you?" He stared at the dog as he tore another finger off the glove. "Where did you find this?" He glanced around the barn. "And when?"

***

Melanie stared at the beautiful dresses in the magazine Lacey plopped on the table in front of her.

"These are more western cut dresses. Now, if you want a more traditional cut, we can look those up online," Lacey said, sitting down on the couch next to her and pulling a computer onto her lap.

"I've never really thought about a wedding dress." She flipped through the pages. They were all beautiful and so not her.

"What did you wear for your first wedding?" Lacey tapped on the keyboard.

"Jeans and a sweatshirt."

Lacey stared at her. "No dress?"

"We were married by the Justice of the Peace."

"No family?"

She cringed. "I didn't have anyone I wanted to be at the wedding. And now I don't have any family. My mother passed away five years ago."

"I'm so sorry," Lacey said solemnly. After a short silence, her face brightened, and her eyes sparkled. "My dad will give you away and we will make this a wedding to remember."

Melanie swallowed the lump of emotion in her throat. She didn't know what to say. Everyone in this family had welcomed her even with all her baggage. Growing up, she couldn't find a person to befriend her, and now, without looking, she had a family and a whole community watching her back.

"I didn't mean to make you cry." Lacey wrapped an arm around her shoulders.

"I've never felt so welcome as I have since setting foot in Duncan. And now, with all you and your family, and even the law enforcement, are doing for me, I don't know how to repay any of you."

"Raise robust boys and girls to take the high school teams to state and carry on with the ranch and the excavation company." Lacey said it with such conviction, Melanie started laughing.

"You laugh, but this community judges the families by how many strapping children they have that can give the town bragging rights to state pennants and put the town's name on the map." She pointed at her chest. "Look at me. If Jared and I moved to Duncan after getting my name in the Rodeo Hall of Fame, I'd have the whole town eating out of my hand." She frowned. "But I don't want that. I didn't ride bulls to get handouts. I rode bulls to prove women are as tough, and in most cases, tougher than men." She stared into Melanie's eyes. "And don't you forget that."

Without saying it, her friend had just told her she was stronger than the man they were all protecting her from.

"What do you think? Western or traditional?" Lacey shifted the computer on her lap to show a variety of wedding dresses.

"Traditional, even though the wedding will be here at the ranch."

***

Brett had finally wrestled the glove from Kool and took it to

Dillon. They'd watched the recordings of the footage the day he'd chased the man to see if he'd dropped a glove. They couldn't find any evidence that he had.

"You're sure this isn't one of yours or a family member's glove?" Dillon leaned back in the chair, rubbing his eyes.

"It doesn't belong to a family member. Kool wouldn't have chewed it up if it had." Brett paced the small area in the cabin that wasn't covered with tables and monitors or the bed. "I don't like it. It means someone has been here since then." He pulled on his coat. "I'm going to go walk through the path of all the cameras, you make sure you see me in all of them."

"Ok, but I think you're overreacting." Dillon picked up his phone and Brett's rang.

He talked on the phone to Dillon as he walked in the path of all the cameras set up around the house, barn, and cabins.

"They're all working. Go in and visit with your bride to be." Dillon closed the connection.

Brett entered through the back door, wondering if it was a good idea to keep it unlocked during the day even though there was a camera aimed right at it. Once inside, he flipped the lock.

Voices in the kitchen drew him and Kool to the warm wonderful scents of cooking. "What are you making?" He kissed Melanie's cheek and sniffed the pot steaming on the stove.

"Beef soup and fresh bread." Melanie handed him a cup of coffee.

"And toffee bars," Lacey said, licking her lips.

"I was so smart to hire you and fall in love with you," he said, wrapping his arms around Melanie.

"I agree," Lacey said. "Come on, Kool. Let's go watch T.V."

His cousin always knew when to disappear. He spun Melanie in his arms and captured her lips. He'd planned to keep the kiss light, but worrying about who could have left the glove, he kissed her as if he'd never see her again.

She broke the kiss and gasped for breath. "What was that about?" Her eyes were filled with uncertainty.

Damn! He'd made her suspicious by not holding back. "I wanted you to know how much you mean to me."

"I already know that. You've told me many times. Why was it so important now?" Her gaze roamed his face. "What have you found?"

"Nothing of importance."

"Don't tell me nothing after kissing me like that." She backed out of his arms.

"Kool found a glove." He ran a hand through his hair. "I don't think it belongs to anyone who has been here."

"As in family?" Fear started to creep into her eyes.

"Yes." He put a hand up, brushing his fingers across her cheek. "Don't get scared. Dillon and I checked all the cameras before I came in. No one will get in here and hurt you."

"What about you? When you're out doing your chores. Steve could do something to you."

"I'm always watching. I'll be fine." He nodded to the soup. "When will dinner be ready?"

She glanced at the timer on the oven. "Fifteen minutes."

"I'll let Dillon know." He pulled his phone from his pocket and walked out of the kitchen, dialing his brother to tell him to stay put until he brought dinner to him.

Chapter Twenty-six

Melanie woke with a start. A sound had awakened her. There it was again, a shrill scream.

"Brett, Brett! Wake up, something's wrong!"

Brett rose off the bed in one movement and stood, raking a hand through his hair. "What?"

"Listen."

There was the sound again.

At the same moment his phone rang, Lacey threw the door open. "The barn's on fire!"

Brett was already half dressed.

Melanie pulled on sweat pants and a sweatshirt, slipping her feet into slippers. All three barreled down the stairs and stood in the back porch, pulling on coats.

"You stay in the house with the doors locked," Brett ordered when she shoved her foot into a boot.

"I can help you," she insisted.

"You'll be a target out there. This had to have been set to lure you outside." He kissed her cheek. "Stay. It will be one less thing for me to worry about."

She nodded and locked the door behind them, watching out the pane glass window as flames licked out through the window in the back of the barn. Tremors shimmied up her spine as the horses' frightened nickers grew louder.

Flashing and bobbing lights made the barn appear to spin like a disco ball. Help was coming.

How had the fire started? She wandered into the kitchen to fill the large coffee pot they used when guests were at the ranch. She also whipped up a batch of banana bread and pumpkin bread. Setting the timer on the oven, she heard what sounded like breaking glass on the back porch.

No one would have broken the window on the door to get in. They would have called out to her. She slipped quietly through the swinging door into the dining room and out the door on the other end of the room into the hallway just before the stairs.

She stopped in the hallway, listening. Someone was opening and closing doors in the back of the house. She stepped out of her slippers and ran up the stairs and into their room.

The light was still on from them dressing. Would anyone notice if she turned it off? Or would it be best to leave it on?

"I know you're up here, Mel." Steve's deep, nasty voice and the name he'd always called her lodged fear in her chest and froze her limbs. She heard his footsteps creaking along the hallway.

"Melanie!" Brett's voice bellowed through the house.

Fear for him shoved her own terror to the side. She plunged her hand under the mattress on Brett's side of the bed and brought out the handgun he'd placed there after they'd learned Steve had disappeared.

"Melanie!" His call was more frantic.

She slipped the gun in the pocket of her hooded sweatshirt and opened the bedroom door. Steve was moving carefully down the hall toward the stairs.

"You looking for me?" she asked softly, to catch his attention but not let Brett hear her. She hoped he thought Steve had taken her away. That would keep him out of danger.

Steve spun around, a wicked smile on his face. "That's sweet of you, getting my attention to save your lover." He strode toward her. "I think it's only fitting he watch me kill you before I kill him."

"You won't get away with this," she said, trying to step out into the hall, but he was too quick. He shoved her into the bedroom. She landed on the floor with her hand twisted under her hip. Pain radiated up her arm.

"You really thought you could get away from me?" He stood over her, holding a gun much like the one in her pocket.

"I did get away from you. And, I am no longer your wife." She remembered Dorothy and Lacey's words about strength. She had strength. She'd gotten away from this man and she'd rid herself of him legally.

"You will always be my wife, even in death." He raised the hand with the gun.

Everything went black.

***

Brett ran up the stairs at the sound of a man's voice. He flew through the bedroom door as the son-of-a-bitch struck Lacey in the face with a gun.

He roared and flung his body at the man, driving them both to the floor. The hard length of the revolver barrel lay against his chest between them. He hit the man in the face with his fist, hoping to knock him unconscious.

Melanie needed him, but he couldn't let this maniac loose. Perret had a gun. Brett could tell by the crazy in his eyes, Perret would kill them both, damn the consequences.

They rolled.

Brett swung and caught the man's jaw.

Perret cursed and shoved the barrel of the gun under Brett's chin. "I'd kill you right now, but I want you to watch me kill the woman you stole from me, then I'll kill you."

Brett shoved the man and rolled away from the barrel.

Perret raised his gun.

A boom rang through the room.

Perret's eyes widened and his body slumped to the floor.

Melanie's head and her small hands, clutching his revolver, were all he saw of the woman over the top of the footboard. Blood streamed down her face, the palest he'd ever seen her.

He stumbled to his feet, kicked Perret's gun under the bed, and took the revolver from Melanie.

Lacey and a deputy ran into the room.

His cousin pulled them both into a hug as the deputy dug through

Perret's pockets.

He flipped open a wallet. "Steven Perret. The man who vowed to kill his wife?"

"Yes." Brett could hardly get the word out. The man had almost succeeded, if not for Melanie's strength.

The deputy took one look at him and Melanie and nodded. "Looks like he got what was coming to him. Lacey would you take your cousin and Mrs.—"

"Melanie," both he and Lacey said.

The deputy nodded. "Miss Melanie down to the great room. I'll need their statements."

Brett picked Melanie up in his arms. "I kicked his gun under the bed. I wasn't sure if he'd come around or not."

The deputy nodded and pulled out his cell phone.

"Come on." Lacey led the way to the great room, then headed down the hall. "Let's put her in the bedroom back here. All the people who came to help put out the fire will be filing in here for coffee and the goodies Melanie has in the oven."

He liked the idea of the two of them having a private space. Melanie hadn't stirred since shooting her ex-husband. He wasn't sure if she was in shock or if Perret's blow to her head had done significant damage.

"We need a doctor to look at her," he said, placing Melanie on the bed.

"I'll make the phone calls. You stay with her. I'll bring tea soon." Lacey left, closing the door behind her.

Brett sat on the edge of the bed, holding her hand and whispering how much he loved her.

***

Melanie couldn't stop shaking. Cold, she felt so cold.

A hand pushed her hair to the side and a voice she knew penetrated the fog she was drifting in.

"Melanie, honey. The doctor is on his way." Brett's soft voice slowly pulled her eyelids up.

She stared into his worried eyes. Her left wrist and head throbbed. Keeping her eyes open made her head hurt worse. She closed her eyes and the vision of Steve slumping to the floor shot them back open.

"Did I kill him?" she whispered.

"No. But he's got a nasty gut shot and from what the sheriff tells me, a lot of years in jail for arson, attempted murder, and violation of a restraining order." Brett kissed her forehead. "Dr. Taves is here to check you out. Mom, Dad, well, everyone but Jared, are in the great room enjoying the coffee and snacks you made."

"The barn?"

"We managed to get the worst of it out right away. When I saw things were under control, I came back to the house and found the backdoor window broken." Sadness dulled his eyes. "When I realized he was in the house and I'd left you there…" He kissed the hand he held. "I was kicking myself up one side and down the other for not keeping you by my side. Then I heard him threaten you and saw…" He closed his eyes, then kissed the throbbing spot on her head. "I thought he'd taken you from me."

She squeezed his hand. "I put your gun in my sweatshirt pocket and called him into the room. I didn't want him to hurt you."

"We nearly got killed trying to protect each other." He kissed her lips. "We don't have to worry about him anymore. We can start our family and live without fear of the unknown."

"Ahem. I realize you were both in a life or death situation, but I really should take a look at your injuries." An older man with white hair and sparkling eyes behind round-rimmed glasses smiled down at her. "Your injuries appear to be the worst. Let me take a look at you, my dear."

Epilogue

Melanie stood at the top of the stairs of the lodge at the Tumbling Creek Ranch. Allan Wallis held his arm out to walk her down to her groom, waiting for her by the large river rock fireplace. Her heart was full of love, not only for the man she was about to marry, but his family as well.

They had all pitched in and helped tend to the guests while her wrist and head healed. Brett had kept her sequestered in their bedroom, bringing her meals and bridal magazines while the guests came and went, and she never saw a single one.

But today, the house was overflowing with family, friends, and even special guests, like Mr. and Mrs. Barnes.

They descended the stairs, her in her empire waist, silk dress with a gauze overlay embellished with small clusters of pearl beads.

Brett wore a western cut jacket, jeans, and his town boots. Her heart thudded against her ribs at the sight of her handsome groom. His gaze latched onto hers and there wasn't another person in the room.

She barely remembered saying her vows. Staring into Brett's eyes, all she wanted to do was get whisked away to their honeymoon at a secluded beach resort in the Caribbean. A place she'd never been but always wondered about.

The reception was a success. Dorothy and Carolyn made sure all the punch bowls had been kept filled, the cake didn't tip over when some rowdy youngsters ran into the table, and Kool behaved himself.

Finally, the time had come when they could leave the ranch and head to the airport for their honeymoon. They snuck up the stairs to their room to change and grab their bags.

Brett helped her out of her dress. "You know, we have enough time we could make love for the first time as a married couple in this bed."

She wrapped her arms around his neck and kissed his lips. "I would love nothing better, but with the house full of your family it wouldn't be long before someone would come looking for us."

He grinned. "True."

Staring into his eyes, she had to say what had been on her mind ever since he told her he wanted her for his wife, whether she was free or not. "I am so thankful that even after knowing all my past and baggage, you could love me, anyway."

He walked over to the door, locked it, and they made sweet love as husband and wife.

The Wrong Cowboy to Love

Chapter one

Ruby Cutter stood outside the salon wondering how she'd let her cousin Jackie and Arlene, her cousin's maid of honor, talk her into getting a make-over for the bachelorette party tonight. She was self-conscious of the short bob the hair-stylist insisted would look wonderful on her. Her long neck always made her feel like a baby giraffe in a human body. Her long thin arms and legs didn't help that feeling any. But to have her neck exposed and no long, stringy blonde hair to hide it, she felt as if she stood on the street naked.

And people were gawking. Her face heated and the tips of her ears burned.

"Look at all those men giving you the eye," Arleen said, hooking her arm through Ruby's. "You're going to have all the men at The Crystal Bar watching you."

"I don't want all the men at the bar to watch me. I want my hair back." Ruby stood up the collar of her button-up shirt to hide her exposed neck.

Jackie turned her collar down. "You have a graceful neck. Men love a long-necked woman." She grinned. "Anyway, Thad likes my long neck, he says it gives him more to kiss."

Ruby studied her cousin. They were the same height, but her cousin had a curvy, filled-out form while she had minimal curves. "I don't—"

"Stop don't-ing. We're going to get you a fun outfit." Arlene led her down the street to an upscale boutique.

"I can't afford whatever is in there," Ruby said, digging her heels in. She had lived in Bozeman the last four years working as an I.T. person for a large law firm. She didn't spend her money frivolously on clothes she couldn't wear to work. She spent her money on fun technology.

"You can't go out with that hair and makeup without a new outfit." Jackie dragged her into the boutique.

***

Four hours later her stomach gurgled from hunger, but Jackie and Arleen had managed to make her look like a runway model. She had on high-heeled boots of soft leather that went up to her knees. Her flowy, flowery skirt was a good six inches above her boots. A teal, silky, boat-neck top covered her upper body while bangle bracelets jangled on her wrists and a bulky necklace with the same colors as in the skirt lay on her chest. She had to admit, she loved the big, bright-colored hoop earrings Arleen talked her into purchasing. She felt daring and vivacious as they walked into the crowded bar.

She glanced at her cell phone. It was only seven and the place was already full. "Don't you want to party somewhere with less people?" she asked Jackie.

"No. They have an out of town band playing. I heard them once before. The lead singer is cute and has a good voice."

She stared at her cousin. "You aren't planning on running off with this singer and leaving Thad standing at the alter?"

Her cousin laughed. "No. I would never leave Thad. He's my soulmate. But I can fantasize about what life on the road with a singer would be like."

Arleen found a table with two chairs. She promptly struck up a conversation with three guys at a table with four chairs.

Ruby sunk into one of the chairs, glad to not be towering over most of the people. She looked up and realized she was alone. A man with a short, neatly trimmed, graying beard hovered not far from the table. When she made eye contact he smiled and started her way.

She wasn't a bar person. Her first instinct was to jump up and run, but then her friends wouldn't know where to find her. And this was Jackie's night.

"Hello," the man said.

"Hello." She glanced up at him then back down at her hands, twisted together in her lap.

"Care if I join you?" He put his hand on a chair.

"I'm sorry, this is a girls only party," Arleen said, placing a third chair at the table and sitting down. "But if we see you on the dance floor later, we'll dance with you."

The man bowed his head and walked away.

"Thank you!" Ruby said, willing her racing heart to stop. She didn't know how to send the man away.

"All you have to do is tell them to buzz off and they will." Arleen glanced back over at the table where she'd commandeered the chair.

"You know I don't even tell off the jerks at work that act like I don't know anything because I'm a woman." She sighed. She really had to grow a pair of balls and not worry about hurting people's feelings.

Jackie returned with three huge glasses of an icy, fruity looking drink and a basket of wings. She placed the tray on the table and picked up a glass. "Ladies, a toast to my last party night as a free woman."

They clinked glasses and drank.

Ruby enjoyed the cool, sweet drink. She slurped it up and ate two wings as the drone of voices ebbed and flowed. "This place is loud," she shouted at her friends.

"Wait until the music starts." Jackie finished off her drink and waved over a waitress. "Three more."

"If there's alcohol in this, you're going to have to pack me out of here." Ruby picked up another chicken wing and tried focusing on the cardboard characters tacked to the ceiling. "Is that really Luke Skywalker?" she asked, pointing with the wing.

"Yes." Arleen put her hand down. "You might want to eat more chicken and drink less or you'll make our night end early."

She nodded.

When the waitress returned with drinks, Arleen ordered more wings and a basket of fries.

Ruby hadn't eaten this much greasy food in a long time. After half the basket of fries was consumed, she needed a trip to the restroom.

Arleen escorted her through the crowd. "You know how to get back?"

"I can make it back." Ruby pushed her way into the ladies' room, took care of business, and splashed water on her face, trying to clear her head.

She shoved the door to the dark hallway open and heard it hit something.

"Damn!" a masculine voice cursed.

Her first instinct was to flee back into the sanctuary of the restroom, but the door opened wider and she stared into a pair of angry eyes under the brim of a cowboy hat.

"I'm so sorry. Did I break anything?" She put her hands out to touch him and swayed forward.

Chapter Two

Dillon Wallis grabbed the tall, pretty blonde by the arms to stop her from toppling forward. The only thing she'd damaged was the outside of this guitar case. The door had startled him more than doing any real damage.

"Hey, you're a little unsteady. You might want to slow down on the drinks." He eased her back down the hall, away from the restroom doors and closer to the staircase leading up to the second floor stage.

"I've only had one," she said, grinning like the one drink was an epic accomplishment.

"Well then, I'd say one is your limit." He grinned back at her. She had a cute little dimple on her left cheek.

"My cousin, it's her bachelorette party, just bought me another one. Have you had a fruity drink before? They're good." She wiped a long hand across her forehead, jangling bracelets.

"Maybe I should escort you back to your cousin." Dillon set his guitar case on the stairs and took her hand in his. She stood a few inches taller than him. He glanced down. The lower half of her long legs were encased in leather boots with four-inch heels.

"Where is your cousin?" he asked, leading her toward the packed room.

"We were over there, under Luke Skywalker."

He glanced the direction of her raised hand. Sure enough, there was a cardboard cutout of the Star Wars hero. With her using an intergalactic character to navigate by and her lack of consuming alcoholic beverages, he had a feeling she didn't usually hit the bar scene.

She followed alongside him through the maze of people, mumbling "excuse me" every time she bumped someone.

A blonde with similar facial features but a curvier body jumped up as they approached the table.

"Ruby, we were just wondering if we needed to send out a search party." The woman's smile turned all teeth, and her eyes widened. "But it looks like you found a handsome man to keep us company."

"No, Ma'am. I'm just helping Ruby back to her table. We bumped into one another. I could see she wasn't in any shape to navigate the floor on her own." He settled the woman called Ruby into the empty chair. "Maybe I'll get a chance to catch up to you later." He gave the hand he held a squeeze.

Ruby smiled at him. "I'd like that. And I owe you a drink for banging the door into you."

"You don't, but I'll see about taking you up on that. I have to get back to work." He departed before the other two women could quiz him. It had been a rule of his since he'd started traveling to gigs, not to give out any information about himself. He didn't want some woman thinking he needed a roadie.

At the stairs, he picked up his guitar and took the steps two at a time to the second floor. This venue was a first for him. The band had been here before but with a different lead singer. He'd just booked this gig last week. The drummer was an old friend. He'd called up saying they needed a singer for this weekend in Bozeman, and could Dillon do it?

He didn't even have to think about it. The only way to make a living as a singer and get his songs heard was by hitting the road, making demo tapes, and hoping the right person saw him. He'd called his cousin, Lacey, and asked if he could crash with her and her husband, Jared, for the weekend. She never turned down family and it saved money.

They planned to come listen to him tomorrow night.

"Where you been?" Barry, the drummer, asked.

"Helping a drunk chick find her way back to the nest." He didn't bother saying anymore even though he could tell Barry was pondering the comment.

As soon as all the introductions were made, and the instruments tuned, they played the first song.

As he sang, his eyes wandered to the threesome at the table under Luke Skywalker. He saw the minute they recognized who he was. He grinned and saluted, singing about how a woman had broken his heart.

Chapter Three

Ruby couldn't believe the man she'd hit with the door was the lead singer of the band. She leaned close to Jackie. "How come you didn't tell me he was the singer?"

Jackie shook her head. "He's not the guy they had the last time they were here. But he is dreamy."

She could agree with her cousin on that. Not only was he nice to look at, his voice, especially when he looked at her and sang, made her warm in all the right places. She was going to take his advice. The next time the waitress came by, she ordered a soda. Only one fruity drink for her.

Jackie and Arleen were dancing when the man with the beard came back to the table.

"I see your friends are off having fun. Care to dance with me?"

He seemed like a nice enough guy, but her heart was set on a boy from high school and until she ran into him again, she really didn't want to give anyone the wrong idea. "I'm sorry. I don't like to dance. I'm just here supporting my cousin who's getting married next weekend."

The man shrugged and wandered back to the bar. She felt sorry for him. He seemed to be here alone, but she wasn't sorry enough to dance with him.

"We're going to take a fifteen-minute break," the singer said and the band members all stood up and disappeared from view.

Jackie and Arleen returned from dancing and started sucking down their third fruity drink.

"How can you two drink that and not be flat on the floor?" Ruby asked.

"Practice," Arleen said, and the two started laughing.

Ruby didn't know what was so funny. She stared at her two friends and plucked a cold fry from the basket in the middle of the table right next to her slushy second fruity drink.

The waitress came over and set another soda on the table.

"I didn't order this," Ruby said, pushing the drink back across the table toward the waitress.

"It's from him." The woman nodded toward the end of the bar.

The singer raised a glass of what appeared to also be soda.

She smiled and raised her glass.

"It appears you have an admirer," Jackie said, sliding off her stool. "Want me to invite him over?"

Ruby wasn't sure what she wanted. "I-I don't want him to think—"

"That's the fun of a night like this, you don't think." Arleen slid off her chair and marched straight over to the man.

His eyes narrowed as Arleen approached.

Ruby would have liked to slither under the table. She hated being embarrassed.

***

Dillon hadn't planned on anything coming of his sending a soda to Ruby, but here came one of her friends, marching across the room like she was on a mission. He glanced past her to the tall blonde. Her dimple was gone. Her pale skin was red and her eyes wide like a frightened calf. She hadn't sent her friend over, that was clear.

"Hello, I'm Ruby's friend, Arleen," The woman put a hand out.

Dillion grasped her hand. It was smaller and plumper than Ruby's. "Dillon."

"Ruby's shy. And doesn't usually drink. We're here having a small bachelorette party for Jackie. If you could maybe find a way to dance one dance with Ruby, it would make her night."

He stared into the woman's eyes. She was drunk, but he also saw sincerity. She thought her friend, the one that looked as if she'd stepped out of a fashion magazine needed her ego propped up.

The fifteen minutes was up. "I can't make any promises." He put his glass down on the counter and followed the other band members back up to the stage.

As he sang the next set of songs, his gaze had a mind of its own, finding Ruby and watching her turn away man after man who approached her when her friends were on the dance floor. The woman sipped her drink, nibbled on the wings, and watched the people. She appeared uncomfortable.

The more he watched her, the more he wanted to know her story. She was gorgeous but acted as if she didn't want anyone to see her. A couple times, she made gestures that made him wonder when she'd cut her hair.

His curiosity got the better of him. On the next break, he picked up his soda from the bar and wandered over to the table under Luke Skywalker.

He made eye contact with Ruby and the other two were a blur as they retreated from the table.

"I'm Dillon," he said, holding out his hand.

"Ruby," she said, a bit shaky. "I'm really sorry about hitting you with the door. I didn't realize—"

"Hey, no harm done. It hit my guitar case and that's what it's for, to protect my instrument." He released her hand when he had the urge to continue holding it. Canned music played while they were on break. The dance floor was just as crowded as when the live music played.

"Want to dance?" He put his drink down and slipped her hand from her glass.

Her eyes lit up at the request, but she said, "I-I'm not very good."

"It's a slow dance. There's not much to it. Come on." He waited for her to slide off the tall chair. Her hand gripped his tight as he led her to the dance floor.

He stayed on the edge of the crowd, already conscious of her anxiety. Dillon placed her arms over his shoulders. He put his hands on her slim waist. "Now just sway to the music," he said in her ear.

He held her away from him, where he could see her face. Her concentration was killing him.

"Do you like music?" he asked.

"Yes."

He shook her hips. "Loosen up. Just let your body move to the beat." His grasp on her hips was light as he slowly made her sway with the beat. "Now slide your feet to the beat, one by one to the left, and I'll guide you." He liked holding her, gazing into her big blue eyes.

She continued to bite on her lower lip and concentrate much too hard. The song finished and a fast one started. The fear in her eyes had him leading her back to the table.

When she had slipped back onto her chair, he glanced at his watch. "I have five minutes. Do you live in Bozeman?"

She nodded and sipped her drink.

"Are you between jobs?"

Her brow wrinkled, and she stared at him. "Between jobs? What do I look like, a hooker?"

"No! I thought you were a model." He definitely hadn't phrased that right.

"Model?" She started laughing. When she caught her breath, she shook her head. "I'm not a model. This…" she waved her hand up and down in front of her "…is all my friends doing. I'm a computer geek. I don't haunt bars and this is the only time anyone will ever see me in this."

"That's a shame." He meant what he said. She was a knockout whether she believed it or not. "I have to go. It was nice dancing with you."

Dillon wound his way back to the bar, left his glass, and headed up the stairs. No wonder Ruby looked so out of place even though she was dressed for a night on the town.

Computers. They had more in common than she knew.

Chapter Four

Jackie and Arleen were full of questions when they returned to the table. And she couldn't answer a single one of them.

"I don't know where he's from. I didn't ask, and he didn't say." She was a little bummed that she hadn't learned more about him. He'd been so patient with her inability to dance. She loved music, she just didn't have any rhythm, or so her grade school music teacher told her, and she believed it to this day.

"Did you ask him to be your plus-one for my wedding?" Jackie asked.

"No. I barely know him. I'm coming alone." She hadn't told her cousin that Thad's good friend, who'd offered his Dude Ranch for the wedding, was a cousin to the man she had loved and lusted over since high school. And the day he'd stood in front of her in P.E. and someone pulled his shorts down, she'd had an excellent view of his tight buns with a dusting of hair. She'd been mortified, but he'd pulled up his shorts, turned around, apologized for his friend's bad behavior, and winked at her. She'd just about melted into a puddle of teenage goo.

Every time she thought about the possibility of Nate being at the wedding her whole body went up in flames.

"No one comes alone to a wedding. How about I find you a hunky guy?" Arleen said.

"No. I'm hoping to meet an old acquaintance at the wedding. I want to be unencumbered." She smiled at her cousin and friend.

"Who?" they both asked at the same time.

"I'm not telling. You'll do something like you did tonight to that poor singer." Her gaze drifted up toward the stage where he was singing a foot stomping song. "I think you embarrassed him as much as you did me."

Arleen stopped sipping her drink and narrowed her eyes. "He didn't need much encouragement."

"That's because he thought I was a model." She snorted. "Me, a model."

Jackie pushed the short bangs off Ruby's forehead. "Cousin, with this haircut and those clothes, you do look like a model. When are you going to realize you are a great catch for any man?"

"I don't want any man. I have my eyes on a certain one." She smiled, but the smile wavered as the singer started a soft slow ballad. She glanced up and found his gaze on her.

Arleen started laughing. "I think that's a fine man to have your eyes on."

Ruby startled and picked up her soda. "I'm not talking about him." She changed the subject. They strolled out of the bar around two in the morning as it was closing down. She stole one last look at Dillon as he bent to put his guitar away. He had a pretty nice butt as well.

***

Thursday morning Ruby stood in front of her apartment, her bags packed and waiting for Jackie to pick her up. They were headed to Tumbling Creek Ranch today to make sure all the wedding preparations were being done to Jackie's specifications.

Her cousin pulled up in a small SUV and hopped out to help load the two suitcases and Ruby's computer bag.

"You know you're only going to be there three days technically," Jackie said, placing the largest bag in with four other bags already in the vehicle.

"And you?" Ruby asked, pointing to all the bags her cousin brought.

"I'm the bride. That box is my dress, that one decorations, that bag has my clothes while I'm at the ranch and that bag is for my

273

honeymoon." She pointed to the computer bag Ruby still held. "Why did you bring that? You aren't supposed to think about work, only my wedding."

"I brought it in case." She never went anywhere without her computer. She never knew when someone would call and need tech support or her specialty of finding records others couldn't.

"There better not be an 'in case'. This weekend is about me, Thad, and our wedding. And as one of the bridesmaids, it is your duty to make sure it goes smoothly." Jackie smiled, flipped up her sunglasses to peer into her eyes and then slid into the driver's seat.

Ruby sighed. Her cousin wouldn't become a bridezilla, but she was determined that Ruby would have a good time while at the ranch. She planned to have a good time. Especially, if Nate showed up.

They talked about the wedding plans. Jackie had been to the ranch when she and Thad checked it out. She filled Ruby in on the owner, Brett Wallis and his wife, Melanie. "They run the ranch with the help of family and some hired help. They are a cute couple and have only been married less than a year. But Melanie has some great ideas. The wedding will be in the barn in case a spring rain decides to pop up. I guess they can just all of a sudden burst out of the clouds when you're that high up in the mountains."

She glanced over. "What am I telling you this for, you grew up in Duncan. Did you know Brett?"

"No, he was out of school before I went to the high school. His brother, Garth, and their cousins, Lacey and Nate, were in school when I was." She hoped she hadn't put too much emphasis on Nate's name. She didn't want her cousin thinking she needed to play matchmaker.

"Lacey, she's the female bull rider. Brett talked about her a lot." Jackie wrinkled her nose. "I don't know why a woman would want to ride a bull."

Ruby understood. It was the thrill of doing something as well or better than a man. She'd been told her whole life she could never measure up to her brothers. She couldn't in sports, but she'd outscored them on all the intellectual tests and went on to be the valedictorian of her high school and college classes. She earned more money than her brothers and spent all her spare time making sure she kept up to date on all computer technology.

"I think what she did was a huge step for women." Ruby would never back down on women's equality.

"I know, you are the wrong person to talk about this subject with."

They entered Duncan, a town Ruby hadn't returned to since graduation. Her parents had moved her junior year, but she'd wanted to stay and finish in Duncan. More for the fact she couldn't bring herself to leave Nate, even though he'd barely talked to her all through high school other than the one day she'd witnessed his perfect ass.

As they drove down the main street, a lump rose in her throat. There was the café where the math club would meet on Wednesday afternoons. The small theater where she and her friend Dottie went once a month to watch a movie and wish they were the girls with the boy's arms wrapped around their shoulders. She had lost track of her friend. Maybe while she was here, she could ask around and find out where she was.

They left town and headed down the county road toward what she'd known as the Wallis Ranch when she was in school. There had been several school picnics held at the ranch. She'd gone to one. After falling in a creek and having to sit in the house by the fire to dry off, she decided not to go on any other outings. She wasn't clumsy when sitting in a chair working computer codes.

Thirty minutes later, they drove under an archway with the words, Tumbling Creek Ranch spelled out in iron.

"Oh, Jackie! It's gorgeous! I don't remember it looking like this before."

"That's because when Brett took it over, he made some major changes to make it into the best dude ranch resort in Montana." Jackie pulled up to the front of the main house. A dog ran out to the car, barking with joy.

Ruby had always felt this building had the most inviting front porch.

Thad burst out of the main house doors and straight to the driver's side of the vehicle.

Jackie opened the door and was caught up in his arms.

"I thought you would never get here." He accented his comment with a long sloppy kiss.

Ruby exited the vehicle. The dog ran around her barking.

"Kool, I see we have company," a woman said from the porch.

Ruby walked up the steps to the woman, close to her age with long brown hair, a welcoming smile, and noticeably pregnant belly.

"Welcome to Tumbling Creek, I'm Melanie Wallis. My husband and I own the ranch."

"I'm pleased to meet you, Melanie. If you could tell me where I'm staying and where the bride is staying, I'll get our things tucked away." Ruby shook hands with the woman.

"There's no need. Thad and Brett will take care of your things. Come in and get something to drink. It's been an unusually warm spring." Melanie led the way into the main building.

The great room was inviting with throws, pillows, and overstuffed furniture. The large river rock fireplace was just as Ruby remembered from standing in front of it, trying to dry.

"Is this your first time to Tumbling Creek?" Melanie asked, motioning to iced tea and lemonade.

"Lemonade, please. No. As a student in Duncan we had a few picnics out here." The large dining room was as inviting as the great room with fresh-cut flowers, games and books on a bookcase, and pretty tablecloths on the long family style tables.

"You grew up here? Then you know the Wallis cousins?" Melanie poured a lemonade and an iced tea, before taking both drinks over to a table. She sat and indicated for Ruby to sit, too.

"I knew the younger ones. I don't remember Brett. But Garth, Nate, and Lacey were in high school when I was." Ruby sipped the beverage and was surprised at the prefect combination of tart and sweet. "I was actually in Nate's grade." She worked hard to keep from getting excited over the boy she'd not seen in eight years.

"I'm sorry." Melanie laughed. "Just kidding. He's still a handful that's for sure. From the family stories I've heard, he was and is a lady's man."

She couldn't stop the blush that heated her cheeks. A lady's man. He'd have no use for the geeky girl who'd hung on his every word. But it also brought back memories of girls giggling in the restroom talking about Nate this and Nate that.

"Will he and Lacey be at the wedding?" She didn't want to sound overly excited, so she'd tacked on Lacey to her enquiry.

"Yes, as will Garth and Dillon. When there is a big event like this, the whole family pitches in." Melanie rose. "And here comes the bride."

Ruby let the information sink in. The whole family. She remembered Mrs. Wallis, Lacey and Nate's mom, was a nice woman. She had sat with Ruby as she'd dried out that day.

"Hi Melanie. Do you mind if I steal Ruby? I want to show her the barn." Jackie was as animated as ever.

"That's fine. Go ahead. Brett and Garth are going to start putting up the altar and decorations tomorrow. You and Ruby can oversee and help." Melanie stood. "When you finish in the barn, I'll be doing the final touches on the cake if you want to see it."

"I would! Thank you, Melanie. I don't know how you can make all the food for the reception, the cake, and handle all the people who will be staying here this weekend." Jackie hugged Melanie.

"Because this family works together. Brett's mom and his aunt will be here all day tomorrow helping me with the last minute food prep and meals for your family and bridal party." Melanie picked up the glasses and exited through a door at the end of the dining room.

"Come on!"

Ruby grinned and followed her cousin. This was going to be the best weekend.

Chapter Five

Dillon parked in front of the barn. He'd promised Brett he'd set up the sound system tonight for the wedding and the reception. He had a gig in nearby Elkton on Friday night but would be back Saturday morning to help with final preparations and sing the song he'd prepared for the wedding couple.

He did a double take when two women walked out of the barn. It couldn't be? Opening the pickup door, he caught their attention.

The tall body and pale face under the short blonde hair was familiar. She wasn't made up today, but in his estimation, that only made her more striking.

"Ruby?" he called.

She put up a hand to shield the late evening sun and a grin spread across her face. "Dillon?"

He started toward her. Jackie said something and continued to the house.

"What are you doing here?" they both said at the same time and laughed.

"Jackie is getting married here on Saturday," Ruby said.

He could see the wheels behind her eyes churning.

"I promised Brett I'd set up the sound system tonight. I have a gig in Elkton tomorrow night." He couldn't stop his gaze from taking in every nuance of her face. This fresh, unpainted version of her was stealing his senses.

"Dillon Wallis?" Her eyes lit up as she made the connection. "Oh, when Melanie mentioned a Dillon, I never dreamed it would be you, the singer from the Crystal Bar."

"I hope you're not disappointed."

"Oh, no. I'm pleased. We never really had a chance to talk." She glanced at the speakers and stands in the back of his truck. "Would you like me to help you? I'm pretty good with electronics."

Only an idiot would turn down the chance to hang out with this woman. "I'd be obliged. It's more than a one-person job, but Garth had a class tonight." He walked to the back of his truck and opened the tailgate.

He'd never been as excited about setting up a sound system. "Now that you know my last name, what's yours?"

"Cutter." She picked up two of the stands and carried them into the barn.

He'd known a Ron and Rich Cutter. They were his and Brett's age. "Did you live here?" he asked when he carried one of the speakers into the barn.

"Yes." She exited the barn, and he hurried to catch up with her.

"Are Ron and Rich your brothers?"

She frowned. "Yes. Those two athletic bozos are my brothers." She picked up more stands and headed into the barn.

Dillon picked up another speaker and packed it inside. "Didn't your family move when Rich graduated?"

"They did, but I stayed to finish high school here. I lived with Dottie Kelly and her family." Ruby stopped and faced him. "I was captain of the math team."

"And valedictorian of Nate's class." He grinned. Now that he knew who her family was, he could see the resemblance. And understood where her height came from. He also remembered Nate's graduation. Ruby had not only graduated as the valedictorian but had also left the gymnasium with just about every scholarship given at Duncan High. "Where did you end up going to college?"

Her cheeks turned a bright pink. "M.I.T.," she said quietly as if embarrassed.

"Really? And were you top of your class there, too?"

She ducked her head and walked out of the barn.

He didn't understand why she appeared embarrassed. At the truck, he put a hand on her arm. "There's nothing to be embarrassed about being smart."

"Yes, I did graduate at the top of my class, but some of my male classmates started rumors that I only made it there by sleeping with the professors." Her face had turned a dark red. "That was my first and not my last introduction to men who can't stand it when a woman is as smart or smarter than they are."

"I'm sorry you were in college with dickheads." He slipped his hand down her arm, linking his hand with hers. "There is nothing wrong with a woman with brains. I prefer it. Then I don't have to figure out the tip when we go to dinner."

She laughed.

His chest warmed with the accomplishment of taking her mind off the dickheads from her college.

"Come on. If we can get this unloaded before dinner, I can set it up afterwards." He released her hand only because it was hard to carry a speaker with one hand.

She smiled and picked up more equipment.

***

Ruby glanced around the big table. Brett, Melanie, Thad, Jackie, Arleen, who'd arrived while she was helping Dillon, Mack, Thad's best man, and Jackie's mom, Aunt Cassandra, were all sitting at the table, along with her and Dillon.

Jackie was on her left and Dillon on her right. Jackie thumped her with her elbow and leaned close. "What a coincidence. You and Dillon, here for the weekend." She winked.

Ruby shook her head. She liked Dillon. A lot. But her heart fluttered when she thought of Nate. When would he arrive?

"Do you think you'll get that sound system set up tonight?" Brett asked.

Dillon glanced at her and grinned. "Ruby offered to help me after dinner. I think with her brains and my brawn we'll get it done."

Everyone laughed, and Ruby's ears burned.

"I can't believe that you two met last weekend and here you are at the same wedding," Arleen said, drawing attention to them.

Once that was said, everyone wanted to know how they'd met.

Jackie started, "We, Arleen, Ruby, and I, were at the Crystal Bar for my bachelorette party."

"And Ruby hit Dillon—" Arleen started.

"Hey, that's not fair." Ruby cut in. "I don't drink, usually, I'd had one fruity drink and was a bit tipsy while leaving the restroom and I slammed the door open into someone and they swore."

"Let me take over," Dillon said. "I was walking down the hall from the back of the establishment to the stairs to the stage when the ladies' restroom door flew open and hit my guitar case. Yes, I said, damn, then Ruby fell into my arms."

"I did not!" she objected.

"You did. I had to set you back on your feet and suggest you not drink so much." He grinned, and she felt her neck and face growing warmer.

"I'd only had the one drink and not enough food," she insisted.

"That's what she told me. And when I asked her where her table was she said under Luke Skywalker."

Everyone laughed, and her face burst into flames. She explained how there were cardboard characters and actors on the ceiling of the bar.

"And then on his first break, he sent a soda over to Ruby," Arleen said, insinuating something had happened.

"I was only making sure she didn't have any more alcohol and end up falling off the tall boots she was wearing." Dillon winked at her.

Heat rose up her neck at his playful ribbing. She'd never had a man tease her like this before. She was used to her brothers badgering her and males at work making remarks about her clumsiness and brains.

"So… did you go over and talk to her?" Aunt Cassandra asked.

"Arleen came over and suggested it would make Ruby's night if I danced with her." Dillon said.

"She what?" Ruby had never felt so mortified. "Our dance was a pity dance?" She stood, knocked the chair over, and stumbled from the room.

Dillon had no idea what that was all about. He'd been the envy of every man in that bar.

"I better go talk to her," Jackie rose.

"No, let me. She was no way a pity dance." Dillon righted the chair and shifted his attention to Melanie. "What room is she in?"

"Two-oh-five," Melanie said, nodding her head.

He strode out of the room, checked the great room, and headed up the stairs. Mumbling could be heard behind the door of room 205.

"Ruby, can I come in?" he asked, at the same time he knocked softly on the door.

"Why? You want to give me more pity?"

He tried the knob, it wasn't locked. Shoving the door open, he was hit in the face with a pillow.

"Pillow fight, huh?" He picked the pillow up from the floor and launched it at her.

The pillow hit her smack in the face and fell to the carpet. She didn't even get her hands up in time to knock it out of the way.

"Go away," she said, dropping onto the bed.

"No. Not until you hear me out." He grabbed the chair by the small desk and placed it in front of her. Taking the seat, he captured one of her hands. "I did not ask you to dance with me out of pity. I asked you to dance with me because you are a beautiful woman and I wanted to learn more about you."

She sniffed and studied him from under downcast lashes. "That person, at the bar, that wasn't me. That was a person my cousin and friend made up."

"But today, when you are being yourself is when I made the decision to get to know you better." He put a hand under her chin, making her look into his eyes. "Today, when I saw the real you, without the makeup, four-inch heels, and sexy clothes, I fell under your spell more than the night at the bar."

Her eyes widened. "My spell? What are you talking about? I'm just a brainy, bean pole of a woman, who can't walk across a room without tripping or knocking something over."

"No, you are a slender, intelligent woman, who could use some dance lessons."

The corners of her mouth started to twitch. "I'm sorry I was such a poor dancer. So few people have ever asked me to dance I've not made it a priority to learn."

Dillon stood, pushed the chair behind him, and using the hand he held, pulled Ruby to her feet. "Here's your first lesson."

"We don't have any music." She crossed her arms.

"There is always music." He gathered her close and sang one of his standard ballads.

She swayed as he sang and slowly moved her around the small area in the room. When the song finished, she remained swaying in his arms, her eyes closed, and her blonde lashes rested on creamy white cheeks.

He wanted to kiss her, but knew it was too soon. She'd think it was a pity kiss. The thought made him chuckle.

Her eyes popped open. "What's so funny?"

"That you thought I asked you to dance with me out of pity. I was shaking in my boots when I asked you. I saw all the men you'd sent away all night long. Why did you dance with me?"

The beautiful blush he'd come to look for rose up her long elegant neck. "I turned the others away because I can't dance. But when you asked, you'd been so kind up to that point, I figured you wouldn't stomp off the dance floor when I proved my clumsiness."

He shook his head. "You do know the only reason you are clumsy is because you think so. Use that smart confident brain of yours and realize that every time you say it, you're setting yourself up to fail. If you think you're clumsy, you will be."

Dillon began another song, pulling her up against him. This time she caught onto the rhythm quicker and relaxed more in his arms.

At the end of the song, she took two small steps back. "Thank you."

"You're welcome. Shall we go finish our dinner and get that sound system set up?" He walked over to the door.

Chapter Six

Ruby fell into bed happy and exhausted. The sound system wasn't all set up until eleven, and then Dillon had insisted they needed to try it out. He'd plugged in a country CD and they'd danced. The others heard the music and soon there was an impromptu dance being held in the barn. It was after midnight when Dillon said he had to go. He had to work and then play at a bar in Elkton. If not for the rehearsal dinner, she could have gone with him.

***

She woke Friday morning to a rooster crowing and the sounds of footsteps in the hall. A glance at the clock said it was six. It would be a long day with only five hours of sleep, but she was too excited to stay in bed. She dressed and headed down to the dining room.

Dorothy Wallis, Lacey and Nate's mom, was setting out the morning beverages. "Good morning, Ruby! I couldn't believe it when Melanie and Brett told me you were part of the wedding party." The woman wrapped her in a hug. "It was a long time ago when we kept each other company in front of the fireplace in there."

"You remember that day?" Ruby asked, surprised by the warm welcome and memories.

"It's a day I'll never forget. You wandered up to the house looking like a drowned puppy. When I asked you how you got so wet you were reluctant to tell me." Mrs. Wallis bustled around the dining room, setting out silverware and napkins.

Ruby filled a cup with coffee and sat down. She'd tried to forget how she'd ended up in the water that day, but it all came rushing back. "Did I eventually tell you?"

Mrs. Wallis faced her. "Yes, you did. Boys at that age are so full of hormones they say and do stupid things."

She nodded in agreement. She didn't even remember which boy had said, "Let's push her in the water and see if she has any boobs under a wet t-shirt." Ruby pulled the sweater she wore over her t-shirt tighter around her.

"And if any of those boys saw you today, they'd all be falling at your feet." Mrs. Wallis pushed the empty cart to the kitchen door.

Jackie wandered into the dining room. "You're up early."

"The rooster woke me. I figured I might as well get the day started." Ruby was still reeling from the woman's memory of her. She'd always felt she was invisible.

"We have the decorating to do and then the rehearsal tonight." Jackie filled a cup half full of coffee and the other half cream and sugar.

Arleen dragged into the room. "We do get a nap later today, right?"

Jackie laughed. "If you work hard and we get the decorating finished before the rehearsal, you may nap."

Ruby watched the two as she sipped her coffee. Arleen and Jackie had been friends since junior high. And despite their many differences were the best of friends. She'd never had a best friend. Her IQ had not only scared away boys, but the girls as well. These two were her closest thing to friends. And she only saw Jackie during family get togethers and Arleen when she came with Jackie.

That was why she worked all the time. She didn't have time to think about how sorry her life was.

"Hey, why are you looking so gloomy? You were dancing and spent the whole evening with a handsome, yummy man," Arleen said, sitting down with a cup of coffee.

Her neck started heating. Man, she'd love to not get embarrassed so easily. "He was fun. I think we're becoming friends."

"Friends? Is that what you call a man who chases after you when you've embarrassed yourself?" Arleen stared at her over her cup.

"Why didn't you tell me you had asked him to dance with me? That is a pity dance." Even though Dillon had told her dancing with her had been something he wanted to do, she still felt like an idiot that Arleen had gone over and made her sound like a loser.

"But he didn't have to ask you to dance. And he didn't walk over then, he came by later. He had to have wanted to dance with you pretty bad to ask, when he knew you'd been turning other men down." Jackie nodded her head. "That was no pity dance."

Her cheeks warmed. "I know. He told me the same thing. And he didn't care that I couldn't dance."

"You looked like you had the hang of it last night," Arleen said.

"That's because Dillon is a good teacher." The minute the words came out she regretted them.

"He is? What else did he teach you?" Arleen didn't know when to quit.

Mrs. Wallis pushed the cart through the kitchen door, thankfully interrupting the conversation. It was laden with cinnamon rolls, eggs, ham, fruit, and biscuits. She placed the food on the table where they sat, along with a stack of plates and basket of silverware.

"Enjoy. Melanie is a wonderful cook." Mrs. Wallis retreated with her empty cart.

The three dug into the food and were just about finished when Thad and Mack entered the dining room.

"I can't believe you are all up so early," Thad said, kissing Jackie.

Mack took the seat next to Arleen. "Brian should be here by noon."

The third member of the groomsmen. Ruby hadn't met him or Mack before.

"You and Brian will have a lot in common," Mack said. "He does some kind of coding for NASA."

Ruby was intrigued but knew she didn't want a man who talked computers all the time. She worked enough that her down time was spent doing anything but talking about computers.

"I don't think Ruby will be interested in Brian. She has her eye on someone else," Jackie said and winked.

She wasn't sure what her cousin meant. She hadn't told her about her infatuation with Nate.

"Yeah, she and Dillon were looking pretty cozy last night," Thad said.

Ruby stood. "I'd prefer if you'd all just mind your own business." She walked to the dining room door. "I'll be in the barn putting up decorations."

Why did people feel the need to fix her up with anyone who knew computers or looked at her for more than five seconds? She strode out to the barn. Kool ran out of the barn to greet her. She bent to pet his head before entering the building. Brett and another person were putting together the altar.

When the man turned, she realized it was Garth. She hadn't seen him since high school but there was no mistaking his red hair and stout body.

"Ruby, are you the first one up this morning?" Brett asked, as she walked over to where the two were sorting lumber.

"The others are in finishing up breakfast and should be out here soon." She stared at the white pile of boards. "Is this the altar?"

"Yes. It is. We just have to remember how it goes together." Brett motioned to Garth. "This is my brother Garth."

She nodded and smiled. "Yes, he was in high school with me."

Garth studied her a minute then smiled. "Ruby Cutter! The smartest person to ever graduate from Duncan High."

Heat crept up her neck. "I'm not the smartest—"

"Yes, you are. What are you doing these days?" Garth leaned on a board.

"I work for a law group in Bozeman." She scanned the area for the boxes of decorations she'd noticed the night before.

"Law? I thought you went into computers?" Brett picked up two boards and held them together.

"I troubleshoot the technology in the office and find information for their cases." She spun away from them. Talking about work wasn't in her plans for the weekend.

"Are these the decorations?" she asked, pulling white tulle from a box.

"Yes." Brett knelt on the ground and started fitting boards together and the talk ended until the rest of the crew arrived. Then the chatter and badgering continued as they worked to make the barn look like a bridal venue.

At noon, they all tramped back to the main house for lunch. Melanie, the two Mrs. Wallis, and Cassandra joined everyone at the table. The conversation was flowing when Brian and Thad's parents arrived.

Ruby finished eating and wandered into the kitchen with her dishes. Dorothy, Caroline, Brett's mom, and Cassandra were in the kitchen cleaning up and working on food for the rehearsal dinner.

"When are your parents and brothers arriving?" Ruby's aunt asked.

"I'm not sure. Ron and Glenda aren't coming until tomorrow. They both had to work today. Rich and Steph are coming after work tonight. Mom and Dad, they weren't sure if they'd come tonight or tomorrow with Ron." She and her family didn't call each other every day. Ever since her decision to stay in Duncan her junior and senior year, she and her family weren't as close. They all felt she'd abandoned them when she hadn't wanted to start all over in a new school.

"I thought they might want to come early so you could all visit." Cassandra didn't look at her.

"You know they don't go out of their way to see me. I'm the black sheep of the family." She left the kitchen through the back door and walked out to the barn to work on decorations on her own. She didn't need her family, and she didn't need to watch other close families and realize how she'd sacrificed that for a boy who didn't even know she existed.

She was brooding and hanging white honeycomb bells when she heard a vehicle drive up and a door close. It was either another guest or someone Brett had hired to help.

The sound of cowboy boots on the wood floor had her twisting her head to see who it was.

Her heart stopped, and all her blood heated as Nate Wallis, even better looking as a man, walked straight toward her.

She attempted to step off the bench she stood on and ended up making it wobble and her body fall toward the floor.

Strong arms caught her.

"Now that's something I don't get to do every day." Nate's face was level with hers, his mischievous brown eyes scanned from her forehead down to her sneakers. "Who are you and why haven't I met you before?”

Her heart began working again. She had enough sense to wiggle out of his hold and land on her feet. She took a step back and then another, putting space between them.

“I’m sorry. I didn’t mean to frighten you. I’m Nate Wallis.”

“I know who you are.” She glanced at the doors, willing someone to walk through and end her awkward torment.

“You do? Then you have me at a disadvantage.” He took a step forward and extended his hand. “You are?”

She held her hands to her chest. “Ruby Cutter,” her name came out on a whispered breath.

“Well, Ruby Cutter, I’m pleased to meet you.” He glanced around. “Where is everyone? I was told to be here at one to help decorate for the wedding tomorrow.”

Her heart nearly ripped in two. He didn’t even remember her name. She hadn’t expected him to know her by sight, but that her name didn’t even register… Sucking up her dismay, she said, “They hadn’t finished eating when more people arrived. I’m sure you can find them all in the house.”

“I’ll go check on them. Nice meeting you, Ruby.” He winked and gave her another up and down scan.

This time her body didn’t heat. She felt the same revulsion she did every time a man scanned her that way. Checking her out as if looking to find missing parts and pieces like a used electronic device.

When the echo of his boots faded in the open barn, she sat on the bench and stared at the altar Brett and Garth had made. Her hopes of a wonderful weekend and finally having the boy of her dreams notice her, was gone. He’d noticed her all right, but not the way she’d dreamed. The boy hadn’t changed. Why had she thought he would? She’d fallen in love with his charisma, smile, and derriere. She’d just witnessed that he had the charisma, smile, and derriere, but remained just as unconcerned for others. He didn’t even remember her name. They only had forty high school graduates the year they graduated. And her name had been called enough times graduation night, she would have thought the name would have rung a little bit of recognition.

She sighed and returned to stand on the bench and finish the string of bells.

Chapter Seven

Dillon had told Jackie and Thad that he might not get by the ranch before heading to Elkton, but he couldn't get Ruby off his mind. He thought he'd run by, see how things were coming along and use the excuse of wondering if Jackie wanted to hear the song he'd prepared, today. rather than just at the wedding.

As he pulled up to the house, he spotted Nate's truck. He loved his cousin, but the man was a womanizer, and he didn't want him setting his hooks in Ruby. Nate loved them until he got what he wanted, a night in his bed, then he dumped them. He'd been doing it since high school and no matter how many times he'd been lectured on the proper way to treat a woman, Nate wanted to have a good time and damn the consequences. He dated for the thrill, like his sister rode bulls for the thrill.

Hoping to catch Ruby, Dillon headed straight for the barn. He stopped in the doorway. The place had transformed from the day before. White tulle was draped from beams, white bells hung from posts, and white chairs were set up. The altar, covered in flowers and pine boughs, was colorful and festive. He spotted someone moving around behind the altar.

Dillon walked into the barn, his gaze on the person. She stepped out from behind the altar and it was the woman he had hoped to see.

"Ruby."

Her body twisted as she stared toward him, squinting.

The sunshine behind him from the doorway had to make him hard to see, but the sunlight gave her an angel's halo. "The decorations look great."

She stepped to the side, and a smile slowly tipped her lips. "Dillon. I'm surprised to see you today."

"Is it a good surprise or a bad surprise?" He stopped in front of her and before he realized his actions, his hand swept a short strand of hair behind her ear.

"A good surprise." She frowned. "The bad surprise was earlier," she mumbled.

"Bad surprise?" He studied her. Her neck grew pinker.

"That wasn't for you to hear and doesn't matter. Everyone is inside resting up for the rehearsal and rehearsal dinner." She pushed another vial holding daisies into the green foam he could see under the pine boughs.

"You didn't need to rest up? We were up late last night." He picked up the box she had bent over to pull another vial from and held it while she eyeballed the altar.

"I was up early, but I felt like some quiet time." She shoved the vial in and picked up another one.

"Would you like me to leave?" He didn't plan on leaving, he could tell she was upset about something.

Her gaze flashed to his face. "No. You're fine. Arleen keeps trying to throw me at all the unattached men here. Jackie keeps asking me what's wrong. My aunt keeps asking me questions about my family that I don't know the answers to." Her gaze flit to the altar, and she worked another bundle of daisies into the garland. "You don't push me." She glanced at him. "I like that."

Hearing her say that made his stop worthwhile.

"You are going to save a dance for me tomorrow at the reception, aren't you?" He studied her as she took her time answering.

"You're probably the only person who would tolerate my dancing." A smile slipped across her lips. "Will you be here for the wedding?"

"I have to be. I'm singing a song."

Her eyes widened. "Oh, is that why you're here? For rehearsal?"

He hadn't planned to stay for rehearsal, but he could head out as soon as they finished and still make Elkton in time. "Yeah. How about we go get something to drink while we wait for rehearsal to start?" He set the box on the bench and grasped her hand.

Her cheeks reddened, but she nodded her head and walked beside him.

He hadn't expected everyone else to be in the dining room when they entered. He'd released her hand to open the door for her. When Ruby saw all the people, her feet stopped. Dillon put a hand on the small of her back, easing her into the room and to a table that wasn't occupied.

"Sit, I'll get us some lemonade."

She nodded and had to have seen the raised eyebrows on the women present. He also noted the challenge in Nate's eyes. It wouldn't be the first time his cousin had tried to steal one of Dillon's girlfriends.

He said hello and shook hands when introduced to people he didn't know as he made his way to the beverages. When all the greetings were finished, he filled two glasses and headed back to Ruby. Nate was sitting at the table.

Dillon handed a glass to Ruby and took the seat beside her.

"Surprised to see you here, Dillon," Nate said.

"I have to be at the rehearsal, too. I'm singing for the wedding." He sipped his drink and watched Ruby sip on hers.

"I understand you and Ruby met last weekend," Nate said, his gaze hovering on Ruby's face. "I've known Ruby since grade school, isn't that right, Ruby?"

Her pale face scrunched into a scowl. "How is it you know that now but didn't have a clue who I was when we met in the barn earlier?"

Dillon couldn't stop the grin that spread from ear to ear. He should have known Ruby wouldn't fall for Nate's pretty boy charm.

Nate sat back. "Is that the impression you had? I was so taken with your beauty and thinking Ruby Cutter grew up to be a gorgeous swan, I forgot my manners."

"Meaning you thought of me as an ugly duckling in school?" Her eyes narrowed.

Nate beamed at her with the look and smile that melted females.

"No, you were never an ugly duckling. You were timid. I do remember that."

Ruby's neck and face grew crimson with embarrassment.

"I'd think Brett would have something for you to do," Dillon said, trying to remove Ruby's discomfort.

Jackie stood and clapped her hands. "Time for rehearsal. Everyone to the barn, please."

"We'll have the dinner all set up when you get back," Melanie said, standing by the kitchen door, one hand rubbing her pregnant belly.

Ruby was thankful Nate wasn't in the bridal party. She stood at the same time as Dillon.

"I'll save you a seat next to me for dinner," Nate said, winking.

There was a time when she would have been overjoyed to have Nate save her a seat. Right now, she was embarrassed and didn't respond, only followed Dillon out of the dining room. Thank heavens for him.

"You know, after the rehearsal you don't have to go to the dinner. You could come with me to Elkton," Dillon said as they walked to the barn.

The voices of the others trailed behind them. His offer was something she was tempted to accept.

"Can I think about it?" She glanced over at him.

"You can think about it right up until I climb in my truck and head to Elkton." He grinned and bumped her shoulder with his.

Why was it so easy to talk with Dillon, and Nate, who she'd thought of as her soul mate for years, upset her so much she couldn't find words? "Thanks."

Dillon walked to his truck and pulled a guitar case out of the passenger seat. Ruby waited for him at the entrance as everyone walked past, chatting.

"What song are you singing?" she asked.

He grinned. "It's a secret. You'll find out when everyone else does."

"You mean Jackie and Thad didn't tell you what song to sing?" She studied him. Was he fooling with her?

"No. They each told me about a date and what they loved about the other person." He shrugged. "And I wrote them a song."

Her jaw dropped open and she stared at him.

He laughed and lifted her chin to close her mouth. "Don't look so surprised. It's what I do. I'm a songwriter."

Ruby studied Dillon. No wonder he always knew exactly what to say to make her feel better. He was a wordsmith. "I look forward to hearing the song."

"Everyone in the bridal party, up here please!" Jackie called out.

Ruby left Dillon to tune his guitar and walked up to the altar. She was paired with Brian, the last of the groomsmen to arrive. He was tall and broad, with a round face, small eyes, and fleshy lips. She smiled but didn't hold eye contact. Her mind was on how Dillon could write a wedding song.

She walked over to Jackie. "I thought you didn't know Dillon?"

Her cousin stared at her. "I didn't."

"Did you know he wrote you a song for your wedding?" Ruby watched her cousin. She looked as shocked as Ruby had when Dillon had told her.

"Thad said he had asked someone who was recommended to sing at the wedding. He never said anything about it being an original song. Oh my! I hope it isn't something he repeats over and over."

Ruby had to stand up for Dillon. "From what he said, I think you're going to love it."

"Really?" Jackie peered at her groom as he visited with his groomsmen. "Thad did ask me a lot of personal questions a month ago and wouldn't tell me why. I thought it was for our vows."

"I have a feeling they were put into a song."

The preacher arrived and began explaining how the ceremony would unfold. When he finished, the women were ushered outside the barn to come in as they would tomorrow. Ruby had to walk in first. Her neck, face, and ears burned as the groom and his two groomsmen, the preacher, and Dillon watched.

One foot in front of the other, she told herself trying not to fall and make a fool of herself. She made it to her spot by the altar and watched as Arleen and then Jackie entered. Both walked in as if they did this kind of thing every day.

"We'll ask who gives this woman," The preacher said. "Then your vows, and then I understand there will be a song."

"Yes," Thad said. "Dillon has written a song for us."

"Do you want to sing it now or wait until tomorrow?" the preacher asked.

"That's up to the bride and groom," Dillon said.

"Will it make me cry?" Jackie asked.

"I'm not a bride, but it might," Dillon replied, making eye contact with Ruby.

"Then I better hear it now, so I don't cry as much tomorrow." Jackie grasped Thad's hands as if she needed him to ground her.

Ruby was glad Jackie requested the song. She was curious to hear it and would wonder about it all night if she didn't hear the lyrics now.

He strummed the guitar with a sweet, lilting melody before his warm voice filled the barn.

The song was the story of Jackie and Thad meeting, a couple of dates, and Thad proposing. Not only was it beautifully told but the chorus had her heart squeezing.

You walked into my life.
You opened my eyes to all the beauty in the world
 and filled my heart with joy.
Your love found and completed me.

He ended the song with the chorus and everyone had tears glistening in their eyes.

Jackie released Thad's hands and ran over, hugging Dillon. "That is beautiful!"

Dillon smiled but appeared a bit uncomfortable. "Sorry, I can't stay. I have a gig in Elkton." He eased out of the hug and put his guitar away. "You want to come, Ruby?"

She glanced at Jackie who nodded her head.

"You're sure there's nothing else I need to help with?" Ruby asked.

"Go! You did more decorating than anyone else and you helped set up the sound system. I think you deserve a night of fun." Jackie linked her arm with Thad. "But we expect you to have her back here as soon as you are through. She needs to look her best tomorrow."

Dillon saluted. "She'll be here no later than three."

"Three!" Ruby wasn't sure she could do two late nights in a row.

"You can sleep on the drive back from Elkton. It takes about an hour to get there." Dillon picked up his guitar case.

"But I need to change," She looked down at her dirty shirt and jeans.

Dillon scanned her. "You look fine to me, but if you want to change, you have twenty minutes."

Arleen grabbed her arm. "Come on." As they jogged out of the barn, Arleen said over her shoulder, "Don't leave without her."

"I don't need you to help me put on a clean pair of jeans and a shirt," Ruby said.

Arleen held the main house door open. "You need makeup and your hair fluffed."

Ruby huffed. "I'm not going there to attract anyone."

"No. But you want to make Dillon proud you are with him." Arleen pulled her up the stairs. "Go wash up and change your clothes, I'll get my makeup and curling iron."

It seemed like a waste of time to put on makeup and fix her hair. She didn't want to attract anyone. She was going to listen to Dillon sing.

After washing up, she put on her best pair of jeans, a long sleeved dark blue blouse that buttoned up the front and her sneakers. The only other shoes she'd brought were the fancy ones to wear with her bridesmaid dress.

Arleen burst through the door with a cosmetic bag in one hand and a curling iron in the other. "Come over here." She placed the items on the dresser and plugged the curling iron in.

"You really don't need to do all of this." Ruby ran her fingers through her hair, fluffing it.

"Yes, I do." Arleen spread foundation on Ruby's face, then blush, and eye makeup.

All Ruby did for work was lotion on her face and mascara on her eyelashes.

When Arleen finished, she looked like the person who had walked into the Crystal Bar a week ago.

"This isn't me."

"Yes, it is. It's just an enhanced version. It's the version that caught Dillon's attention last week." Arleen picked up the curling iron and soon Ruby's short hair was full and looked like it had been styled by a salon.

"Now, you may go." Arleen waved her hand to the door.

Ruby rolled her eyes, picked up her purse, and hurried down the stairs.

Nate walked out of the great room as she headed for the door. He whistled. "Where are you headed looking like my fantasy?"

She stopped in her tracks. Nate fantasized about her? She tried to wrap her head around how he could fantasize about her when he hadn't known she existed until today.

"Want me to take you to dinner?" He moved closer and put a hand on her hip.

Two steps put her closer to the door and away from him. "No. I'm going to Elkton to watch Dillon sing." She stepped out the door and closed it, taking a big breath. The man she'd wanted since high school just asked her to dinner and she'd turned him down.

What is wrong with me?

Dillon stood out front by his truck.

That was what was wrong with her. She found being around Dillon more pleasant than being with Nate. She smiled and walked down to the truck.

"You didn't have to get that gussied up," he said. "I have to sing tonight, not keep men from hitting on you."

Her neck heated as well as her cheeks. "It wasn't my idea. It was Arleen's."

He held the driver's door open for her.

One glance and she saw his guitar was in the passenger seat.

"I hope you don't mind sitting in the middle," he said as she climbed in.

"I don't mind as long as it doesn't hinder your driving." She scooted over towards the passenger side.

Dillon slid in and grasped her leg, pulling her to the middle. "I don't bite, and the seatbelt won't feel good if you're sitting half in the middle and half to the side." His gaze held hers a moment before she grabbed the seatbelt and clicked it.

He pulled his on and started the truck.

She noticed Jackie and several others watching them drive away. What were they thinking? She glanced sideways at Dillon. What was his reason for inviting her? She'd jumped at his invitation to avoid her family and the rehearsal dinner. She didn't know how to fit in at family settings.

"You're sure you don't mind me coming along?" Ruby wasn't

sure if this was a date or a friend thing.

"I wouldn't have asked you if I didn't want you to come with me." Dillon smiled at her and returned his attention to the road. "As quickly as you accepted, I had a feeling you didn't want to stick around."

"I know I'm a bridesmaid and should be laughing and having a good time at the rehearsal dinner, but I really didn't want to feel like the odd woman. I never do well in party environments. I don't drink, I don't dance, and I prefer to sit in a corner and not have to carry on a conversation." She'd never told anyone about her introvert self.

"That why you studied computers? To not have to deal with people?" Dillon glanced at her.

"I do spend seventy-five percent of my time dealing with computers and not people. But some of my work is talking people out of smashing their computers."

Dillon laughed. "I can see that. There's not a week goes by that mom or Aunt Dorothy don't want to throw something at the computer at work."

"Where's work?" She wanted to hear about him and not talk about her.

"My day job is helping at the Wallis Excavation Company. We rent out big equipment and do jobs for people. Garth's the mechanic, Nate drives the trucks that deliver the equipment, and I run equipment and help out at the shop. Pop and Uncle Allan help Garth and show people how to run the equipment they rent."

She studied him. "I didn't think your family would ever leave Tumbling Creek. It's so beautiful."

He shrugged. "Not all of us wanted to ride horses, round up cattle, and put up hay. In fact, Brett and Lacey are the only two who thrive on that. But it also wasn't sustaining both families. Brett bought Uncle Allan out and made the place a dude ranch. We all get to come back and help with events like this wedding and can stay there any time we want."

"Giving you the best of both worlds."

"I guess." He didn't sound like he had the life he wanted.

"What do you want? I don't think it's working for the excavation company the rest of your life." She sat a little sideways to study him better.

"I want to do more demo tapes and get my songs into the hands of the people who can get them to the public." He sighed. "But it takes me two months to save up enough to make a demo. I have to rent a studio and an audio technician. Then I have to send it out and wait for someone to hear it and believe it's good enough to sing."

"Do you play your originals when you're at a bar?" She tried to remember if he had sung something she didn't know last weekend.

"I can on nights like tonight when I'm singing just me and my guitar. But gigs like last weekend, with a band, I have to sing what they know." He pulled onto the highway and picked up speed.

"Have you tried to start up your own band and go on the road?" She didn't think she'd make a good roadie, but she'd be willing to help him when he was in the state of Montana where she could still get to work on Monday.

"I don't want to do the band thing. I don't want to be a lead singer. I want to write songs."

She put a hand on his arm. "If all your songs are as wonderful as the one you wrote for Jackie and Thad, we need to get your songs into the right hands."

He peered into her eyes. "You want to help me?"

"Don't sound surprised. The law firm I work for has some clients that are in the music business." She started ticking off the ones she remembered.

"You'd be willing to slip them a demo?" His gaze remained on the road as he put a hand on her leg. "I can't thank you enough for offering to help."

"I haven't done anything yet. When the wedding is over, you can give me some demos and I'll see what I can do."

Chapter Eight

Ruby was taken by the old-fashioned façade of Elkton. She loved it the second Dillon drove down the main street. When he parked in the lot next to the Elkton Inn, a large log building that looked as if it had been built when the area was first settled, she had goosebumps.

"I love this town," she said.

Dillon grinned and helped her out of his truck. "It's one of the oldest towns in the state and they are proud of their history."

"I can see why." She continued to gawk at the store fronts as he retrieved his guitar from the passenger side and captured her hand.

Dillon introduced her to the owner and the bartender then placed her at the end of the bar. She'd have a good view of the small stage where he would be playing.

Earl, the bartender, wiped the bar in front of her and placed a coaster down. "What'll you have?"

"Ginger Ale, please."

He pointed at her with his hand in the shape of a gun. "You got it, kid."

She giggled and watched Dillon tune his guitar.

By nine when he was to start playing the place was packed.

"Are there always this many people on a Friday night?" she asked.

"Nope. It's usually like this on Saturdays, but when Dillon is here, he packs 'em in."

That was good to know and something he needed to use… An idea came to her. "Is there a place where I can video him singing and still get some of the crowd?"

"Sure. Give me a minute."

She nodded and pulled out her phone. Good thing she had put it on the charger while she was working today. The first and second songs Dillon sang were from other artists.

He started talking about being a teenager and how he'd fallen for a girl in a higher grade. "And this is the song I wrote when she rejected me."

Ruby saw Earl was busy. The only way she could see to get a good video was to sit up on the bar where she would be above the other patrons. She did just that, even though for any other reason she would have been embarrassed to make such a spectacle of herself. She had the phone pointed at Dillon and videoed the whole song. He'd noticed her the second she'd sat up on the bar, but he only grinned and kept on singing.

When the song finished, Earl walked over to her before a couple of cowboys stumbling her way could reach her.

"Come on. The boss doesn't want you giving other people ideas." Earl waved her down and she followed him to a door that had a set of stairs. "Go up them stairs. You should be able to see and hear everything from a window. That was where the ladies of the evening stood when this place was a bar and brothel."

Her cheeks heated at the thought she'd be hanging out in a window like an old west prostitute. But if she could get good footage of Dillon playing his own songs that she could upload to the internet, that would get him the best attention and possibly noticed by the right people.

She went up the short set of steps and walked to the one window that wasn't covered. From this vantage point it appeared she was over the bar. There was enough noise down in the bar that no one heard the racket she made getting the old window to raise. She found a wooden chair in the corner of the room and brought it over to the window.

Dillon was just announcing another of his original songs. She turned on the video and enjoyed the song. The crowd went crazy when he finished. She made sure that was at the end. He sang two more standard bar songs and told the crowd he was taking a fifteen-minute break. She wasn't sure whether to stay here or meet him at the bar.

He must have spotted her because he motioned he'd come to her. She gave him a thumbs up and sat back, watching the people in the bar.

A few minutes later, Dillon walked through the door carrying two sodas.

"Thank you," she said, taking one from him.

"You hiding out from the drunks?" he asked, crouching next to her chair and looking out the window.

"No. I'm taking videos of your original songs. We can put them up on the internet and get followers and then, when you send in the demos, you can say, you have this many likes and followers. That's how singers get on a lot of the singing shows is by the followers they gain through the internet." She grinned.

He studied her. "That was quick thinking on your part. I especially liked you sitting on the bar. If that wasn't the hottest thing I've ever seen."

Her heart started racing. She wasn't sure whether she was upset by his comment or pleased.

He leaned close. "Can I kiss you?"

She gulped and peered into his eyes. "I-I guess so."

He grinned and brushed his lips across hers.

The hair stood up on her arms and her mind went numb. She'd only been kissed a couple of times over the years. Usually as a good-bye after a lousy date. This soft caress of lips turned her senses upside down.

Dillon stared into Ruby's eyes. He could see she was excited about the kiss but also trying to rationalize it. Before she decided it was a bad idea, he put a hand under her chin and held her lips up to his. He covered them, sealing her sweet mouth to his. As he'd presumed, she'd not kissed many men. He'd keep this kiss platonic. But the next one, he planned to show her what she was missing.

He leaned back. "I have to get back down there."

She nodded, her gaze still locked with his.

Dillon kissed her lips one more time chastely and stood. He walked out of the room with the stiffest hard-on he'd had in a long time. Walking down the stairs, he did his best to make it go away. No one needed to see him coming from the old brothel rooms with a bulge in his jeans.

***

By midnight, Dillon no longer caught sight of Ruby in the window. He took another break about twelve-thirty and wandered up to the room over the bar. She was asleep on the floor. He wished he had a coat to make her a pillow. Even though his fingers itched to touch her, he let her be. She'd worked hard all day and been up late the night before.

He finished out the night and at two, after putting his guitar in the truck, returned to the empty bar and woke Ruby.

"Ruby? Come on, angel, we need to get you back to the ranch."

She wiggled and wiped a hand across her face. She left a streak of dust.

Dillon put an arm around her shoulders and eased her to a sitting position. He thought about picking her up and carrying her out to the truck, but didn't want anyone getting the wrong idea, including her.

"Come on, sleepyhead, you need to wake up enough to walk to my truck." He kissed her cheek.

She smiled, and her eyelashes fluttered up. Her gaze took in the room. She started to shoot to her feet, but Dillon held her tight.

"Shh. It's okay. You fell asleep up here. Are you ready to go home?"

"What time is it?" She ran a hand through her hair, spiking it up.

"Close to two-thirty. We need to get going or your family will call out a search party." He eased her to her feet.

"They won't care. But Jackie will kill me if I'm not 'fresh as a daisy' for her wedding." Ruby took two steps toward the door and turned around. "My phone!"

He spotted the phone on the chair she'd used while filming. Dillon walked over, plucked it off the seat, and held it out to her.

Ruby tucked it into her back pocket and continued out the door.

Dillon followed behind, hoping she'd awakened enough to navigate the narrow stairs.

At the bottom Earl stood waiting. "I was beginning to think I'd have to charge you for the room." His eyes sparkled.

"Very funny!" Dillon slugged the larger man in the shoulder and directed Ruby out of the building and over to his truck.

The cold air seemed to awaken her. She stood straighter and her eyes were brighter.

"I can't believe I fell asleep on that floor." She brushed at the dust on her clothing.

"I can. You were up late the night before and worked hard all day."

She slipped into the middle of the seat, and he followed her.

Starting the truck, he said, "You can lean on me and sleep some more if you want." He liked the idea of Ruby leaning into him, maybe even entwining their arms.

"I don't want you falling asleep on the drive. I'll stay awake." She pulled out her phone. "I can see how good of a videoing job I did."

On the drive he heard the songs he'd written in a whole new way. He couldn't believe how well the music translated through the speakers on her phone. "What kind of phone is that?" he asked between songs as she messed with the screen.

She grinned. "One I've made some tweaks to. You and your songs sound wonderful. I'm sending these to my computer. That way I can make sure they are enhanced, and I put only the best videos up."

"What do you mean by tweaks?" Her intelligence intrigued him.

"A cell phone minus the actual calling part is a small computer. I've loaded only the fastest, best application to my phone to listen to music and make videos." Her head bent as she continued to move things around on her screen. "When I use the applications on my computer these will look like full blown music videos by a producer."

Dillon whistled. "You can really do that?"

She smiled at him. "Yes."

"You might just be my lucky charm." He kissed her cheek.

They turned onto the bumpy county road, and she shoved the phone into her pocket. "Thank you for asking me to go along. That's the first time I've had fun at a bar."

He grasped her hand. "It's the first time I've had someone sit on a bar to get my picture."

Ruby laughed. "I would have never done that if I hadn't been so focused on getting a good video of that song."

"That's what surprised me when I saw you up there. I knew that wasn't something you would have done if your mind hadn't been occupied." He sighed. "And you were one pretty picture sitting up there." He had to let that image go or have a bulge in his pants when he left her off at the ranch.

She leaned her head on his shoulder. "No one has ever told me I'm pretty and you've told me that twice tonight."

He couldn't believe no one had seen the beauty he saw even when she wasn't wearing makeup. "You're kidding me? Didn't your mom or dad tell you that when you were growing up?"

"No. The boys were handsome and strong. I was smart. They always called me smart, never pretty." She sighed. "At the time I didn't care. I wanted to best them with what I had and that was brains. But now, as an adult. It's nice to have kind words said that doesn't have anything to do with my mind."

Her head resting on his shoulder made him happier than any woman he'd ever kissed. There was something about her that set real well with him.

"At work my co-workers, men and women, never say nice blouse or I like your hair. Even after I had my hair cut and went to work, no one said anything. I figured at least the receptionist would say something but it's as if I'm invisible."

"Do you think it's because you have been trying so hard to make yourself invisible that people are ignoring you?" He knew his suggestion might upset her, but from the short time he'd been with her, she seemed to prefer not to be seen, but at the same time she was human and craved some positive reinforcement.

She snuggled her head against his shoulder. Where their hands were still clasped, she rubbed her thumb across his knuckles. "Yes, it's probably my fault. I have preferred to be in the background and let others shine."

"When do you want to shine?" he asked, raising their clasped hands and kissing her fingers.

"When we get your songs noticed."

He wasn't going to let her get away. That first night she'd drawn him in with her innocence, and now he couldn't wait to show her life was full of wonderful things.

Chapter Nine

Knocking on the bedroom door woke Ruby. She glanced down at her dusty clothes and rolled off the bed. The mess on the quilt made her feel ill. "I should have at least stripped to my underwear." She groaned, and the door opened.

"What are you doing still in those clothes? And why are you so dirty?" Jackie entered the bedroom, her brows drawn together in a frown.

"I fell asleep in a room above the bar. And now I've transferred all the dust to the quilt." She brushed at the fabric, trying to clean the cover.

"Forget that. You need to shower and get over to my mom's cabin. That's where we're all dressing and doing our hair." Jackie picked up Ruby's toiletry bag and robe, shoving her out the door.

Ruby hurried down the hall to one of the bathrooms. She scrubbed and washed her hair. Pulling on her robe, she gathered all her dirty clothes and her small bag. One step out of the bathroom and she stopped.

Nate stood at the end of the hall, knocking on her door.

Before she made up her mind to duck back into the bathroom, he noticed her.

"Ruby, look at you looking fresh as a daisy." He advanced on her, stopping within arm's reach.

"I'm sorry, I have to hurry, Jackie and everyone are waiting for me at Cassandra's cabin." She didn't like standing in front of this man with only a robe.

His gaze tended to roam, and there it went to the V of skin between her breasts, left by her gapping robe. She grabbed the front, closing the gap and shifted to walk around him.

He put out an arm. "You are going to dance with me at the reception. I'd love to hold you in my arms."

His dark eyes turned to dollops of chocolate. She'd never seen the likes in a man before. His intense gaze had her stomach fluttering. Maybe he was still her soulmate, she just had to be around him a little more.

"If I promise you a dance will you let me go?"

His grin widened. "I'll take that to mean you'll dance with me. I'll be the luckiest man at the wedding." He stepped aside.

Ruby headed to her room, dumped off her dirty clothes, stepped into her underclothes, and picked up the box holding her bridesmaid dress and shoes.

She found the cabin where the bride and bridesmaids were dressing. Giggles and women flowed in and out of the small building. She started to walk toward the building when a voice called out.

"There you are! We were beginning to think you hadn't returned last night," her mother said by way of a greeting.

She stopped and stared at her mother. "What do you mean by that?"

"Well, you leave your cousin's rehearsal dinner to go with a man you barely know, and you've made yourself all up, like a woman on the hunt for a man."

Her mother's words hit her as physically as if the woman had raised a hand and slapped her.

"Just because I cut my hair and Arleen is heavy-handed with the makeup, doesn't mean I'm sleeping around. You raised me. I am your daughter."

"I didn't raise you the last two years of high school or college. Who knows what loose morals you picked up?" The expression on her mother's face said she meant every word.

Tears burned and started down her cheeks. "Well, now I'm glad I lived with people who showed me kindness." She pushed the cabin door open, dropped her box on the nearest piece of furniture, and went straight to a chair in the corner. Ruby dropped her face into her hands and tried to pull herself together. This was Jackie's big day. She didn't want to bring any sorrow to her cousin. She was the one family member who had always been there and cared about her.

"What's wrong?" Arleen asked, crouching in front of the chair.

"Nothing. I'll get it together in a minute." She didn't uncover her face.

"Too much to drink last night?" Arleen questioned.

"No. All I had was soda." She drew in a deep breath, scrubbed the tears from her face, and peered at Arleen. "Did you know that Dillon is a song writer? He played half a dozen songs that he wrote last night, and the crowd loved them."

"Really? All I know is that Jackie hasn't stopped raving about the wedding song he wrote. Come on, we'll start with your hair."

Ruby stood and followed Arleen into the bathroom. She spotted Jackie being dolled up by her mother. A pang of sorrow pierced her heart. It wouldn't be her mother helping her on her wedding day. It would probably be Aunt Cassandra.

***

Dillon arrived earlier than he'd been instructed to arrive. He couldn't wait to see Ruby. He knew she would outshine the bride.

On his way into the main house he noticed Mrs. Cutter deep in discussion with her husband. He wondered what that was all about but had another Cutter woman on his mind. The male family members not in the bridal party were sitting around in the dining room. He spotted Ruby's brother Rich at a table with a woman and two children.

"Hi Rich." Dillon held out his hand. He wanted to make sure he was in good with the Cutter family. He'd like to keep Ruby in his life.

The man held out his hand, but it was plain he didn't have a clue who Dillon was.

"Dillon Wallis. We went to school together," he said, to help the man's memory.

"The one who kept Ruby from the dinner last night and didn't get her home until early this morning?" Rich stood. He was six-foot-four and broad as a barn.

"Hey, I don't know why you're going Neanderthal on me. Jackie told her to come with me, and I had Ruby back here when I told Jackie

308

I would." He wasn't going to fight the man, but he wasn't going to be treated like someone who was irresponsible. That was Nate.

As if he'd conjured up his cousin, Nate walked into the dining room.

Dillon met him halfway. "Any idea what our jobs are today?"

Nate narrowed his eyes. "Stick to your singing and stay out of my way with Ruby."

He should have known Nate would have put his sights on Ruby after the attention he'd paid her yesterday and the woman went to Elkton with Dillon.

"Don't use Ruby the way you have all the other women. She isn't experienced and will get hurt." He didn't know why he was saying this. His cousin had never listened to a word anyone told him about women. And telling him she was off limits would only make her more attractive to his need to conquer.

Nate grinned. "She already told me she'd dance with me at the reception." He put a hand out, shoving Dillon's shoulder out of his way as he walked by.

He didn't need all this grief. Dillon strode out of the dining room and over to the kitchen door. Melanie and his mom were busy getting the food for the reception plated.

"Where's Brett or Garth?" he asked.

"They should be down by the barn, parking the guests." Melanie glanced at him. "You look like you lost your best friend. Didn't last night go well?"

He walked over and hugged Melanie and then his mother. "Last night was great. It's the accusations I'm getting this morning that are getting me down."

"Anything we can help you with?" his mom asked.

"I'm not sure. What do you know about the Cutters?" He picked up a carrot from the vegetable plate his mom was putting together.

"Mr. Cutter's job transferred him out of here after the boys were out of school and Ruby stayed. Before that they seemed to put all their efforts into the boys. They live not far from the youngest one, I've heard." Mom put a hand on his cheek. "If she's the one, don't let her family be a problem. We have enough love around here to share." She winked at Melanie and gave her a one-armed hug.

"From what Ruby said and now the way Rich treated me, they

aren't a close family, but they seem to think the worst of Ruby. Which I don't understand. She is the sweetest, purest woman I've encountered." He also didn't like the way Nate was after her. "And Nate seems to have made her a crusade."

Mom shuddered. "We won't let that happen. He's hurt too many girls and women with his amorous ways."

"Thanks. You cheered me up. I'm going to see if I can help park cars." He picked up another carrot stick.

"I'm looking forward to hearing you sing. Jackie hasn't stopped talking about it." Melanie handed him a cupcake as he walked by.

"Thanks, sis." He kissed her cheek and headed to the pasture below the barn. It was where the cars parked during an event in the barn.

On his way, he noticed all the activity around cabin number two. He found his feet carrying him that direction before he realized it. A quick chat with Ruby to make sure she remembered her promise to dance with him seemed like a good reason to see her.

"Where do you think you're going?" a woman he hadn't met yet asked as he walked up to the cabin door.

"I'd like to speak with Ruby."

The woman looked him up and down. "Are you the one she stayed out all night with?"

He didn't know who she was and didn't think she needed any information from him.

"I'm a friend."

"How many male friends does she have?" The woman seemed overly excited.

"I'm assuming any man she meets, because she is a sweet woman."

"I knew it! I knew it! She denied it, but my daughter sleeps around."

Dillon had no idea where this came from but figured out this was Mrs. Cutter. "I'm pretty sure, Ma'am, that your daughter doesn't sleep around."

The door opened, and he'd never been so happy to see Arleen. "Could you let Ruby know I'd like to talk with her a minute?"

"Sure thing." The young woman disappeared.

Ruby stepped out the door and frowned when she spotted her

mother.

"Can you go for a short walk?" He liked the pretty violet dress she wore.

"I can't go very far in these shoes." She raised one of her feet.

"I promise to stay on the path." He held out his arm and she slipped her hand through his crooked elbow.

He ignored the woman standing by the cabin with a pinched expression. "You look lovely," he said, when they were far enough away the woman couldn't hear his words.

"Thank you. This dress is gorgeous."

He stopped at the last cabin and faced her. "You make the dress gorgeous." He meant what he said. He'd never seen a lovelier sight.

A blush rose up her neck.

"How's it going?" He didn't think now was the time to mention her brother or her mother's accusations.

The happiness dulled in her eyes. "It's been a trying morning. But I'm looking forward to the wedding to hear you sing and the reception to dance with you."

"You just made my day," he said, wanting to lean forward and kiss her, but he restrained.

"I might have to dance once with Nate. He cornered me upstairs when I was coming from the bathroom and the only way I could get rid of him was to promise him a dance."

"He stopped you in the hall and coerced a dance from you?" He didn't realize his cousin would stoop that low.

Her blush bloomed to her cheeks. "If I had had on more than my robe, I would have never given in. But I just wanted to get to my room."

Anger burned in his chest. He'd have a word or two with his cousin. "If he made you uncomfortable to get you to dance with him, he doesn't deserve a dance."

"But I promised." She glanced over his shoulder and then back to his eyes.

"That isn't a promise you have to keep, and I'll see to it." He saw movement out of the corner of his eye.

Mrs. Cutter was striding this way. "What does she want?" he muttered.

"Probably wants to humiliate me some more." She kissed his

cheek. "I'm looking forward to hearing your song again." Ruby strode by her mother and down the path to cabin two.

The woman stopped in front of him. "You think you can fool me by being all proper while I'm watching. I learned you are the man who kept her out nearly all night."

"Mrs. Cutter, you need to get your facts straight. I'm not going to defend myself or Ruby to you. You and your son seem to have your minds made up and I'll not be a part of your witch hunt." He walked by the woman and headed to the parking area. There he would find agreeable company—his brothers.

Chapter Ten

Ruby was pleased to see Dillon sitting off to the side of the groomsmen when she walked down the aisle toward the altar. Her fears were chased away by his smile and nod.

When Jackie and Thad held hands and exchanged vows, she allowed her gaze to travel to Dillon. He locked gazes with her. She didn't hear anything the bride and groom said. Her senses were concentrated on the man beyond them.

Dillon moved, walking up to stand between the couple. He strummed the guitar and soon his warm voice surged through the speakers as he sang the song written for the bride and groom.

Ruby couldn't take her eyes off him as he painted pictures with the music and lyrics he fused together.

His voice died in the openness of the barn rafters. Sniffing and shuffling could be heard before Dillon walked back to his place and the preacher pronounced Jackie and Thad husband and wife.

She moved to the middle and walked beside Brian, following the bride and groom to the front of the barn. They stood in the processional line while the guests filed by, expressing their congratulations to the couple.

Ruby scanned the barn looking for Dillon. His presence had become important to her. He understood her better than anyone she'd ever had in her life.

"Hey, gorgeous. How about you come with me to check out the hay loft?" Nate asked, catching her from behind.

"Get your hands off me!" she said, batting at his hands.

"Is this your boyfriend?" Brian asked.

"No!" Ruby didn't like the way Nate's fingers had moved up to her ribs and too close to her breasts for her liking. She stomped on his toes with her pointy-heeled shoe.

"Hey!" He released her and hopped on one foot.

"Keep your hands off me," she said, not caring if she made a scene. He might have been her infatuation through high school and beyond, but she didn't like the man he'd grown into.

"See, I told you she lets men grope her." Her mother said to her father. They both stood in front of her, disapproval etched on their faces.

It shouldn't have surprised her that Nate took that moment to disappear.

"Mother, Father, will you be staying the night?" she asked.

"We haven't decided," her father said, looking at her as if she were a hooker on a street corner.

She'd forgotten how prejudiced her parents were to anything they deemed unsuitable. It all came back to her why she had wanted to stay in Duncan for her last two years of high school and never visited her family.

"You'll need to make up your minds soon enough that Melanie can get a room ready for you." She turned her attention to Dorothy Wallis who waited patiently behind her parents.

"You look beautiful in that dress, dear," Mrs. Wallis said, loud enough for her parents to hear as they congratulated Jackie.

"Thank you." She hugged the woman. "Could you please tell your son I'm not interested in him. He keeps making a spectacle."

"I'm sorry. Nate's always been competitive when it came to his cousins." Mrs. Wallis shrugged and moved along the line.

Ruby wondered what the woman meant by her comment.

Mr. Wallis, Dorothy's husband, gave her a hug and complimented her.

Next came Dillon's parents.

"You look beautiful in that color," Carolyn Wallis said.

"Thank you."

"I can see why my son's taken a shine to you," Mr. Wallis said.

Before she could ask what he meant, Garth gave her a hug and a wink. She didn't know what that was about and continued nodding at the people passing by to get to the bride and groom.

She looked down the line and spotted Dillon at the end.

Within minutes, he stood in front of her and grasped her hand. "Come on."

He led her by the others still chatting in line and out into the wonderful summer sunshine.

"Where are we going? These heels sink in the ground." She reached down to remove her shoes.

"Leave them on. We're only taking the long way into the reception."

His words stopped her enthusiasm. She thought he was going to take her on a walk. "Oh."

"Did I say something wrong?" He faced her.

"I thought we were taking a walk or petting horses. Anything but going into the reception." She hated that she wanted to avoid her family. But their comments and actions proved she was better off without them.

"I can understand you want to stay away from your family, but it's Jackie's wedding, she's your family, and she loves you. You can't let her down." Dillon put a hand under her chin and caressed her cheek with his thumb. "Show your family you aren't what they think."

"How can I do that when Nate grabs me in front of everyone."

"He what?" Dillon dropped his hand from her chin as his fingers curled into a fist.

"Right before my parents appeared in front of me, he grabbed me around the waist and his hands slid…" Her cheeks darkened.

"I'll rip his head off!" Dillon stalked away from her, then back. He had to get his temper under control. His cousin would get what was coming to him when Ruby wasn't around.

"Dillon, no! I stomped on his toes with these pointy heels." She put a hand on his shoulder and raised her foot behind her, showing him the heel. "I don't think he'll be doing much dancing this afternoon."

He glanced down at her shoe, then scanned her bare leg. Raising his gaze to her face, the dimple that drove him crazy winked at him as she tried not to smile. He'd dreamed about kissing that dimple last night along with discovering if she had any dimples anywhere else on her body.

"Let's go mingle." He grasped her hand and led her to the house. The large dining room doors were wide open to allow guests to mingle back and forth between the great room and the dining room.

Ruby pulled back when he started into the dining room. He spotted her family in a cluster by the punch and spun around, leading her over to the fireplace in the great room.

"You sit here. I'll bring you something to eat and drink. I want you fortified when we dance." He squeezed her hand and peered into her eyes. The gratitude shining there made him wish he could do something else to ease her troubles.

On his way to the punch, he asked Garth to keep Nate away from Ruby. She didn't need him giving her any more grief with her parents.

With two cups of punch and two plates loaded with everything, he maneuvered around the other guests. He'd kept an eye on Ruby from across the two rooms, making sure no one was bothering her.

Nearing the fireplace, he glanced up and his heart lurched. Patsy Boyle was sitting with Ruby. He'd dated Patsy for several years in high school. After graduation she went off to beauty school and came back hotter than when she'd left and looking for trouble. She got it after hooking up with Nate and several others. But she'd named Dillon the father of her baby when they hadn't even slept together after she came back. He'd had to force her to do paternity tests to prove he wasn't the father and didn't have to provide child support.

He'd also had to prove to his family he wasn't shirking his duty as a father.

"Dillon, how sweet of you to bring me something." Patsy reached toward the drinks.

"These aren't for you. Ruby, I think we'll be more comfortable over there." He pointed to a low table with foot stools beside it.

"I should have known you'd pick up any new pretty girl that came along. All you Wallises are alike," Patsy said, loud enough to gain the attention of half of the room.

Ruby sank down on a footstool and relieved him of a cup and plate. "What was all of that about?"

Dillon didn't even look back to see if the woman was telling her story or not. "We dated in high school. She went away. When she came back, she became pregnant and named me as the father."

Ruby shook her head. "But you weren't."

"No, I wasn't. I had to pay for paternity tests to prove I didn't need to support the baby." He glanced at Ruby. "It was mainly for me, I needed to prove I wasn't a deadbeat dad."

"You would never be a bad dad. You've had good role models. Parents who would have stood behind you no matter what."

He saw the minute her words sunk in.

"But it's different with my family. They don't believe me, and they only care how my actions affect them, not me." She glanced over where her family was huddled around a table. "You know, this is sad, but I have never once missed them. Not in high school when I stayed here or in college or even now. I've not gone home for any holidays or birthdays. I don't feel welcome with my own family." She nodded toward his parents. "I would go home for the holidays if they were my parents."

"Yeah, I was lucky when they passed out parents." He bumped his knee to hers. "I'll lend them to you."

She laughed, and that dangerous dimple knocked the wind out of him.

Chapter Eleven

Ruby had never had as much fun at a function as she'd had today. The reception had moved back to the barn for dancing. Swaying in Dillon's arms to a slow dance, she placed her head on his shoulder and didn't worry about where her feet were or if she looked awkward. Dillon had eased her nerves about dancing and kept her laughing most of the evening.

"Having a good time?" he asked.

"Yes."

"Good. When do you go back to Bozeman?"

She raised her head and peered into his eyes. "Tomorrow afternoon."

"I'll spend the night at the ranch. We can go for a horse ride tomorrow morning."

The idea swelled her heart. "It's been a long time since I've been on a horse."

"It's just like riding a bike, they say."

Laughter bubbled up her throat.

"I think it's about time I had my dance." Nate's voice cut off her laughter.

"Ruby, do you want to dance with Nate?" Dillon asked, not stopping their swaying bodies.

She peered into the eyes of the man she had believed was her soulmate. "No. I don't dance with men who don't respect a woman's space."

Dillon swirled her away from Nate and across the dance floor toward Jackie and Thad.

"That was rude," she said, without any remorse.

He laughed. "Only to Nate. He hasn't treated you properly and doesn't deserve to dance with you."

"You two look like you're having fun," Jackie said as Dillon stopped them in front of her.

"Keep Nate away from Ruby. He isn't playing nice. I have to visit the little boy's room." Dillon gave her hand a squeezed before releasing her.

"What does he mean by that?" Thad asked.

Jackie jumped in. "Didn't you see how Nate grabbed Ruby in the reception line? And everyone was talking about his obnoxious behavior." Jackie linked her arm with Ruby. "We'll make sure he doesn't take off with you." She peered into Ruby's eyes. "That is if you do like hanging out with Dillon."

She knew her cousin was fishing for information. "I do like him. He's considerate and fun. I videoed him singing at the bar last night and plan to upload it to the internet to help get his songs noticed."

"It sounds like you two are a good fit." Jackie grinned and hugged her arm.

"It's time to cut the cake," Jackie's mom said, waving the bride and groom to follow her.

"Come with us," Jackie said, not releasing Ruby's arm.

"I can't be in the middle of your cake cutting." She scanned the room. "I'll go stand with Mrs. Wallis."

"Ok, but if Nate comes near you, you scream, and I'll come running." Jackie took off her shoe. "These heels are deadly."

"Jackie!" Cassandra called.

Ruby pushed her cousin toward the groom and the three-tiered cake.

She pivoted to walk over to Mrs. Wallis and nearly bumped her nose into Nate's chin. Before she could step backwards, he grabbed her arms.

"You promised me a dance this morning."

"You know I would have said anything to get you to leave." She jerked her arm loose.

"What do I have to do to get you to dance with me?" Nate started to put a hand on her arm.

"Stop touching me and acting like I'm a possession you can do whatever you want with." She crossed her arms and wished Dillon would return.

"Touching is a sign of interest." He leaned forward. "And I'm interested in everything about you."

She took a step back. "No, you aren't. If you were interested in me, you would treat me with respect. You get in my space, you touch me, and you haven't even asked me what I do or where I live."

"I don't have to know that to be interested." His gaze drifted down to her feet and back up to her face.

"With me, you do." She spun away and spotted Dillon making his way around the edge of the crowd. They met close to the cake table.

"What happened to your body guards?" he asked, glaring in the direction of Nate.

"They had to cut the cake." Ruby nodded toward the table with plates of cake. "Let's get some and go sit down by the creek."

"That's a good idea." Dillon picked up two pieces.

She grabbed two plastic forks and napkins and followed him out of the barn. The evening was cooling down but after the dancing and all the bodies in the barn, the fresh air was welcome.

Dillon walked through the small meadow to a downed log next to the creek. Kool ran ahead of them to the creek, lapped the water, and headed back to the barn. Dillon waited for Ruby to sit before handing over a piece of cake.

"This is so peaceful," she said.

"I've written quite a few songs sitting alongside this creek, but farther up, by the waterfall. That's where I want to take you on our ride tomorrow." He forked cake into his mouth.

"That sounds wonderful. I'd love to see where you compose songs." She stared into the bubbling water. "I have a confession to make." It had been gnawing at her since seeing how angry Dillon was with Nate earlier.

"I'm not a priest." His eyes crinkled at the edges from his grin.

"Not that kind of confession." She thought a minute. "Well,

maybe kind of."

He set the cake plate on his lap and shifted to face her. "What do you mean? You don't have a boyfriend you've neglected to tell me about? A husband? A child?" His brow furrowed.

"No. Nothing like that. The reason I stayed at Duncan High when my family left was because I was in love with Nate." She studied Dillon.

His eyes twinkled, and he picked the cake back up. "Is that it? Every girl in high school was in love with Nate."

"But I saw his naked butt in P.E. and knew we were soulmates." She had to make him understand she'd come to this wedding in hopes of having Nate for her boyfriend.

Dillon spit out cake and laughed so hard his eyes watered. "You fell in love with his ass?"
He stopped laughing. "That makes sense. He is an ass."

"It's not funny. Ever since my sophomore year I've been in love with Nate. I've dreamed about him and wanted him to see me for who I am. I went along with Jackie and Arleen's plans for the makeover in hopes of catching his attention and spending the whole weekend with him." She peered into Dillon's eyes as he stared at her.

"Are you telling me, you'd like me to take you back to the barn because you want to dance with Nate?" Dillon stood.

"No. I'm telling you this because…" She didn't want to tell Dillon she had feelings for him. They lived miles apart and she wasn't sure how he felt. "Because, you've become my friend and I want you to know the truth. I lusted after your cousin from afar."

Dillon studied Ruby. She really thought he needed to know she had pubescent lust for his cousin. He knew from his cousin's actions this weekend he'd burst her teenaged fantasy.

"And you told me about Patsy and I thought I needed to tell you about my…past." Her blue eyes were wide and held sincerity and relief. "Because that's what friends do."

He set his cake plate down and grasped her hand. "I have more in my past than you'll ever be able to match. All you have to do is listen to my songs to learn about it."

She gave a small nod. He wasn't sure if the nod was to acknowledge he'd led a more promiscuous life or that she'd listen to his songs.

"I'm willing to start with us being friends. But down the road, I'll be a mite happier if we become a couple." He raised the hand he held, placing a brief kiss on the back of her hand.

"I'd like that, too." Her eyes had darkened.

He saw the fire of a woman he'd like to undress and pleasure.

"Shall we go back and throw bird seed at the happy couple?" He rose and drew her up alongside of him.

"Wouldn't want the birds to go hungry." Her eyes sparkled like the tumbling creek beside her.

"No, we wouldn't."

They arrived in time to be handed a small scoop of birdseed. Everyone was lined up along the path from the main house to the driveway. Thad's SUV sat waiting for them to drive off. Streamers and cans were tied to the vehicle and *Just Married* was written across the back window.

"Here they come!" shouted Arleen.

Jackie and Thad dashed by the line as birdseed pelted them. Jackie stopped long enough to hug Ruby and said something in her ear. Ruby nodded, and Jackie sent Dillon a grin before dashing to the SUV and driving off.

"What did she say to you?" Dillon asked.

Ruby smiled. "I'll tell you when the time is right."

He could tell it was something that made her happy and that's all that mattered to him.

"Dillon, time to get to work," Brett said, walking up beside them. "People are leaving. We need to get the sound equipment packed up and the barn cleaned."

"I'll go change and I can help," Ruby volunteered.

"You're a guest. There's no need for you to help," Brett said.

"I'd rather help than have nothing to do." Ruby released Dillon's hand. "I'll be down there in ten."

He grinned and slapped Brett on the back as Ruby hurried into the house. "She'll be down here in five. It doesn't take her long to throw on work clothes."

Brett gave him a sideways glance. "You and Ruby have been spending a lot of time together."

"Yeah, we've become friends." Dillon spotted Nate by the barn. "And Nate needs to learn to keep his hands off her. She doesn't like it."

"I can have a talk with him," Brett offered.

"Like that's going to do any good. Just give him a job that keeps him away from the sound equipment and Ruby."

Brett nodded as they entered the barn.

Garth, their dad, their uncle, and Nate were all busy pulling down decorations and putting tables and chairs back in the storage rooms.

Dillon unplugged cords and packed speakers to the door.

Ruby entered the barn, her makeup washed off, wearing a pair of jeans and a t-shirt.

This Ruby was more fetching to him than the dolled-up one. She immediately began rolling up the cords and stacking them by the speakers.

They didn't speak, just exchanged glances as they worked. When everything was at the door, he grabbed her hand. "We need to go get my pickup."

She didn't say a word, falling in step beside him. His truck was parked at the far end of the field to allow the older people attending the wedding to not have to walk so far.

Moonlight lit their way across the packed grass field. It was a good thing grass bounced back this time of year.

Ruby stopped in the middle of the field and released his hand. "This is so beautiful. The moonlight on the mountain tops over there, the dusting of light on the trees by the creek." She faced him. "This place has always been one of my favorite places to come."

His heart stuttered. Had Nate been more than an infatuation? Had he brought her here? "When have you been here before?"

"In school. It seemed like every time there was a school picnic it happened here on the Tumbling Creek."

He grinned, remembering his classes and his brothers' classes that had come here for picnics. He'd forgotten all about how much this ranch had meant to the community when he was growing up. "I'd forgotten about those. When did you come out here?"

"I think in fourth grade and then in high school." Her happiness faded.

"That would be the junior class excursion." He remembered kissing Patsy up by the waterfall. He'd make a new, better memory up there tomorrow.

"Yeah. That sounds about right." She continued walking.

"I take it that doesn't have pleasant memories for you?" He caught up to her, capturing her hand.

"The only pleasant memory was visiting with your aunt. She made me forget the taunting I'd received."

Dillon put his arm around her shoulders, hugging her close. "Kids can be cruel."

She leaned her head on his shoulder. "Yeah."

They walked this way to his truck. He opened the driver's side and she slid in.

He climbed in, twisted to face her, and grasped her chin. "Don't let things in your past ruin your future." Staring into her eyes, he couldn't stop the downward motion of his lips.

He brushed his mouth against hers, heard her sigh, and deepened the kiss. He captured her lips under his, brushing his tongue along the seam.

She gasped and her lips parted. It was the invitation he'd been waiting for. His tongue delved into her sweet warm mouth. He felt her hesitation at his entry.

Easing back, releasing her mouth, he stared into her eyes. He saw excitement sparking in their depths as she licked her lips.

"Do you want to continue?" he asked.

She nodded.

He placed a hand at the back of her head and settled his mouth over hers again. Since his first kiss in high school, he'd never had the pleasure of introducing a woman to the joy of kissing. His heart beat against his chest like the ringing of a huge church bell. He wanted the kiss to introduce Ruby to the intimacy, but his body wanted more.

Chapter Twelve

Ruby's heart raced as if she'd been scared out of her wits. The caress of Dillon's lips and tongue made her body ignite like a hot circuit board. Her body wiggled closer to him. His hand, holding her head, was gentle. His other arm came around her, drawing her body against his. His strength added another thrilling nuance to the kiss.

Now she knew what her friends meant when they'd talked about a good kisser. Everywhere Dillon touched her, her body came alive. Her sensitive skin heated and pressed to him.

His hand on her back, moved up and down, pooling heat down low in her body. She moaned.

Dillon released her lips and pressed his forehead to hers. "Angel, you don't know how sexy you are." He kissed the tip of her nose and released her.

"I've never…" How did you tell a man who'd just kissed you breathless that it had been your first real kiss?

"Me either." He started the truck. "You're the first woman to make me forget where I'm at when I kiss you." He put his arm across the back of the seat. His fingers traced a circle on her neck. "We need to get the sound equipment loaded and you tucked away in your room."

She had a feeling that if she'd been kissing Nate like that he would have taken her on the truck seat. Ruby leaned her head against Dillon's shoulder. He was the perfect man.

At the barn everything was cleaned up and put away. Nate stood by the sound equipment, a scowl on his face. "Where have you two been? It doesn't take that long to get a truck."

"Ruby stopped to watch the stars," Dillon said, slipping out of the truck. He grasped her hand, easing her out. "Why don't you go on in? Nate's here. He can help me load the truck."

She was reluctant to have this be the way the night ended, but she liked the idea of staying away from Nate. She kissed Dillon's cheek and headed to the main house. Her footsteps felt lighter, her heart tap danced in her chest. If she hadn't thought she was falling in love with Dillon before, the last thirty minutes confirmed it.

Ruby entered the main house and found Arleen and the groomsmen in the great room visiting. She wandered over to the small group.

"We were just talking about going for a ride tomorrow morning before we leave. Do you want to go?" Arleen asked.

Heat rose up her neck. "I already have a ride planned."

Arleen's eyes lit up. "You do? On a horse or…" she glanced over at the men.

Now Ruby's ears burned. "On a horse. Dillon invited me."

"You and Dillon seem to be getting along quite well." Arleen leaned closer. "Any details?"

"No details. We're friends. I'm going up to my room. I have videos to clean up." She left the room, her face still warm. The men had been watching her as intently as Arleen.

In her room, she put on her pajamas, crawled into bed, and pulled her computer onto her lap. Cleaning up the videos of Dillon singing wasn't a hardship. She enjoyed listening to his voice, but this time she also listened closely to the words, since he said his songs were his story. There were only six songs on her phone and now computer. They were but a fraction of his life. His songs reflected a slow pace, family, and sorrows when it came to love.

She never wanted him to write a song of sorrow about them.

***

Dillon jumped in the back of his truck. "Start handing me the speakers," he said to Nate.

His cousin grudgingly handed him a speaker. "I don't understand why Ruby is pushing me away."

Dillon grabbed the speaker and stared at Nate. "Dude, you are not God's gift to every woman. Ruby has barely dated. You come on too strong and scare her. Not every woman likes a man who treats them like property."

Nate glared at him. "That's the same thing she said."

"Then I guess you need to think about it if two people are telling you the same thing." Dillon took the next speaker out of his hands. He hoped Nate didn't change his tactics with Ruby. Given what she'd told him about believing Nate was her soulmate, if he started treating her better, she might decide she'd been right all along. That thought soured his stomach.

They finished loading the truck and Dillon tarped it while Nate wandered off to his truck to head home.

When Nate's truck disappeared down the road, Dillon headed to the main house to find out where he could bunk for the night. He found Brett and Melanie in the kitchen doing the last of the dishes. Kool lay on the floor by the back door.

"I thought you'd left. I saw Ruby go up the stairs a while ago," Brett said.

"Nate and I loaded up the sound equipment. Any chance I can sleep here tonight? I'd like to take Ruby on a horseback ride tomorrow morning before she leaves." He picked up a cookie from a plate sitting on the work station.

Melanie stopped washing a bowl and faced him. "Taking her on a horseback ride on your childhood stomping grounds. Is this getting serious?"

He shrugged. "I can't say from her side of things, but I'm thinking she's the one."

Melanie took the three steps between them and hugged him. "She's a wonderful woman. I hope she sees you're a great catch."

Brett slapped him on the back. "It's about time you found someone to help you get your dream."

"Thanks, but this could be premature." He didn't want to get his hopes up, but her taping him singing and the kisses they'd shared out in his truck, had his heart doing cartwheels.

"You can sleep in cabin four. It's not cleaned up, but I can give you fresh sheets," Melanie said, moving to the door that led to the office, supply room, and the room where their hired help stayed.

"I appreciate this. I'll clean the room before I leave tomorrow. It's the least I can do." Dillon caught his brother watching him.

"What horse were you planning to put her on? The bridal party want to go for a ride tomorrow morning."

"I thought I'd use mom's old horse."

Brett nodded. "And did you plan to go up to the waterfall by the Indian drawings?"

"Yeah."

"I'll keep my ride down lower then. Wouldn't want to interrupt anything." Brett slugged him in the shoulder as Melanie entered the room with sheets.

"Thank you, both of you." Dillon didn't know what he'd do without his family. It saddened him to think Ruby was so alone.

"Enjoy your ride tomorrow." Melanie said as Brett rubbed her back.

***

Ruby dressed in jeans, a t-shirt, and her sneakers. She didn't own a pair of riding boots. Then she packed her bag and boxed her bridesmaid gown and shoes. Everything was packed and sitting by the door when she went down to breakfast at seven.

The only person sitting in the dining room was Dillon. She grabbed a cup of coffee and sat down across from him. She'd replayed their kiss many times while falling asleep last night. Every time she'd had the same warm all over sensations and her heart sped up. Now, staring across the table into his eyes, she couldn't have been happier.

"You're up early," he said, picking up his mug and sipping.

"I could say the same for you."

They locked gazes over the rim of their cups.

The kitchen door opened.

Melanie rolled out a cart filled with breakfast foods. "It looks like you two want to get an early start on your ride." She handed them each a plate and waited for them to pick the foods they wanted from the cart.

"Thank you. How do you do all of this cooking and keep up these hours? It looks like you're going to have that baby any day," Ruby said.

"I love to cook. Making meals is a joy even though my husband keeps telling me to slow down and let our new help learn some of the kitchen work." Melanie placed the platters of food on the sideboard. "Enjoy your ride."

"We will," Dillon said, digging into his food.

Ruby hesitated to take a bite. "How does she know about our ride?"

"I was talking to her and Brett last night when I asked them where I could sleep." Dillon studied her. "It wasn't a secret."

"No. I wondered how she found out. I guess Arleen, Mack, and Brian are going riding today, too. Do you think we'll run into them?" She didn't want her last hours with Dillon spoiled by other people being with them.

"I told Brett where I planned for us to ride. He'll keep the others away." He grinned at her. "I don't want anything to interrupt our time together."

She sent him a reciprocating grin. "That's how I feel."

"Eat up, so we can get going."

Ruby began eating and not talking. There would be plenty of time to talk when they were riding. She finished, picked up both their plates, and put them in the tub for dirty dishes. She dropped a napkin. Picking up the napkin her sneakers came into view. "Will I be able to ride with these shoes?"

Dillon walked up beside her. "What size shoe do you wear?"

"Eight." She wiggled her toes inside her shoes.

"Come to the back porch." Dillon led her into the kitchen.

"Do you need more food?" Melanie asked.

"No, Ruby needs boots. I think mom's will fit her." Dillon continued to a door at the back of the kitchen. This opened onto an enclosed porch. There was a row of cowboy boots along the wall. He picked up a dark brown, worn pair. "Try these."

She slipped off her sneaker and slid her foot into the leather boot. "I don't think it's big enough."

"Grab those ears on the sides and shove your foot down as you pull up on those. A boot needs to fit snug. That way you don't get blisters from it rubbing."

She did what he said, forcing her foot into the boot. And sure enough, once she made it past the curve, her foot fit in the boot just fine. She shoved her left foot into the other boot and straightened.

"You look good in boots," Dillon said as he walked over to hats hanging on the wall. He plucked a red one with a string off the hooks. "See if this one fits. It's one of Lacey's old hats."

Ruby plunked it on her head. It was a little big but the string tightened and held it on.

Dillon grabbed a hat on the end. He looked every bit a cowboy. "Let's hit the trail."

Laughing, Ruby followed him out the back door and down to the back of the barn.

Brett was at the corral in back saddling horses. "Morning," he said, nodding to them. "I caught your horse and mom's."

"Thanks." Dillon led her along the row of horses to a brown one and a gray one. He put his hand on the rump of the gray one. "This is Riffle. He doesn't get excited about anything and will not let anything happen to you."

"Hi Riffle." She stroked his back. "What's your horse's name?"

"Jig. He's a good old boy." Dillon entered the back of the barn and came out with blankets. "Put this on Riffle. But watch me." He placed the blanket he kept on his horse.

She did the same with Riffle.

"Good. Come in and get your saddle."

She followed him into a room with two dozen saddles and blankets on rails. Bridles and halters hung from hooks on all the walls. "How many horses go out at one time?"

"Depending on who is staying here, Brett can wrangle up to twenty people, but he needs help to take that many out." Dillon put his hand on a saddle. "Use this one."

She picked the saddle up the same way he had and felt the weight pull on her arms and shoulders. "Who helps him?"

"It depends. Sometimes Melanie, sometimes Lacey, sometimes Garth or me. It depends on the timing and what everyone has going on." He carried the saddle out to his horse.

He waited for her to get next to her horse. "Now lift it up and put it on the horse's back. Then make sure everything is hanging loose."

She did as he explained and waited for his next instruction.

"Reach under the belly and grab the cinch hanging down on the other side." He reached under his horse and grasped the ring hanging down.

She did the same. Following all of his instructions, she saddled her horse.

They were soon meandering through the meadow alongside the creek.

"How far are we going?" she asked, riding alongside Dillon and Jig.

"To the third waterfall. It has something I think you are going to like." Dillon shot her a mischievous grin that melted her heart.

Chapter Thirteen

Dillon took his time on the way, stopping at both the lower waterfalls only long enough for Ruby to stretch her legs and take photos. He wanted to be to the upper waterfall by ten, giving them over an hour to enjoy the spot before heading back down.

They emerged from the trees at the small clearing before the waterfall.

"This is breathtaking!" Ruby exclaimed.

Her immediate joy upon seeing the place, made him smile.

He dismounted and took her reins as she dismounted and pulled out her phone.

"If only you had your guitar. This would be a beautiful place to do a video of you singing." She stood near the edge of the water, filming the water frothing over the rock rim above.

He tied the horses to a log and joined her. Placing his arms around her middle, he drew her back against him. He'd been wanting to take her into his arms all morning.

She dropped her head back against his shoulder. "This place is beautiful and peaceful. Thank you for bringing me here."

"You're welcome to come here any time you want." He spun her in his arms. "I mean it. Any time you want to come here, call up Melanie and let her know. They'll find a room for you."

She shoved her phone in her back pocket and placed her hands on his shoulders. "You being here with me is what makes it so special."

He peered into her eyes and saw a reflection of his own emotions. Dipping his head, he captured her lips and drew her body against his.

Her arms wrapped around his neck as she kissed him back with passion.

His hands roamed up her back and down to the top of the curve of her bottom. He wanted to feel every curve but was cautious of scaring her.

A bird screeched, and she ripped her lips from his, but stayed in his arms.

"What was that?"

"A hawk." He continued moving his hands up and down her back. She leaned into his hands, her body making the motion of a cat stretching and pushing her pelvis against his groin.

Her actions made his hard-on ache. He slid his hands all the way to her bottom. Holding her still against his aching cock.

Her eyes widened. But she didn't move. "Is that…?" She swallowed, and her gaze shot down and back up to his eyes. "Do you have?"

He grinned and nodded.

Her neck, cheeks, and ears were a charming crimson.

"I've…I've…" She swallowed but her body remained still.

He released her and backed away. When her gaze shot to his bulging crotch, he just about came in his shorts.

"Why don't we take a little walk? There's something I want to show you." He held out his hand.

She grasped it and followed him along a barely discernable path away from the waterfall. He'd only brought one other woman to this place. It was as special to him as it had been to the Blackfoot.

He rounded the boulder and faced the carved pictographs.

Ruby stared at the rock. "Who?"

"The Blackfoot Indians. This was where they summered. The carvings show what they killed to eat and how they fought their enemies." He drew her closer to the rock. "This has been a secret of our family. If others found out about it, they could come up here and destroy it."

She shook her head. "I won't tell a soul. This…" She spun in a circle in the small, secluded area of the rocks and bushes. "This is a special place. Do you write songs here?"

"I've written a couple." Her curiosity about his song writing tickled him.

"What was the last song you wrote here?"

He studied her staring at the pictographs. "It was about how nature is as fickle as a woman."

She faced him. "Really? Can you sing it for me?"

He'd never sung one of his songs without his guitar to accompany him. But the hope shining in her eyes, gave him the courage to try it. "Sit down." He captured her hands and drew her to a sitting position in front of him.

She settled on her bottom, her legs crossed in front of her. He sat the same way. They held hands as he sang the song that had been written as he sat here strumming his guitar.

When he finished, Ruby stared at him for so long he thought she was trying to think of something nice to say.

"It's just a—"

"True comparison. The words, the nuances. That should be the first song you send out as a demo." She raised his hands to her lips and kissed them. "I've never heard anything so poetic."

He lay backwards, pulling her on top of him. "You keep talking like that, and I'll start getting a big head."

She placed her forearms on his chest and looked down at him with her dimple twinkling. "I just tell things like I see them."

"I'm beginning to think you're just hanging around with me because you think I'll be a big star one day." He raised his eyebrows as if questioning her.

Ruby laughed. "Not think. I know."

"You going to be my roadie?" He liked the idea of her coming to his gigs with him.

"It depends on what it entails." She was running a finger lightly back and forth over his bottom lip.

The softness of the touch had his cock growing again.

"You help me set up my equipment, take videos, and caress my ego afterwards." He nipped her finger.

She pulled it back. "I might be able to do that, if the gigs aren't too far from Bozeman."

"There's one more requirement," he said, grasping her bottom and sliding her body up his so he could kiss her.

"What's that?"

"I need lots of these." He kissed her, long, wet, and breathless as his hands kneaded her hips and sides. He felt her nipples pebble through his cotton shirt as her weight pressed down on him.

He came up for air, and she mewed like a kitten when his lips left hers. A quick roll and she was under him. His forearms were on either side of her holding his weight off her. He captured her lips once more before dropping kisses down her neck to her t-shirt collar.

Her hands skimmed his neck as she played with his hair.

"I think we could negotiate a deal," she said breathlessly as he ran kisses back up her neck.

"What kind of a deal," he asked, lingering with his lips barely a hair's breadth from hers.

She licked her lips. Her tongue skimmed his mouth.

He didn't wait for an answer. Dillon captured her mouth again, this time, tasting her fully and dallying with her tongue as he cradled her head in his hands.

Ruby's senses were sparking, and her mind had gone from coherent to zeroing in on all the pulses, throbs, and yearnings in her body. Dillon's kiss had her gasping for air but not wanting to break the kiss. His tongue had triggered sensations not only in her head but her breasts and her mound that had become sensitive to his hardness pressing against it.

Even as she rationalized all the sensations and realized the parts of her that were awakening, she knew this wasn't the place she wanted to make love to Dillon. She wanted it to be where they could stay and revel in the aftermath. Not have to dress, hop on a horse, and ride for two hours.

She released her hold on his neck and with reluctance drew out of the kiss.

Dillon raised his head and peered into her eyes. "Too much, too soon?"

She started to say yes but changed her mind. "No." She brushed his lips with hers. "I want more, but I don't want it here, rushed." Her neck started heating.

Dillon cooled her heated skin with wet kisses before saying, "I understand." He rolled off her and to a sitting position. He picked up his hat and placed it on his head.

She sat up.

He plopped her hat on her head and grinned. "I don't have another gig for a couple of weeks. I could come visit you next weekend."

Her cheeks burned, thinking about Dillon staying with her at her apartment. The idea was appealing. She didn't have a roommate and the weekends were usually spent cleaning and buying groceries for the week. "I don't have any plans."

He stood, reached down, grasped her hand, and pulled her up into his arms. "Then it's a date."

"Bring your guitar. We can take some shots to add to the videos." Why not make it more than just them getting together to make love. Her face heated at the thought of seeing Dillon naked.

"I can do that. It pretty much goes everywhere I go." He kissed her on the mouth and released her. "Let's get back to the ranch. Do you know what time Arleen was planning on driving back?"

"She said we'd leave at one." Ruby followed Dillon back to where the horses stood.

"Then we better get on down the trail." He stood at Riffle's head while she mounted.

Dillon swung up onto his horse, and they started back down the trail they'd used to get to the waterfall.

Ruby noticed there were still parts of her body throbbing. The rocking in the saddle wasn't helping the problem. She shifted, trying to ease the sensation. They couldn't get back to the ranch any too soon.

Dillon slowed his horse and rode beside her when the trail wasn't narrow. He put a hand on her leg. "Are you doing okay? Your face looks pinched."

Heat once again crept up her neck and into her cheeks. She didn't know what to say.

"What's wrong? Something's wrong because you're embarrassed."

"I-my…" She stood up in the saddle to stop the rubbing on her crotch.

"Is your bottom sore from riding? We can get off and walk."

"It's not my bottom. Well, not my rear end." Rather than have to tell him, she decided to walk for a bit. "I'd like to walk."

He had a puzzled expression but stopped his horse and dismounted. Dillon stepped around his horse and bumped into her as she slid her feet to the ground.

"I can massage—"

She pressed her body to his and kissed him. If he knew how volatile she felt at this moment, he wouldn't say a word.

His hands grabbed her backside and kneaded. She moaned into his mouth and rubbed her mound against him. It was all instinct that had her doing what it took to ease the needs taking over her good sense.

One of his hands moved to the front, rubbing her mound and between her legs, touching the spot that throbbed. She cried out as his touch sent electrical charges shooting to her limbs and blanking her mind. Sagging against him, her hands clutched his shoulders and she rode out the sensations.

His arms circled her, holding her close as he kissed her neck.

Her legs finally gained strength. The realization of what had transpired had her burying her head in his shoulder.

"Are you better now?" he asked, no hint of joking in his voice.

She didn't know how she'd found the courage to look at him, but she tilted her head and peered into his eyes. All she saw in their depths was caring.

"The rocking of the horse made it worse." She didn't know what else to say.

He kissed her cheek. "I didn't know you were that turned on."

"I've never had that happen before." The sensations were everything she'd ever heard girlfriends talk about. But to actually experience it… She would be ready and willing to do it again when he visited. And do it together.

"That was just the beginning of the wonders I'll show you about your body." He released his embrace. "I promise you will be the most loved woman in Montana."

Her cheeks heated.

Dillon laughed. "Come on. We need to get you down this mountain."

He helped her back up in the saddle.

He remounted, and they rode side by side, talking about the trees, flowers, and mountains until they came to the meadow by the barn. There Dillon kicked his horse into a lope and hers followed.

At the barn, he took hold of her reins.

"Why don't you go in and clean up for your trip home. I'll take care of the horses and see you off after lunch."

She nodded and headed to the house.

Chapter Fourteen

Ruby paced between her tiny kitchen and the front door, waiting for Dillon to arrive. It was Friday. She was done with work, and he had left an hour early from work to drive down here and get in at a decent hour. They'd talked on the phone several times during the week about his visit and how he would show her new things. The conversations had left her aching for his touch. But now that he was about to arrive, she was nervous. There were going to be a lot of firsts this weekend. She worried, she might not be what he expected.

She'd worked every evening on the video and was anxious for him to see it before she put it up on the internet. The folded piece of paper on the counter caught her eye. She'd talked one of the lawyers out of a couple of names and phone numbers of clients that were in the music business.

A knock on her door startled her. Ruby scanned the small apartment. It was neat and tidy, ready for company. She walked over to the door. A quick peek out the peephole and her heart started racing. Dillon.

She opened the door wide. "Welcome."

Dillon stepped in, set his bag and guitar on the floor, and swooped her into a hug and a mind-numbing kiss.

"Ahem!" Someone cleared their throat loud enough to catch the attention of anyone in the building.

Dillon's arms relaxed, and he continued the kiss for a minute longer before releasing her. They both looked out her still open door.

Her next door neighbor, Mrs. Perch, stood in the doorway, her perpetual scowl scrunching up her face.

"Good day, Mrs. Perch," Ruby said and shut the door.

"A friend of yours?" Dillon asked.

"She's the neighbor next door. Don't make me moan loudly or she'll be over here rapping on the door with her cane." She covered her mouth, surprised she'd said something so flirtatious.

Dillon burst into laughter.

Her neck and cheeks heated. "Stop laughing."

"What happened to my timid computer geek?" He pulled her back into his arms. "I'm kidding. In case you couldn't tell, I missed you."

Her body warmed and her heart raced. "I missed you a little, too."

"Only a little?" He peered into her eyes and within seconds his lips captured hers, kissing her until her knees grew weak. He eased her down onto the couch, pulling her into his lap.

She wrapped her arms around his neck and dove into the kiss and all he wanted to give her. Time didn't matter. They had until Sunday afternoon when he had to leave.

His hands roamed under her shirt and she didn't care. The sensations that followed the tracing of his fingers heated her body and drove away all thoughts but Dillon and how he made her feel.

Ruby kneaded his shoulders and slipped a hand between the snaps on his shirt. She slid her fingers through the hair on his chest as she skimmed across his muscled pecs.

She wiggled closer. He grabbed one of her legs and turned her. She now sat with a leg on each side of his. His hands returned under her shirt, skimming across her back and arching her. He trailed kisses down her neck and using his teeth began unbuttoning her shirt. She still had on her button shirt and slacks from work.

When her shirt lay open, he stopped.

She peered down at him. His hands had moved to her sides. His thumbs moved back and forth at the edge of her bra. His gaze was on her face.

"You are the most beautiful woman I've ever laid eyes on."

The sincerity in his tone and eyes put a lump in her throat. No one had ever made her feel as beautiful as he had from their first meeting.

"Those words will get you whatever you want," she said softly before capturing him in a kiss. She was a quick learner and teased his tongue as he had hers on Sunday.

This time he moaned and took over the kiss as his hands unfastened her bra and divested her of her shirt and undergarment.

He released her lips and began teasing one nipple and then the other.

Ruby moaned and dropped her head back. She'd never known how sensitive her breasts could be. His hand traced a line from her lips, down her chin, along her neck, between her breasts and over her belly button to the top of her slacks. The soft skimming motion set her body on fire.

She put her hands on Dillon's shirt to unsnap it, but he caught them and shook his head.

"This is the appetizer before I take you out to dinner." He held her wrists behind her back with one hand and continued teasing her nipples with his lips and tracing the fingers of his free hand over her naked body.

Her body tingled and sparked like an overloaded motherboard. She didn't want the sensations to stop.

Dillon had told himself, this weekend was all about Ruby and making sure she received all the pleasure, but suckling her beautiful breasts, tracing her creamy skin, and hearing her purrs of rapture, his pants were getting tighter and tighter. He either had to bring her to completion soon or stop.

He turned her around on his lap, kissed her neck and slid his hand down her belly and under her slacks. Her mound was warm, her clit was plump and ripe. He only had to stroke it a few times and her body shattered. His hand remained stroking her as he played with a nipple and continued kissing her neck. She had two more smaller climaxes and slumped on his lap with a sigh.

A smile curved his lips against her neck. She'd be ready for the real thing later. He eased his hand out of her slacks, his fingers sticky. He nipped her shoulder. "You might want to clean up before I take you to dinner."

She nodded but didn't make any move to get off his lap. He sucked her ear lobe and played with her breast until she finally pushed off him and walked into what he presumed was the bedroom.

That had been quite the welcome. Dillon grinned. Just as he'd hoped, she was going to be a firecracker when it came to making love. He washed his hands and picked up his belongings, packing them into the room where Ruby had disappeared.

It was a small bedroom with a queen-sized bed and a miniature bathroom to the side. Ruby was in the bathroom. He could hear the shower running. As much as he wanted to peek in, he knew they wouldn't get out of here for dinner if he stepped in that room.

She had a colorful patchwork bedspread, a small dresser, and opening a narrow door, a tiny closet with slacks and button up shirts like she had on when he'd arrived. While he'd found her fetching in jeans and a t-shirt, seeing her in the business clothes had overloaded his senses. She was one sexy package, and he was glad he was the one who saw it first and let her know.

The water turned off.

He stood at the end of the bed wondering if he should step into the other room or…

Ruby walked out of the bathroom, holding a towel around her. It started at her nipples and ended just above the tuft of blonde hair between her long legs. Her eyes widened at the sight of him in her bedroom. Her gaze dropped to the bulge in his pants and a sly smile lit up her eyes.

"Want to watch me dress?" she asked, putting a foot on her bed and running the towel up and down as if drying while the rest of her was naked as a babe.

"I'll wait out here or we won't get to dinner." He took one long look and stepped out of the bedroom. His heart raced, and his cock had grown to an uncomfortable size. He walked over to the kitchen, grabbed an ice cube from the refrigerator, and held it on the back of his neck. It was either that or drop it in his pants.

By the time Ruby walked out of her bedroom in a halter-top sundress, he'd gotten his body under control. He was glad the dress came to the top of her knees and the halter-top covered her chest. The vision of her standing with a towel that barely covered her flashed in his mind and his cock twitched.

"Let's go." He opened the apartment door and whisked her down to the parking lot and his truck.

"Where are we going?" She slid in the driver's side even though there wasn't a guitar in the passenger seat.

He grinned when she sat close to him, her hand on his thigh. What a difference a week made. He'd never moved this fast with a girl before, but he'd never wanted to make her happy and make sure she had eyes for only him. With Ruby's long fantasy of being with Nate, he had to make sure he had her heart, body, and soul.

"I thought we'd go someplace quiet and romantic." He'd looked up all the Bozeman restaurants on the internet and had decided that one of the Italian ones looked like the best option.

When he parked across the road from the restaurant, Ruby stared at the building.

"We're eating in there?" she asked.

"Yes. I made a reservation on Monday." He opened the door and helped her out.

"I've always driven by and wondered what the food was like. It's a place you don't really want to go in alone." She wrapped her arm around his. "And now I'm not alone."

He kissed her temple. "You definitely are not."

They enjoyed a delicious meal and talked about the things she'd accomplished this week for him and he told her about mishaps at the excavation company.

Back at the apartment, Ruby pulled out her computer and showed Dillon the video. He couldn't believe how she had turned a phone video taken in a bar into something that looked like it had been mastered by a film crew.

The video ended. He read the credits. She hadn't put her name anywhere on the video and she had done all of it.

"You don't like it?" she asked, the insecure Ruby emerging for the first time that night.

"I love it. But why didn't you give yourself credit for the wonderful work you did? You made me look good. Made my song sound incredible." He set the computer off her lap and faced her. "Why isn't your name on this?"

"I don't need credit. I just want people to see what a wonderful song writer you are."

He shook his head. "You can't remain invisible forever. I don't want the video on the web unless you take credit."

She started to shake her head.

"Why don't you want your name on there? Or take credit for the work?" He studied Ruby.

Her eyes were downcast, her body appeared to be shrinking before his eyes. What was she so afraid would happen if her name was seen by millions?

"I just feel that taking credit for the video might make my bosses think I don't want to work for them if they see it. I don't want to lose my job." She picked at her cuticles. "I like my job. It isn't hard, but it's challenging. I can work all weekend if I want or I can take the weekends off. It's become my life and I'm not sure I want my life to change."

Dillon picked up one of her hands. "I'd like you to find there is more to life than working with computers. Would you please put your name on my video? And *if* your bosses find out, you can tell them you did it for me, your boyfriend." He nudged her chin up with their linked hands. "I want you as my roadie. I can't think of doing another gig without you helping set up and being there when we take down and drive home."

She grinned and her eyes became animated. "How soon do you know the dates?"

He pulled out his phone, and she dug hers out of her purse. He told her the dates and places he had through the summer.

"I can make all but this one." She pointed to a date in August. "I have a conference I have to attend."

"Where's the conference?"

"Denver."

"That's too far. I was going to say I'd come get you." The date was two months away and he already missed her.

"It's okay to put this video on the internet?" she asked, tapping her computer.

"If you put your name in the credits." He was adamant that would happen.

She pulled the computer onto her lap and opened it. He watched as she opened the video app and added her name as the producer of the video. She clicked save and immediately opened a site on the internet.

Several clicks later, she smiled, blinking her charming dimple at him. "We'll check in the morning and see if anyone found you overnight."

"Are you trying to make me an overnight sensation?"

She closed the computer and faced him. "You already are to me."

He pulled her onto his lap and kissed her with the passion and admiration he had for her.

Chapter Fifteen

Ruby snuggled against Dillon. They'd made love twice before falling asleep. Her body still tingled from his touch and the explosions he'd brought to her body. She'd held out all this time waiting for Nate, but she had never fantasized that making love to him would be as mind-blowing as it had been with Dillon. He'd been conscious of this being her first time and took things slow and easy. Preparing her for his entry. And then! She giggled. He'd looked so shocked when she'd grabbed his bottom and sunk him in all the way.

He'd aroused her body to the point she couldn't see from the sensations rampaging her body so fast and furious. All she could think was to get him in her to ease the pressure that had built. But having him fill her had only added to the sensations. Her first climax had nearly taken her head off with the explosion of lights, tremors, and electricity.

Dillon's arms wrapped around her, one hand grasping a breast and the other on her belly, pressing her bottom against his hard-on. He nibbled on her neck as his body rocked against her.

"This is a nice way to wake up," she said, turning her head and meeting his lips.

Their tongues tangled, and he continued rocking against her until she throbbed with need. Spinning in his arms, she faced him, raising a leg over his hips. It was all the invitation he needed. Dillon reached to the bedside table, grasping a condom package. As the night before, he opened the package, and she rolled it down his magnificent length.

Once the protection was in place, Dillon captured her lips in a hot, wet kiss and entered.

Her body greedily rocked with him in a dance of passion. Her heart soared at the way their bodies moved in unison and they climaxed together.

Lying in his arms, feeling their bodies tremor and relax, she didn't want to experience this with anyone else.

"Are you doing okay?" Dillon asked.

She raised her eyelids. The concern in his dark eyes made her heart skip a beat. "I'm fine. Never better." She stretched, rubbing her body against his. Her nipples scraped against his chest and shot a tingle to her toes. He'd super-charged every inch of her skin to ignite when she touched him.

"Good. Since it's your first time, I didn't want to make you sore." He ran his fingers through her hair and cupped the back of her head. "I want you to find making love to me satisfying."

She pushed up, pressing her lips to his. "You make it very satisfying," she said against his lips.

He growled, rolled her onto her back, and kissed her until her body sprang back to life.

She reached under him to see if the kiss was affecting him, but he slid out of bed. Which gave her a wonderful view of his body in the morning sunlight filtering through the lace curtains of her bedroom. She sighed. He had muscles in all the right places, not too big, but enough to let her know he could take care of her. And he had been aroused by the kiss as much as she had.

Dillon walked into the bathroom, and called, "Where are your towels?"

She grabbed two off the shelf in her closet and walked into the bathroom. "Here."

He raised one eyebrow. "You know this shower isn't very big."

"But won't it be fun to see how clean we get?"

Grinning, he started the water, and when he deemed it warm, he pulled her into the three by three shower with him.

Oh, the titillation of soaping up his body and him soaping up hers.

The small area made it impossible to move without rubbing together. His slick soapy body called to her hands. She traced his muscles and slid her hand up and down his length, enjoying the feel of it surging and growing in her hand. She'd never dreamed touching a man with abandon could be so freeing and wicked at the same time. Her life had always been cautious and proper.

Dillon lifted her up. She wrapped her legs around his waist, and he pressed her against the side of the shower as he entered. She moaned and rode him hard, reveling in the wildness she felt.

Stepping out of the shower, her legs wobbled like jelly.

Dillon handed her a towel and pushed her into the bedroom. "Dry off and get dressed out there."

She grinned at him over her shoulder and shut the door. She dressed quickly and headed to the kitchen to make breakfast. How was she to get through a week without him when in just one night he'd settled in her heart and mind and she didn't want to ever be parted from him.

Dillon walked into the kitchen. His breath whooshed out of his lungs at the site of the Ruby. She stood barefoot, in crop pants and a tank top, no makeup and he'd never seen anything as beautiful. That they'd just had a night of all consuming love making added to his love and infatuation with the woman. He'd been with half a dozen women since graduating from high school and none had exhilarated him or taken him on the ride he went on last night.

The woman standing barefoot in front of the stove flipping pancakes had stolen his mind, his body, his soul, and his heart.

He walked up behind her and started to put an arm around her waist.

"Uh-uh-uh. You start that and the pancakes will burn."

He kissed her cheek and backed off. "What can I do?"

"The coffee is brewing, but you can get out plates and utensils." She placed pancakes on a plate.

When the coffee was ready, he poured a cup for him and one for her. He placed hers next to the stove and leaned against the counter, studying her face as she took a sip and concentrated on flipping pancakes.

"Do I have flour on my face?" she asked, wiping at a cheek with the back of her hand.

"Nope. You're perfect." He kissed the cheek she'd wiped.

She snorted in a very unladylike way. "I am far from perfect."

"In my eyes, you are exactly what I want and need." He hadn't planned to announce that so soon, but he wanted her to know, this wasn't a one weekend deal. He'd be back on her doorstep next weekend and the following and the following until he figured they knew enough about one another to make it a commitment.

Ruby placed the pancakes on the plate and faced him. Her gaze searched his. "That was exactly what I was thinking."

He put his coffee down, took the spatula out of her hand, and kissed her with the promise of many more.

Releasing her, Dillon picked up his coffee and the plate of pancakes. He placed it all on the table and waited for her to join him. They sat and stared at each other.

A grin played across his lips. "We can't just stare at each other all day, though I like what I see."

Her dazzling dimple appeared, and her eyes sparkled. "Did you make plans for today?"

"I have one thought, but you need a rest." He raised an eyebrow in challenge.

"We can come home early." She put a bite of pancake in her mouth.

"Come home from where?"

"The Farmer's Market. I go there every Saturday. I buy produce this time of year and I look around for items for my apartment."

"That sounds like fun."

She wiggled her eyebrows. "And it only lasts until noon."

Dillon laughed. "Then we won't be coming home early from it, since it's nearly nine now."

"True. Eat up so we can go."

Within twenty minutes they were in his truck headed to the market at the Gallatin Fairgrounds. By the time they drove in the parking lot, he could feel Ruby's excitement.

"What is it about this place that gets you so excited?" he asked, helping her out of the truck.

"The atmosphere. Everyone acts as if you are family. And there is so much creativity under these canopies and in the buildings." She linked her fingers with his, and they walked into the grounds.

Ruby had her own set path she took. And each one of the vendors remembered her and chatted with her. They all eyed him. It was evident he was the first man she'd brought with her to the market.

At a flower vendor, he purchased a bouquet of daisies. "This will remind you all week that I'm coming back," he said as he handed them to her.

Her eyes lit up and she kissed his cheek. "Thank you."

She purchased vegetables and looked at handmade jewelry, scarves, and pillows. All of a sudden, she stopped and sucked in air.

"What's wrong?" He scanned the area for anything that looked like a threat.

"We forgot to check your video this morning." She reached for the phone in her back pocket.

"Hey. That can wait. I'm having too much fun with you right now to worry about if one person saw the video yet." He plucked her phone from her hand and dropped it into the bag of vegetables he carried.

"What if I get an important phone call?" She stood in front of him, peering up into his eyes.

He saw the glint of mirth in their depths. "I'll take your mind off of it." In the middle of the market, with people walking around them, he wrapped an arm around her and kissed her until her body sagged in his arm. He eased away from her lips, kissed her forehead, and led her over to a bench. They sat down, holding hands, and watched the other market goers wander by.

This was the type of Saturday he'd known he was missing but had tried to rationalize that he wasn't really this type of guy. He wanted late nights, later mornings, and the music scene. But he didn't. He wanted time with a wife, and one day, children that he loved and writing music for others to go out and sing on tours.

He squeezed her hand. "How about a picnic?"

"Where do you propose we go on this picnic?" She stood up.

"Palisades Falls. I saw it's only about forty minutes from here. What do you think?" He grasped her hand, and they headed toward the parking lot.

"I haven't been there in over a year. I'd like that."

Chapter Sixteen

Ruby couldn't believe that it was Sunday afternoon already. Dillon had his bag packed, sitting by the door with his guitar.

"This weekend went much too fast," she said, standing by the door wishing he didn't have to say good-bye.

"I'll call every morning and night, and I'll meet you in Helena Friday at six. We can drive to Big Lake together. We'll spend the night there Friday and Saturday and I'll bring you back to your car on Sunday." He wrapped an arm around her, holding her tight to his body. "As long as we call and meet every weekend, we'll make this work."

"I know it will work. It's just that I already miss you." She put her arms around his neck and clung to him as their lips met, fused, and expressed their intentions in a long drawn out kiss.

Dillon broke it off first. "I hate to leave, but I have to get back."

His phone buzzed that he had a text. "It can't be family, they know when I'll be home." He glanced down at the number. It was unfamiliar. He read the text. "It's someone who wants to talk to me about writing songs." He glanced at her. "How come he contacted me like this?"

"It's the only way I knew for people who wanted your songs to contact you." She released his neck and took a step back, wondering if she'd gone too far with the whole video thing. When they'd checked the numbers that morning, he'd had nearly a hundred thousand hits. "Do I need to change it? Do you have a website or an email?" She picked up the notebook that sat on her coffee table for notes.

"I don't have either one. All I've done is write songs and sing them at bars." He glanced down. "There's another one. This isn't going to work."

"As soon as you leave, I'll take your number off the video. Do you want me to make a website and set up an email? I can do that this afternoon. I took enough photos of you this weekend and can put them up and only a chorus or first lines of songs so no one can steal your songs." She was talking fast to prove to him she hadn't done all this to take away from his song writing.

He put a finger to her lips. "Get my number off the video. Make whatever you think I need but send it to me and let me look at it before you put it out on the net."

She smiled under his finger. "Got it."

His hand slid through her hair and cupped the back of her head, bringing their lips together one more time.

He groaned. "If I don't leave now, I'll never leave."

"That's not such a bad idea," she said, meaning every word.

"And you don't help." He kissed her quick, grabbed his stuff, and opened the door. "See you Friday and talk to you tonight."

"Yes." She watched him walk to the stairs. When he'd disappeared, she closed the door and ran to the bedroom window that looked down on the parking lot. He must have seen her in the window. After he stowed his bag and guitar, he walked to the driver's door and waved. She waved back already feeling loneliness creeping up on her.

She pulled out her computer, removed the contact information, and reloaded that version to the internet. Then she started on a website. At least she'd spend the rest of the day looking at photos of Dillon and listening to the videos she made of him in the bar and when he sang to her at the falls.

***

Dillon pulled into Duncan an hour later than he'd planned. He'd stopped on the highway and helped an elderly lady change her flat tire. He was dirty, sweaty, and missing Ruby more than he'd thought possible. How could one-and-a-half days with someone make him want to be with her even more? He'd called Ruby after helping the woman because he'd be getting here later and didn't want her worrying. She thanked him for the call and started rattling off all the things she'd been doing since he left and all of it had to do with him.

He parked his truck by his folk's garage. The rooms over the garage worked well for him. Being gone so many weekends and working all week it didn't make sense for him to have an apartment. He paid rent on the room and bath above the garage, and it was half what he'd have to pay for a place in town.

Their old dog, Boone, woofed at him as he rounded the truck to get his things out of the passenger seat.

Dad walked out of the garage, wiping his hands on a rag. "Did you have a good time?"

"Yes, I did." He was old enough his dad knew he'd spent the weekend with Ruby and that they'd slept together. But while that was wonderful, that wasn't the best part of the weekend. He'd enjoyed every minute of everything they did together. "We went to the Farmer's Market and Palisades Falls."

"Sounds like a full weekend." Dad stood there studying him.

"It was. I can't wait to see her next weekend." He pulled his bag and guitar out of the truck.

"Next weekend? Didn't I see where you have a gig then?"

"Yes. Ruby's going to meet me in Helena, and I'll take her with me to Big Lake." He walked to the outside stairs leading up to the room. "Dad, she's the one for me. Wait until I show you the video she made of me singing one of my songs. It's on the internet."

"We saw it. Garth showed it to us this morning." He nodded. "That girl does good work."

Dillon nodded. "I think so, too." He continued up the stairs.

"Your mom has leftovers if you're hungry," Dad offered before going back into the garage.

Dillon nodded but he wasn't hungry. He wanted to talk with Ruby and go to sleep. He dropped the bag by the door and packed his guitar over to the stand where it stayed when he was home.

His phone buzzed. There had only been ten more texts from people before Ruby had taken down his number. This time it was Garth.

Nate's looking for you, he texted.

Why? Dillon texted back.

He found out you spent the weekend with Ruby. It wasn't me who told him.

Why does he care?

You know Nate. We can't have a girl he hasn't already seduced.

Thanks.

Dillon disconnected the chat and wondered why Nate thought he had to get his hooks into Ruby. He was ninety-nine percent sure he had Ruby's heart, but her confession of Nate being her soulmate, had him worried his cousin might swoop in and take his girl, again.

***

The days dragged for Ruby. Dillon called her in the morning as she woke. Hearing his voice first thing every day got her up and out of bed. But then the hours dragged on waiting for him to call in the evening. They usually talked for half an hour in the morning and two hours at night.

Friday morning, she was up and packing when he called.

"Morning, Angel," he greeted her.

"Good morning. I'm packing for the weekend. Is there anything special I need to bring?" She looked at her drawer of underwear and put her laciest ones in her bag.

"All I need is you. You don't know how empty my arms feel without you in them."

Her body heated knowing he missed her as much as she missed him. "I'll see you at six and then we'll have two days and two nights together." Her heart spun with the excitement of having his hands and lips all over her again.

"Call me when you leave and don't drive too fast. I want to make sure you arrive safe." Dillon's concern warmed her. It had been years since someone cared about whether or not she made it anywhere in one piece.

"I'll be careful, and you do the same."

They finally ended the call. She finished packing, ate a quick breakfast of cereal, and took her bag, purse, computer, and lunch out to her car. This was going to be the longest day of the week. She just knew it.

***

Dillon had okayed it with Uncle Allan and his dad that he would leave work today two hours early to meet Ruby in Helena. Just as he was clocking out, Nate walked up.

"Why are you clocking out early?" he asked, with even more animosity than he'd been showing all week.

"I have a gig in Big Lake." He hung up his overalls and put his clean cap on his head.

"I know for a fact you aren't gigging anywhere tonight. You might be singing at some low rate bar tomorrow night but not tonight." Nate stood with his hands on his hips.

"What does it matter to you?" Dillon had tussled with his cousin many times over the years, but never over a girl. He always let Nate have them, but this time he was in with his heart and he wasn't about to give up to him easily.

"I heard you spent last weekend with Ruby Cutter. Are you spending this weekend with her too?"

"Not that it's any of your business, but yes I am. She's going to the gig with me to get more videos." He wasn't ready to tell his cousin he and Ruby were getting closer by the day.

"Get videos. You didn't let her dance with anyone else and kept her to yourself the weekend of the wedding. You're not letting her see if there might be a better choice for her." Nate crossed his arms. "Like me."

"You only want Ruby because she likes me. Go take out someone who is more like you. Ruby is far from your usual type of woman." Why he was telling this to his cousin, he didn't know. "I have to go." He shoved by Nate and climbed into his truck.

On the drive to Helena he thought about how Nate was pushing so hard to keep him and Ruby apart. His cousin had never cared in the past. He always just took the girl away, never tried to wedge his way between them. What made him act differently with Ruby?

Chapter Seventeen

Ruby stood in the window of the room Dillon had rented at a resort on the edge of the lake. It was picturesque, romantic, and he'd taken her to new heights the night before once they arrived and were tucked in this room. She glanced over her shoulder at him still sleeping in the big king-sized bed.

His curly hair was tousled, and the covers were down around his waist, revealing the sprinkling of hair across his chest and the ridges of muscle on his arms and stomach. He was hers. She walked back to the bed, slipped his shirt, she'd been hugging around her, off her shoulders and to the floor and lay down on top of Dillon.

He'd brought out a naughty playfulness in her she would have never believed existed.

His eyes opened slowly as his hands ran up and down her body from her shoulders over her bottom and down to her thighs. "Good morning, Angel. This is how I'd love to wake every morning."

She pressed a kiss to his lips and answered, "Me, too."

His eyes lit up. "This is a bit early since we've only known each other about a month but I've been thinking I'd like to make this permanent." His hands stopped roaming and rested on her lower back.

She twirled her finger in the sprinkling of hair on his chest. "You mean like a ring and a wedding permanent?"

He rolled her to the mattress and raised up above her. "Yeah, like that kind of permanent." His gaze held hers.

Ruby didn't know of any reason to say anything other than, "I think that's a wonderful idea."

His eyes blazed with heat as he gathered her in his arms and kissed her until her breathing was ragged and her heart thudded against her ribs.

He came up for air and she didn't give him a chance to catch his breath. Rubbing against his growing length and making sure he knew she wanted more from him than a kiss. They made slow love until her stomach growled.

"You need breakfast, and we'll look for a jewelry store," Dillon said, slipping out of bed and heading for the bathroom with a jacuzzi tub large enough for the two of them. He'd promised her they would romp in there tonight after his gig.

She joined him in the shower. "You don't have to buy me a ring right now."

"We both just agreed to getting married. I want to get you an engagement ring that you like. It's best to do that while you are with me. And next weekend, when you come to Duncan, we'll figure out the date for the wedding." Dillon soaped her up and rinsed her as he talked.

His touch was becoming something she expected rather than craved. The way he caressed her and made her feel special warmed her heart.

She returned the favor. "Where will we live when we marry? I can't just leave my job, we might need the income while you peddle your songs."

He turned, his gaze studying her. "I'll give up my job and move to Bozeman. I'll have to find something during the week to pay for studio time and help with bills until I get my break." He feathered a finger across her cheek. "Would you be okay with me living with you? Or we could find a small house."

She shook her head. "We'll wait on a house until you are selling songs. We'll wait to start a family until then, too." Ruby ran her hands over his abs and up to his chest.

"You keep gliding your hands over me like that and we'll be starting that family right now." He captured her mouth in a knee-buckling kiss.

He wrapped her legs around his waist and pushed her against the wall.

She grabbed his head. "You kissed me like that just so you could have your way with me."

He grinned. "Do you mind?"

Her response was to raise herself up and lower onto him. The ride was as wild and exhilarating as the last shower they'd taken together. And as with that one, Dillon pulled out before he released. She had to admit, she liked the way he slid in and out without a condom and made a mental note to visit a doctor and get contraception. That way they could make love without the latex between them.

When they were cleaned and dressed, Dillon led her out of the room, down the stairs, and out to the parking lot.

"I saw a pancake place when we drove in last night. We'll go there, then find the jewelry store." Dillon settled her in the middle and slid behind the wheel.

"I'd eat a burger if you find a diner. You give me a lot of exercise." She placed her hand on his thigh as he started up the vehicle.

"I think it's the other way around." He kissed her cheek as he backed out of the parking spot.

Within minutes, they pulled into the parking lot of the restaurant. They both ate a large meal then sat back, relaxing and digesting.

The waitress brought the ticket. "You two are some of the few who can clean our plates that well."

Ruby glanced over at Dillon and started laughing. She wondered if the other people who cleaned up their plates had a raucous night of sex like they had.

Dillon nudged Ruby with his knee and paid the waitress. "Thank you. We worked up an appetite last night."

"Good for you," the waitress said, smiling at them both and walking away.

He was rewarded with the red creeping up Ruby's neck and rouging her cheeks.

"Why did you say that?" Ruby asked in a low voice.

"You can't deny it was what you were thinking." He placed his cap on his head and grabbed her hand, tugging her out of the booth.

"I was, but you didn't have to tell her." Ruby walked close to him.

He nodded to the waitress who beamed at them as they walked out of the restaurant.

In the truck, he pulled out his phone and searched for jewelry stores. There was one only a few blocks from here. He handed his phone with the map app open to Ruby and they navigated to the right street.

Dillon started to open the truck door and Ruby grabbed his arm.

"I don't want an expensive ring. If I like one that is out of your budget just tell me. And on the same token if I like one that doesn't cost very much don't make a fuss about it not costing a lot. It's not the price that matters. It's that it's a symbol of our lo—" She stared at him.

"What's wrong?" He held her hand in his. Something had snagged in her intelligent mind.

"We said we wanted to get married, but you...I...never said—"

He peered into her eyes. He knew the words she needed to hear, and he needed to say. "Ruby Cutter, I love you. I have from the moment you slammed the restroom door into my guitar case."

Relief washed into her blue eyes and the dimple he'd been kissing a lot lately bloomed on her cheek. "I love you and have since the weekend of the wedding. You did so many little things that warmed my heart that weekend."

"Then we're agreed we love each other and a wedding is what we want?" He studied her face, watching for any hesitation.

"Yes." She leaned into him, initiating the kiss.

Dillon enjoyed the times she asserted herself. This kiss was one to go down in the books as a moment that sealed her more in his heart.

Ruby leaned back, her eyes glazed and her breathing ragged.

He drew in gulps of air and hoped one of these days his body wouldn't react so quickly to hers.

When they were both breathing normally and his cock had calmed down, he slid out of the truck, her with him.

In the store, he stood back, letting her browse and see if she saw anything.

A woman in her fifties approached them. "May I help you?"

Dillon glanced at Ruby. She straightened and pointed to a bridal set with hearts engraved in the band and one single diamond on the engagement ring. "What is the price of this set?"

A smile grew on the woman's face. "I wondered if you were

wedding ring shopping, but I didn't want to assume." She pulled the set out, flipped the tag over, and showed them the price.

Ruby cringed.

Dillon took the set from the woman and held it out. "Try it on."

Ruby slid her finger into the set and it looked perfect on her hand.

"We'll take it," he said.

"Dillon, this is a lot of money." Ruby pulled the rings off.

"No. It's what I thought it would be. I was with Brett when he picked out the rings he gave Melanie." He took the rings. "Would you take the tags off and give Ruby the engagement ring?" he asked the clerk.

The woman beamed. "I agree they looked stunning on her long fingers." She clipped the price tag off, shined up the engagement ring and handed it to him rather than Ruby.

He grasped Ruby's hand and placed the ring back on her finger. "Since we've already discussed we're getting married, there's no sense in asking you." But he did pull her into his arms and kiss her.

"My, you are one lucky lady," the woman said, polishing the wedding band and putting it in a box.

Dillon handed the clerk his credit card and waited for the transaction to go through, watching Ruby stare at the ring and grin. His heart did a flip at the happiness gleaming in her eyes.

Leaving the jewelry store, he asked, "Do you want to call your family and tell them?"

She stopped. "I should, shouldn't I?"

He nodded. "How about we go back to the resort and take a walk on their paths? You can talk to your family, and I'll call my parents."

Ruby stared at the ring and didn't say anything all the way back to the resort. He hoped her reaching out and telling her family the news would start a dialog between them that would heal whatever preconceived notions they had built up about her.

Chapter Eighteen

Ruby knew Dillon was right. She needed to call her parents, but she'd not shared anything with them since they'd moved from Duncan and severed the family ties.

At the resort, Dillon led her to the back of the building. They started down the wood chip pathway leading out into pine trees and down to a lake.

Dillon stopped at a bench. "You want to sit here and make your call?" He kissed her briefly as if he understood her hesitation.

She nodded. Not really wanting to call her mother. She opened her contacts and Jackie's name was at the top. Happiness bubbled in her chest. This was someone she could call who would understand her joy.

The phone rang, and Jackie's voicemail answered.

"You started something," Ruby said in a happy voice. "Give me a call."

While she was on the high of her good fortune even if she hadn't been able to tell Jackie everything, she pushed her parents' home phone. It was Saturday. She couldn't think of any place they would be.

Their answering machine came on. That was better. Easier. "Hi Mom and Dad. I wanted to tell you Dillon and I are engaged. I'll let you know when we decide on a wedding date." She hung up, happy she hadn't had to answer any questions.

Dillon stood about twenty feet away talking on his phone. He was animated, his smile huge. He glanced at her and winked.

Her insides fluttered. Seeing his joy in reporting their news to his family lifted her spirits. His big loving family would be hers after the wedding.

He put his phone in his pocket and walked over. "How did it go?"

"I got my parents answering machine and Jackie's voice mail. I'm sure they will be calling me back." She stood. "Since we're out here, let's see where this path takes us."

"That's a good idea. We just have to get back to the resort in time to grab dinner before we go to the bar." He grasped her hand, and they headed on the path around the lake.

Before they'd gone a hundred feet, her phone rang. Excitement bubbled when she saw Jackie's name.

"Hello," she answered as calmly as she could. Dillon squeezed her hand and walked down to the lake's edge and tossed rocks in the water.

"What are you talking about?" Jackie asked. "What did I start?"

"Dillon and I are engaged!" she blurted it out.

Jackie squealed. "I knew it! I knew it! I could tell you two were made for each other. When is the wedding? You will make me the matron of honor?"

"Yes, you'll be the maid of honor. We haven't picked a date yet. We just talked about it this morning, and Dillon bought me a gorgeous ring, and now we're telling our families." The last word came out slow and not as excited.

"What did your parents say?" Jackie's sympathy reached through the phone.

"They weren't home. I left a message." She sighed. "After the awful things my mother said to me the day of your wedding, they'll probably think this quick of an engagement and wedding means I'm pregnant. Another disappointment."

"Oh, Ruby, you are anything but a disappointment. You have a better job than your lunkhead brothers. You have a great man. And soon you'll have a better family," Jackie said it all with conviction.

"This is why I love you and am glad every day you are my cousin." Tears burned her eyes. Jackie was the only family she had that believed in her and was always there for her.

"I feel the same. Let me know when the date is, and you know I'll help you with the wedding." Jackie's voice faded. "Sorry, I've got to go, we have some of Thad's co-workers here for a barbeque. Call me tomorrow."

"I will. Say hi to Thad for me."

"He says back atcha." Jackie laughed. "Gotta go."

The line went dead. Ruby smiled. She could always count on Jackie.

"That wasn't your parents," Dillon said, walking up beside her.

"No, that was Jackie. She's excited. Says she knew all along we were a good match." Ruby looped her arm through Dillon's.

They continued around the lake and ended up back at the room. Dillon put on a fancier snap-front western shirt and cowboy boots that were less scarred. Just before they left the room, he plopped a cowboy hat on his head and picked up his guitar.

"Did you see any place that looked good for dinner?" he asked as he placed his guitar in the passenger seat.

"I don't remember." She hadn't paid much attention to what they'd passed after they'd bought the ring. While looking for the jewelry store, she'd been watching the navigation map on his phone.

"We'll drive toward the bar and see what we find."

***

Dillon hadn't played this bar before. It was large, dark, and packed full. His first concern was what to do with Ruby. He knew she was uncomfortable sitting in the bar area alone. All the single men would hit on her.

He scoped out the area where he'd be standing. It was a raised platform with tall wide speakers on each side. He could put a chair behind one and Ruby could sit, kind of backstage.

After checking in with the bartender and the manager, he asked if it would be all right with them if he put a chair on the stage for Ruby. The manager said he didn't care as long as it didn't cause trouble.

Ruby spoke up. "I video Dillon when he sings his original songs. Would it be okay for me to include some of your bar and the patrons?"

"If you're going to do that you can't hide behind a speaker," the manager said.

"I will have to come out from behind the speaker to get good footage." She scanned the room as she talked.

"You walking back and forth from behind the speaker is going to attract attention. And could cause trouble." The way the manager kept mentioning trouble, Dillon wondered if this bar was known for fights breaking out.

"I can stay out of everyone's way if you'll let me sit on the stairs beside the bar."

Dillon looked where she was pointing and discovered a set of stairs leading to the second floor to the left of the bar.

"Those go to the liquor storage and my office." The manager eyed her. "You'll just sit on the stairs?"

"Except when Dillon takes a break. I'll stand at the bar with him then." Ruby smiled, and her dimple flashed.

"Okay. But you start trouble—"

"I know. No trouble." Ruby kissed Dillon's cheek, walked behind the bar, up the stairs, and sat on the fifth step, putting her above most of the heads of the people milling around.

"That's some girl you have there," the manager said.

"I know. That's why I put a ring on her finger today. I don't want to lose her."

The manager slapped him on the back. "Good idea. Now go sing. I heard you're a crowd pleaser. Show me."

***

Ruby sat on the steps filming more great footage to mix with other she had. Dillon announced his first break. She made her way down the steps and stood at the end of the bar.

He came over, kissed her cheek, and ordered them both sodas. "How's the filming going?"

"Good. I can mix this in with the same songs I recorded before and this will be an even better video." She sipped her drink and watched the cowboys and men in sneakers and slacks mingle together vying for the attention of the women in clusters about the room.

"I'm glad I don't have to worry about that anymore." She glanced down at the ring on her finger.

"What?" Dillon asked.

"Having to walk into a bar and sit alone."

He laughed. "You didn't do that before. Except the night I met you."

"That was the best night of my life." She leaned over and kissed his cheek. She had been fighting Jackie and Arleen all day over the makeover, the clothes she'd never wear again, and the packed bar. But that fruity drink that night had brought her and this handsome man together.

"Best night of my life, too." He drew a long drink, kissed her lips, and headed back to the stage.

Ruby just settled on the step and her phone rang. She glanced at the name. Her mother. It was too loud in the bar to try and carry on a conversation. She sent it to voicemail. But she'd have to call her mother back in the morning for sure. By the time they finished tonight it would be too late.

Dillon finished a usual bar song and started talking. "I wrote this particular song, in the last week. I fell in love and couldn't be with my girl and it was killing me." He glanced her direction and her heart squeezed with happiness.

He'd written a song for her!

"This song is called, *You Stole My Heart*." He strummed the guitar and his warm, sexy voice began telling her about how her innocence, intelligence, and dimple stole his heart.

When he finished, the crowd erupted, and he blew her a kiss.

"Dang!" She looked down at the small camera she'd brought along to use to video. She'd been so wrapped up in the song, she'd forgotten to video. And that was one she wanted played at their wedding.

His next break, she flew down the stairs and into his arms. "That was the most beautiful thing anyone has ever done for me." She kissed him, not sparing any of the emotions bouncing around inside her.

He returned her kiss and stood at the bar with his arm around her waist. "I guess you liked the song?"

She hip bumped him. "You know I did." She glanced down at the video camera she set on the bar. "But I was so busy listening and watching I didn't get it videoed."

"That's okay. That song is only for you." He nodded to the bartender and two more sodas were placed in front of them.

"Didn't you see the crowd go nuts when you finished? They loved it."

He shook his head. "The only person I care about liking that song is you. It's our song."

She didn't agree but loved that he wanted to keep it theirs.

It was two-thirty by the time they returned to the resort. Ruby kicked off her sneakers and headed to the bathroom to shower. The large jacuzzi came into view, and she remembered what Dillon had said. She leaned over, plugged the tub, and started the water running.

"I should have known you wouldn't forget," Dillon said from behind her.

"It's not every day a girl becomes engaged and has the chance to soak in a tub like this." She scanned the area. "Do you see any bubble bath?"

Dillon reached into a shelf under the sink and brought out a small bottle. He poured a small amount in the tub and set the bottle on the sink.

Ruby undressed and slid in, enjoying the slosh of the warm water as she watched Dillon undress and climb in. He sat across from her, his legs on the outside and hers together down the middle.

Since meeting Dillon she'd experienced more intimate encounters than she'd ever thought possible. Sitting in the tub, as the water splashed, staring into his eyes and scanning his body, none of it felt awkward.

He grabbed her foot and pulled her toward him. The water was up to her waist. She went willingly, wrapping her legs around him as he moved forward. They sat in the middle of the tub, body to body, their legs folded behind the other.

"How's this for your first co-ed bath?" He scooped the warm water up, pouring it on her back.

"I like it. Very personal." She kissed him, showing her appreciation for him and all he did for her.

The water splashed around her shoulders.

Dillon leaned forward, dipping her into the water as he shut off the faucet.

She knew he wouldn't dunk her face under. He was too considerate. She clung to his body and nipped his shoulder.

The air jets started, water pulsed around them, and bubbles grew. The movement of the water and Dillon's hands roaming her body, along with his tongue and teeth teasing her nipples and nipping her neck started the sensations she'd come to expect every time he touched her skin.

She ran her hands over his body and grasped his growing length.

He captured her lips, tangling their tongues as he raised and then lowered her onto him. Every time he filled her, her heart said she'd come home. Her love for him grew with his every action, whether it was writing her a song, or filling her and taking her to the stars.

When they were both spent, Dillon helped her out of the tub. They took a quick shower to shed their bodies of bubbles.

And fell into bed and slept.

Chapter Nineteen

At eleven Sunday morning, Ruby's phone rang. They'd spent the morning in bed, watching television, reading the paper that had been put in front of their door, and enjoying one another. She glanced at the name and reluctantly hit the answer button.

"Hello."

"Why didn't you call me back after leaving that message?" her mother started.

Ruby grimaced.

Dillon reached over, pulling her back between his legs and holding her against him.

His support bolstered her. "I'm sorry. When you called back last night Dillon was performing at a bar and it was too noisy to talk."

"You can't leave a message about being engaged and getting married and not answer the phone." Her mother huffed. "Who is this Dillon?"

"Dillon Wallis. The man I was with at Jackie's wedding. The one who sang the wedding song?" She rolled her eyes. The whole family had been at the wedding and knew the Wallis family. It was typical that her mother acted as if she didn't have a clue.

"The Wallis boy who thinks he's a singer?"

"No, the Wallis boy who is a singer/song writer."

"You'll be supporting him. Is that what you want to do? Your father wants to know why you are talking wedding already? Are you pregnant? We knew you staying in Duncan in high school you'd pick up bad morals."

"I'm not pregnant, and I don't have bad morals." Except she was sitting naked in bed with the man she was going to marry. But her mother didn't need to know that.

Dillon snickered.

She elbowed him.

"We haven't set a wedding date, but I'll let you know when."

"We can't afford anything big. You keep the budget down." Mother's tone had gone squeaky.

"I don't expect you to pay for any of the wedding. We'll take care of it."

"How will that look if you pay for the wedding? We'll pay but you can't be elaborate."

Ruby dropped her head against Dillon's shoulder. This was exactly the conversation she'd wanted to avoid.

"We have to get on the road. I'll talk to you later." Ruby didn't wait for her mother to say any more. She hit the off button and tossed the phone to the foot of the bed.

"You know we can have the wedding at the ranch and it won't cost us anything." Dillon kissed her neck.

"I would love the wedding there, but we'll still have to pay for food and decorations." She spun, curled her legs, and snuggled against his chest. "Do I have to invite them?"

Dillon laughed. "You technically don't have to, but they are your family."

She sighed. "Yeah." The constant thump of his heart under her ear was comforting.

"I know you used the excuse of going to shorten the conversation, but unfortunately, we do have to get going. I don't want you driving from Helena to Bozeman too late." Dillon lifted her head and kissed her lips. "It's going to be hard to spend another week without you."

The idea of five days and nights with only the phone to connect them was hard to think about. She forced a smile. "But we'll be together on the weekend again."

He hugged her tight then released her. "We better get going."

She climbed off the bed and dressed. Dillon did the same. They didn't say much as they packed and carried their bags and his guitar to his truck.

***

Dillon arrived at work Monday morning knowing he'd be hammered with questions about his quick engagement. Garth and Uncle Allan slapped him on the back and congratulated him. Mom and Aunt Dorothy hugged him and said he'd picked a good wife. His dad quizzed him about how he planned to support a wife. And Nate, he wasn't as gracious about the engagement.

"I understand you bedded her and popped the question. An innocent girl like her is going to jump at the first man who pays attention to her." Nate's comment was made when no one else was around.

"She's not as innocent as you think, and she picked me because she loves me, and I love her." Dillon didn't know why he felt compelled to defend their choice.

"How do either of you know it's love? You've only known each other a little over a month. I can't even decide if I like a woman in that short of time." Nate walked off to take a truck somewhere.

Dillon was glad his cousin would be gone most of the day. He asked for jobs away from the shop for the rest of the week.

As Friday rolled around, his biggest concern was deciding where he and Ruby could stay. He knew she'd be embarrassed if they stayed in the room above the garage, knowing his parents knew they were up there together. He decided to call Brett and see if they could have one of the cabins at the ranch.

"I heard the good news," Brett said when he answered his phone.

"Thanks. I'm a happy man." Dillon smiled. He was a happy man. His conversation with Ruby every night and morning kept them connected. They'd also decided there was no reason to wait on the wedding. They knew what they wanted. Spending the weekend at the Ranch would give them a chance to talk with Melanie and Brett about a date that would work for them.

"Is there a chance you'd have an empty cabin this weekend for Ruby and me to use? She's coming here because I have a gig in Elkton again on Saturday and we wanted to talk with you and Melanie about dates for the wedding."

370

"Just a second. I have to ask the boss." Brett chuckled, and he heard muffled voices talking. Brett came back on. "She said cabin four would be available, but she'd love it if you could clean it up when you leave. We have someone coming in Sunday night and the new help is either going to have to learn to move faster or be fired. With the baby due next month and some of the chores getting harder for Melanie to handle, we need help."

"Not a problem. We can clean any others that need it Sunday afternoon." Dillon had helped enough since Brett opened the Dude Ranch that he could handle any job but the cooking.

"Then it's yours. Will you be here for Friday dinner?"

"No. Ruby won't get here until eight." Dillon hated that she had to drive three hours by herself, but he didn't have time to pick her up and take her back to Bozeman.

"We'll have the cabin ready."

"Thanks!" Dillon clicked the off button, excited to be able to tell Ruby they would be staying at the Ranch.

***

Friday night, Ruby drove up to Tumbling Creek Ranch excited to see Dillon and talk to Brett and Melanie about the wedding. She'd gotten off work an hour early. It was seven, but Dillon had said he'd be at the ranch when she arrived.

She didn't pull up to the house, she drove her car over to cabin four. Dillon's truck wasn't by the cabin. She'd told him she'd be early.

Parking the car on the gravel to the side of the cabin, she grabbed her small bag and tried the door. It was unlocked. She stepped in and was surprised to find Nate sitting in a chair.

"What are you doing here?" she asked, dropping her bag on the bed.

"I wanted to make sure you knew what you were doing." He stood and took several steps toward her.

Ruby backed up. She remembered how uncomfortable he'd made her the weekend of Jackie's wedding. "I know exactly what I'm doing. I'd like you to leave."

He grinned. "This is my family's ranch. I can do whatever I want here." He took another step toward her.

She backed up, putting the chair between them. "I don't understand this," she waved her hand up and down, "man you've become. In high school I wanted you to notice me. I wanted to be your girlfriend. I've thought of you as my soulmate and wanted desperately for you to notice me at Jackie's wedding."

"I knew you preferred me over Dillon." He sidestepped the chair.

"I don't prefer you to Dillon. I love Dillon. You give me the creeps." She moved to the other side of the chair.

"Creeps? What's wrong with a man showing you how much he wants you?" Nate stared at her.

"You aren't. You're acting like a stalker. It's creepy." She stared him in the eyes. "I don't understand what I thought I saw in you in high school. I feel nothing for you and everything for Dillon."

Nate's predatory stance and gleam in his eyes faded. "You really love Dillon? After only knowing him for such a short time?"

"I started falling for him the first night we met. Then here, at the wedding, I knew I'd fallen all the way." She held up her hands. "I hope one day you don't come on so strong to a woman and she can see you might just be the love of her life."

Nate walked up to her. "I'm sorry if I made you uncomfortable. I've never had a woman turn me down as flatly as you did, and I didn't want to believe it." He put out his hand. "Friends? After all, you're going to be my cousin."

Ruby held out her hand. "Cousins."

He grasped her hand and pulled her into his arms. But it was an honest hug. He didn't grope or try anything that offended her.

The door opened.

She pulled away and found Dillon standing in the doorway. His face was pinched and red. His eyes drilled into Nate.

Chapter Twenty

Dillon couldn't believe his eyes. Ruby had told him she found Nate creepy and here they were hugging. He flashed back to when she told him she had thought Nate was her soulmate.

"What's going on in here?" he asked.

"Dillon it's—" Ruby said, taking a step toward him.

Nate wrapped his arm around Ruby's shoulders. "Just congratulating Ruby on picking the better man." The shit-eating grin on his cousin's face was more than he could take.

Dillon spun around, slammed the door shut, and strode toward the barn. He climbed on the four-wheeler and took off out through the meadow. He should have known better. Years of pining for a guy, and she fell for whatever pretty picture he painted. His mind flashed over all the time he'd spent with Ruby. He knew they'd only known each other a little over a month, but he knew everything that made her tick. Everything that upset her, everything that made her giddy.

He gunned the machine and headed for the falls. How could he have thought a month would wipe out a lifetime of wanting someone?

***

Ruby slugged Nate in the belly. "What have you done?"

He doubled over and peered up at her from under his hat. "What do you mean?"

She hit him on the head. "You know exactly what I mean. He took what you said the way you meant it to sound." She grabbed a jacket and marched to the door. "I've a mind to…it's not worth it." She slammed the door just like Dillon and ran to the main house.

There were people sitting around in the main room, talking and drinking coffee. She poked her head into the dining room. Some kids were playing board games. Ruby headed on down the hall to the kitchen doorway.

Here she found Melanie rubbing her lower back, and the young woman they had hired bent over the sink washing pans.

"Ruby? Dillon just went to the cabin to see if you were here," Melanie said, picking up a glass of water.

"He was there. But he saw Nate being a butt and took off. I'm pretty sure I know where he's going, but I'm not sure what horse to ride or if I can saddle it." Ruby had a pretty good idea that Dillon went to the waterfall where he wrote songs. She bet he was working on one about a low-down sneaky backstabbing cousin.

"Brett took some people on a hike right after dinner. There's a four-wheeler beside the barn you could use." Melanie sipped the water.

"How are you doing? You're looking close." Ruby liked Melanie. Dillon had told her that Melanie had lost a child in a previous marriage, which made the family worry about her.

"I'm fine. Doctor says the baby could come any day." She eased down into a chair.

"Good. I better get going before Dillon makes up his mind what he saw is what I get." She winced at the thought and went out through the backdoor and down to the barn. She didn't see a four-wheeler.

"I bet he took it." she said, kicking at the dirt.

"Took what?" Nate's voice put her on the defensive.

"The four-wheeler." She stared at Nate. "Can I trust you to help me saddle a horse, so I can go talk to Dillon?"

He took a step towards her. "You can count on me for anything."

She narrowed her eyes. "No, I can't. You made the man I love think I had chosen you."

"Fair enough. I'll get Riffle saddled for you. Do you need me to help you find him?"

"No, I remember the way." She waited beside the corral while

Nate saddled the horse she'd ridden when Dillon took her to the falls.

She mounted up and headed at a lope across the meadow. Inside the trees, she kept the horse at a trot where the trail was safe. Dusk was starting to fall when she noticed the trail was forked. She didn't remember that.

Ruby couldn't see the side of the mountain for the trees. She remembered the waterfall being on her left when they approached it. With that as her guide, she took the left fork. As the path grew darker, birds flapped in the trees, noises seemed to grow louder, and Riffle walked slower.

***

Dillon sat at the waterfall thinking about what he'd seen at the cabin. Jealousy had kicked in the minute he'd spotted Nate. Ruby had tried to say something, but Nate had spit out his comment. Had he taken it wrong? He found it hard to believe Ruby would declare her love for him and take his engagement ring only to turn around and decide Nate was the man for her. They'd discussed how she felt about Nate now. She didn't love Nate. She loved him.

He started up the four-wheeler and headed back to the ranch. It was nearly dark. He had to pick his way through the trees with care. How could he have been so stupid? Ruby would never be that cruel.

When he drove up to the barn all the lights were on and Brett and Nate were saddling up horses. Kool ran towards him barking.

"What's going on?" he asked as the two walked toward him.

"Kool, quiet," Brett said, before asking, "Where's Ruby?"

"She's here." The minute the words came out, he could tell by the look on his brother's face that wasn't true.

"She had me saddle a horse to go get you. She said she knew where you'd be and how to get there." He pointed to Riffle, mud to his knees, standing at the hitching rail. "Riffle came back without her."

"Hell!" Dillon flew off the four-wheeler and into the corral to get his horse. He had the animal saddled and ready to go in minutes.

"What are you waiting for?" Dillon took off across the meadow at a lope. He had a pretty good idea what had happened. She had to have taken the wrong fork in the path. Why hadn't she called out when he drove by with the four-wheeler? Maybe she did, and he didn't hear it over the noise of the machine. He flogged himself for being an ass.

***

Ruby sank down on the ground and wrapped her hands around her throbbing ankle. She hadn't seen the creek until poor Riffle had walked in. The mud had sucked around the animal's legs.

Remembering how terrified she'd been for the horse, lessened her fear at the moment. She'd managed to get Riffle out of the mud but had lost her sneakers and twisted her ankle in the process. She'd tied the horse's reins up and hoped he'd find his way back to the barn, and they would know to look for her. She hoped the mud would give them a direction to go.

While she grew up in Duncan, she'd been a town girl. Since letting Riffle loose, it seemed like every creature that ever lived was in the woods making noises.

She wanted to cry over her predicament and the fact Dillon was sitting somewhere thinking the worst about her. Her heart ached at the knowledge Nate's actions had caused him pain. And that he didn't believe in their love enough to know she would never turn to anyone else.

A tear slid down her cheek. She swiped at it and felt the grit of mud on her face. "I should get up and walk," she told herself. She pushed to her feet and tried a couple steps. Her ankle wasn't the worst of her problems. Being in socks, every stick, thorn, and rock poked her feet.

She sat back down, wishing she'd thought to bring her phone. But it was in her purse in the cabin.

"Ruby! Ruby!"

She listened.

"Ruby!"

It was Dillon!

"Over here! Over here!"

She stood and spotted light bobbing through the trees.

"Over here!"

"Slow down Dillon, you're going to kill yourself!" Brett shouted.

Something small and dark came running down the path.

"I'm here!" she called again.

Kool ran up, licking her hand and whining.

Jig and Dillon trotted down the path toward her. Dillon dismounted before the horse stopped and caught her in his arms.

"Ruby, I was so scared." He kissed her cheeks and her forehead before kissing her lips.

She clung to him. He was here. He'd come looking for her.

When he drew out of the kiss, she grasped his ears. "I wasn't doing anything with Nate when you walked in. He was giving me a hug and congratulating me on our engagement. You, Dillon Wallis, are the only man for me." She couldn't see his eyes.

He hung his head. "I was stupid. I've been letting what you told me about your infatuation with him in high school and beyond sway me into thinking you've wanted him a long time and haven't known me very long."

"I don't love him. He was a childish crush. You are the man I love and want to spend my life loving." She kissed him, showing him how much she wanted him and only him.

Rays of light appeared and grew brighter.

"Looks like he found her," Nate said.

"Yeah. About time. I thought he was going to kill himself," Brett said. "Load her up and let's get home."

Dillon scooped her up and placed her on his horse. He mounted behind her and held her to him all the way down the mountain.

When the other two rode to the barn, he took her to the back door of the main house. "Melanie can take a look at your ankle."

Dillon dismounted and lifted her down from the horse but didn't set her on the ground. She dropped into his arms, and he carried her to the door.

Ruby grabbed the handle, opening the screen and the door. Dillon carried her through the porch and into the kitchen, placing her on a chair.

"You've got mud all over you," he said, squatting next to the chair. He scraped it off her cheek.

"I hope Riffle made it back safe. He was stuck in the mud. I got him out but lost my shoes and twisted my ankle." Ruby peered into Dillon's caring eyes. "All I could think of was you sitting up there by the waterfall and making up a song about me breaking your heart. I never want to do that."

Dillon leaned close and kissed her. "You didn't do anything wrong. Nate had been telling me how we were moving too fast, and I wasn't the right person for you. He got into my head. Then his crack standing there with his arm around you…I let all that fuel my jealousy and didn't think with my heart. It was sitting at the waterfall and thinking about all our time together that I realized how stupid I'd been."

Brett walked in the kitchen. "Where's Melanie?"

"She wasn't here when we came in." Ruby shot to her foot. "Did something happen?"

Brett took off through the house, calling as franticly for his wife as Dillon had called for her.

"I hope she's okay. All this turmoil can't be good for her." Ruby gave Dillon a push. "Get a towel and get it wet so I can get this mud off. Then go see if Brett needs help."

Dillon did as she asked. He exited the kitchen door and within seconds returned. "Brett found her. She was sound asleep on their bed. She's exhausted." He scooped Ruby up in his arms. "I'll take you to the cabin to shower. Then I'll call mom and Aunt Dorothy to come help."

"We can help." Ruby offered.

"We will, but I don't think you know how to cook meals for fifty people."

Chapter Twenty-one

Sunday, Dillon stood on the porch of the main house, his arm around Ruby and waving to Brett as he drove Melanie to the hospital to have the baby. His mom and Aunt Dorothy stood beside them.

"Any chance you two can help out here for a few days?" Aunt Dorothy asked. "I don't know why those two didn't take less bookings, knowing that baby would be coming."

Dillon peered into Ruby's eyes. "Can you take the week off from work?" He'd like nothing more than to spend the whole week, here, on the ranch, with Ruby.

"I can call my boss and tell him it's a family emergency." She pulled her phone from her back pocket and walked down the steps to the driveway.

"Dillon, that one is a keeper," Aunt Dorothy said.

"That's why I put a ring on her finger." He put an arm around his aunt and his mother. "Is there a chance you two could pull a wedding together for next weekend? Nothing big or fancy. Just family."

"We'd be delighted, wouldn't we, Dorothy?" Mom said.

"Does Ruby know about the sudden plans?" Dorothy asked.

"She will when she finishes her call if you two are willing." Dillon watched Ruby walking up the driveway with a big smile on her face. He wanted to see that the rest of his life.

"He told me I could take as long as I needed." She stepped into his open arms.

"Good. Mom and Aunt Dorothy say they can put a wedding together for next weekend. If you took another week, we could go on a honeymoon." Dillon let her go when she pushed out of his arms and faced the older women.

"You could do that? This coming weekend?"

"We certainly could," his mom said.

She flew back into his arms. "Then let's do it!"

***

Ruby stood in the same cabin she'd stood in a little over a month before with Jackie and Aunt Cassandra. This time she was the one in the white dress and being pampered.

"This dress is perfect for you. Where did you find it?" Jackie asked as she buttoned the tiny buttons that went from the base of Ruby's spine all the way up to the nape of her neck.

She'd bought the dress because Dillon had made a comment about what he could do after unbuttoning each button. "It was at the Duncan Thrift shop. Dorothy made a few alterations and it fits perfect."

"It does! The short skirt shows off your long legs and the sleeveless, high neckline shows off your shoulders, long neck, and arms." Jackie finished the buttons and Cassandra placed a halo of forget-me-nots on her head.

"Dillon's mouth is going to drop open when he sees you." Jackie gave her a hug.

"I'll go see if they are ready for us," Cassandra said, walking to the door. She stopped at the door. "You know, it was short notice." She disappeared out the door.

Ruby shook her head. "Your mom is always trying to make excuses for my parents. But the simple truth is they didn't come because they are afraid their friends will think this was a quickie wedding because I'm pregnant." She stared at her reflection in the mirror. Loving Dillon made her a stronger person. "I don't need them. I have you, your mom, and all off Dillon's family. They see the worth in me and I don't need people around me who don't."

Jackie hugged her. "That's my strong cousin. I'll always be here for you."

Dorothy Wallis stuck her head in the cabin. "They're ready. Oh my! You are gorgeous, Ruby. Dillon is one lucky man."

Tears of joy trickled down her cheeks. "Thank you, Mrs. Wallis. You don't know how much that means to me."

"Don't cry now, you'll ruin the makeup," Jackie chided her, and they walked out of the cabin and over the driveway to the barn.

She'd told them not to go to the fuss of decorating the barn, the great room in the house would have been good enough, but the Wallises didn't listen.

Brett stood by the door waiting for her. He'd offered to walk her up the aisle to his brother.

He held out his arm, and she looped hers through it.

"You're holding up pretty good for a new dad," she said.

"Being a dad is the best feeling in the world." He squeezed her hand. "You're looking pretty good for a woman about to marry my thick-headed brother."

She laughed. "That's because this is the happiest day of my life." Ruby looked up the aisle and her breath stopped. Dillon stood beside the preacher, in his cowboy hat, shiny boots, fancy shirt and jeans. His smile was as big as she'd ever seen it.

Today she would become Mrs. Dillon Wallis.

Dillon knew the dress would look great on Ruby when his aunt finished with it, but he'd never in his wildest dreams realized how sexy it made her look. And she was his from today forward.

Brett brought her up the aisle and handed her off to him.

"You are gorgeous," Dillon whispered.

"You're not bad yourself, cowboy," she whispered back.

The preacher took over. They said the vows they'd written and then Garth handed him his guitar and Jackie brought over a stool for Ruby to sit on. She sat, and he played the song he'd written for her. The dimple that drove him crazy winked at him the whole time he sang and even captured a tear or two.

When he finished the barn was silent.

Ruby sprang off the stool, wrapped her arms around his neck, and kissed him.

The crowd roared to life, clapping and whistling.

Melanie and Brett's baby, Josie, started crying.

This was what family was all about. Dillon returned his new wife's kiss with vigor and looked forward to their honeymoon at the resort where they'd become engaged.

Ruby leaned out of the kiss and said, "I'm glad I realized Nate was the wrong cowboy to love."

***

About the Author

Thank you for taking a journey with Jared and Lacey in *8 Seconds to Ride*, Melanie and Brett's story in *Love me Anyway*, and Ruby and Dillon's story in *Love Me Anyway*. I had fun making up the Tumbling Creek Ranch and populating it with the Wallis family and the people they fall in love with. There will eventually be 6 novellas in the Tumbling Creek Ranch series. You can find me at these places:

Website: http://www.patyjager.net
Blog: https://writingintothesunset.net/
FB Page: https://www.facebook.com/PatyJagerAuthor/
Amazon: https://www.amazon.com/Paty-Jager/e/B002I7M0VK
Pinterest: https://www.pinterest.com/patyjag/
Twitter: https://twitter.com/patyjag
Goodreads:
http://www.goodreads.com/author/show/1005334.Paty_Jager
Newsletter- Western: https://bit.ly/2JVGe4j
Bookbub - https://www.bookbub.com/authors/paty-jager

I love to hear from fans. You can contact me through my website, blog, or newsletter.

All my work has Western or Native American elements in them along with hints of humor and engaging characters. My husband and I raise alfalfa hay in rural eastern Oregon. Riding horses and battling rattlesnakes, I not only write the western lifestyle, I live it.

<u>Other Contemporary Western Romance</u>

Perfectly Good Nanny

Bridled Heart

Thank you for purchasing this Windtree Press publication. For other books of the heart, please visit our website at www.windtreepress.com

For questions or more information contact us
at info@windtreepress.com

Windtree Press
www.windtreepress.com

Hillsboro, OR 97124